GOING
HOME

MIKE HURLEY

This is a work of fiction. Unless otherwise indicated, all the names, characters, businesses, places, events and incidents in this book are either the product of the author(s) imagination or used in a fictitious manner. Any resemblance to actual persons, living or dead, or actual events is purely coincidental.

All rights reserved.
Copyright © 2024 Mike Hurley
ISBN: 9798395146885

DEDICATION

I would like to dedicate this book to my friends Jim Clark and Ashton Baskette.

Their constant support, editing, and encouragement were invaluable, and to my dog Rosie who spent countless hours on my lap, helping me write. Rosie crossed the Rainbow Bridge after the last chapter was written.

CONTENTS

1. FIRE 7
2. PROMISES 24
3. SAYING GOODBYE 42
4. WYOMING BOUND 53
5. INVESTIGATION 70
6. LOVE AND KISSES 97
7. FAMILY DINNER 112
8. YOU'RE UNDER ARREST 126
9. HER NAME IS HOPE 139
10. LET'S GET MARRIED 161
11. MY CHERIE AMOUR 185
12. MAMA MOOSE 204
13. YOU'VE BEEN SERVED 222
14. DAVID AND GOLIATH 245
15. SHERIFF ARLO WOLFF 270
16. 10,000 MILES TO BOSTON 297
17. SKIPPING STONES 313
18. FALL FESTIVAL 330
19. U-TURN 355
20. HIGH OCTANE 375
21. JE VOUS AIME 393

CHAPTER 1

FIRE

So the rumors were true.

What Sherry had been discounting as the idle chit-chat of the old biddies at Edith's Diner in Hope Valley was actually true! To think that she, Sherry Whitmore, an esteemed trial attorney from New York City couldn't separate fact from fiction in what the likes of Edith Smith, the proprietor of Edith's Diner and self-appointed mayor of Hope Valley had said, rattled her. That her parents were separating?

It was preposterous. After all, who got separated after being married for fifty-five years? For sure, yes she had wanted her parents to move off the old dilapidated farm that was their home to a nice little retirement community in town for years, but she had never expected her mother would move, and her father would stay. If they couldn't take care of the farm together, her father certainly wasn't going to be able to take care of it by himself.

Sherry's father was reading the newspaper in his family room recliner chair. While Sherry stood in her mother's bedroom, trying to stop her from packing suitcases and boxes.

"I still don't understand why you just can't stay here," Sherry said. "You even have your own room, you wouldn't even have to see Dad, and I'm sure I can convince him to move, I just need some time."

Her mother stopped packing just long enough to give Sherry her famous death stare. "Sherry, what your father and I are going through, it's just beyond that, that's why." We're separating, followed by a divorce a year later.

There comes a point when you realize the ship is sinking, and no amount of life rafts will save us.

"Beyond what? Sherry asked, realizing she sounded a bit like when she had been a whiny teenager. Being home always did that to her.

When her mother didn't answer her,...Sherry said, "You and Dad have always had fights and I understand he can be a bit stubborn and difficult, but moving out? Don't you think that's a bit extreme?"

"No, I don't," her mother replied, grabbing the few remaining hangers from the closet and stuffing them into a reusable shopping bag. "Now Sherry, if you can't support me I'm going to kindly ask you to just get out of my way," and she waved her hand dismissively at Sherry and began rolling the suitcase out of the bedroom. Sherry couldn't believe this was happening. Was her mother seriously going to move out of the home she had lived in for fifty-plus years? When Sherry came home for her obligatory two times a year, on Christmas and another holiday, her mom always greeted her with homemade pies, but not this!!

Her mother, Connie was eighty-one years old for goodness sake! It was patently absurd. Sherry had to stop her. After all, Sherry was a trial attorney who won fifty million dollar judgments against corporate juggernauts, she could do this.

"Mom! Mom!" Sherry called out as she followed her mother out of the room. "Mom, listen to me, we can work this out," Sherry said, and she gave her father who was sitting in his armchair calmly reading a newspaper as if it was just another day a look that said help me but he barely looked up.

"Mom," Sherry said again, "can you just stop for a minute and listen to me?"

Reaching for her mother's hand, but her mother brusquely pushed her away, and looking Sherry squarely in the eyes, she said, "No, I cannot.

I have given that man a child,...you!! And many good years of my life, and if he wants to choose this farm over me so be it. And if you can't understand that Sherry so be it, but since you haven't lived here since you were 18 I don't see what right it gives you to tell me what to do."

"But I went away to college and law school and then to a job Mom, you are married to Dad. this is your home," Sherry said, gesturing to the kitchen and living room. Her mother's mouth was a hard line. "Not anymore," she replied and strode out of the house pulling her suitcase behind her.

Sherry looked at her father helplessly but he just licked his finger and turned the page of his newspaper. "Aren't you going to do anything?" Sherry asked him.

He shrugged. "She wants to leave, so let her go," he replied.

Sherry sighed. It was like her parents had conspired to drive her insane. Yet she knew it had to be killing her father to see her mother just walk out the door like that, but he was stubborn as an ox and wouldn't budge if his life depended on it. It was up to her to fix this. She stared at him, reading the newspaper like he didn't have a care in the world.

"I'll go talk to her," Sherry muttered darkly and threw a cardigan over her shoulders, and stepped out into the chilly morning air.

Her mother's friend Alice was standing in the driveway in front of the house, next to her VW buggy, and helping her mom put her things in the trunk. "Alice, could you try to talk some sense into her?" Sherry said to her mom's friend as her mother went to sit in the passenger side of the car.

Alice just gave Sherry a faint smile and said, "It's what she wants dear," and that was that.

They got in the car and her mother gave her a wave as Sherry watched in disbelief as the two ladies drove off down the winding dirt road that led away from the farm, the little VW kicking up dirt behind it until it disappeared in a small dust cloud. As far as Sherry knew her mother was going to live in a small studio apartment in

Alice's building in the town of Hope Valley, which was ten miles and a universe away from the farm. Alice lived in the little downtown area that was for all intents and purposes though not in name, a retirement community mostly composed of 70 and 80-something women, with the occasional young person moving in and out.

Sherry sighed and went back into the house. She was surprised to find her father putting on his boots.

"Well, Mom's gone," she told him, her voice cracking a bit. She looked around the kitchen. "Now what are we supposed to do?" she asked him. "I don't know about you but I'm gonna go out and close up the coop and make sure the animals all have water," he replied.

Sherry looked at her father. Of course, he would say that. For a wild second, she had thought maybe he was getting ready to go after her mother. But she should have known the animals always came first for him, no matter what.

It wasn't that she didn't understand, after all, he had run a large sheep farm and orchard for almost his entire adult life and had grown up on the property as well. The farmhouse in which she stood was part of a hundred acres of mountainside and flat land, perfect for a sheep farm and carding mill which her father and mother had run together for almost fifty years.

Until now.

Sherry pulled out her muck boots or yuck boots as she called them and followed her father out to the chicken coop. She had grown up with chickens of course but had grown unaccustomed to the sights and smells of the coop living in New York, and now the smell of it mixed with the smell of sheep dung which was enough to make anyone no matter how used to it. want to vomit. But she had to help him. How was he going to manage on his own? Yes, he had pretty much single-handedly taken care of the sheep and the chickens and the rest of the farm but he had never cooked, vacuumed, or paid bills. Yet she couldn't just stay here indefinitely, she had to get back to New York, she had only taken a few days off after all, and her fiancé Cooper, a paralegal at the firm she worked at, was anxiously waiting for her return too.

Did her father even know how to clean a toilet, Sherry wondered, as her stomach turned into a knot. Her father handed her a filthy chicken waterer.

"Fill this up will ya Sherry?" he said.

She took it trying not to look at all the chicken poop clinging to its sides. Gross!! She whispered to no one!!

This is why she left the farm in the first place. Sherry tried to hold her breath as she walked to the garden hose on the side of the barn to clean out the feeder. In 5 minutes, she had it full of fresh water for the chickens.

Sherry was almost back to the coop when she saw something red and flickering in the distance. It was off to the back of the property which was heavily wooded. She heard the sound of a tree crashing down and then saw smoke.

It was a fire!!

Fire

She dropped the chicken waterer and ran into the coop he wasn't there.

"Dad! Dad! she yelled running back into the barn where she found him. "Dad! There's a fire!" she told him. "Where?" He asked.

"In the backfield, near the carding mill," she explained and then grabbed her cell phone and started dialing 911. She added, We should probably just call Arlo.

Just then she heard the sound of a truck peeling away and she had a glimpse of her father peeling out of the driveway too in his truck. She wondered how an 81-year-old man could move so fast. And who was in the first truck. an arsonist?

"Where are you going?" she yelled after him, but she already knew where he was going. She knew her dad enough to know that the farm was everything to him and that he was heading straight to where the fire was. What exactly did her father think he could do by himself against a raging fire in the woods? He was going to get himself killed. But 'Windy Hill Farm' was his family. It was in his DNA!!

There was no answer on her 911 call, Sherry swore to herself. Of course, she had forgotten there was hardly any reception for cell phones at the farm, let alone a way to call 911. She would have to call the Sheriff instead so he could notify the fire chief. She groaned. Sherry knew the Sheriff, Arlo Wolff quite well, which would be a good thing in an emergency, usually, but in this case not so much!!

Sherry had dated the Hope Valley Sheriff in high school. One, Arlo Wolff. It hadn't ended well, and he was one if not the most annoying person she had ever met. She heard a large cracking sound and was terrified to see a tree fall in the distance near where the fire was raging. Could her night get any worse? She tried calling 911 again....

"Come on! Come on!" Sherry said to herself as she mumbled "answer the phone!"

Finally, she heard a voice but it wasn't Sheriff Arlo, it was a female voice. Is this 911? Sherry asked.

"Yeah sort of, maybe what do ya need"?

Aren't you supposed to ask what my emergency is?

"Is this Sheriff Arlo Wolff's residence?" Sherry asked in an impatient demeanor. The female voice replied in a slow drawl, "Who is this?

"Look, is this Sheriff Arlo's house or not?" Sherry asked angrily. If Sherry had the wrong number, this lady was wasting valuable time. "I need emergency help at Windy Hill Farm".

Sherry added...

"What do you want again?" the female voice asked, in a 'drunk as a skunk' voice.

Sherry swore again and replied slowly, in a succinct and sarcastic voice, I need a fire engine. There's a fire at Windy Hill Farm. Are you a fire fighter?

But more specifically......

"I'm looking for the sheriff of Hope Valley,

"Do I have a wrong number or what? I want Sheriff Arlo Wolff!"

You don't have to be rude!! The lady announced. Hang on...I think he's bottling wine he grows grapes you know.

Sherry snuffed out a scream of agitation as she saw the mills roof collapse in a stew of flames. Her thoughts ran like wildfire....

She remembered calling 911 last year in Manhattan, her co-worker was in cardiac arrest......

By the time Sherry said her name, and the words 'heart attack' the 911 operator had clicked on ambulance and fire engine icons and calmly announced: Emergency Personnel are in route to your location, and began asking more questions. But this was not Manhattan, and

FDNY / Battalion 10 / Engine 22 was already on a call, on West 57th Street. Sherry heard a shuffling of the phone.....

......"Sherry?" A familiar male voice replied to her. She recognized the voice as Arlo's. "So you want Sheriff Wolff do you?," Arlo chuckled, "I knew you would come to your senses one day."

Sherry didn't have time for Arlo's typical ridiculous banter, "Arlo, please concentrate. This is serious, there's a fire over here at Windy Hill." "What?" Arlo became all business in a second. "Where?"

"The back area, near the carding mill," she said. "My dad went down there and.." she looked down towards where the fire was raging, now getting so close she could smell the char coming off the burning wood.

"Do you have any idea how it started?" he asked , grunting and sounding like he was getting his shoes on.

"I don't know, I just looked out the window and there it was, can you just get the fire chief down here quick? I mean I tried to call 911 and no one even answered!" "That's because the fire chief gave his secretary and 911 operator Denise the day off. Arlo replied.

'But what if there's an emergency then? The fire chief is obviously a complete idiot!" Sherry cried. "Ouch, well that hurts. I'm also the fire chief," Arlo replied wryly.

"I thought you were the police chief?"

"I am," he replied, "I'm the police chief and the fire chief. And Sherry, all our 911 calls roll over to Casper Police and Fire one more ring and they would have answered.

Patience is a virtue, Sher!"

Of course. Leave it to Hope Valley to have no emergency services of their own today, and the police chief was also the fire chief who routinely gave his 911 operator the day off. Now Sherry remembered why she had wanted to get out of Hope Valley so desperately after high school.

"Arlo, just get a fire truck down here right away!"

"Okay, I'm on it," Arlo said, "you always did like to make a big ta do about nothing, just like when we were dating. Wait!! Arlo commanded. Someone else called this in 6 minutes ago....and....

Casper Fire and Rescue is 4 minutes out!

Just stay calm Sher, I'll be right there, to give the Casper boys a hand" And with that, Sheriff and Fire Chief Arlo hung up.

Sherry looked at her phone and almost threw it down in dismay. "Stay calm? Stay Calm?" How was she supposed to stay calm with a raging idiot running a fire department. And a fire heading towards the house? And leave it to Arlo to bring up how they dated for two weeks back in high school. And how long was it going to take Arlo to get here, he'd probably stop for a burger and fries. Sherry moaned.

She couldn't just sit around and do nothing. So Sherry jumped in her car and sped in the direction of the fire.

She hadn't gone even two hundred feet down the bumpy winding dirt path that her father used as a farm vehicle road, when she saw the fire moving even faster now.

And fortunately the two big flocks of sheep were in distant fields today.

What if Sheriff Arlo and the Casper FD didn't get there in time and the fire reached the barn, or worse yet, the house?

Sherry steered her car to park next to her Dad's pick up. She jumped out. The fire was not even 100 feet from where she stood and engulfed full trees in a fiery blaze. Waves of heat roared out like monsters in a horror movie. And flames shot up, like one of the USS Missouri's massive 16 inch guns.

"Dad!" she shrieked and immediately coughed as she took in a lungful of black air.

She fought the urge to jump back in her car and high tail it away from there as fast as possible. "Dad!" she yelled again even more desperately. She walked along the edge of the road back and forth. Nothing and no one.

There was a loud crack that made her jump and she was terrified to see a tree with a fireball on it falling in her direction. Even though the tip of the tree fell more than ten feet away, fire started to creep off its leaves and onto the ground very quickly. This situation was getting more and more dangerous fast. She knew the safest thing to do would be to jump in her car and drive away fast. But she couldn't just leave her dad there, she had to find him. And where the hell was Arlo?

"Dad! Dad!" Sherry screamed. Fond memories of fishing with her father in Nebraska when she was a little girl exploded in her mind.

Sherry adored her father, tears began running down her face. She climbed up on an old picnic table, took a deep breath and screamed loud enough to wake the dead ....."DAD!! WHERE ARE YOU?"

Fire

She stumbled off the picnic table, in a fury of coughs from the thick smoke. Her eyes burned.

It was then she saw her father's boots, lying askew in the grass on the other side of the road. She rushed over to see her father lying on the ground, his face ghostly white. She put her hands to her mouth in horror.

He looked…dead.

Parts of his sleeves and pants were smoldering.

Sherry shoved her meticulously manicured and perfectly painted fingernails into the soil and threw handfuls of dirt onto him from head to toe. She quickly snuffed his clothing fires out and saw burned skin on his neck, face, and arms.

She hated this farm and all the hardships it had thrown at her family for decades.

For no apparent reason, Sherry laid her hand on his forehead.....he felt hot. She knew little about first aide, and had no idea how to treat a burn victim. Then his shirt reignited, from some dying ember in his chest pocket.

Sherry stood and yelled "HELP!"

She was overwhelmed way past her comfort zone.

She saw a teenage girl running towards her carrying two heavy buckets of water. "You can't fight this fire with 2 buckets!"

Sherry screamed as the girl kept running towards her like an unstoppable Sherman Tank. "Stand back please!" The girl yelled and poured the buckets on Sherry's dad.

He groaned and moved a little.

"Rory?" He mumbled. "God that cold water feels soooo good!

Rory! Is that you?"

He asked through smoke clogged eyes, as she knelt and felt his pulse.

"I'm here Hank! Sherry's here. Everything's going to be ok. Why did you run into the fire?" Rory asked. She spun the cap off a bottle of water, and helped Hank sit up, and take a drink.

"I was worried Jerry and Snowball were inside. Jerry reads books in the office some days, when it's raining. Snowball doesn't like his tail getting wet." Hank replied between clusters of coughs.

"Jerry is home cleaning his room.

I asked him to call 911 and report the fire. He was nervous but he did a good job!" Rory replied, then added...

"We need to move you Hank. away from the fire.

Sherry, grab his other hand please!"

Rory requested and the two women began dragging him away from the fire. They stopped and let 2 big fire engines drive by.

A rescue vehicle stopped, and two EMT's began triage on Hank.

Sherry took Rory's hand and said; "thank you! And who are you again?" "I'm Rory I'm your father's neighbor.

We live in that blue house down across the alfalfa field. Jerry is my little brother and Snowball his pet rat." "Rory! OMG, I haven't seen you in years, you're a beautiful young lady now, your long red hair is so stunning!" Rory blushed and whispered; "thank you!"

"How did you become adept in rescuing grandfathers from fires?" Sherry asked with a grin. Rory smiled, and replied;

"I'm a teen volunteer on the Hope Valley and Casper Fire Departments.

I can't fight fires but we wash and clean the engines and stow away the hoses and learn how to keep everything ready to go out on a call. We take college credited classes about strategies in fighting fires, first aid, and calming victims of fires. I want to get my bachelors degree in Fire Science, from the University of Wyoming. But I'm only 15. Actually 16 in a few days. With a four year degree in fire science I can get a job as fire chief, at any fire department in the US and Canada. Then I'll get my Masters Degree from the University of Alberta. The Canadian's wrote the book on fighting forest fire safely.

But I'm torn because my real passion is classical music and how it still influences every genre of main street music today. And I'm fluent in French so part of me thinks I should attend the Université de Paris, and get a music degree."

Sherry smiled, and hugged Rory.

"Our world needs more brave young women like you."

Sherry was an emotional wreck. Her parents derailed marriage had about derailed her.

She watched the EMT's and firefighters work, and marveled at how a 15 year old girl knew just what to do, and say, to keep everyone calm. "So how did you know we had a fire?"

Sherry asked Rory.

I just got home from school and saw the flames, from our family room window. I knew Hank would run into the fire. That's the kind of man he is. He and your son are very much alike, you know, they care about people!"

Rory paused and brushed the hair out of her face, and became slightly nervous, as she asked Sherry… "Is Tom coming for a visit?

I haven't seen him in over a year."

"I think so." Sherry replied. Tom was her high school son. Senior year and handsome as hell. And Sherry sort of guessed Rory and Tom would make the perfect couple.

"Tom's really cute, and handsome! I can't wait to see him!"

Rory said with a big smile, then blushed.

"Thank you Rory!" Sherry mumbled, as the EMT's loaded Hank onto a stretcher.

"Can you leave me yours and Hank's vehicle keys, the fire fighters will want them moved away from the fire." Rory asked. "Sure honey." Sherry replied as she climbed into the back of the ambulance, and passed out the keys.

Rory waved to Hank and smiled at Sherry, then sprinted over to Hank's big pickup and drove it up to the house. "The girl doesn't even have a drivers license and she can speak French and drive a manual transmission!"

Sherry mumbled to herself, as she watched out the window.

Sherry was worried about everything. Her Father's burns, her Mother's obstinance, the destroyed mill, Tom, and a plethetera of other issues. But Sherry couldn't get Rory out of her mind...

For such a young girl...almost 16, Rory was a very impressive young woman. Sherry wondered if Tom might notice Rory, and how she's become such a pretty girl.

Chapter 2

PROMISES

A strong breeze from the Harbor blew west across Boston, Massachusetts. It was a sleepy and cool Monday morning, but the city was wide awake. Tom sat on a frumpy old green sofa, in the waiting room of the Counseling Dept.

He attended the elite:

Massachusetts Prep Institute, (MPI), a high school, catering to the upper class. But his family was upper middle class, at best.

He wondered why they had such an old sofa in such a fancy school. He looked at his watch, It was 7:39 a.m., and Erik MacDavey was always late. Even when Erik was early, he was late.

But most days at MPI, Tom felt like a fish out of water, his mother grew up on a sheep farm in Wyoming. Tom's estranged father was an officer in the Marine Corps for 8 years, and now lived somewhere in New York City, where it was thought, he owned an independent car repair shop.

Or maybe he was an attorney or both. Tom could never get a straight story about him, from his mother. She despised Tom's father and had enough legal documents drawn up to confetti Michigan Ave in Chicago.

Tom and his father were strictly forbidden from contacting each other.

Oddly, the only thing Sherry Whitmore ever told her son, about his father, that was true...

He was awarded a Purple Heart for injuries, and a Navy Cross for heroism under fire in battle. He single-handedly eliminated 9 enemy combatants and rescued 7 of his men pinned down by enemy fire. That was all Tom knew about his father.

Sherry rarely talked about her ex-husband.

But when she did, nothing good was ever mentioned. And his battles with PTSD, she found embarrassing, a real man should be able to put all that aside. But of course, Sherry had set foot in a hundred different courtrooms, but never onto a real battlefield. where brave men fought and died.

Tom wondered who gave his mother the right to judge a man's battle with PTSD.

She had never seen her friends blown up by a grenade or fought the enemy in hand to hand combat. There were many things about women and moms, Tom didn't understand.

Tom's blood was part blue-collar, and all the students at school knew it.

Tom's mother, Sherry felt MPI was a launch pad for a career as a lawyer, or medical doctor. Tom suddenly looked up, and said "hey".

"Good morning Tom!"

Erik MacDavey replied as he stood in the doorway, looming over the room at 6 feet, 11 inches. A former center for the Boston Celtics. Everyone called him 'sir', except Tom.

They were good friends. The only friend Tom had at school was Erik. The two men were close like brothers, with enough years between them to be father and son. Erik motioned for Tom to follow him.

"Come in the office Tom, I've got the results from the disciplinary board, and it's a bunch of BS I'm afraid. I've got a meeting with

Principal Robert's. I'll see what I can do, but I can't promise you anything. You beat up the school's star quarterback. There's no way the school board will expel him. So it's you.

Just take a deep breath Tom, these are the curve balls of life that separate the boys from the men." Erik said as he stared out the window. "The star quarterback attacked a 15-year-old female student, and you stopped him cold. You're the hero Tom, and you know what? If they don't remove this incident from your records I'm quitting.

My integrity is more important than some rich kid quarterback!"

"Erik, I can't believe rescuing a freshman girl from a creep, is considered fighting, I wish you could have seen her eyes when I told French to leave her alone. He turned to face me and she ran. She was crying, Erik! She was crying like a girl cries when she's terrified."

Erik understood Tom's anger and replied.

"Well, sexual harassment officially doesn't occur in this school, so to bury the problem the solution is expelling you, Tom.

French is the football team's star quarterback, so the school deflected to the path of least resistance. If this was a public high school, French would have been expelled.

It's total crap, Tom! I don't blame you for being upset. I'd be furious; Eric replied.

"I wasn't born yesterday you know, and some guys, no matter how affluent their families are, well, they're creeps!" Tom said while looking directly at Erik.

Tom sunk into a chair, and let off more steam.

"French was kissing her and she fought hard to get away, but he's a big guy! He was acting like a gorilla and dragged her into an empty classroom. I followed them in and ended it.

But you know what?

If I had been in ROTC, what would they have done? If I was an Eagle Scout, they would have called me a hero and pinned a medal on my chest. But, no, I'm just some stupid kid with family in Wyoming who owns a sheep farm.

I wish I went to a normal school, with kids whose parents were electricians, bankers, plumbers, doctors, and farmers. You know everyday Americans!"

Erik knelt next to Tom and calmly said. "I'm very proud of you, and what you did to help that girl was awe-inspiring. You're far beyond an ordinary American Tom." Tom looked into Erik's eyes and smiled, then said "You're the only friend I have here."

Tom stood and looked out the window at the Bay. He was in no hurry to leave Erik's office this morning. In a moment, he turned to Erik and said;

"I don't belong here! My parents adopted me from Korea when I was a baby. They wanted the best for me, but sometimes 'the best' isn't what a guy needs. Look, I'm not into whining, but I've tried to make friends here…I have!

But, everyone's busy yachting, flying to Europe to see a soccer game, or they private jet up to Toronto to go shopping. I asked a girl out once, Cindy Marsh, she looked embarrassed I was even talking to her.

Like I had a contagious disease.

I've worn these same tennis shoes for over a year, this shirt is from Costco. The other kids think Costco is a store for homeless people.

If this is such a great place, with mature, and driven students, then why was the starting quarterback trying to force that freshman girl to have sex with him? Why wasn't he aspiring to the school's code of conduct?

He wanted way more than a kiss you know, she was pretty, like gorgeous pretty.

If I wasn't dating Trinity, maybe I'd ask her out, her smile about stops a guy's heart." Tom exclaimed.

Erik sat perfectly still and listened intently. He was a famous basketball player but also had a Master's Degree in Psychology. Erik knew where Tom was heading with this conversation.

Tom looked his high school counselor in the eyes and said, "I'm out of here, they can't expel me if I quit, can they?" "No". Erik replied soberly. "Where will you go?"

"Maybe I'll keep working at Trinity's hamburger joint," Tom replied sullenly. I've been there for over a year, I could go full-time!

"You're getting straight 'A's here Tom, you could get into MIT or Harvard. You're 4.0, personable, and handsome. Girls at MIT would line up to ask you out. And it's not full of rich kids. But you're going after a career of flipping burgers? That's crazy!"

Erik replied.

"Ok, whatever, maybe I'll do my senior year of high school in Wyoming.

I can get straight 'A's in Wyoming, and they have pretty girls there too". Tom replied. "When are you leaving?" Erik calmly asked.

"By the end of the week, maybe Trinity will go with me, her parents drive her nuts." "Do you love her?" Erik asked.

"You know I do, she cares about me. She's kind and smart, she's beautiful. She's spunky, and I'm quiet. What's not to like?" Tom replied emphatically, as he walked out into the waiting room, pacing nervously.

"Come for dinner tonight Tom, you and Trinity, Lily will love to see you both!" Erik said.

"That sounds nice, but do me a favor Erik, please don't tell my mom any of this stuff, she'd freak." Suddenly, a knock on Erik's office door...

"Come in!" Erik blurted out.

The door creaked a bit, just as Tom looked up into the pretty blue eyes of a young freshman girl. She smiled at him. Not any old smile, but a pretty smile that meant something.

Tom's heart stopped cold. She was drop dead gorgeous.

And he stood a mere 8 feet from her. There was no terror or tears in her eyes. She was stunningly pretty. "Good morning Mr. MacDavey!" The girl politely said as she turned to look into his office.

"Oh hi, Claire! Thank you for coming.

I think you know Tom". Erik said, as he stood, and walked out into the waiting area. Tom's eyes were now the size of silver dollars; his heart was racing like a Ferrari.

It was her, the pretty girl he beat up French to rescue.

Claire was only 15, but he couldn't take his eyes off her. She was a red rose at dawn. She turned and stepped close to Tom, and said...

"Hi, I'm Claire Renault, I don't believe we've been formally introduced." "Hello, I mean Hi! I'm Tom."

"Do you have a last name?" Claire asked quietly but with a teasing grin. "It's just I want to write you in my diary."

Claire's eyes wouldn't let go of Tom.

"Sorry, Tom Whitmore," he replied nervously.

"Mr. MacDavey said I could find you here." Claire returned. "My father owns the

Boston Celtics, he asked me to give you these.

They're season tickets for you and your family, for 5 years. Not many people impress my father, but he'd like to meet you, and thank you for your courage." She handed him an envelope.

Their fingers touched but for a moment. "It was nothing," Tom replied dismissively.

"Kindness and bravery are far from nothing."

Claire replied as she glanced at his chiseled chest and shoulders. "It looks like you work out."

Tom shook his head yes and stole a glance at Claire's pretty young figure. There was an instant attraction between them, and both Tom and Claire felt it.

Claire stared at the floor, searching for the courage to continue, finally she looked up into Tom's eyes and softly said,

"You were very brave Tom Whitmore, thank you for saving me. I was terrified, I kept telling him to leave me alone. What you did I normally see only in Superhero movies. But…you're the real deal!" Claire smiled again. Tom's heart stopped again.

"It's no problem, I'm just glad I was there." Tom replied. He tried to look away but couldn't.

"French is way bigger than you, and you gave him 2 black eyes and a broken nose. You didn't have a scratch on you. Why? Are you Superman in disguise?" She asked with a giggle that usually turned young men to applesauce.

"Do you have a cape beneath your shirt?" Claire teased and gave Tom a little push. She couldn't peel her eyes off him.

Tom blushed as he tried to explain,

"I'm Korean, and I'm a small person. I used to get picked on when I was in middle school.

My mom enrolled me in boxing, martial arts, wrestling, and dance. I was taught to avoid an enemy's frontal attack and be fast with my responses. Wrestling is a mental game, anticipate, and intimidate.

Martial arts is a game of deflection, to tire your opponent out, and walk away. Dance brings strength and coordination. But boxing is where I excelled, and combined with speed and nimbleness, I never stood still.

You know sting like a bee."

Their eyes wouldn't let go of each other.

Claire had been schooled in the elegant sophistication of European gentility. She spent 2 summers in Austria, and had a kindness in her eyes, accompanied by a quick wit to disarm a knight.

Tom had been brought up with the precepts of kindness and humility. Hard work, and using the Golden Rule as a compass in life. His father, the retired Marine would be very proud of him.

But it was his Grandpa Hank who had chiseled Integrity, honor, and the importance of a man's word into Tom. Tom and Claire had traveled different highways in life, yet their passions were the same.

He could have kissed her, she could have taught him to dance a Polish Waltz, in a castle at sunset. But their song was not to be.

Yet their hearts shared a moment, that time would never forget. Somehow, this humble young man reminded Claire of her father.

Claire stepped forward and kissed his cheek. She slid a note with her phone number into his hand, and whispered, "I'd like to see you again, that is if you're not dating anyone." Her fingers lingered in Tom's palm, they were soft and lovely.

She smiled at Tom and thanked Erik, then quietly walked out of the office. Like the last scene in a Shakespearean play.

The door closed and Tom wanted to go after Claire, to escort her through life, to kiss her, and to be her man. Her composed elegance was that of a swan on a silent lake. But she was fun too.

Claire fit perfectly into Tom's heart….

"Wow!" Tom exclaimed.

"She's amazing, and gorgeous and sweet and lovely rolled into one. I didn't know girls like Claire existed!

And she seemed incredibly intelligent, and much older than 15! Do you think I should ask her out?"

Tom asked. "I think she likes me!"

"Ya think!" Erik laughed, then replied, "I'd be real careful if I were you. Dating two women at once can be a deadly affair. Somehow they sense each other, women have radar you know.

In Claire's world, honor and integrity are worn in private and public every day. Tom, you'd have to break up with Trinity before pursuing Claire.

Furthermore, her father would have a background check run on you. Are you ready for that level of intrusion in your life? And you'd have to learn how to dance. Like at White House State Dinners. Her father is a first cousin of the President, and they're close like brothers. And don't ever piss off a Secret Service agent.

Can you handle all that with grace and charm?" "My middle name is Fred Astaire."

Tom quipped.

"Get out of my office, and don't be late for dinner!" Erik teased with a big smile.

"Oh, and full disclosure here, Claire is very serious about dating you. She's much more than a pretty girl, she holds a 4.0 GPA, like you. She'd be quite the catch.

She asked about your family." "What did you tell her?" Tom asked.

"Oh, all about your mom being a powerful Manhattan attorney, your grandparent's sheep farm, and your father the Marine holding 2 medals from combat." "Well, what did she say?" Tom asked impatiently.

"Claire is hoping to major in history and teach. She was most impressed by your father.

Claire understands the significance of being awarded the Purple Heart, and the Navy Cross. Those medals define your father, and you, Tom.

Do you know whose image is on the Purple Heart?" Erik asked solemnly. "No." Tom replied.

"Well, Claire does.

And she thinks you, my friend, walk on water." Tom grinned and departed Erik's office on cloud 9. He couldn't get Claire out of his mind.

But Tom had a quality he shared with his father: integrity. He would never cheat on Trinity.

Not in a million years.

***

Trinity closed the tiny manager's office door in Handy's Hamburgers store # 93, and sat at her desk. The phone was to her ear, her father on another one of his 'suck it up, and grow up' rants.

He was a seasoned businessman who played to win. His daughter received no special treatment.

She was just another store manager, with the same expectations as everyone else. She was getting a lecture, and rolled her eyes with drama!

She doodled her name and Tom's, and drew a heart in between.

The call passed 6 minutes, and Trinity knew this was the perfect time to scream into the phone. He was a man, and a screaming woman unsettled them instantly. It was a known fact!

She had watched her mother use this tactic on him for years.

But Trinity was working hard to shift her tactics. Manipulating a man with the intrinsic superior intellect of a woman, was much more satisfying. Like a lion tamer, who carried calm confidence into every cage, redirecting the mental energy of roars and lunges, into a quiet subservience.

Estrogen mastering testosterone.

College psychology classes and dominating the game of chess had taught Trinity new and subtle ways to manipulate a man. Redirecting a man's mind was an art form as complex as the instincts required in the martial art form of Wing Chun. Mental acuity and reading a man's body language were key. Changing a man's mind such that he took the credit for his change of course, was essential, and always subtle.

Trinity believed a woman often needs to be an invisible puppet master in a man's world. She counted to 10, then pounced....

"Dad! You never listen to me!

I don't want to be CEO of Smithe Enterprises in 15 years.

I don't want to run your 159 fast-food restaurants, 322 hotels, and 17 golf courses.

What you do is just not me! But I can be your partner and greatly increase our bottom line! Dad, your businesses have excelled for one reason, your passion to succeed.

Well, I have inherited your same passions, but in a creative and artsy way. Please just give me the money to rent a warehouse to explore my creativity!

I'd like to design and sell Christmas ornaments, online. I can buy the basic bulbs from a supplier, and then with a few employees, we custom paint and decorate them. An online tool says I could gross a million in the first year!

We could add that to our family portfolio, We win Dad!

You and me, think of how much I could learn from you Dad! All I need is a warehouse to set up shop!"

Trinity smiled like a fox, she had backed her father into a corner with the finesse of a lion tamer. She smelled the fear of a male suddenly realizing he was trapped by the superior intellect of a female.

Trinity calmly listened to his insane response, then

2 minutes later, pressed end on her cell phone, and screamed! Her father was a man and drove her nuts!

"I'm not silly and immature," she yelled at her phone!

Trinity walked around the block to let off steam, then called Tom, "Hi Sweetie, I just had a ridiculous call with my father. He thinks he knows everything! He makes me so mad!"

"What did he say Trin?" Tom asked.

"It doesn't matter Tom, I need to get out of this restaurant for a while, and you're off today. Do you feel like doing a walk and lunch at the Bay right now?" Trinity asked.

"With you?" Tom replied.

She smiled and said, "I'll pick you up, where are you?"
"At school, I just had a meeting with Erik."

"How'd that go?" Trinity asked.

There was a long pause and finally, Tom replied;

"They're going to expel me, so I quit, and I'm moving to Wyoming for at least the summer. But I don't want my mom to know they tried to expel me." Trinity started her car and zoomed down

Midway Blvd towards Tom's school as he spoke.

Butterflies flew into her stomach. She felt sick as she asked, "What about us?" "I was sort of hoping you'd come with me Trin.

It would be good for us to get away, together." Tom replied hopefully.

"I can't Tom, I start Harvard next week, and I can't get out of that. My dad is paying for everything. He already hates me!" "Babe, he doesn't hate you!"

Tom heard Trinity crying as her car squealed to a halt by the flagpole. Tom jumped in and kissed her, and tasted her tears. Trinity quickly shifted into 4th and merged onto the highway. She took his hand and said;

"I just assumed you'd be here in Boston. My dad rented me a townhouse halfway to Cambridge. I thought we could live together. But now you want to move to Wyoming." She sighed and darted between cars at a high speed, as her emotions crashed all around her.

Tom could see what was happening and softly said, "Trin, let's take a long walk, have lunch, and clear our heads. We've both had stressful mornings." Trinity shook her head yes and roared onto an exit at 95 mph. Speed calmed her emotions.

In 8 minutes they parked and began a long walk along Boston Harbor. Both keenly aware that a goodbye for them might end their relationship.

**

They began a 4-hour walk, along the water. Friends told them they looked good together. So this afternoon, hand in hand, with a clear sky, and a gentle breeze, they were a young couple in love.

The two passed a playground and spent 30 minutes on the swings. They held hands as best they could, but smiles and laughter resonated with the young couple, reminding them why they loved being together.

Each time Trinity swung up to the highest point of her arc, she'd let go of the chain with one hand, throw Tom a kiss, then scream in delight! Trinity loved swings.

They slowed and stumbled off the swings and collapsed in a cuddle of laughter in the grass. They kissed as long as it took 3 clouds to cross the sky.

They walked awhile and bought hot dogs, German potato salad, and iced teas from a sidewalk vendor for lunch.

In a little while, Trinity asked Tom if he felt like sharing an ice cream cone.

He didn't, but bought one anyway.

Rocky Road was her favorite. They both took a bite and immediately the ever-spontaneous Trinity kissed the usually reserved Tom, right in front of hundreds of strangers. Melted ice cream dripped between their tight kiss, and onto their chins, and soon both were laughing.

Trinity chased Tom around a duck pond, as he masterfully balanced the ice cream cone in his right hand.

A cool breeze followed them as they walked some more, then played frisbee for a while, but sadness had moved into each of their hearts. Tom saw goosebumps on her arms and led Trinity to a bench looking out across the bay. She sat on his lap as Tom took off his jacket and set it across her shoulders.

Trinity stared at a little mound of ants, each ant looked so all alone and lost in animinity.

When she first met Tom, Trinity had been adrift in a family of no love. Her father, regularly berated her, calling her stupid, and lacking in fortitude. Her mother, too busy to hug her children., and ask about their day.

Tom had built up Trinity, with praise, and encouragement. Even offering to come over and confront her father, during one of his rants. Tom was only 17, but he believed in building people up, not tearing them down.

Trinity fought back tears as she looked at Tom and asked, "when do you leave?"

"I don't know, soon is all I know". He replied sadly. She knew he was upset, and her heart was already shattered.

Trinity laid her head on his shoulder, then slid her hand up inside his shirt, and felt for his heartbeat. Trinity had no idea how she could live without this young man. No one had ever loved her, like Tom.

Chapter 3

SAYING GOODBYE

"Dr. Sasha Vuong, to Emergency, Dr. Sasha Vuong," the loudspeaker blared.

Sherry sat up with a jolt, opened her eyes, and saw Hank was awake in his hospital bed. "You're awake Dad, that's great. How are you feeling?" Sherry asked.

"Better, though I've got enough bandages to play a mummy in a horror movie."

"Well you were burned pretty badly," Sherry reminded him. "Dad, do you remember anything about what happened?"

"Dad, I didn't mean it that way," Sherry replied. "It's just I was so scared when I saw you lying there like literally on fire and unconscious, but then Rory showed up, Hank gave her a look. "Yes Sherry I remember, there was a fire on the property near the carding mill. I might be 72 but I'm still all here thank you very much…despite what your mother thinks."

She was dressed like a fireman. I've never seen a girl so young take charge in an emergency. She's a very pretty girl Dad, with long chestnut hair, and bright blue eyes. Do you think Tom will notice her next time he comes here?"

"I just want to get out of here Sherry, I have things to do. Farms don't run themselves you know, and Tom is capable of finding a girl all on his own."

"Dad, did you know I had to call Arlo like six times this morning to get help to the farm? And it seems his girlfriend sort of answers the 911 calls. Hope Valley is very unprofessionally run." Sherry moaned.

"Well, our tax base is low and Arlo does the best he can. Casper wants to annex us and we've voted it down several times. Now their 911 network covers Hope Valley, so they're just trying to sweeten us up. But Arlo keeps things running." Hank replied.

"He's a serious pain in the ass Dad."

"Well maybe so but he cares about people..more than, well I see your mother's not here."

"I haven't had time to contact her," Sherry said, but that was a lie. She had in fact texted Connie three times to let her know what had happened but never got a reply.

Suddenly, Sherry's cell buzzed, it was her mom. "See!" Sherry said to her dad, showing him the phone, "she cares." Sherry answered with speaker phone. "Hi, Mom, thanks for calling me back," Sherry said cheerfully.

"So the old coot's in the hospital is he? He's gone and burned down the farm? I knew it would happen one day!" Connie cried. Sherry looked at her dad who rolled his eyes at her. "Yeah she sounds really concerned," Hank said in a sarcastic tone.

Sherry took her phone off speaker and went into the hallway to talk to her mother. If her parents had conspired to make things as difficult for her they couldn't have done a better job.

"Mom will you just listen," Sherry started but Connie was on a rant and in no mood to listen to anyone.

"No, I will not listen! When are his games going to stop Sherry? We're both too old for that damn farm and I tried for fourteen years to get him to retire. He's stuck in a rut, him and his sheep! He loves those damn sheep more than me! Well, now he can deal with whatever comes his way!"

"Dad's in the hospital with second-degree burns and you're his wife! Don't you care? Please come down here!" Sherry pleaded. "No, I will not Sherry!" Connie cried, "This is yet another one of his games to control me! I've got to go unpack, and put up curtains." "Mom don't do this, you know dad loves you!" Sherry cried.

"When I left he didn't even try to stop me! That's grounds for divorce honey!" "Mom, listen to me!" Sherry pleaded.

"Sherry, I'm through listening. Goodbye!" Connie practically shouted, and she hung up the phone.

Sherry was shocked. She had thought for sure her Mom would come straight to the hospital to see her Dad. But instead, Connie seemed annoyed by Sherry's call. Sherry had heard her Mother angry before, but never this angry. Sure Connie had been complaining off and on to Sherry about the farm and all the work to do on it over the past few years, but Sherry hadn't paid it much mind. She had been so busy trying to become partner at her law firm.

And she had to admit her mom was right about one thing. It was obvious Hank couldn't handle the farm alone. What if during the fire, Hank had been alone at the farm? A picture of his unconscious face and smoldering clothes came to mind. She shuddered to think what could have happened to him. And then there was the old crumbling farmhouse, the sixty-five acres of overgrown land, the fifty or so odd animals on the property, not to mention Sherry was pretty sure her father had never cooked a meal in his life. No, he certainly couldn't live out there alone.

A thought suddenly came to Sherry. What if there was another way she could convince Hank to sell the farm and move to town with her Mother? Some kind of reverse psychology!

Her phone rang again. For a second, Sherry had a wild hope it might be her mom calling back, but instead it was her boyfriend Cooper. "Hey doll," Cooper drawled. "How's your pops?"

"He's okay, luckily, just a minor concussion and burns. I was so scared, I thought he was dead. I don't know what I would have done."

"Well, one thing you could do babe is get back here. Attorney Federman isn't very happy with how you just took off to the Wild West on vacation." "Cooper I didn't just take off, it was a family emergency, and my parents run a sheep farm, in a quaint little town, it's hardly the Wild West."

Sherry complained.

"Ok whatever, but we're supposed to put some big bucks down on that condo on 52nd babe, how are we going to have the moola together for that if you're off in Idaho instead of billing for hours here?" Cooper whined.

"It's Wyoming, not Idaho, Cooper!"

"Well whatever Sher, but I heard Wyoming has more tumbleweeds than Texas. You need to get your dad a robot nurse and get home!" "No, I've got to figure this out. Look, I just need a couple of days, to make sure my dad's okay and try to get him to sell."

"But why does it have to be you that does it? Why don't you get your ex-husband Matt to handle things? You always said he's a deadbeat. Give the idiot something to do Sher!"

"No, definitely not him," Sherry cried. She wasn't interested in having her ex-husband Matt involved with her parents or in any other part of her life. But then she suddenly had a light bulb moment...

"Cooper, you're a genius! I think you've figured out a way I can get back to New York ASAP!"

"A genius you said? Well, some have described me as a card-carrying genius. And I'm glad to be of service babe, anything to get you back from Kansas," Cooper simpered.

"Man Cooper, you sure get your states all mixed up for a genius!" Sherry teased. "But Look Coop, I gotta go."

"Okay babe, see you soon," Cooper replied. "Yes, bye… and I love you," she said.

"Right back at you babe," Cooper crooned, as he returned to building a giant Lego city, in his Manhattan 58th-floor attorney's office. Sherry looked out the hospital window and smiled. She'd make a phone call to Boston in a few hours and launch her plan....

***

Hank was soon discharged and Sherry drove him home with little conversation. She pushed the front door open and helped her father into the farmhouse.

After an early and quiet dinner, Sherry got Hank all tucked in, kissed his forehead, took the picture of her mother off the dresser, and tossed it into the closet. She heard the glass break and didn't care.

Sherry did the dishes, cleaned the kitchen, vacuumed, and washed both bathrooms.

She had no control over her parent's marriage or its demise, but she could control the cleanliness of the home she was raised in.

As she cleaned, Sherry was surrounded by mostly warm memories of growing up in this house. The many years of affection between her parents made Sherry feel safe. She was loved and held an integral position in her family.

By high school, lots of her friends were the product of split-up families. Sherry found it ironic, that now, her aging parents were taking her down that same path. Sherry stopped to check on her father and found him asleep. Her mother still had not called to check on him.

Sherry drank a cup of hot tea, put on her pajamas, and a movie, downstairs in the family room. It was only 7:05 p.m.

In her mind, Sherry ran through her new plan of getting her father out of this old house. She thought of every possible argument he could present and smiled. Her plan seemed foolproof. Sherry decided she'd make her phone call in the morning, and officially set things in motion.

***

Rory sat at her bedroom desk, scrolling through photos from last summer. Her homework was done, and she had made lasagna for dinner. Jerry helped her do dishes and jabbered on endlessly about the incredible meals pirates ate on their pirate ships in the 1800s.

Jerry rambled on most evenings with diatribes about the most mundane of subjects. But to a 9-year-old boy in Wyoming, pirates in the Caribbean could fill his sails for days.

The music of Wolfgang Mozart poured from Rory's headset. She could easily get lost in the harmonies of classically composed music.

But on her bedroom wall was an old LP album cover, she found on a rare family weekend trip to Colorado last summer.

Rescued from obscurity in a musty old forgotten basement record store, on Denver's 16th Street Mall. It was now her prized possession.

Stevie Wonder's rhapsodic poem about an eponymous new love. Dressed up in a joyous celebration, 'My Cherie Amour' was the one song that could lift Rory's heart on the darkest of days.

Soon to be 16, young Rory was just another teenager. Full of the joys and sorrows of adolescence. Yet in many ways, she saw herself as a big sister who had been thrust into caring for her little brother, as a mother would. She had teen and adult responsibilities, as her mom was rarely home.

But tonight, Rory's memory was full of 4 unforgettable hours last summer. She volunteered to work on the Hope Valley Sophomore Float for the 4th of July parade. And she spent one Saturday afternoon attaching skirting with the most amazing young man she had ever met. His name was Tom Whitmore. He was visiting his grandparents for 6 weeks. They lived just across the alfalfa field on a big sheep farm.

Of course, Rory had known Tom for many years, but just a polite hello or two was all that ever passed between them.

He attended high school at some prestigious institution in Boston. A place normally inhabited by stuck-up and privileged rich kids. But Tom was different. He asked Rory all about school,

her hobbies, her family, and her dreams. He had an easy laugh and a fun smile she could still see tonight. Plus he was incredibly smart, handsome, and strong.

She about fainted when they completed the skirting work and he hugged her goodbye and kissed her cheek. He was a gentleman, in a world of goofy young boys. Finally, she found the group photo,

11 freshman students, soon-to-be sophomores. and Tom.

He was a junior that year, all the way from

New England, and he stood next to Rory looking like her best friend. Rory closed her eyes and said a prayer… that she'd see him again this summer. He was gorgeous.

10 minutes later, Rory, pushed open the bathroom door. Her little brother went off on her.

"Hey! Would you close the door! I don't have any clothes on!" Jerry scolded, as he grabbed a towel to hide behind. "What are you doing in here?" Rory demanded with an authoritative inquisition.

"What do you think I'm doing, I'm getting a shower!" 9-year-old Jerry blasted. "What do you want?

Can't a guy shower in peace!"

"You're not a guy, you're a boy, and there's a big difference." Rory teased and tried not to laugh. She loved getting Jerry all worked up.

"Just cause you're a 16-year-old girl, you think you're like sooooo hot!" Jerry replied, now agitated. "What does a 9-year-old boy know about hot?"

Rory laughed in reply.

"Get out of here!" Jerry yelled as he threw a wet hand towel at her.

"You don't need to be all rude about it Jerry, I used to change your diapers!! I'm your sister, ya know. And just so you know, I'm going to Shania's house, I'll be home late, so keep the doors locked!

If you get scared text me, I'll come home and scare you more!" Rory laughed again as she headed out the front door.

Jerry stood on the toilet and yelled. "I'm not scared!"

"Whatever." Rory replied from the door.

"No....you whatever!" He shot back at light speed.

Jerry stepped into the shower just as his sister closed the front door. "Ok, Mom!" He mumbled sarcastically, Jerry hated being left home alone. And he was scared with no one else in the house.

***

Trinity spent the night at Tom's tiny apartment. She couldn't handle her parents yelling at each other for hours.

Trinity liked to cook and make dinner, while Tom washed dishes and Googled all the colleges in Wyoming and Colorado she could attend.

They fell asleep all cuddled up together on the sofa. But at 2:00 am she awoke and watched Tom sleep till dawn. Tears fell from her cheeks all night long. Tom was her knight, she loved him, and saying goodbye was going to kill her.

Chapter 4

WYOMING BOUND

Tom looked at Trinity, she stood at the left register, counting and loading cash and change. He could see her tear-filled eyes. Trinity was trying her best to put on a cheerful face at work. But Tom knew she was devastated he was moving to Wyoming.

"You ok Trin?" Tom gently asked as he slipped his arm around her thin waist.

The store was opening in 18 minutes and Trinity was busy, getting ready. But she stopped, looked at him and said, "my brother Jamee just called and said my parents had World War 3 late last night in the kitchen. My dad told my mom she was a spoiled brat, so she opened the cupboards and threw all the dishes on the floor, and then started screaming.

I can't live there any longer Tom, yelling and fighting freaks me out! It's like a war zone. What am I going to do with you gone, Tom?

And we're getting a bus full of old bowlers for lunch, they're headed to Toronto for a tournament. Did you know they have bowling tournaments, it's a thing I guess." She wiped her tears on his shirt and kissed him.

Then said, "I need to look happy! We're Handy Hamburgers and we're always happy!" She rolled her eyes and asked, "Your grandparents farm…do they have a big barn?"

"Yes, why?" He replied. Trinity did not reply and went to the other register, with a handful of cash. Tom returned to wiping the front counter and soda machine when he got a call on his cell.

"Mom?" Tom hadn't heard from his mother Sherry in almost three months.

"Is everything okay?" Tom asked gingerly, as he walked out the back door and into the alley.

He stopped breathing and waited for a verbal assault from his mother about being evicted from school. Most moms had ways of finding out everything about their kids.

Tom knew his mother had very high expectations of him, and MPI High School was a launch pad to any number of Ivy League colleges. "No, everything is not okay Tom, it's your grandfather," his mom said.

"Grandpa?" Tom asked dumbfounded. Well, that was not what he was expecting. "Wait what? What's going on with him?" Tom kicked an empty can of green beans down the alley and tried to restart his brain.

Why wasn't his mom exploding at him about school?

He quickly found an image of his grandfather in his memory. Tom's last moment with his Grandpa Hank was a bear hug, in the passenger drop-off lane at

Denver International Airport, last summer. He spent at least a month every summer in Hope Valley, for years.

"There was a fire on the property, and your grandfather received some burns. He's going to be okay, but he keeps asking for you, Tom." "Oh no! What about grandma?" Tom asked.

"She's fine Tom. She wasn't even there. That's a whole other thing. Look, Tom, I'm just going to tell you. Your grandmother has moved off the farm and into town. She separated from your grandfather. It's just totally crazy here. The farm was getting too much for her, and you know how stubborn your grandfather is, he won't move. But with this fire happening and everything I'm starting to realize it's really too much for either of them, you know what I mean? And that's what I need your help with."

"My help?" Tom almost laughed. Truthfully he didn't really understand what his mom meant. He remembered loving the farm and his grandparents seemed so happy there. But Tom wasn't even doing a good job of managing his own life, he wasn't sure how he could help with his grandparents.

"Yeah, I know if anyone can convince your grandfather to move, it's you. I know it's a lot to ask because you have school, but this is an emergency. So can you come up here just for the weekend? It's Thursday, so you'd only miss a few classes."

Tom hesitated. Should he tell her that he had left school? Would that be the right thing to do? Give her more bad news while she was dealing with all the drama going on in Wyoming?

"Tom?" his mother said. "I know I shouldn't be asking you this but it will make a big difference. Your grandparents are always bragging about their grandson who's a straight-A student at an exclusive prep school on his way to Harvard!"

Tom swallowed. Oh, God!! He decided against telling her anything about being evicted, or quitting, or Trinity, or that she sometimes sleeps at the apartment his mom pays for. Or his plan to move out to Hope Valley. Tom quickly raised his shields and put on a team player persona…

"Mom, it's fine, I'm a part of this family and we all need to step up and help when needed.

I love Grandpa and Grandma, and you, so I'll fly out there ASAP. So you're there in Hope Valley now Mom?" Tom asked. "Yeah, I'm staying with your Grandpa and caring for him. He's a stubborn old goat you know!"

Sherry replied.

Tom grinned and added, "you're stubborn just like him Mom."

Sherry laughed and sighed. She was so relieved her plan was falling into place. "I love you Tom." Sherry softly said.

"I love you too Mom, have you told Dad about Grandpa?" He asked nervously.

"No Tom, and I don't intend to, your father is no longer a part of this family. He's a jerk, a loser, and last I heard, he's homeless and living on the streets like a rat." Tom wanted to protest, but he bit his tongue and said, "Look Mom, school starts in a few days and I need to take care of some stuff, you know, like books, and meal tickets, and all that. It might be like almost a week before I can fly out."

"That's fine Tom, your grandparents will both be ecstatic you're coming. I'll email you an absence explanation you can give to the school office." Mother and son said their goodbyes and both were delighted their plans were playing out perfectly.

Tom tossed the green bean can into the recycle dumpster, then stepped into Handy's and wondered how a man with a Navy Cross and Purple Heart could be homeless. It made no sense, and he refused to believe his mother. Tom promised himself he'd find a way to contact his father by the end of the year. His dad was family too.

Tom walked up front to find Trinity. She was in the kitchen flipping burgers with Marty, the assistant manager. Tom was shocked to see Trinity doing actual work. Though her father had made her the general manager since she graduated the year before and refused to go to college, (her reasoning being genius entrepreneurs didn't need any college), she usually just talked on her cell and filed her nails.

But a month ago, Trinity's father made her attending college, a condition of employment. What Tom wasn't surprised to see was Marty hanging out with Trinity. It was obvious Marty was almost thirty, with dirty hair and a hybrid dork/geek personality. He was a complete loser, but his eyes were all over Trinity.

Almost every guy that met Trinity liked her. She was eighteen, charming, and fun. Tall, but thin, with a pretty figure that turned guys' heads. She had a winning smile, there was nothing not to like, except even Tom had to admit that sometimes she was a bit flighty.

With her long blond hair, she looked stunning driving her white BMW at lightning-fast speeds about town. She had even raced a few Corvettes on the Interstate. "When's the bowling bus arrive?" Tom asked. "They're running late, so you'd better get to work, Tom. The bathrooms need cleaning!" Tom ignored Marty and turned to Trinity.

She wore a fake smile and was trying to be happy.

"Hey Trin," Tom said, "I need to talk to you," then looking to the front of the empty restaurant he added, "And there's no customers so why are you guys making all these burgers?"

"Tom there you are," Trinity said, turning from the grill to give him a quick peck on the cheek, then she continued, "You're not going to believe this! I came up with the best idea. It's definitely going to be the next big thing in fast casual dining....a green melon burger! You take a melon and mash it up, fry it on the grill, and voila you have a healthy meatless burger," she held up a brown round disc and broke it in half, "and look at this, it's green inside! Isn't that great? Want to try it?" She held out the melon disc to Tom.

He resisted the urge to vomit. "Uh, no thanks. Look, Marty, I need tomorrow off," he said.

"Uh, no, you don't get special privileges just because you date the owner's daughter," Marty replied snidely.

Tom took a deep breath. "I'm not trying to get special privileges, it's my Grandfather, I need to go see him, it's a family emergency. He just got out of the hospital." Tom said as calmly as he could.

Marty laughed. "Yeah right, likely story!

He was in the hospital on Sesame Street right!"

"Shut up Marty," Trinity interrupted her assistant manager and said to Tom, "What's wrong?"

"It's my Grandfather Hank, he got into an accident or something. I don't know exactly, my mom was sort of unclear, I think she said something about a fire, and he's asking for me."

"Is he dead?" Trinity cried, putting her hand to her mouth in horror.

"No, he's not dead, Trin! But I don't know, I think he must be in pretty bad shape. My mom rarely calls me!

I'm going to fly out a day or two early I guess. My mom says she needs my help. I've got a ton of stuff to do like clean out my apartment, pack, get a haircut, say goodbye to Erik, on and on."

Trinity stepped away from the grill and began pouring more oil into the French fry machines. Tom pulled her arm and looked into her eyes.

"Did you hear what I just said?

Look, Trinity, I need to quit like right now. I'm sorry but I can't give 2 weeks' notice. I'm very sorry. But my Grandfather is important to me Trin."

Trinity stared into his eyes and blurted out...

"I love you, Thomas Whitmore. You're more a family to me than my own family. If you're going to Wyoming, then so am I," Trinity said in a determined tone, as she fought back tears.

"Please hold me Tom."

Tom led Trinity into the manager's office and closed the door. She felt his powerful arms wrap around her small figure and sighed. Tom gave Trinity a minute and felt the stress leave her body. Finally, he said,

"Wyoming is very different than Boston Trin, are you sure you want to do this?"

She looked up into Tom's eyes, then kissed him deeply. "Has your mom ever thrown every plate in the kitchen on the floor, and broken them to bits?" She asked him in a whisper.

"I'm sorry Trinity, my mom is far from perfect but she would never break dishes in a fight.

I'll come with you to your house and help pack up your stuff. I don't want you there alone." "I'm scared Tom," Trinity whispered as she felt the strength in his shoulders.

Tom sat on the office swivel chair and Trinity on his lap. He could feel her trembling a bit as he imagined going to her house and beating up her father. No one would ever hurt Trinity again!

Tom promised himself.

But he worried about bringing a girl home when he was supposed to be comforting his family. Would his mom be angry and make calls and figure out he got expelled?

But Tom felt it was his place to protect and care for Trinity. It's what boyfriends do. "I'm really glad you're coming we me, Trinity! We should buy airfare today Trin." She grinned and replied, "OK Mr airfare man, but I'm taking a private jet!

And I'm selling seats. 1 seat to Wyoming will cost you. oh look! The fare just went up!

Looks like it's ten kisses to sit next to me on a Leer Jet. Eleven if you want to hold my hand. And twelve if you want a bag of pretzels, oh my!"

Tom tickled her. Trinity screamed and ran out of the office laughing. Suddenly she was ecstatic to be leaving Boston, and her crazy parents behind.

They finished their shift at Handy's and spent that evening and the next day packing, running errands, cleaning Tom's apartment, Trinity's bedroom suite, and doing everything one does to end a chapter of their lives and begin another.

Tom accompanied Trinity to her home, at a time when no one was there. She emptied drawers and closets while he ran to the basement looking for suitcases. On the way back up, he took another stairway and stepped on broken dishes in the kitchen.

Tom took multiple trips to Trinity's bedroom with enough suitcases to move a family of elephants.

Then he returned to the kitchen, found a broom and dustpan, and secretly swept up the broken dishes on the floor. If asked, Tom wasn't sure why he cleaned up the brokenness of a family's life.

Somehow he felt sorry for them, and appreciative too that in their shattered marriage, Trinity's parents had raised Trinity to become the beautiful young woman Tom had fallen in love with.

An hour later, Trinity walked through the once joyful house and looked into all the rooms.

Her happy childhood memories now were gone. She walked through the kitchen and wondered who cleaned up all the broken dishes. She opened her heart and left an honest note for her mother.

"You ok?" Tom asked as she closed the garage door and slid into the passenger seat of her BMW. She didn't reply but stared at an old swing set in the backyard as Tom drove to the small county airport. Slowly she left behind her old life and as they pulled into the airport.

Trinity put joy on her face and was excited to begin a new life with Tom. But a storm was still swirling in her heart.

They parked and found two luggage carts, for Tom's 2 duffle bags and her 11 large Samsonite hard-shell suitcases. Trinity had packed up everything in her bedroom suite.

Including her extensive collection of Madame Alexander Dolls from her grandmother. And an 1829 antique miniature tea set from her other grandmother.

Secretly Trinity was fearful her mother would find and destroy them in a rage.

Trinity smiled at a young skycap and pointed to her father's 18 million dollar Leer jet. He took the luggage carts while she ran around the parking lot looking for a grated and deep storm drain.

"What are you doing?" Tom asked as she looked behind bushes and parked limos.

"I want to drop my car keys into a deep storm drain so my Father will get a headache when his concierge locates my BMW, without the keys. They'll have to call the county to pull the grate covers off all the storm drains and spend hours fishing for the keys."

"Wait, why are you being so mean to your father?" Tom asked in disbelief.

"Because he's an ass and has never had a kind word for anyone. He never once told me he was proud of me or congratulated me for high grades, getting accepted into Harvard, or being the manager of the most profitable Handy's in

North America. That's why Tom!" She replied with glaring eyes.

"Don't do that Trin, being mean and getting even, never produces positive results. My Grandpa always says if you throw weeds into your neighbors' yard, the seeds will blow back into yours."

"Well, look at you, 'Saint Thomas of Boston' all holy and righteous. So pray tell what should I do with my car and keys? Sir Tom." "Why are you acting like this Trinity?"

"Because I'm sad and scared to leave my family, and they don't love me, Tom. They probably won't even realize I'm gone. I miss my grandma, she died 2 years ago and gave me like over 50 Madame Alexander dolls. Packing them up brought back so many good memories of her Tom. She really really loved me. And now, you're the only one who loves me, Tom. Even when I'm having a meltdown in an airport parking lot. You're right beside me!"

Tom watched as crocodile tears fell from her eyes. She fell into Tom's arms and cried her heart out. After a few minutes, Tom gently talked to her about life, love, and their future together.

Finally, Trinity softly asked, "what should we do with the BMW?"

"We'll need a car in Wyoming Trin, couldn't you leave the keys at the airport's front desk and have your father's concierge ship the BMW by rail out to Casper? Trin, just because your father is an ass doesn't require you to be one."

She stared at him with another temper tantrum brewing in her mind. But finally, Trinity handed the keys to Tom and stomped off in a huff to the jet.

Tom locked the BMW and ran the keys into the airport office, then sprinted back to the Leer just as the door was closing. He quickly called Trinity's father's concierge and gave the necessary instructions per Trinity.

Tom fastened his seatbelt and cautiously glanced at his girl. She took his hand and whispered, "I love you for being you!" Trinity had long seen the kindness and respect for everyone in Tom's young heart.

In a family of shattered dishes and lack of love, she clung to him.

"I'm sorry for being a brat," Trinity whispered as the 22-passenger Leer jet leaped into the sky. He kissed her forehead and pulled her close.

"I love you, Trinity Smithe!"

She kissed Tom and snuggled into his strength.

"So you said your Grandpa has a big barn, I mean like how big is it? Do you think there'd be enough room for me to launch a business like a dance and yoga studio?" Trinity asked while combing his hair with her fingers.

"Yeah, it's huge Trin, with a big empty hay loft upstairs you could put on a square dance with 100 people." Trinity sighed and smiled. Moving to Wyoming was the best decision she'd ever made.

After the flight attendant served dinner, they found a movie to watch. Halfway through Trinity curled up into Tom's lap and fell sound asleep. He pulled a blanket over them and kissed her cheek. She was a handful on a good day, but Tom loved her deeply. He looked out into the darkness for a while. The flashing navigation light on the wing lulled Tom asleep.

A few hours later, the Leer jet gracefully touched down on a short runway in a tiny airport in Casper, Wyoming. They were home.

***

The second the Leer jet wheels touched the runway....

8 miles away, Rory jolted up in bed from a deep sleep. She got up and stared out her bedroom window. Wondering what woke her. She snuck into Jerry's room, pulled his blanket up, and kissed his forehead. She looked out every window and saw no one. Finally, Rory crawled back into bed and noticed the photo of her and Tom on the wall was the only photo lit by a moonbeam.

She stared at the photo for a long time, then fell back asleep.

***

Tom and Trinity stood outside the tiny terminal with 2 carts full of luggage, realizing they had forgotten to arrange a ride to Hope Valley, which was just 8 miles away via back roads.

"I guess I'll try for an Uber or something," Tom mumbled, starting the app on his phone.

"Don't bother, I just used my Father's concierge app for a ride, while you were in the restroom, a car is on its way," Trinity said matter of factly, as she yawned. It was 5 minutes after midnight, local time. Tom smiled, she might be flaky but she definitely made a good travel companion.

Tom could see a black vehicle approaching them at a distance. When it got closer he realized it was a limousine. "That's not a car Trin, it's a limo," he said.

Trinity shrugged. "It's a type of car," she replied and hopped in as a dark-suited chauffeur opened the back door for them.

Tom crawled in and wasn't ready for the type of fancy it was. Plush leather seats that still had that new car smell, a fridge to one side, a sink- who put a sink in a car? And a television set.

"See, isn't this better than an Uber?" Trinity asked him, settling into the crook of his arm. "Uh, yeah just a bit," Tom replied with a grin.

A window opened to the front of the car and two eyes peered back at them. The chauffeur asked, "Where to?"

Tom took his cell out of his pocket, "Uh, Windy Hill Farm, it's 504 Rural Route 9 in Hope Valley," he said. The limo made a U-Turn and headed for

Hope Valley. Thanks for getting us a ride Trin!" Tom said as he yawned.

"Of course sweetie, that's why you have me," Trinity replied.

She snuggled even more into his shoulder, then asked, "Now tell me more about your grandfather, the man who doesn't throw weeds over the fence."

Tom thought for a minute. "Well, I don't know, he's got a lot of land, but it's way out at the edge of town. My grandmother and he used to run a carding mill together."

"A what?" Trinity asked as she slipped off her high heels.

"It's a place where you take sheep wool and turn it into usable wool fiber, you know, to make stuff, like wool thread."

"Oh like wool to make those super trendy Irish sweaters I've seen on TikTok?" Trinity asked. She pushed her phone screen into Tom's face.

Tom squinted at the screen. "Uh, yeah like that. Anyways, they have a bunch of sheep and then they get them sheared like once a year and make wool out of it." "Hmmmm, why not just hire some people for that," Trinity mumbled as Tom looked out the window and wondered if her father's concierge service knew of people to work in a carding mill.

He hoped Trinity would fit in at his grandparent's place. They had no money for a concierge or to hire a limo at midnight. They'd probably put Trinity in the small guesthouse. In contrast, her bedroom back in Boston had an attached sitting room, an office, and a huge private bath.

Soon Tom and the driver stacked the huge pile of luggage on the farmhouse's front porch.

All the lights were out, and his mom and grandpa were sound asleep. Trinity handed the driver a generous tip and he sped away.

***

"Can you believe we're in Wyoming, I mean it was 36 hours ago I told you I wanted to come." Trinity said as she looked up at the night sky and a billion stars twinkling down at her.

"Can we sit out here for a minute, I've never seen so many stars!" Trinity asked as she sat on top of the pile of suitcases.

She raised her arms for Tom to sit next to her, and then screamed as all the suitcases slid off the porch, and down the stairs like snowboards on moguls. In a second she lay on the front grass and watched their heaviest piece of luggage slam into the mailbox and knock it over.

Tom stumbled down the stairs trying to reach Trinity but he was knocked over and broke the handrail. 'Tom!!" Trinity screamed out in horror as he fell next to her. They made enough noise to wake the dead!

Chapter 5

INVESTIGATION

Sherry grabbed the shotgun off a basement shelving unit, then ran into the laundry room.

She opened the 3rd drawer of an old dresser next to the dryer, and grabbed a box of shells and a flashlight. She loaded both barrels and ran up the stairs into the kitchen.

"Dad, I've got the shotgun, let's go!"

"I'm doing this alone Sherry, go get in your bedroom, and crawl under the bed!"

"No, for God's sake Dad, I'm not a little girl, we're going out together. Here, take the shotgun and I'll carry the flashlight." "It's that damn bear again, I'm sure of it!"

Hank rattled off as he checked the safety on the gun. "But I heard a woman screaming Dad!" Sherry said nervously. She opened the door and Hank stepped out first, with the double barrels leading the way.

"Shine that light, Sherry, I hear laughing, and what's all this luggage doing on the porch, and stairs, and damn!! Someone knocked my mailbox over." "What luggage?" Sherry asked as she tripped on a big hard case and fell, then rode the piece of luggage down the steps.

She came to a stop and shone the light into a sea of suitcases and saw a pair of tennis shoes and a pair of high heels. Laughter leaked out of whoever they were. "What's going on here!" Hank hollered out in a thunderous volcanic voice. Tom and Trinity were drowning in laughter, and tickling each other.

"Hands in the air, you're on private property!" Sherry yelled out half hysterically. She shone her light on two people, lying in the grass, giggling, laughing, and tickling each other. Suddenly one of them stood, still smiling and blinded by the light.

She was tall, thin, and lovely, with long blond hair and galaxy-blue eyes. "Don't shoot! I'm with Tom!"

"You're a girl!" Sherry exclaimed.

"Last I looked I was!" Trinity said with a smile as pretty as a peach. "I'm with your grandson, my name is Trinity.

I'm so sorry for all the commotion, it was an accident, and I'm Tom's girl." "Oh my God, he's got a girlfriend!" Sherry whispered to herself.

Trinity reached for Tom's hand and pulled him up. She brushed leaves and stuff out of his hair and shirt. He stood, still laughing, then composed himself and said.

"Mom, and Grandpa, I'd like you to meet my girlfriend, Trinity Smithe."

"It's nice to meet you, ma'am and sir." Trinity softly said as she pushed the hair out of her face. Tom was shocked to see Trinity nervous, he had never seen her nervous before.

She started setting all the suitcases upright, then walked up to Sherry reached down, and helped her up.

"I'm so sorry!" Trinity said, now appearing flustered. Sherry hugged Trinity and said, "my name is Sherry, and this is Tom's Grandfather, Hank. And we're delighted you're here Trinity. Tom's never brought a girl home before.

You sort of surprised us, and you're gorgeous, like a movie star!" Trinity blushed and softly replied, "thank you, but I'm just me." "Come on, let's get you a cup of tea Trinity.

That's such a pretty name!

The boys can bring the luggage in."

Sherry led Trinity around to the side door and into the farmhouse's kitchen. They never locked their doors. "Is Grandma sleeping? Where is she?"

Tom asked, refusing to believe his grandmother moved into town. "Your grandmother?"

"Yeah, Grandma always greets me with hugs and a couple of cherry pies." Tom replied, with sadness in his eyes. "I realize we're a few days early."

"Cherry pie has always been your favorite, we must have enough cherries in the basement freezer to make 90 pies. Winter was mild so we probably won't get many cherries this summer.

All fruit trees require a certain number of hours of chill, below 45 degrees to rest and produce a good crop the next year. Sour cherry trees like our 3 meteor trees require about 1200 winter chill hours….."

"Grandpa…….where's my grandmother?" Hank paused, then said;

"Thomas, she moved out, and wants a divorce.

She had enough of me and this farm, she wanted us to get a place in town. Son, moving me off this farm is like moving those 3 cherry trees to the moon.

I told her I couldn't, so she got in a mood like all women get you know. But, a man has to let a woman simmer for a while, and then eventually they all come around, a cherry tree can't live without sunshine, and a woman can't live without a man. That's a fact, Google it!"

"Geez Grandpa, don't say that in front of Mom or Trinity!"

***

"Honey, just call me Sherry, it's easier that way." "Are you sure?" Trinity asked sincerely.

"I'm sure, I like being called Sherry and not all the Mrs crap." Trinity smiled, so far, after just

30 minutes she liked Tom's mom a lot. She was nice, down-to-earth, and perceptive. "So, tell me about yourself?" Sherry nervously asked.

Trinity smiled and replied, "There's not much to tell actually. I'm 18, born and raised in Boston, I love sailing and hiking, and your son, but not in that order!" Trinity giggled and continued.

"I'm close to obtaining my black belt in

Jui Jitsu, I've been studying the art of self-defense since I was 8.

My 15-year-old cousin Tara got attacked in a parking garage and my mom freaked. A day later I was the Karate Kid!"

My last job was manager of a fast food restaurant, and I needed a change in my life. I'm delighted to have come here with Tom and finally meet you. Tom talks about you all the time."

Sherry beamed at Trinity's hidden compliment, then asked, "what about your parents?"

"My parents are both very driven people, to a point, I question why they had kids. My 2 brothers and I have almost raised ourselves. My mom is never home, and all my dad does is yell at me. Tom is the first person who's ever really loved me, for who I am, well except for both my grandma's. I was especially close to my father's mom. But both my grandmothers are now deceased.

I'm sorry to drop all that on you." Trinity said as she teared up. "Oh honey, it's OK, come here."

Sherry said and wrapped Trinity in a big hug. "We all struggle with our parents, my mom up and got mad at my dad and moved out.

I can't even talk to her about it. Just give your mom some time honey. Are you sure you're not hungry, I'll cook up anything you want."

"No, I'm good, thank you." Trinity replied with a pretty smile. "Trinity, we'd better get you to bed, your body clock is still on EDT." Sherry suggested.

"We need to get the men to bed too."

Sherry got up from the table and put a few things away in the kitchen, then asked Trinity;

"So, when you're ready, I'll take you out to our guest house. I think you'll be comfortable there. It's a cozy little house. Thanks, Sherry!! That sounds lovely. We got up early and I'm exhausted.

Trinity stood and walked into the living room.

Hank was asleep in his lazy Boy chair, and Tom stared at the wall like he was in a trance. Trinity gasped when she saw his tear-drenched face. "Honey, what's wrong?"

"My Grandma is gone, she actually moved out, I just can't believe it." Tom moaned as Trinity held him on the sofa. "Well, what if we go visit her tomorrow Tom, and you can ask her about it." Trinity softly suggested.

***

Trinity's mom Carol parked her new electric Lucid sedan in the garage and looked over at Bay 7. Trinity's car was gone, and it was very late.

But Carol wasn't worried, her mind wandered to the speech she was writing for a fundraiser dinner. She was president of the 'Boston Women's League'.

She set her stylish $1200.00 purse on the kitchen desk and picked up a note from Trinity. Odd though, it was sealed in an envelope, with 'Mom' written on the front. Trinity was never one for formality.

"Oh my God!!" Carol mumbled aloud as she began to read....

Dear Mom,

I'm being smothered in this house. You don't seem to know who I am, and I can't live in Dad's shadow any longer. I'm not sure he realizes I'm still his daughter. Once I turned 18 he treated me like an employee. You never ask how I am or seem to care about any of my struggles. All you focus on, are yelling at Dad, your charity groups, and your duties as president of that stupid women's league thing. You used to hug me and ask how I am. I'm your daughter. But you don't remember me.

So I moved out.

I still miss Grandma and now I'm crying as I write this. Grandma loved me for who I am, why can't you and Dad love me too? I'm your daughter. If I had a daughter I would spend all my time with her.

I appreciate how hard Dad works, and his vision to build a business empire. But I have my own dreams to explore, I've asked him for a small warehouse to start an internet business. He thinks I'm immature and silly.

I'm going away for a while to try my wings and test my ideas. Please don't worry, I'm with Tom, I love him and he treats me like a princess. Please don't try and find me.

Sincerely, Your daughter, Trinity Smithe

Carol set the letter down as tears streamed down her cheeks.

She opened her iPad photo app and typed

'Trinity' into the search bar. In seconds hundreds of smiles flashed up on the screen.

"Trinity," Carol whispered as her eyes touched each photo. Her daughter was beautiful and reminded Carol of her mother.

In a moment Carol walked into her daughter's bedroom suite. The bed was made up with clean sheets, the furniture had been dusted and the carpeting vacuumed. 'Why?" Carol muttered, wondering who Trinity thought was going to use this room.

Carol opened the spacious closet and gasped. It was almost empty. She began writing Trinity a text message.

It was 2:40 a.m. in Boston, as Carol typed.

"Trinity, I miss you. I can't sleep, I'm sitting on your bed, praying you're ok. I'm sorry if I haven't been the kind of mother you had hoped for. I know I get way too involved in my charities!! Please call me, all your stuff is gone. You couldn't even say goodbye?

I'm glad you're with Tom. I like him, he's a responsible young man and I know he'll keep you safe.

I just want to know you're ok. Trinity, you're my first child, I will always love you! You're a part of me!! Mom."

Carol added a heart emoji and pressed send. Her iPad was drenched in tears.

***

It was late as Sherry got her father back into bed and gave him another dose of pain pills. She was quiet as thoughts of her mother and Trinity ran through her mind. It seemed so ironic her parents were asleep in different homes, while her young son brought home a girl. A real girl!

Sherry wasn't ready for either, as she kissed her sleeping father's forehead and turned out the light. She crawled into bed and stared at the ceiling. Her heart was full of worry.

What if her parents never spoke to each other again? What if Tom got Trinity pregnant?

There was so much now that was out of Sherry's control. She set her alarm for 6:00 and tried to sleep, but her mind was busy. Almost 2000 miles east, another mother couldn't sleep. Carol curled up onto her daughter's bed and sobbed.

A second later, Trinity was awoken by a text from her mom. She glanced at it and set her phone back on the end table. She was in no mood for a chat with her mother.

So far, Trinity liked this place. Tom's mom was wonderful, and she was sure his grandparents could mend things quickly. For Trinity, Hope Valley, Wyoming was a breath of fresh air!

***

The following morning, Hank sat on the front porch and took a sip of coffee. The sun had been awake about an hour, and a woodpecker was just starting his shift, on a dead maple tree 200 feet north.

"Damn rackety bird." Hank muttered.

He smelled bacon cooking and was glad 2 happy women were in his kitchen this morning. He hated to cook and relied on cereal and peanut butter when a woman wasn't around.

Tom stepped out onto the porch, wearing shorts, and a t-shirt, just as a Hope Valley Sheriff's car drove up and parked in front of the house. "Why are the police here Grandpa?" Tom asked.

"The fire." Hank replied.

"Morning Hank!" Sheriff Arlo called out as he closed the squad car door. Deputy Bruce stepped out the passenger side and waved a greeting. "You boys hear about the fire?" Hank asked.

"We did," the sheriff replied, then added: "We need to nip arson in the bud, it can terrorize a community." "What makes you so sure it's arson?"

Hank asked with a frown.

"What else could it be, sheep don't play with matches Hank."

"Oh is that right Arlo? Since when are you an expert on sheep?" Hank snorted in reply, as the two lawmen stepped up onto the porch. Hank and Arlo had a solid friendship but enjoyed acting gruff and teasing each other.

"Well, I'm the sheriff and fire marshal, I'm trained to figure these things out. I took classes and got certified in fire investigations, while you have been snoozing for days on the porch!

Nice to see you again Tom." Arlo quipped.

"Good morning Sheriff, good morning Deputy." Tom replied respectfully.

"Arlo, I took a class on nuclear submarines and got certified to sail the USS Wyoming right here through this pool of crap you're floating." Hank announced. Arlo grinned and enjoyed the creative insult from Hank.

Tom moved and stood behind his grandfather and whispered, "is this rude posturing really needed this morning Grandpa?" Hank ignored his grandson and continued.

Investigation

And you don't need to be wearing Colt revolvers on my porch. "So what exactly do you boys want with us law-abiding citizens this morning?

You dated my daughter, Arlo, were you ever threatened in this home?"

"Hank, you and Connie were always good to me, and Connie's cherry pies are still the best in Wyoming! But you know we always wear revolvers. What about you Tom, do you like your

Grandmother's homemade cherry pie?" Tom smiled but didn't answer.

"Hank, we need to investigate the field and carding mill, and anywhere else the fire occurred."

"You boys aren't setting foot onto my property until you join us for breakfast!" Hank said with a grin. "You cooking?" Arlo asked with a teasing smile.

"Sherry" Hank touted in reply.

"Damn, she's a good cook!" Arlo announced, then turned and faced Tom and asked, "Tom, did you know your mother and I dated in High School? Yup, we dated. I had a ring picked out, I had a speech all prepared to ask your Grandfather for her hand."

"What happened?" Tom asked.

"She had enough credits to graduate in December, our senior year. She was off to College in Chicago by New Year's. I was cold leftovers when she came home in May.

And she had your father's engagement ring on. That's what happened." "Do you know my father, sir?" Tom asked.

"Your father is a good friend of mine, and he's a fine man," Arlo replied. "So my dad is not a homeless person?"

"Good God no! He's a war hero and an amazing man. Wait…..you don't know him?" Tom looked embarrassed and didn't reply.

The screen door opened and Trinity stepped out onto the porch. She smiled her prettiest smile for Tom and stood right next to him. Her hand slid into his.

She lightly kissed his lips and whispered,

"Good morning my love, I dreamed about you last night, and I love it here! The barn is huge and amazing! Why are the police here?" Tom didn't reply, but squeezed her hand 3 times; it was their secret code for 'I love you!"

"Sheriff Arlo, Deputy Bruce, I'd like you to meet my girlfriend Trinity." Tom announced.

The two lawmen politely said hi to Trinity, the young deputy noticing how pretty she was. His eyes lingered on Trinity far too long.

"Breakfast is ready," Trinity announced with her lovely Boston accent. The men followed her into the kitchen and served up scrambled eggs, bacon, hash browns, baked beans with ham, and freshly baked biscuits, with butter and cherry preserves. Arlo sat next to Sherry and turned on the charm, knowing all too well she was divorced. Sherry was polite but raised her shields.

As a contrast, Tom and Trinity held hands under the table, her foot set atop his and she ate a few bites off his plate. Sherry noticed how smitten Tom was with Trinity and wondered how much money she'd need to spend to look young and beautiful again.

After a little while Arlo and Bruce drove out back and surveyed the damage. They took lots of photos and the Sheriff scooped up assorted suspect piles of ash. After an hour, they drove back up to the farmhouse and announced their findings, they had a suspect in the arson.

"Well, let's have it Arlo, who is the son of a bitch, who lit the fire?" Hank asked.

They were assembled on the front porch. Hank sat in his chair. Everyone else stood and stared at the sheriff, who pulled out a cigarette, lit it, and drew a long pull of smoke into his less-than-healthy lungs.

"I need to stop smoking." He said to himself.

He looked up at the Rocky Mountains, flicked some ash into the bushes, then turned and looked at Hank. "Hank, you're a smart cat, you served our country as an officer in Army Intelligence.

But intelligence is my middle name. Oh sure, you could fool any number of fire investigators from Cheyenne to Denver. But not here, and not now."

Arlo took another long puff giving Hank a chance to interject.

"You know Arlo, your best drama is laced with BS, cut to the chase man!"

Arlo exhaled up towards the porch ceiling, the smoke was full of hot drama. He swung his eyes around to Hank and said.

"You Hank, are my prime suspect, logic decrees you want the insurance money on this place. You're under house arrest until I can further investigate this." "Wait just a minute Arlo! You obviously suffer from dementia or insanity!

Why would I want to damage my place?

When I die, I intend to leave this property to my daughter and grandson. This ranch is their inheritance! I love Windy Hill, and I suggest you remember my hospitality to you, and get your sour ass off my property!"

Trinity pulled on Tom's hand and looked into his eyes. She whispered, "did you know you're inheriting this place? We could build a brand new barn for me to launch a business in! Take me downstairs and kiss me!"

Tom ignored Trinity, let go of her hand, and followed the Law out to their patrol car. "Sheriff Arlo, could I talk to you for a minute, sir?" Of course, Tom, what's up?"

"Sheriff, I agree with my grandfather. He would never set fire to anything he loved, especially this farm. It's been in his family for generations! My ancestors are buried up top of that hill beneath those 5 old oak trees. I'm only 17, I'll be 18 in a couple of months, but I'd like to ask you to please reconsider your decision. There must be other suspects! What about that Brady kid, I think he's a senior in High school. I heard he vandalized the school and set the science lab on fire. Then there are all the developers dreaming about buying this land and building homes. Maybe one of them did this?" Tom's eyes pleaded with the Sheriff.

"You bring up some good points Tom, there are other suspects, but let me ask you a question.

Do you think there's any chance your mother would go out on a date with me? She smiled at me twice this morning at breakfast and she's still the girl I fell in love with!"

Tom couldn't believe what he was hearing.

"Well Sheriff, I can tell you, from my perspective, she dates intelligent and kind men. But they have to have a backbone and stand up for what's right. But sir, I know my grandfather has always respected you and called you a fair-minded man. So I can put in a good word for you with my mom."

Deputy Bruce kicked a rock across the driveway, then looked at the front porch and saw Trinity watching him. He tipped his hat to Trinity and stood tall like a peacock showing off his feathers.

The sheriff shook Tom's hand and replied, "You're a breath of fresh air in this town Tom. You're not afraid to call a spade a spade.

I might be looking to hire another deputy in 2 years. You should finish school and send me your resume! Our town needs more young men like you!"

Deputy Bruce walked to the patrol car and inhaled another long look at the gorgeous Trinity. Her lovely young figure had intoxicated him. Arlo shot the young deputy a disapproving glance, and whispered, "Put your eyeballs back in your head Bruce!

You're 24 and she's a teenager!"

Trinity waved and smiled at Bruce, she loved a handsome young man in uniform.

Tom said goodbye and walked back to Trinity. She wrapped an arm around him and said, "What was that all about?"

"I just asked the sheriff the appropriate way to kiss a pretty girl." Tom replied, trying not to laugh.

Trinity grinned and ran her fingers up his ticklish ribs, he laughed and ran towards the backyard. She followed him like a cheetah chasing a rabbit.

Sherry looked out the kitchen window and watched the beautiful Trinity chasing Tom and wrap her arms around her son and take him down. Trinity lay on top of Tom and stared into his honest black eyes, then kissed him deeply.

Sherry looked away and realized it had been quite a while since she had felt the strong arms of a real man hold her.

And she hoped her handsome son and his gorgeous girlfriend were being careful!! The last thing she needed was to host a baby shower! "I love you!" Tom whispered to Trinity.

Investigation

She blushed and giggled and searched desperately for the courage to tell Tom she loved him too, but couldn't find the words. Instead, she traced his eyebrows and said,

"I know you don't like bullies, and you told me if you had been there when my dad was yelling at me and making me cry, you would have put a stop to it. I'm thinking just now, you went and talked to the Sheriff and put a stop to his ridiculous accusations towards your grandfather. Am I Right?"

"My grandfather can take care of himself." Tom replied straightaway.

Trinity kissed his nose and softly replied….

"You're a brave man, Tom, I feel safe and protected when I'm with you." Trinity took a deep breath and closed her eyes.

Tom watched as she struggled with her emotions.

"I love you!" Trinity blurted out, then laid her head on Tom's chest and cried. "Why are you crying, Trin, what's wrong?" Tom asked with a worried voice.

"I just feel like crying Tom, I'm a girl and we do that." Tom massaged Trinity's back and then held her tightly. In a minute she sat up and looked into his eyes, while her tears fell.

"You know what?" Trinity asked. "Tell me," Tom replied.

Trinity wiped away her tears and whispered,

"It's hard for me to say; I love you. My family never used that phrase."

Tom and Trinity closed their eyes and cuddled together in the grass for over an hour. Both still tired from their trip. "Tell me something new?" Trinity whispered into Tom's ear. He smiled and kissed the end of her nose, and said,

"You're beautiful!" "No, something new silly!" She replied.

They both laughed and loved being together. Finally, Tom put on a serious face and said,

"Arlo told me he knows my father, they're friends. And he said my dad is an amazing man, and not homeless." Trinity smiled sincerely and replied,

"Amazing, just like his son."

***

That afternoon, Connie began hanging window curtains, and one for the shower. Her phone beeped with a text, it was from Tom.

"Grandma, my girlfriend Trinity and I arrived a few days early, we spent the night at the farm, and we're on our way to see you. My mom gave us your address. See you soon!"

Connie smiled and was in a rare happy mood.

She turned on some music and minutes later, while hanging her bedroom window curtain she heard a knock on the door, followed by a sudden explosive hammering on her wall, that startled her into a fall off a stepladder.

Tom and Trinity were at her door and heard it all.

Connie fell onto her oak dresser and bounced off, then ended up on the floor, in a world of hurt. She cried out as her right knee exploded in burning pain. She screamed and then yelled:

"Help! Help me!" She screamed again as another loud jackhammering noise tore into her wall. "Tom, did you hear that? A woman screaming and crying for help!" Trinity blared out.

"That's my Grandma and the door is locked." Tom replied in a calm panic.

"I'll run to the office for help and ask for a key." Trinity replied.

"No, we don't have time for that, I'll kick the door down! Stand back!! I saw a Marine do this in a movie!" Tom yelled. "What are you doing? You're not an army guy!"

"I'm kicking the door down!" Tom replied as he backed up and slammed his shoulder into the wooden door. It groaned while wood splinters shot out everywhere. Next, he kicked the handle with his boot, then stepped back and rammed the door hard like a Denver linebacker.

With a crash, he burst into the apartment, tripped over a box of kitchen gadgets, and fell to the floor with a groan. Trinity stepped over Tom and mumbled.

'Boys!"

Using her blooming women's intuition, Trinity dashed into the bedroom and found Connie in a heap on the floor. "Hi! You had a fall, your knee is hurt. Everything's going to be ok, we're here and I know first aid!"

"Who are you?" Connie asked while tears fell down her cheeks, from the pain. "I'm Trin, Tom's girlfriend."

"You're a girl!" Connie replied in shock.

"Yeah, last I checked, I was!" Trinity said with a giggle. "Can you straighten your knee?" Connie stared up at Trinity and her pretty long blond hair and bright blue eyes and said:

"Yes, I can bend my knee, and, oh my, you're absolutely beautiful!"

Trinity beamed at the compliment, and put her thumb on Connie's wrist, to check her heart rate. "I think you got a bad sprain is all," Trinity said with a comforting smile.

Tom limped into the bedroom and hugged his grandmother. "Your grandson put on a cape in the hall and kicked your door down." Trinity giggled and rolled her eyes.

Connie rested while Trinity and Tom hung the curtains and helped unpack. In a little while, Trinity announced: "I'm hungry." "What do you feel like?"

Tom asked.

"What's around here?" Trinity replied as she unpacked a new box of dishes, and asked Tom for a kiss. "So do ya want to make out or eat?" He replied.

"I'm going to eat you!" Trinity growled with a grin.

"Um, there's a couple of burger places, a Dairy Queen, a diner, The Valley Smokehouse is a bar and serves barbecue." Tom pulled some money out of his wallet and handed it to Trinity.

"Babe, why don't you choose, and bring me a carry-out, whatever looks good. I'm going to go check on grandma, I'll text you with whatever she wants to eat." "K," Trinity replied, followed by, "your grandma is nice, I like her. She said I was beautiful, was that just something to say to a strange girl or a real compliment?" "My grandma is a straight shooter, she never just says stuff, ya know," Tom replied.

"Did you tell her how upset you are, she moved out of the farmhouse." Trinity asked. "No, not yet."

"Why not? You're sort of a straight shooter too." Trinity said with a wink, and added, "You know, Wyoming is the 'Cowboy State'… I think I'm goin' get me a cowboy hat and have a shoot out!

Maybe line up bottles on a fence and shoot 'em up! I might need cowgirl boots too!" Trinity exclaimed.

"You think I should?" Tom asked.

"Should what?" Trinity inquired as she pulled an imaginary pistol out of her front pocket with lightening speed, and shot a lamp. "Ask my grandma, why she moved out?"

"You should do what you think is right Tom, you want a Dr Pepper?" "Yes please." He replied.

***

Trinity walked 5 blocks to the burger joint for 3 meals, and bumped into the town's high school bully on 2nd Street, in front of the auto parts store. He wasted no time revealing his reputation.

"Hey baby, looks like you're walking right into my life! How about a kiss to get us acquainted?"

Trinity completely ignored him and continued walking at the same pace. She had a brown belt in martial arts and knew how to defend herself. Trinity also had prior experience with young men with his SAT score.

"Hey chickie, I'm talking to you." Brady announced as he ran ahead and stood in her way on the sidewalk. She walked around him, totally oblivious to his existence. Brady's two friends stood to the side and laughed. Brady grabbed Trinity's arm and forcefully spun her around to face him.

She now stood inches from the thug's face and looked up into his eyes. "What kind of kiss do you want?" Trinity asked matter of factly. Brady and his 2 friends laughed and exchanged goofy immature hand gestures with each other.

Brady grinned, knowing he was going to get way more than he ever dreamed of from this girl. She didn't even put up a fight. Brady couldn't stop laughing as Trinity asked him again.

"I've got things to do, just tell me what kind of kiss you want. Maybe my arms around your neck, for a little intensity? Do you know how to kiss a girl?" Trinity asked with a pretty smile. She looked into his eyes as Brady leaned down to kiss her.

When his lips were one inch away, Trinity slammed her knee up into Brady's groin, then punched him hard in the throat. Instantly the 6 foot, 2 inches, 225-pound bully bent over in excruciating pain. Then crashed to the sidewalk, barely able to moan.

"Are you done, or would you like another kiss?" Trinity asked Brady. "I'm sorry!"

He whimpered in a flurry of coughs and groans.

She looked over at the other two, and softly said, "would you boys like a kiss too?"

They ran off just as a police cruiser pulled up onto the sidewalk and an officer jumped out. He saw everything and immediately cuffed Brady, got him up, and called him by name.

"I'm calling your mother Brady!" "You ok Miss?" The Deputy asked.

Trinity shook her head yes and asked if she could go on her way. "Do you want to press charges?"

The tall and very handsome officer asked.

"No sir, I'm sure this young man had me mixed up with someone else. Thank you, Deputy Bruce." Trinity calmly retorted, then glared at Brady with laser eyes. She turned and continued walking to the burger joint. The deputy's eyes were glued to her lovely figure.

"Wait, please, can I have a word?" The young deputy asked.

Trinity walked back to the patrol car and waited quietly.

Brady was frozen in pain and groaned as Deputy Bruce guided him into the back seat of his police cruiser. "Please don't call my mom!" Brady pleaded in a whisper. He stared at Trinity and wondered how a beautiful young woman could take him out in mere seconds.

The young deputy closed the rear door, looked at Trinity, and asked; "Brazilian Jiu-Jitsu?" "Yes sir," Trinity replied, with a pretty grin.

"You're a skilled student, Brady is a big guy, and you had him incapacitated in under 3 seconds! Your form was perfect, and fluid.

A very impressive real-life maneuver!

I'm Officer Bruce Marsdan, and you are?"

"Trinity Smithe." She replied. "You don't remember, but we've met before."

"Yes! At Hank's house, Arlo and I stopped by for an arson investigation and stayed for breakfast. Trinity, I'm sorry I didn't remember you!"

"No worries, I'm wearing a different color sun dress today…..surely that's why!" Trinity replied, teasing him, with flirting mixed in. She noticed his powerful male torso, and chiseled jawline, hot enough to stop a girl's heart.

"What belt do you train for?" He asked.

"Black," Trinity replied softly, their eyes locked in a trance of attraction. "So you're currently a brown belt, aka level 4 out of 5?"

"Yes sir," Trinity answered with a gorgeous smile, and wondering why all the questions.

Deputy Bruce walked closer to Trinity and leaned against the patrol car. His immaculate white shirt and blue tie mesmerized Trinity. While his gentle confidence and commanding presence took her breath away.

"Can I explain, why all the questions."

He asked her. Trinity's adoring eyes said yes. "I recently earned my black belt and I'm trying to open a Jiu-Jitsu Academy in

Hope Valley. I currently drive to Cheyenne for training. In 2 weeks I'll become a Professor of Jiu Jitsu.

Would you be interested in helping me run the academy? It's about 5 minutes from here, and I've got 55 students signed up from all over the county. You could work for your black belt, and become a Professor too."

Trinity stood perfectly still, as her long blond hair blew across her face, and asked, "what will you pay per hour, I need a job at least till I get my small business up and running. I'm new in town."

"How much do you want?" He asked.

"35.00 an hour, and 50.00 an hour when I become a Professor." Her pretty blue eyes were focused on his adorable green eyes. Deputy Bruce grinned and replied.

"You drive a hard bargain!

You're hired! Will you stay for a year if I give you a 500.00 hiring bonus?" Trinity smiled at Bruce, she saw the desire in his eyes.

But Trinity knew how to play with a man....she abruptly turned and continued to the burger place. Bruce's eyes followed Trinity until she crossed the street. He was mesmerized by her brash, yet playful personality. He wanted to handcuff her deadly smile. And Bruce was positive Trinity Smithe was the most beautiful girl he had ever seen.

"Hey!! I need to use the bathroom, can you hurry it up! You'd think you never saw a girl before." Brady yelled from the back seat.

Chapter 6

LOVE AND KISSES

The next morning, Trinity walked with Tom down the corridors of Hope Valley High, towards his classroom. It was the first day of school, his senior year. She popped into a restroom and Tom stood in the hall waiting for her.

"I thought I smelled sheep poop in here!

If it isn't Tom the farmer! Are you here to mop floors and clean toilets? I heard they're looking for an assistant janitor. Brady walked up and shoved Tom into the wall. Boston sheep farmers are not welcome here!" Brady announced.

"You do that again Brady, and I'll have you kissing the floor!" Tom retorted.

"Is that right, you little worm, did your mommy not change your diapers this morning? It sort of stinks in here." Brady shoved Tom into the wall again.

Tom, punched Brady and flipped the big linebacker onto the floor.

Just then Trinity walked out of the restroom and glared at Brady. "Are you back for more?" She asked in a sarcastic tone.

Brady turned pale and motioned for Tom to stop, he stood, and walked backwards away from Tom and Trinity. "Is she your girlfriend?" Brady asked in an alarmed voice

"What's it to you?" Tom asked as he began walking toward Brady. "You keep her away from me Tom!

She's a menace to society!"

"You scared of girls now Brady?" Tom jeered. "Let me see your phone Brady." Tom said.

"Why do you want my phone?"

"I just want to put my cell # in your phone, so you can text me, I'll fight you anytime and anyplace Brady, just you and me! How about today 3:00."

Trinity stared at Brady and walked right behind Tom. She exuded a quiet confidence that scared Brady to death. Suddenly he turned and ran out of an emergency exit, terrified of Trinity and her martial arts.

The doors fire alarm began blaring. "You ok?" Tom asked Trinity.

She proceeded to tell him about her sidewalk encounter last night, and the job offer. "Brady touches you again, Trin, and I'll kill him!"

Love and Kisses

She giggled and kissed Tom passionately, then said.

"You're the first guy who's ever wanted to protect me! I'll see you tonight! My knight!"

***

After class, Tom headed to the exit, but a pretty voice followed him and called out. "Hey Tom, wait up!"

Rory watched his eyes automatically check out her pretty young figure and beautiful long red hair. "Hey Rory! How have you been?"

"Good, Tom, this is my friend, Shania!Shania, this is Tom, he's from back East but spends lots of summers here at his grandparent's place next door to us." Shania stared at the floor, and softly said "hi," she was shy, especially around good-looking young men.

"Come join us for lunch Tom! We're headed to the diner, you know, 'Earlee Mug' diner on Main."

Tom agreed and enjoyed a fun lunch with Rory and Shania, but he had to work hard to keep from staring at Rory. She was gorgeous! After lunch and a couple of video games, Tom had to leave.

"Hey! It's nice seeing you again Rory!

Bye Shania, it was nice to meet you!"

The moment Tom stepped out of the restaurant, both girls screamed. "He is soooo hot!"

Rory watched Tom out the window, and softly said, "by the end of the year, I'm going to kiss him!"

***

Later that afternoon, Rory reflected on her life, as she finished the barn chores. Her imagination had flown back 16 year's to the day she was conceived.

Her mother was 'dating' 5 different men in Casper. An accountant, a cowboy from Montana, an attorney, a Vietnam veteran drifter, who worked at the bowling alley, and a mechanic at the shop she took her car to.

Problem was she had no idea who Rory's father was. She was too embarrassed to ask 5 men for DNA samples and 2 of them had left the state, by the time she discovered her pregnancy.

Her mom didn't understand why Rory was so upset, but for Rory, not knowing who her father was, disturbed her on many levels.

Rory had met Trinity and the two young women had an instant dislike for one another. Not much was said, but there was bad chemistry between them. They seemed natural enemies, like lions and hyenas. But they both had eyes for Tom.

And to Rory's chagrin, Jerry introduced himself to Trinity in the barn, and shook her hand. They somehow liked each other, and chatted about the best properties to hold on the board game, Monopoly.

***

2 hours later, Tom heard voices and ran up the basement stairs. He walked up to the side door and stood be-

Love and Kisses

hind his grandfather. "What do you mean he's missing?" Tom asked with a worried look.

"I can't find him anywhere!" Rory blurted out. She wiped away tears and continued.

"My mom is working and sleeping in the city like she always does. I'm in charge and Jerry's only 9 you know. His stupid rat is gone too.

He drives me nuts, he's a goofy little boy and I'm afraid I've been hard on him the last few weeks, he mumbled something this morning about running away, and I just laughed it off.

Are all 9 year old boys so scattered and goofy?" "Have you called the police?" Hank inquired.

"No, not yet, Jerry comes over here a lot when he's upset and your animals comfort him." Rory looked into Tom's eyes and softly said:

"He's my little brother, what am I going to do?"

Tom stepped out onto the porch and saw Rory's eyes were full of rattled emotions. He grabbed her hand and ran down the stairs, "come on, let's go look in the barn!"

Moments later, Tom slid the big barn door open and felt for the light switch.

"I already looked in the barn!" Rory exclaimed as she tightened her grip on Tom's hand. "We'll look again, I'll go upstairs in the loft and you look under the cars, tractors and trucks."

Tom turned and looked at Rory, her eyes were glued to him. She was even more beautiful with teary eyes. The male in him wanted to kiss her. "I'm so scared!" She whimpered right into his heart. Rory knew Tom was attracted to her and she played right into Tom's testosterone filled mind. "Can't we look together, I feel safe with you Tom!"

"Ok, let's look upstairs first, come on."

Rory followed and held tight to Tom's hand, as he led her up the big front staircase. "Aren't you scared?" She whispered into his natural instincts to protect her.

Tom ignored her and yelled out. "Jerry! Are you up here?"

They searched everywhere and Tom saw several folding tables Trinity had set up for her small business.

He stopped and glanced at a sheet of paper where she'd been writing ideas for her new company name, 'Sheepland Flowers' and 'TNT Flowers' seemed to be her favorites. Both were circled many times. Rory laid her head on Tom's back. Her left hand wrapped around his abs.

Her right hand touched the letters 'TNT'.

She studied them intently, trying to ascertain their significance. Tom suddenly seemed in a trance as he turned and stared at Rory.

Her pretty young curves, long chestnut hair and effervescent blue eyes teased his young male mind.

Rory looked up to ask about 'TNT' and saw his eyes locked onto her. "Tom?" She whispered as she squeezed his hand and smiled in a way she knew, intoxicated guys.

"Are you ok?" She asked softly, caressing his imagination even more.

Tom, awoke from his trance and met her eyes. He blushed and realized, Rory knew what he'd been thinking. "Um, I'm guessing 'TNT' means Trinity and Tom." He replied nervously, as he looked away.

Rory knew Tom felt something for her, it was obvious by the way he stared at her, they had a real chemistry. A woman knows these things. She stepped closer to nuzzle up to him, but suddenly a voice flew up from downstairs. "Tom, are you in here?" Trinity asked.

Her pretty eyes saw them upstairs in the loft. She had seen Tom staring at Rory and was fuming mad. "Yeah, we're upstairs, um looking for Jerry."

"Well is he up there?" Trinity replied like a sarcastic machine gun. "Uh, no, he's not here."

"Well maybe you should come down, and look elsewhere, who's up there with you?" Trinity asked in an odd voice that precluded she already knew the answer. "We'll be right down"…….Rory replied as her eyes stared into Tom's, dreaming of leaving a note in his heart.

Rory stepped back, Tom was blushing, and embarrassed for his split-second gushing over her. Then his eyes met Trinity's, over the loft balcony rail, but instead of a look of indignation, Trinity simply said;

"Maybe we should all split up and start looking for Jerry!"

"Come on!" Rory took Tom's hand and led him to the stairs. They passed under a bright lightbulb at the top of the stairway, she let go of his hand and saw the deer in the headlights look still in his eyes. Rory grinned slightly, she was relatively new to this ancient game of flirting with a man. But she was shocked at the power she held over Tom.

Rory ran down the stairs and forced several tears to come, she spread sadness over her face, like sunscreen, and sniffled, just as she emerged from the creaking stairway, and into the suspicious gaze of Trinity.

Rory ran past Trinity's menacing eyes and out the door, then dashed into the fields to find Hank's flock of sheep. Jerry might be reading them a story. But in Rory's heart, she knew Jerry was fine, as her imagination was still upstairs in the loft, kissing Tom.

Trinity walked quickly out of the barn. Tom pivoted and ran after her. "Trin!! Wait!"

She ignored him, and marched post haste to the chicken coop. Her emotions were on fire with rage. She thought of sharp jagged words to stab Tom's heart with. Trinity had learned to control the explosive anger she'd inherited from her mother. But right now she soooo wanted to punch Tom with a diatribe of indignation, maybe something like,

How dare you flirt with that girl Tom, she's only a sophomore!! A mere child! And you were drooling all over her!

Instead, beautiful Trinity took a deep breath and gazed across the chessboard of her life. She understood the wandering eyes of young men, and let Tom's fascination with Rory slide right into the trash.

Right now, Trinity's entire existence was dependent on Tom, and his half-crazed family. Burning bridges was not in her best interest.

She cherished Tom's love for her, his constant protection, and his unwavering devotion. Trinity knew all too well, risking a breakup with Tom, would leave her all but homeless and possibly sleeping in an alley and begging for food.

She had burned the bridge with her parents and right now, lived in a new land, with a generous and kind family. But a new and more powerful rage for Rory, burned in Trinity's mind. She knew Rory wanted Tom, and it infuriated her.

Trinity felt Tom reaching for her hand, she stopped and fell into his arms. Overwhelmed with emotion, tears trickled down her cheeks. "I love you" he gushed into her ear.

Trinity kissed Tom with a deep and passionate kiss that spoke volumes of her love for him.

In just over 30 seconds, she ended their kiss and touched her nose to his. She knew he was squirming inside and listened as he blurted out, "That was nothing you know, just a supportive hug. Rory had been crying Trin.

I had to do something, and I've known Rory since she was a little girl. I'm like a big brother to her, you know! She was scared of losing Jerry. And women are just, well they're all just suitcases of emotions!"

"Is that right! Suitcases of emotions, you say. Well, who was calm and controlled when we found your grandma lying on the floor? Huh! I was in her bedroom caring for her while you were Superman, all crashed on the floor. I told you kicking down the door was a stupid macho thing to do. But no!

You had to play GI Joe, like a 7 year old boy!

Kick the door down, toss in a grenade, storm the fort, kiss any girl named Rory, and hoist the flag. Beat your chest and hurrah for men!

You can be sooo immature at times Tom. You're 17 going on 12!"

Trinity stared into Tom's eyes, and realized she had said too much. She hurt his feelings, and bruised his heart. Tom did not need the heavy hand she had used with her father. Tom was a kind and sensitive man who constantly fussed over her. Right now he looked like a man who lost his dog and got punched in the gut.

His eyes were misted over, and full of hurt. "I'm sorry Tom, I shouldn't have said all that."

Love and Kisses

Trinity whispered to him. "I'm so sorry! Please forgive me Tom! I love you so much!"

Trinity held Tom and caressed his heart. In a moment, Tom said…..

"I'm sorry too Trinity, the last thing I want to do is hurt you!"

"Are we having our first real fight?" She asked. Trinity had succeeded in sending a shot across his bow, a warning, but she went too far. Right now she had to re- boot his heart and be certain her name was the only female on his hard drive.

"Jerry is a delightful little boy. But Tom, you're a guy, and you may not understand this, but try ok honey.

Rory is no longer a little girl, I saw in her eyes, a desire for you. You're an attractive man, and maybe I'd have tried to kiss you if I was in her shoes.

But I think you need to be certain, Rory understands that I'm your girlfriend. You're off limits to her. And I have one more thing to say, then I'll let it go, a young girl like Rory has no idea how to keep you happy. And I do."

She kissed him gently, then whispered, "Come to the guest house tonight at 11:00. We need some time alone."

***

"Would you two love birds, get out of the way!"

Hank moaned as he squeezed past Tom and Trinity and pushed open the chicken coop door. "Jerry!" Hank exclaimed. "What are you doing in here with the chickens?"

Jerry sat on the coop floor with 15 hens standing around him. He looked up in shock as Hank stood towering over him. "We're having a family meeting, me and the chickens." Jerry said matter of factly with a tinge of sadness in his voice. Tom and Trinity peered around Hank and said hello to the boy.

"A family meeting about what?" Tom asked.

"I don't want to say, cause it's a secret meeting." Jerry replied stoically.

"Tom, he's crying," Trinity whispered as she slid past the two men and sat on the floor next to Jerry, and pulled the boy into her lap. "Well, we all love you Jerry, and we're worried something's got you upset. Can you tell us what's wrong? Please!"

Trinity asked as she rubbed Jerry's tense back, in little circles, while she wanted to scream. 15 chickens were looking at her, and they all had tails. Jerry looked up into Trinity's eyes and began,

"I'm worried Mr. Hank is selling all the chickens, and the whole farm. Grandma wants him to move into town with her. I miss Grandma, she makes me feel special. I don't want Grandpa Hank to move.

All these chickens are my friends and they think I'm cool. And I'm reading them a book about pirates.

And they're scared they might be sold too. Wouldn't you be scared? This is their home, you know!" Trinity shook her head yes, and softly answered . "Yeah, I'd be scared too."

Just then Rory walked into the coop, sat on the floor next to Trinity and plucked Jerry out of Trinity's lap and into hers. She shot Trinity a deadly frown. Snowball poked his face out of Jerry's pocket and launched nasty looks at both Trinity and Rory. They were girls, and girls were trouble!

With groans and noisy knees, Hank slowly knelt next to Jerry. He looked at the little boy for a moment, then said, "I give you my word son, no one is selling these chickens. They're part of this farm, just like you and Rory are, do you understand?"

Jerry looked up into Hanks's kind eyes and smiled. "You hungry," Hank asked, with a grin.

"I'm as hungry as a Tyrannosaurus Rex!"

Jerry exclaimed. "I could eat a million grasshoppers!"

"Ok, you help me up, and let's go get some dinner. My daughter is on her way home from the grocery store and she'll whip something up for us! You and Rory join us for dinner, ok.

You're both part of our family."

***

Rory was tired of being around Trinity, and headed across the alfalfa field, for home. She decided flirting with Tom was not sustainable. Her behavior was manipulative and dishonest, and frankly seemed something Trinity would do.

She needed a strategy that was more straight forward and true to who she was, for any chance to win Tom's heart. Rory decided loving him, and caring for him in a way a true friend should, was the only way he would ever notice her.

She had to be herself, for any hope of an honest and loving relationship with Tom. Rory still had the instincts of a teenager, but she had a wisdom far beyond her year's.

Somehow Rory's desire to be Tom's girlfriend was foremost in her heart, she had never wanted anything more. Except maybe to know who her father was, and what he was like. But Rory would never discover her father's identity, yet she hoped he had qualities like kindness, strength of character, and integrity.

She wanted her father to be fun too,

a perceptive man with a quick smile and an easy laugh. Yet he would stand like a mountain protecting his family. She often dreamed of hiking with her dad, on long interludes with no conversation.

Just the beautiful awareness that he loved her, and would always be her papa.

She imagined too, he was a big and powerful man. Well respected in the community. Oddly, these were the same qualities Rory saw in Tom. She loved all the attention Tom gave to her little brother, and Jerry loved Tom too.

Rory would never know her father, but she could love and care for the young man who reminded her of him. Tom might be small in stature but he was incredibly strong and capable.

A master wrestler, a seasoned boxer, and an affinity for all around martial arts. Rory loved the fact that Tom could take on any adversary and come out on top. Just the way Tom's chest filled out his t-shirts was enough to turn on any girl.

Rory had finally realized, just being herself was the surest way to win Tom's heart. And she had her sails set to be in Tom's arms and kissing him by year's end. "Hey!" A voice called out across the alfalfa field. She turned back and smiled.

"Will you come for dinner?" Tom asked. Rory shook her head yes, and yelled back, "yes, but I'll be over later, I need to be alone for a while." "I'll ask Trinity to keep a plate warm for you!"

Rory smiled and yelled back, "thank-you!"

Chapter 7

FAMILY DINNER

In a few minutes, Sherry walked in the side door and set a bag of groceries on the counter. Trinity was watching a movie in the family room and immediately got up to help with dinner. She stepped over Tom, who was asleep on the floor. Jerry was setting up a game of 'Risk'. He and Tom enjoyed playing all sorts of games together whenever Tom was in town.

Monopoly was their favorite game, and last summer Tom began teaching Jerry the intricacies of the board game 'Risk'. "Hi Sherry!" Trinity exclaimed as she began digging through the grocery bag and putting things away in the kitchen. "Hey Trinity!" Sherry replied with a warm hug.

"What are we having?" Trinity asked as her stomach rumbled. "You like spaghetti?" Sherry asked.

"Yeah, I love spaghetti, I could eat it for breakfast, lunch, and dinner!"

Family Dinner

"Well, I looked in the basement freezer and found a gallon of my mom's homemade spaghetti. It's in the fridge now, could you pop it in the microwave to defrost it. I'm sure it's still mostly frozen.

Then warm it in a big saucepan.

I bought pasta, some broccoli, and dinner rolls. Oh, and butter, my dad likes butter, not margarine. My mom always buys the cheapest margarine she can find. So what about your family Trinity, you haven't talked about them much. Do you miss them?"

Sherry asked as she put spaghetti noodles to boil. "Yes and no, and I don't miss all the arguing.

Before I forget, Jerry is joining us for dinner, Hank invited him. Rory's invited too but there was some drama in the chicken coop earlier and she ran off." Trinity replied.

Sherry rolled her eyes "yeah, that family lives and sleeps drama, but I really like Rory.

The mother is usually gone for weeks at a time. She works at a law firm in Casper, but from what I hear, it's always men who draw her into town. I understand she's slept with every attorney in the state!"

"Does she bring them home?" Trinity asked politely.

"Once in a while, but the real tragedy is Rory and Jerry have been latchkey kids for years. They've been raising themselves." "Should I rinse all the broccoli?" Trinity asked.

"Yeah sure, let's steam it all so we can have leftovers for 2 nights. God knows why my mom freezes spaghetti by the gallon. Who eats a gallon of spaghetti? So, you started to tell me about your family Trinity, you're from Boston right?"

"Um, yeah there's not much to tell, I have 2 younger brothers, my dad owns a bunch of hotels and restaurants and works 24x7 chasing the American dream. My mom discovered charities about 6 years ago and is always gone saving the world.

So, I'm a lot like Rory I guess you could say. I raised myself really, and then I met your son, and I love him. I love being here and being a part of your family! It's very refreshing." Trinity replied.

"Oh, honey, this family is far from normal. My mom moved out and has upset me.

I know my dad is hurting but he never shows any emotion. Typical man you know.

I've got an acupuncture appointment tomorrow to help with my stress. Do you like applesauce?" "I love applesauce!" Trinity replied with a smile.

"Here, can you open this and set it on the table, it's my mom's homemade golden delicious applesauce from last year." Sherry added. "Tom! Honey could you set the table please and ask Jerry to wash his hands before dinner." Sherry yelled into the family room. "Tom's asleep, I can set the table. Right after I pour the spaghetti into this saucepan." Trinity replied.

Family Dinner

"Be careful about pampering your man Trinity." Sherry said, they added,

"I did that with my ex after we married and I became his servant. Well, I'm no one's servant! We had tons of fights over that. Tom's a good boy but he's a man and they constantly take advantage of everyone."

Trinity stayed quiet and polite, but not entering into the conversation about men. Her father had written the book on taking advantage of his wife. But Tom was a man too, and he constantly fussed over Trinity. She was very grateful for Tom Whitmore.

"Hello!" An older female voice drifted up the side door steps. Connie walked into the kitchen and exploded. "Sherry, that's my spaghetti! I'm here to get both gallons and you're serving it for dinner!

No! Get it out of the saucepan and back into my Tupperware! Right this minute!"

Sherry refused to allow her mother any emotional ground and walked to the stove, raised the heat on the burner, and stirred the spaghetti. She tasted it and replied, Mom, this is really good spaghetti! You're the best cook I know."

"Did you hear what I said, young lady!" Connie curtly roared at Sherry.

"Mom, you walked in and immediately started yelling at me, you'd never permit me to act in such a way in this house! Why can't you ask how I am, or inquire about Tom, Trinity, or Dad?

No, everything's about you mom. And I'm not packing up your spaghetti! But I'd like you to help Trinity set the table and join us for dinner. Have you met Trinity? She's Tom's girl.

We're trying to be a family here Mom!" Sherry replied.

"Of course, I've met Trinity, and stop patronizing me, Sherry! That's all you do is push my buttons and start fights! You're just like your father!" Connie retorted. "Mom, could you help Trinity find a pan to steam the broccoli please?"

"This is my house, Sherry!" You don't come in here and order me around! Trinity's a smart girl, she'll find my pans! And they're not your pans Sherry they're mine!" "Mom, if you cannot act like an adult, and be kind and considerate of others, like you raised me. Then get out! Now!"

"Sherry! I'm warning you!" Connie boomed out like a Marine drill sergeant. "Don't talk to me like I'm a child. I'm your mother! And this is my house, so you get out!"

Trinity ran to Tom and shook him. Trinity hated fighting, and her asthma kicked in from hearing Connie and Sherry going at it.

"Tom, wake up! Tom they're yelling! "What! What time is it? I fell asleep! What's wrong Trin, you look all upset! And you're crying! Who's yelling?"

Tom sat up as Trinity replied, "your grandma came a minute ago and she and your mom are fighting in the

Family Dinner

kitchen. I can't handle fighting, and yelling! I'm going to get in the car and go for a ride. I'll be back later! They're yelling at each other Tom! They're being mean, like how my mom and dad fight. I can't handle yelling Tom! I just can't!"

"No, Trinity, you stay here, please!

Give me 5 minutes to talk to my mom and my grandma. I'll stop the fight, everything's going to be ok Trin."
"Tom, don't leave me all alone!" Trinity begged.

Tom held his girl for a minute, then softly said; "Trin, go down into my bedroom and close the door. I'll be right down. I'm sorry they're fighting Trin, but give me a minute ok? You'll be safe downstairs. My sweatshirt is in my closet.

No one's going to hurt you, I promise!"

Tom walked Trinity to the basement stairs, then ran to the kitchen, angry and embarrassed his family made Trinity cry. "You know, I never dreamed my own daughter would cast me aside! After all I've done for you!" Connie shouted out.

"Grandma! What's going on here?" Tom demanded as he walked into the kitchen. "Tom!! How are you, honey?" Connie exclaimed with a big hug.

"I don't know Grandma, you and Mom arguing has upset Trinity. She's crying. I don't like seeing my girlfriend cry. If she's upset, then I'm upset!" "I'm sorry Thomas, I just stopped by to pick up the spaghetti I made, and your mom decided to serve it for dinner. Then she got all huffy with me." Tom looked at his mom, as she grabbed some napkins and silverware to finish setting the table. He knew his Mother was angry too.

"Are you staying for dinner, Grandma?" Tom asked.

Connie turned and opened the fridge and had no idea how to reply. She began moving items and re-organizing shelves to the way she liked her fridge arranged. Without stopping her organizing, Connie answered Tom.

"I'd like to talk to Trinity, then I'll decide." "She's downstairs in my bedroom.

I love her Grandma, and she makes me happy. But she doesn't like yelling and arguing.

You and Mom need to stop! Do you understand?"

Tom looked at both women and continued.

"I came here to get away from the stress of that stupid Boston boarding school. I brought Trinity with me, her parents are explosive and mean to her. I need you both to get along and be nice to her. If you can't, we're leaving in the morning!"

Sherry set a handful of silverware down, and looked at her mother. "I'm sorry Mom! I'm sorry I'm cooking your spaghetti. I should have asked you first."

Connie forced her anger to leave and replied; "I'm sorry too Sherry. You're my daughter, and I love you. I'm sorry I said those things." "I love you too Mom!" Sherry softly replied as she hugged her mother.

Family Dinner

Holding her daughter's hand in a sudden change of heart. Connie looked at Tom and said, "Trinity is a beautiful young woman, and Sherry and I will make her feel welcome here, and loved!"

"Thank you!" Tom replied, then asked his grandmother, "will you stay for dinner, please?" "I'll go down and talk to Trinity, and decide.

She's a delightful girl. Tom, you're only 17 and I have no idea how you ended up with such a smart and gorgeous young woman."

***

Trinity walked into Tom's bedroom and closed the door. She reached into his closet, for his old sweatshirt she loved like a trusted Teddy Bear. She picked up a small framed photo of her and Tom and laid on his bed.

Her face was buried deep into Tom's pillow, soon wet from her tears. She realized by running away from home, she'd sort of burned a bridge with her family. But, oddly, her mother's texts now came every day, begging Trinity to come home.

Trinity looked at her mother's message from yesterday for the third time.

"Trinity, who am I fooling, I know I've been a bad mother, but it's obvious to me now, my begging you to come home is falling on deaf ears. Please call me, and tell me you're ok."

Sincerely, Carol

Trinity stared at 'Carol' and sobbed. Her mother never said I love you, but at least she always wrote 'Mom' at the bottom of her texts.

'Mom' became somehow a comfort to Trinity, that at some level, her mother still cared, and loved her. But suddenly it was 'Carol', like Trinity was now just a friend, or acquaintance.

Yesterday, this wouldn't have mattered, but right now, Trinity was scared. Her fantasy world comprised of Tom's family, had shattered.

Tom's mom and grandma were fighting and yelling at each other in the kitchen. Trinity would forever carry in her mind, the dreaded hours of lying on her bed at home, with her head hidden beneath her pillow. She hated the weekly arguments and yelling between her parents.

Dishes flying, and doors slamming. It seemed every year they disliked each other more. The family who had no idea how to say,

'I love you' had evolved into a family with no love at all.

Tom's family had become an oasis of love for Trinity. A place of safety in a crumbling world. Even with Tom's grandma moving out, at least she had not heard any arguments and yelling. No doors slamming or tires screeching out of the driveway. But now her fantasy of a harmonious Wyoming family had crashed down upon her.

Family Dinner

She held the little framed photo of her and Tom to her chest like it was all she had in life; he was her family now.

One young man loved her, and now some pretty, young chic named Rory was trying to steal him away. Trinity wondered if she & Tom should marry. She lay back on his bed, clung to her small framed photo, and curled into a ball.

Suddenly a knock at the door….. "Come in." Trinity said.

The old wood door creaked open and a cane entered the room and stopped. "Trinity, honey, are you ok?"

Connie asked softly.

"I don't know," Trinity replied. "Can I come in?" Connie asked. "Yes please."

Trinity watched as Tom's grandma walked into the room, and looked at her through old and worried eyes. "You're crying honey, what's wrong? Come here."

Trinity ran the few feet across the bedroom and fell into Connie's arms. She was soft, and warm, but tough too and had stood against many storms in her life. Grandma Connie seemed to know exactly what Trinity needed to hear.

"Honey, I don't know you very well yet, but I do know you're a brave and capable young woman. You ran to me when I had fallen and I had no idea who you were. You helped me sit up, you knew first aid, and you told me everything was going to be ok. I know my grandson adores you, and I'm wondering if my argument with Sherry just now, scared you? Am I right Trinity?"

Trinity shook her head yes and handed her cell phone to Connie and pointed to the text from her mother. "What's this?" Connie asked.

They sat on the bed and somehow Trinity knew she had to confide in Connie. She needed help from a woman who knew all about love, the ups and downs, and everything in between.

"It's my mom, back in Boston, she's never been much of a mom. My brothers and me, are like family pets to her. She always made sure we had food and water, then was gone saving the world. My mom has never told me she loves me. Now she signs her texts, with 'Carol' instead of Mom.

When Tom said he was leaving Boston and coming here, my mom was a big reason why I asked him if I could come along. I needed to get away from her, at least for a while. I have a real hard time telling Tom I love him. I do love Tom, very very much but I can see in his eyes it hurts him when he tells me he loves me, and I can't always say it back. And I saw that Rory girl flirting with him. He says it's nothing, but it's not nothing. I saw him looking at her. You know how guys look at girls they like. I thought about punching her! And then I was setting the table and I heard you and Tom's mom arguing and I got scared. My parents argued and yelled at each other for years and I can't handle that anymore."

"Oh honey, families and love are two of the most complex things we women have to navigate in life. Then you throw in men, and it's a wonder we're not all insane. It's not easy being part of a family, and ours is far from perfect. I love Sherry, she's my only daughter. I'll always love her, but I'm not going to let her run my life.

I know that I frustrate her too. She and I are very much alike, yet, we're very different too. I'm sorry our fight scared you.

And I bet you and your mom are alike in many ways, and you might not understand that for years to come. Maybe your mom can't say 'I love you', but I'll bet she would just melt to hear you say it to her. I can't explain why families fight and argue, but all you need to do is be kind, and brave, not a doormat, there's a difference."

***

They walked upstairs together and Trinity sat next to Connie at the dinner table. Hank said hello to Connie and asked how she was. In a moment, he said a blessing over the meal, it seemed forever and a day since Hank had prayed about anything.

Sherry hugged her mom and thanked her for staying for dinner.

Tom and Trinity got up and took plates into the kitchen, and filled them with noodles and spaghetti sauce, one by one. Warm French bread, butter, and Parmesan cheese were already on the table.

Just then the doorbell rang, and Tom ran to see who it was. Edith stood on the porch with a warm, homemade chokeberry pie. Tom held the door open and invited her in. Trinity came to the door too.

"Edith, I'd like you to meet my girlfriend,

Trinity. Trinity, this is Edith, she owns the diner in town." The women exchanged pleasantries and carried Edith's pie into the kitchen. Sherry insisted Edith stay for dinner.

Trinity gave Edith her spot at the table, then squeezed a chair in next to Tom. Moments later, the table was quiet as everyone began eating.

"Connie, your spaghetti is still the best in the valley!" Announced Edith. Hank agreed and told his wife she looked pretty tonight.

Connie blushed and Trinity slid her hand into Tom's under the table. Soon conversation got around to Edith. "I've heard rumors you're trying to sell the diner?" Hank asked.

Yeah, it's gotten too much for me, I bought it as an interim job and to gain experience in the food industry. I might have some interested buyers, a young couple from Florida fell in love with Wyoming and want to settle here."

"Have you heard any gossip recently?" Sherry asked.

"Funny you should ask! I discovered our resident trouble maker Brady is Deputy Bruce's cousin. Small world isn't it!" "How about some pie or cake for dessert?" Sherry asked.

Trinity helped serve dessert, and coffee, while Edith cozied up close to Hank and showed him her cell phone photos of a dozen homes she's looking to purchase in Cheyenne as rental properties.

Connie glared at the two of them, as Edith was close enough to sit on Hank's lap. Tom and Trinity shared a hazelnut coffee and snuggled up on the sofa together. "So, what did you and my grandma talk about?" Tom asked.

"Oh, just girl stuff, and what a handful men are." She giggled and tried to kiss him.

Instead, Tom tickled her and she laughed, and jumped up, and ran out the front door. Tom was in hot pursuit and caught her by the sheep pasture gate. They collapsed on a hay bale as the sun grew sleepy. Tom pulled his girl close and kissed her.

In a few minutes, Tom and Trinity came back into the farmhouse and began clearing the table, doing dishes, and putting leftovers away. They stood by the sink and giggled, and snuck kisses.

Such was the flavor of love in

Hope Valley, Wyoming, on a cool fall evening.

Chapter 8

YOU'RE UNDER ARREST

Within an hour the chokeberry pie was finished, dessert plates put in the dishwasher, and more coffee made. The adults sat around the dining room table playing cards. Sherry laid down an ace and marveled at how much fun her parents were having with Edith. All animosity had been buried for Trinity's sake.

Tom and Trinity wiped the kitchen counters, poured coffee, and tea into empty cups at the table. Minutes later they lay curled up together on the sofa, searching for a movie to watch.

Trinity's small hand was nestled inside Tom's.

Jerry was asleep on the floor, his head on a family room pillow and Trinity had set a throw blanket over him. No one knew where Snowball was, and no one asked. Suddenly, the side door opened and Rory walked in dripping wet. It was pouring rain outside.

She closed the door and slid her shoes off.

"Hi!! Is Jerry still here?" She asked, intending to take him home for the evening.

"Hi, honey, Jerry is sound asleep in the family room, have you had dinner?" Sherry asked.

"Um, no ma'am." Rory replied. Trinity overheard and jumped up and made Rory a plate from the leftovers. Tom set up a TV tray in the family room for Rory and grabbed her silverware and an iced tea.

"Thank you!" Rory said to Trinity with a sincere smile, and added, "your long hair is so pretty!" "Thanks!" Trinity replied and smiled back.

"Would you like salt and pepper?"

"Oh no, this is perfect, thank you, I haven't made homemade spaghetti in I don't know how long." Jerry awoke, and moments later the 4 young people began watching a movie together.

'A Heartland Christmas'. Starring Amber Marshall, and Graham Wardle.

Connie noticed Trinity's kindness to Rory. She liked Trinity straight away.

The girl disliked Rory and was threatened by her advances to Tom. But tonight, Trinity laid her hostilities to rest…….mostly due to what Connie had shared with her downstairs before dinner.

And Rory was playing nice too.

Several hours later, Edith stood and thanked everyone for a delightful evening. Tom slipped on a jacket and walked Edith to her car. It was a clear but cold night, and the rain had stopped. The north wind blew a chill through the valley.

Tom was wearing a thick jean jacket, but the wind blew right through him. Fall was coming on fast. Tom wondered how bad the winters in Wyoming were, he had only been out to the farm in the summers. "It certainly gets cold out here in Wyoming, and the winds are atrocious!" Tom moaned.

Edith laughed. "You ain't seen nothing yet young man, wait till January!"

"I was just thinking about that," Tom said as they walked toward Edith's VW Beetle. "How brutal are the winters here?" He asked.

"Well, it never gets below -40." Edith replied chuckling. "I remember going out to water my horses one nasty winter and the water in the troughs were frozen!" "What did you do?" Tom asked.

"I used a big bat to smash the ice, and hauled buckets of hot water from the house. And then you'd have to do extra trips because it would be frozen all over again within an hour!"

"An hour?" Tom despaired.

"You're young, you'll be fine." Edith replied.

"Yeah, but I can't understand why my grandfather would want to live like this?"

You're Under Arrest

"Your grandfather has been a farmer for a lot of years Tom, and look at this," she made a sweeping gesture towards the sky and the barn illuminated in the moonlight.

I bet you never had views like this in Boston?" she asked. Tom had to admit, it was nice.

"Sorry about that in there," he said gesturing towards the house, "it's just been hard with my Grandparents, you know." "I know," she said.

"The whole town knows, don't they?" Tom said wryly, "that my grandparents are separated I mean?" Edith nodded. "It's hard to keep news quiet in a small town like Hope Valley,"

She touched Tom lightly on the arm. "But you don't need to worry so much though, I am sure it will all work out for the best. And you're liking it here in Hope Valley aren't you?"

Tom hesitated as Brady's ugly face and threatening fist came to mind. "I guess it's okay."

Tom was startled. Behind all the clownish makeup and silly sweaters, Edith was very perceptive. Then he noticed a car parked at the bottom of the hill, all by itself. No one ever parked down there. "I wonder whose car that is, he asked Edith.

"Gee, I don't know, let's ride down there and we can check it out." Edith said.

Tom got into Edith's car and they drove down to the bottom of the hill where the car sat, only illuminated by moonlight. But when they got closer they could see the bright lights of electronic devices, like a phone or a computer inside the car. There was someone inside the car for sure, but what were they doing sitting there at this time of night in the middle of nowhere?

Edith pulled up beside the car. She leaned over and yelled, "Excuse me, can I help you?"

No response. Tom and Edith looked at each other. "Maybe they didn't hear me?" she said to Tom.

"Uh, I'm sure they heard you, I'll just get out and talk-" he went to get out of the car but Edith put a hand on him.

The black car's window started to open just then. It looked like there were two people, a man and a woman inside, and in the light of their computers, Tom could see they were both wearing white shirts and dark suit jackets on top of that. They certainly weren't dressed like your average Wyoming ranchers. Who were these people?

Looking up at Tom, the woman slowly lowered her car window.

"Can I help you?" Tom asked. "Did your car break down or something?" "No," the man answered curtly as he lit a cigarette.

"Okay then, so are you lost? This is my grandfather's property. The main road is back that way" Tom stated. The two stared at Tom.

"Do you know a Justin Bisone?" The woman in the driver's seat asked suddenly.

Tom was taken aback by the question. "Uh, yeah I know a Justin, but I think his last name is LeClerc, not Bisone. He's renting a couple of horse stalls from my grandfather, why do you want to know?"

The woman acted like Tom didn't even exist. "LeClerc is it?" the woman said, looking at her computer. "It's him," she said shortly to the man. She turned the car on and started backing up.

"Hey, wait a minute," Tom shouted, getting out before Edith could stop him this time. "Where are you going? What's this about?"

But the car had already turned and sped off down the road, leaving Tom and Edith in the quiet dark looking at each other flabbergasted. "What was that all about?" he said, getting back in the car.

"It beats me," Edith replied. "They looked like city folk to me, if they were from these parts I would at least recognize them. Now who's this Justin person they were talking about?"

"He's just some guy my grandfather is renting out part of his barn to. Says he's a vet you know." Tom replied. Edith noticed his change in tone. "Says he's a vet? A veteran you mean? And what, you don't believe him?"

Tom shrugged. "I don't know, something seems off about the guy. But I don't know…I need to tell my grandfather about this, Tom said.

Edith looked thoughtful. "I think your grandfather has enough to deal with right now don't you think?" she said, "how about we keep this between us for now Tom? We can be our own little private investigation team, and if we need to we'll talk to Sheriff Arlo, I hear and see a lot at the diner, Tom, not many that come in and through Hope Valley don't stop by the Earlee Mug..and people tend to let their guard down when they're eating burgers," she added.

"Okay," Tom replied reluctantly. He supposed Edith was correct, his grandfather did have a lot to deal with right now with the farm, and if Tom told him what happened with these mysterious people he was likely to tell Justin to get lost, and that would be a loss of income that the farm desperately needed right then, and Rory would be out of a job as well.

Edith drove slowly back to the house.

"Well, it looks like they're talking now," Tom said seeing Connie and Hank thru a window conversing rather loudly.

"Well, your grandfather is a good man," Edith said, he and I go back farther than he does with your grandmother so she better treat him right." Tom chuckled at that. "Thanks for the ride," Tom said, getting out of her car.

"No Problem kiddo and remember, not a word till we know what's going on," she said.

He nodded and closed the car door. He went up the stairs quickly to see what was going on inside. Tom was chagrined that he had not been gone even five minutes before there was a fight going on inside the house.

You're Under Arrest

If his grandmother was anything like his mom, she wasn't going to let his grandfather get a word in edgewise.

When he got inside he could see that Rory and Jerry were in their coats ready to leave. Rory said, "Oh Tom there you are, we were just waiting for you to say goodbye and thanks for inviting us for dinner."

"Where's Trinity?" He said, noticing she wasn't in the kitchen or living room.

"She went back to the guest house to practice her yoga poses, Jerry said. "Tomorrow is the first day that her yoga center is going to be open."

"Right, I forgot. Are you sure you need to leave right now?" Even though he had told Edith he wouldn't say a word about the mysterious car, he was tempted to at least tell Rory.

But Rory said, "Yeah, we have to go. I have homework and Jerry is getting tired, right Jerry! Time for your nighttime YouTube shows."

"I'm not tired," Jerry declared. "I told you that before, this is way more fun than any old YouTube video!" Tom almost chuckled to see the way Jerry was watching his grandparents fight like it was a fun show. "Let's go, Jerry," Rory said, practically pulling him by the collar. "Say goodbye, Jerry."

"Goodbye, Jerry!" He yelled as his sister half dragged/ half pulled him out the door. Tom shut the door behind them and sighed. Then he steeled himself to join his grandparents and mom in the living room.

"You're being a stubborn old coot is what you're being!" Connie was practically shouting. "I'm just not selling," Hank said.

"But you can't possibly take care of the place yourself," Sherry interjected.

"Who says? There's plenty of farmers who live alone in Custer County," Hank said, "some even older than me if you can believe it. Besides I have Tom here to help me now," he gestured for Tom to come sit on the arm of his chair which he did.

Sherry said, "Tom's going to be off to college in the fall Dad."

"Well I don't know about that yet," Tom said annoyed that his mother was trying to determine his life again. She just assumed he was going to college in the fall without even asking if that was what he wanted to do.

His mom and grandmother looked at him like he had two heads.

"What do you mean you're not sure? Of course, you're going to college. You don't think you can have a career working on the farm here do you?" Connie stated. Tom started to regret coming into the room as it seemed his mom and grandmother's wrath was now turned on him.

Tom said, "I'm not saying that, I just want to make my own decisions." "You're just a child." Sherry started to say.

"Look Mom I'm not saying I'm not going to college but that's up to me to decide not you." "Tom, have you forgotten our deal?" Sherry said.

"What deal?" Hank asked.

"It's nothing," Sherry answered quickly giving Tom a look.

"I haven't forgotten anything, but I should be able to make my own decisions about my future," Tom said. "See what you've done Hank?" Connie cried, "You're making problems for everyone."

"I've done no such thing," Hank replied. "I'm not the one that moved out."

"Well, none of this matters because this is Sherry's property and she thinks we should sell the property to Bob Evans. He's coming to take a look at the property tomorrow."

Hank's face went red at the mention of Bob Evans. "Don't even think about having that man step on this property Sherry, it could be dangerous to his health." "You can't run around threatening to kill people Hank, it's crazy," Connie said.

"It's not in the least bit crazy. it's trespassing and I'd be completely within my rights to shoot the bastard. That is the law isn't it Sherry?" Sherry replied, "Well, I suppose if you felt like you were in imminent danger-"

"Wait a minute, who is Bob Evans? Tom asked.

"A snake and I'd rather die than sell a foot of dirt to that weasel," Hank said.

"He's a developer who takes pieces of property like this one and makes clean organized lots and neighborhoods from unprofitable acreage," Sherry explained. "And where do you expect Orly and the others to live, in a postage stamp backyard? This is their home too," Hank stated.

"They're sheep Hank, not dogs, just sell them. All they do is eat grass and ruin the land with their hooves right now." Connie said. "I've made my livelihood off the backs of those sheep literally for decades now, I'm not about to sell them off now," he replied.

Tom was taken aback. Though his mother had tasked him with convincing his grandfather to sell the farm, Tom had not given much thought about who was going to buy it. He felt a little ashamed to admit he had only thought about the proceeds that would be coming to him from the sale. But now seeing Hank's face when Sherry and his grandma were talking about selling he could tell the farm was more than a place to live for Hank, it was a home for his beloved sheep.

There was a knock at the front door.

"Who could that be at this time of night?" Connie said.

"Probably a neighbor heard your ungodly screaming," Hank replied.

"Give me a break, you know as well as I do that the nearest neighbor past Rory and Jerry is over a half mile away," Connie cried. "And?" Hank said with a shrug.

Tom half smiled at his grandfather though he knew this was a serious situation. Tom knew his mother was the one who actually owned the farm, not Hank. A weird set of family events and negotiations across generations made Sherry the legal owner.

Deputy Bruce stepped into the house.

"Sorry to disturb you all," he said taking his hat off and looking quite sheepish.

"It's no problem, what can we do for you, Deputy?" Sherry asked in an annoyed voice, and added, "Have you and Arlo made any progress on the fire? I hope you aren't still holding onto the harebrained idea that my father had anything to do with it."

"No ma'am, Deputy Bruce said. After examining the evidence at the scene, that theory did not hold water." Sherry snorted. "Of course, it didn't, and please don't call me ma'am, it makes me feel old," she chuckled. "Oh you don't like to feel old Sherry, at least now you know how it feels when folks do that to you," Hank cried.

Sherry just gave him a disparaging look. "So what do you think happened? Was it just a plain accident like I said?" "Well no not exactly," Deputy Bruce looked nervous, "we still think it was set intentionally."

"What? By who? Don't tell me it's those kids Tom told you about?"

The Deputy shook his head. "No, we've spoken to them and they have pretty tight alibis as well."

Yeah right, Tom thought. Maybe Bruce was right and Brady had nothing to do with the fire on the property but in terms of tight alibis he was sure they all just vouched for each other.

"Then who do you think set it?" Sherry demanded to know.

Bruce looked sheepish at her question, "Well, looking at the evidence here," he pulled out an embroidered handkerchief, "we think we have a strong case against the owner of this here."

"Wait a minute," Connie said looking at the handkerchief, "that's mine! It even has my initials embroidered on it. Where did you get that?" "At the crime scene ma'am," Deputy Bruce said, taking out his handcuffs.

"You can't be serious?" Connie exclaimed. "Sherry?" She looked at Sherry who looked so shocked she couldn't utter a word. Bruce stepped towards Connie. "I'm sorry ma'am, but I have to do this. You have the right to remain silent-

"Finally," Hank said and picked up his newspaper.

Chapter 9

HER NAME IS HOPE

When Sherry walked into the police station in downtown Hope Valley the next morning she was greeted by exactly the sight she expected.

Deputy Bruce was sitting with his feet up on his desk reading the newspaper like he didn't have a care in the world. The rest of the police station was empty. Sherry stomped right over and tapped his newspaper. "Boo," she said.

Deputy Bruce sat up hurriedly straightening his shirt and hat. "Oh Ms. Traylor, you scared me," Bruce said.

"I scared you? And It's Mrs. Whitmore, Sherry corrected him, "Traylor is my father's name, Whitmore is my ex-husband's name." "Arlo said you were divorced."

"I am, I just wanted to keep the same last name as my son, you know Tom," she said.

"Oh, yeah, Tom, right? I've been meaning to ask you, is he adopted? He sure doesn't look like you," Bruce replied.

Sherry sighed. "Wow, you must be a mastermind at deduction Deputy. Yes, he's adopted. And I scared you? What if I was a violent criminal?"

Violent criminals don't usually walk into the police department now do they Sherry, and how are you doing this fine morning?" Sheriff Arlo Wolff boomed as he walked in the front door.

"How am I doing??"

How do you think I'm doing? You have my mother locked up in a jail cell and you wouldn't answer your phone last night." "It's not that I wouldn't Sherry, I couldn't,"

What do you mean you couldn't?"

I was otherwise engaged," Sheriff Arlo replied in an English accent. This made Deputy Bruce crack up but Sherry was not at all amused.

"Just stop right there, I don't want to know anything about what you were doing, just release my mother right now." And you know Arlo, my mother invited you to dinner many times when we were dating.

She gave you Christmas presents and threw a big birthday party for you. And this is how you repay her tossing her in jail??

You should be ashamed Arlo Wolff!!

Now release her this minute, with an apology!!

Can't do that, Arlo stated, taking off his jean jacket and putting on his sheriff's jacket. "And on what grounds are you holding her?"

"She's our prime suspect," Arlo said.

Sherry sighed. For about the tenth time since she arrived in Wyoming, Sherry wished she was light years away. "Arlo, I'm trying very hard to be civil to you right now, but you and I both know there's no way my mother had anything to do with the fire at the mill."

Arlo crossed his arms and leaned back on his desk, "Well, the evidence says otherwise. And she also had a motive," "Motive? What motive?"

"Bob Hoffman has been telling anyone and everyone around town that you and your mother want him to buy Windy Hill Farm." Deputy Bruce replied. "Okay, so what? Because If that's how you determine culpability Bruce you are even stupider than you look."

"Sherry, now there's no reason to insult my deputy."

Sherry gave Arlo a dirty look. "You know what Arlo Thanks for reminding me why I dumped you in high school. You haven't changed a bit. Okay, you know what,

I'll just pay the bail to get my mother out."

If Arlo was hurt by what Sherry said he didn't show it. "Fine, so that will be ten thousand dollars."

"Ten thousand dollars?" Sherry repeated stunned by the amount, "What judge in their right mind would post bail on an elderly woman of ten thousand dollars? It's not like she committed murder."

Arlo leaned back in his chair and put his hands behind his head. "Judge Topper, at the county seat, I believe you know him.

Sherry inwardly groaned. She did know Judge Topper. He was the judge she had clerked with when she first finished law school. And the same judge she had left high and dry without a clerk when she'd gotten the call about the job at the Pomfret and Stock in NYC. And now she was looking straight at the face of her old high school boyfriend who she had dumped when she had left for law school. It was like all the Wyomians with vendettas against her were coming out of the woodwork. "Just, whatever," she said through gritted teeth. She took out her checkbook. She just needed to get her mother out of jail, her father off the farm, the farm sold, her son out of Wyoming and to an ivy league college and she could get the hell out of Wyoming and never look back. Just that.

She wrote out a check and handed it to Arlo, Deputy Bruce came over to look. "Aw wee! I don't think I've ever seen a check that big." "I thought you said that was standard?" Sherry cried.

Sheriff Arlo grinned at her. "Follow me," was all he replied.

Sherry followed Arlo down a hallway towards the back of the police station until they reached the holding cell with Connie in it. She was sitting in the cell alone, her arms crossed in front of her.

"Sherry finally, it took you long enough," Connie stated.

"I'm sorry Mom, but I raced down here as quickly as I could last night but I couldn't get in, the doors were locked and there was a big sign on the door saying 'closed'" She looked accusingly at Arlo.

"We're only open from 9 to 5," The sheriff explained.
"You're the police," Sherry stated.

Arlo shrugged. "It's not like we need to stay open. Everyone in town has my number if they need me, and frankly, your mom has been the first person in this holding cell since they redid it four years ago. I mean it is sort of nice don't you think?" He gestured at the furnishings in the cell which included a TV table, bed, and desk." Sherry had to admit that if it hadn't been for the bars on the door it was nicer than her college dorm room.

"That is beside the point," Connie chimed in, "the fact that you even think that I had anything to do with burning down the mill is absurd, she cried. "Then how did a handkerchief with your name embroidered on it end up being used as an accelerant?" Arlo asked.

"Sheriff, you are like a broken record, Anyone could have picked something like that right off the floor of the mill," Sherry said, "and you know it." "Well, how did they get in the mill??

Arlo asked.

"Again, anyone could have broken in," Sherry said. "Like your deputy's little nephew Brady, Tom said he likes to set fires and trespass on property that does not belong to him."

Art shook his head. "Brady has an alibi. Look I understand you're upset but we know the mill hasn't been used for years, and we also know the farm is close to being bankrupt."

"And how exactly do you know that?" Sherry asked. "Ted down at the bank told me," Arlo explained.

Was there nothing sacred in Hope Valley? "Has Ted ever heard of HIPPA?" Sherry said.

"Sherry you're a big New York lawyer, you should know that HIPPA only applies to medical records." "So it's fine to just tell other people's private business all around town?" Sherry asked

"He wasn't spreading around your family's private business," Arlo replied, "he was concerned. We all are." He put his hand on Connie's shoulder. "And we understand that desperate people do desperate things."

"I had nothing to do with the fire Arlo," Connie said stiffly. Now if you'll excuse me, I'm heading back to my apartment for a shower and a rest." "I'll see you soon Mom," Sherry said.

"Sure you can go, Connie, just don't leave town," Arlo told her. "Really Arlo?" Sherry said.

Sherry had had it up to her eyeballs with Arlo's accusations.

She pulled Arlo by the sleeve out of earshot of Deputy Bruce who was still hanging around in the front of the station doing nothing. "Arlo, you and I both know my mother had nothing to do with the fire."

"Sherry, did you know that 80 percent of suspicious fires are set by the homeowners to collect on the insurance?"

"I don't care about your statistics Arlo, you've known my mother practically your whole life, do you really think she's capable of such a thing?" Arlo shrugged. "People change. They do all sorts of things you don't expect." He added.

Sherry had a thought. "Arlo, "is this about me and you? About the fact that I left Hope Valley?"

"No, of course not," Arlo said. "It's about the evidence and motive like all crimes Sherry. Then he added as almost an afterthought, "though I have to say I mean, you never did explain why you didn't call, you didn't write.."

Sherry almost yelled, "I was just a kid Arlo!!

That was twenty-five years ago, you act like it was yesterday!" His cell rang. "I've got to take this."

It was just as well they were interrupted Sherry thought as she walked out of the police department, that Arlo Wolff was some piece of work. He was exactly the same as he had been back in high school, ridiculous and vindictive. She could barely remember what she had seen in him at the time. Sure he could be funny, and even sometimes remotely nice but mostly he was an idiot. It was her fault though. She just had terrible taste in men, look at Matt.

If anything he was even worse than Arlo. At least her current boyfriend Cooper cared about her feelings. Cooper was a paralegal she had recently started dating at the firm. He was fun, and in fantastic shape, and Sherry felt lucky that he had been interested in her, though he was quite a bit younger than her at thirty, but that wasn't such a big deal these days anyways was it? She wasn't looking to get remarried or anything anyways. He made her happy and that was what was important. She was so wrapped up in her thoughts she bumped into someone on the street. "Sorry, she mumbled and was about to keep walking when the person said, "Sherry?" The person who addressed her looked ridiculous piled up in a bunch of blankets with two blue eyes just peering out. Sherry recognized the eyes peering out of the hood as the old librarian from the library in Hope Valley.

She was Meredith, who lived in the same apartment complex as her mother.

"Oh my, Sherry, it must have been at least 3 or 4 years dear since I last saw you. Have you gotten taller since the last time I saw you dear?" "No, I'm not taller," Sherry replied

"Are you quite sure you look taller?"

No, I stopped growing over twenty-five years ago so I'm sure." She really didn't have time for this. "How's your mother?" Meredith asked.

"Fine," Sherry replied. "I mean you live in the same apartment complex so you would know right?" "Yes of course dear but I mean I heard she was in jail?" Meredith

"Yes, it's just you know the problem is Sheriff Wolff. He's an idiot."

"Well I wouldn't say that dear, he got an award last year from the Wyoming police department." "Hmpf," Sherry replied not very impressed.

"Did you know he has a little girl now, she must be around 8 or 9 by now, just the cutest little thing." Sherry was surprised by that. She hadn't known that Arlo had a family. "Wait, so Arlo's married now?"

"No, he didn't marry the girl, she's a waitress out of Casper I believe, the little girl lives with her, but he sees her from time to time. So do you have any children yet dear?"

"Yes Tom, he's a senior in high school, he's going to school In Hope Valley. You met him a couple of years back at my mother's annual Christmas Party on the farm remember?

"Oh yes, the little Asian boy. But no children of your own? Meredith pressed.

"He is my own," Sherry replied, starting to get a bit annoyed. She was so sick of the attitude of so many people that since Tom was adopted he wasn't actually a real son. This attitude she was sure would get worse if she let him stay on the farm with her grandfather like some sort of unpaid farm hand.

"I'm sorry but I have to go, so nice to see you," Sherry lied and went straight to her car and from there straight to the high school. There were kids just starting to trickle out of the building so she shot a quick text to Tom to let him know she was waiting for him. She couldn't believe how old and rundown the Hope Valley high school looked now.

Sherry noted Tom looked tired when he got into the car. He threw his backpack into the back seat. "Hey kiddo," she said.

"So how's grandma?" Tom asked.

"Well, she's not jail bait anymore if that's what you mean," Sherry replied, "I bailed her out this morning, she's safely back at her apartment. She said she was going to rest."

"Well that's good," Tom replied. "I still can't believe that the police just came and arrested her like that.

"Well, not that I condone at all what the police force of Hope Valley do, but they were under a lot of pressure from the insurance fraud division of the company that insures Grove Creek to make an arrest."

"Why's that?" Tom asked.

Sherry made the turn up the Farm road before she answered. "Because that way they don't have to pay for any of the damages. "What? Tom said. "But how is Hank going to pay to fix the mill then?"

Sherry parked in front of the house. She could see her dad in the top pasture with the sheep. She knew he wasn't resting like he was supposed to after his accident but at least he was sitting on a rock, and letting his sheepdog do his job of keeping the sheep out of danger and in one place.

"He won't," Sherry said. "And since Grandma was the one who ran the mill anyways, it doesn't matter. The mill hasn't run in two years, not since Grandma had her heart attack."

"Mom, I know I'm supposed to convince Grandpa to sell and move in with Grandma but are you sure that's the best idea? They don't even seem to like each other."
"That's the way they've always been it will be fine."

"I don't know," Tom replied.

"You don't know what?" Sherry asked. Then she remembered what Tom had said about possibly not wanting to go to college the night before. "What was that all about not wanting to go to college last night? You are so bright Tom, you just fell in with the wrong crowd at school last year." That's not everything, Tom said.

"Well, the money from selling the farm will help with the cost of an Ivy League college. I make a bit of money but Cooper and I want to buy a condo in NY while the real estate market is soft. And it will be so much better for you to be back in New York, with all the culture and stuff that doesn't even exist out here in this hole-in- the-wall town. I'm thinking of you in this Tom."

"You're not thinking about me," Tom said, grabbing his backpack from the back seat and getting out of the car. "And you're not thinking about Hank either. You're thinking about yourself, just like you always do."

"What is that supposed to mean?"

Oh just never mind, Tom said. Just go back to New York yourself if you like it so much. I just find it funny that I've seen you more here in this hole-in-the-wall town as you call it than I ever saw you in New York."

"Tom, that's because I had to work all the time to try to save up money for the condo. If we sell the farm I won't have to do that and you'll see me a lot more, Besides, I'm not going to go back to New York until I know everything is all set here."

"You mean until you convince everyone to do what you want, right?"

Before she could even answer, he slammed the car door and walked off. Was Tom having second thoughts about their plan? Sherry saw Trinity come out from the house to greet him. Sherry's eyes narrowed, she had a feeling this girl was going to turn out to be a problem.

Sherry's phone rang. She looked at the number. It was Cooper. "Hey Cooper," she said, picking up the call.

Hey Dorothy," Cooper replied. "Dorothy?" Sherry said, confused.

"Yeah, like in Wizard of Oz, you know, run into any hurricanes yet?

Sherry finally got what he meant. "Oh, no that's Kansas, honey, I'm in Wyoming and it's tornadoes, not hurricanes." "Oh yeah, yeah, Kansas, but I'm pretty sure it's hurricanes. They're the windy ones right?"

Sherry laughed to herself. Cooper was cute, but there was a reason he was a so-so paralegal and not a crack-shot attorney. He wasn't the brightest person ever. "Tornadoes are windy too hon," she explained, "anyways, how's New York? Can you believe there are no Starbucks where I am for like a hundred miles?"

Cooper laughed, "It's Kansas babe what do you expect?"

Sherry didn't bother correcting him again, instead, she chuckled. How's everything going at HAR?" HAR was the acronym for Harper and Ridley the law firm they worked at in NYC.

She parked her car in the driveway in front of the barn at Hanks house.

"Oh nothing changed at work," Cooper said, "same old, and no fun without you babe. Speaking of that, when are you getting back? I thought it was today sometime."

"Well there's been a slight change of plans, but I'm working on getting back as soon as possible believe me." Suddenly Sherry saw the horse Rory was walking stumble and fall. Sherry gave a little shriek.

"Whoa, babe, everything okay? There's no tornado coming is there?" Cooper asked.

"No, no nothing like that but I've got to go," she said to Cooper, throwing her phone onto the passenger seat.

Sherry jumped out of her car and raced over to where Rory was kneeling beside the grey-dappled horse who seemed to be struggling to stand up. "I saw him fall. What happened?" Sherry cried.

"I don't know, he'd been standing sort of still in his stall but he had seemed fine," Rory cried. Her young face looked red and panicked. "Has he been eating or drinking?" Sherry asked.

Sherry's knowledge of horse issues was limited to what she knew about sheep growing up, but even that had been a long time ago.

But she knew enough to know many things could cause an animal to go down. "Should we call someone? A vet or someone? Or Justin? It's his horse after all." Sherry asked.

Rory grabbed her phone out of her back pocket and punched in numbers quickly all while trying to coax Whisper to stand. "Can I speak to Dr. Thibodaeu?" She asked when someone picked up the call on the other end.

"He's not in," Rory told her when she got off the phone. "Isn't there another vet we can call?" she asked.

Rory shook her head. "Only in Casper."

"The horse was making a really weird whining sound now.

There had to be someone else they could call. Sherry ran to her car to grab her phone. She Googled vets in Hope Valley and she quickly saw that Rory was right, the closest ones were in Casper.

Her Name is Hope

"This is crazy. No vets around? With all these ranches out here? When I was a kid old Doc Maren used to drop by to just check on all the ranches around here. What do people do when their animals get sick now and then and this guy is on vacation?" Text Justin at least."

"Okay," Rory said and grabbed her phone, and started texting someone. "Okay, well I guess it's up to us then," Sherry said staring down at the horse.

Maybe we should just roll and push him up? Rory said. "I've seen this kind of thing on YouTube. They both strained to push him but to no avail.

"He's really heavy, a lot heavier than a sheep," Sherry said, panting. She bemoaned her lack of exercise in years and being out of shape. This is useless, horses weigh about a thousand pounds," Rory mumbled.

That much? Well no wonder we can't budge him then," Sherry replied. You know a lot about horses don't you?"

"Not really," Rory said.

"I think Justin just hired me 'cause I was here and said I like animals." "Oh, okay, hey speaking of Justin, any reply from him?"

No, I'll try him again.

Just then Hank came walking up to them leaning heavily on his cane. "What's going on here?"

"It's Whisper, he was really loopy when I got him out of his stall and then he just fell over," Rory explained. Did you try Eric? Hank asked.

"No, I'll do that now," Rory said, texting rapidly.
"Who the heck is Eric?" Sherry asked.

"He's Ed's boy, the pharmacist." "So he's a vet?"

"No, I just said he's a pharmacist," looking at Sherry like she was being stupid and he walked off towards the barn

"And why exactly are you calling a pharmacist to help with a horse? Sherry asked Rory, hoping she would give her a better answer than Hank's. "Does Whisper need a prescription refilled right now?"

Rory was about to answer when Sherry saw Hank come out of the barn with a big rope. "Now I don't know a lot about horses but they can't be that different from sheep, move over Sherry."

"What? What are you doing with that rope?"

" I'm going to tie it around its neck and try to pull him up that way.

What? No way," Sherry said. "First off you have no idea what you're doing and secondly you're not supposed to be straining yourself, you're not even supposed to be out of bed.

"I can't be lying around in bed when there's so much to do around here. Now move over Sherry!

Just then a small blue pickup truck pulled up beside them and a young boy who looked not much older than Tom jumped out. He was a bit taller than Tom and exceedingly thin, making him move like Sherry imagined a scarecrow would if a scarecrow could walk.

Rory looked up at the blue truck and sighed.

"Eric's here!! He was close by!! He'll know what to do. But he's a pharmacist, I don't understand!!

Sherry whispered as Eric walked up and said, She's a pretty horse.

The young pharmacist looked up at the mountains, then said, Hi, I'm Eric

"Hello," Sherry said, extending her hand but Eric just looked at her hand like she was extending a viper and instead just gave her a short nod of acknowledgment. "So how long has the horse been down?" he asked Rory.

"About 15 minutes," Rory answered. "And he's been drinking fine? He asked

"Yes," Rory nodded, "and he ate all his hay this morning too, he seemed perfectly fine, and then this." How about yesterday?

I don't know, Justin he's the owner. He just brought him here recently. "From where?"

"I don't know, Rory admitted

Sherry was skeptical that this kid was going to be able to help the horse. She interjected, "Why does it matter where he came from?" "It doesn't," he said.

This remark confirmed it for Sherry. This kid knew nothing. They were just wasting precious time with him.

"If he came from really far away like Cheyenne and had no water the whole time, he might have collapsed from dehydration, but he drank and ate today so unlikely. So not colic.

Rory breathed a sigh of relief. "Thank God.

Well, I can't tell for sure, but even if it's not colic it's not good for him to be lying down for too long. Let's try to get him up again." "We already did, he won't budge."

"Did you try a lever?? "A what?"

"A lever, horses are like a thousand pounds. But if you stick a plank under them, you can use the equal and opposite force to get them up." Now it was Sherry's turn to look at Eric like he had two heads.

But Hank had already returned with a long wood plank.

Eric shimmied it under Whisper and then grabbed a big rock and stuck it under the plank too. "Now push him up gently he said, if he wants to get up he will right boy?"

He's a horse he doesn't talk Sherry was tempted to say. Eric reminded her a bit of Hank because the way he talked to Whisper was how Hank talked to the sheep…… like they understood English.

"One, two, three," Eric said, as he pushed down on the plank while Rory, Sherry, and Hank, all tied to coax Whisper up. Sherry was sure this idea of Eric's wouldn't work and was astounded when it did. Whisper stood up like nothing ever happened.

Oh wow, it worked, Sherry marveled. "Good work son," Hank said.

"But is he okay? Rory asked.

Just then Justin's big black pickup came barreling up the drive.

"Hey! Who the hell are you? He yelled at Eric," Get the heck away from my horse!" He grabbed the lead from Eric.

He was just trying to help," Rory said. "Something is wrong with Whisper."

Even though Sherry was a bit disturbed and annoyed with how Justin was acting she tried to remain calm. "The Hope Valley vet was on vacation if you can believe it and Eric here, I guess he knows quite a bit about horses."

"I really don't know much about horses at all," Eric interjected.

Sherry stared at Eric. What was up with this kid? It was like he couldn't understand normal social cues.

"Then why the heck are you messing with my horse?" Justin said angrily to Eric, then he turned to Rory, "And you! I thought I told you only you were supposed to be in charge of the horses, that's why I hired you."

Rory turned even more red but didn't speak, instead her eyes filled with tears. "I'm sorry," she finally choked out. "Next time you just call me, besides he's fine," Justin said pointing to Whisper.

Sherry was surprised when Hank said," You're right Justin, they're your animals, we should have waited for you if there's an issue."

"Damn right you should have," Justin replied. "C'mon," he said to Rory and they led Whisper back into the barn with Rory following dutifully behind. Let me get you something to drink son, Hank said to Eric as they walked towards the house.

"What an ass! I can't believe you let him talk to you like that?" Sherry said to Hank.

"Beggars can't be choosers Hank said. Besides, the animal is his to do with what he pleases right?" I suppose… Sherry said.

She hated that her father was subjecting himself to the likes of this Justin guy to make enough money to keep the farm going. If he wasn't just so damn stubborn he could see that selling the farm and moving to town with her mom was the obvious better choice.

Sherry, Eric, and Hank stood on the front porch of the house watching Justin storm off down the stairs and drive off in his big black pick-up truck, giving them all a last parting angry scowl for good measure.

Sherry turned to Eric, "So I'm a bit confused, you're a pharmacist? Or studying to be a pharmacist?" " I have my Ph.D. in pharmaceutical sciences," Eric replied.

"Okay, but you look awfully young to be a pharmacist," Sherry said. "I'm nineteen," Eric replied.

"You're nineteen and you're already a pharmacist."

"I thought we already went over that," Eric replied not looking Sherry in the eye.

Sherry was about to ask the odd young man another question when Hank interrupted, and said, "Sherry can you just give it a rest for a minute, this isn't one of your courtrooms you know." He also gave her a look that said he would tell her more about Eric later.

"Well, I just want to thank you again and say you're really good with animals," Sherry said.

"I've been told that before," Eric replied. "I better get back to the store, I'm working the front today."

Rory, Sherry, and Hank watched as Eric walked towards his little blue pickup and just as he drove off a white BMW drove up the driveway. "Now who is it?" Hank said. "I live in the country for some peace you know, not this constant circus."

They were interrupted as the white BMW beeped. When the window rolled down they could see it was Trinity inside. "Hi! How do you like my ride?" She asked. "I had it shipped out here by train."

"And look at all the new stuff I got, for my flower business……

Office supplies, a printer, water cooler, a table and chairs, microwave, a lunch table, lamps, plus stationery and business cards, even a blue Lava lamp!! Blue is the color of Tom's eyes.

You do know I love him, don't you?"

Hank looked at Sherry and whispered….. you better hope your son and this woman never have kids!" "Where's Tom?" Sherry asked, noticing he was conspicuously missing.

"He had to stay behind in town with my other stuff. And he has our new puppy!" "What puppy? She has more stuff too?"

Hank asked in an annoyed tone. "You know this girl is going to drive me to hightail the hell out of here Sherry, and I'm not babysitting some goofy puppy who's going to pee on my bed!

I hate puppies!"

"Dad, you need to calm down!"

Sherry smiled to herself. Maybe she had misjudged Trinity. Maybe Trinity instead of Tom was the key to getting Hank to move. Maybe Trinity was good for something after all. And Sherry loved puppies.

"Do you have a name picked out for the puppy?" Sherry asked, with a grin.

Trinity jumped out of the BMW, and excitedly answered…"Her name is Hope!"

Chapter 10

LET'S GET MARRIED

The next morning, @ 7:12 am, Trinity was up in the barn loft, staring at her laptop. She considered options, read reviews, and wondered how her women's intuition worked. Finally, she hit 'accept' in the Findlay Wholesale Flower app and was now committed to buying $500.00 a month in fresh flowers. They'd be delivered Thursdays, in time for Saturday date night, when every guy on the planet bought his girl flowers. It sounded romantic to business-minded Trinity.

And to Trinity, her business model was bulletproof. But, as much as she despised her father, he would have ripped her plan to shreds. Trinity and Tom had bought a used refrigerator at a resale store and it hummed away just 3 feet from the table she sat at.

Trinity stood, and screamed in excitement, Her dream of owning her own business had become a reality.

She ran to the farmhouse, scurried down the basement stairs, sprinted into Tom's bedroom, and leaned over a sound-asleep young future sheep farmer, and kissed him.

"Hey you! Wake up! Guess what?" Trinity asked him. Tom stirred, opened one eye and replied;

"I'm sleeping! Ugh! What time is it?" Trinity excitedly whispered into his ear, "You are dating an entrepreneur first class!

My first yoga class met at 6-am, with 11 people. I ordered my first shipment of flowers!

Aren't you blown away excited? Like..let's dance baby!"

Trinity twirled and ballroom danced with one of Tom's flannel shirts.

"That's nice Trin, can you wake me in an hour! I'm tired! And turn that light off!" "Tom! Wake up and kiss me!

Tell me I'm beautiful, and on my way to being a billionaire! Hey! Why don't you get up now and help me post ads on telephone poles in town and I'll buy you lunch at the diner!"

"Tom sat up and grinned, then replied,

My hair is a mess, I have to put on make-up and paint my nails! And you know what.. You're freaking beautiful!"

Tom collapsed back into his sheets and shut his eyes.

Trinity tickled her young man until he fell out of bed laughing and pleading for mercy.

She opened his dresser drawer, and grabbed underwear, socks, and a t-shirt and threw them at him. "Here! Get dressed young man! I'll be upstairs," Trinity exclaimed. "If you hurry I'll let you drive the BMW! And I'll let you kiss me on Main Street!"

***

Trinity drove her BMW down Main Street, 15 mph over the posted speed limit. Her long blonde hair fluttered out the car window, turning men's heads. Tom lost count of all the guys checking Trinity out.

"How much money do we have Tom?"

"We're down to $139.00 after the refrigerator and all the stuff you bought for your office, and Hope. Did you really need a lava lamp? And like 80% of new business ventures fail in under a year!"

"Tom, there's an old adage 'You need money to make money'. But we're young and just starting out in life, so we need to look like we have money. Good business runs on illusion!

Lava Lamps exude mystique. And all those 80% of failed business were opened by inept idiots!

Running a business is all about genetically inherited instincts. And my instincts Tom are as solid as Goldman-Sachs!" "Who told you all that Trin?" Tom asked,

"No one told me, it's just common sense, Tom! Are you hungry yet?" She asked.

"I'm starving!" Tom retorted as he pretended to faint. Trinity took his hand and made a U-Turn. Do you need mouth-to-mouth resuscitation?" She asked casually. From who? Tom replied with a grin.

"Don't you 'from who' me mister!

I'll make you walk home!"

"After you kiss me!" Tom replied with a squeeze of Trinity's hand.

The Hope Valley Diner was 2 blocks ahead. Tom gripped the door handle as Trinity whipped the BMW into a parking spot like it was a Ferrari "Look at the long wait line!" Tom bemoaned, as he stepped out of the car and was overcome by hamburger and fried onion kitchen smells. "We'll find a table quickly! I promise, I can't have my man fainting on Main Street.

"Here, watch this!"

Trinity snickered as she pressed her lips to Tom's in a heated display right in front of the diner's main window. Her arms wrapped passionately around his neck! Dozens of seated guests stopped and stared at the young couple. Gasping in shock!

"You are one hunk of a kisser Tom, wow!"

Tom, now embarrassed, turned beet red and wanted to crawl into a rose bush!

But Trinity dragged him into the diner, then up to front desk....and said to the young purple-haired girl seating tables; "Hi, we're two of us and looking for a table.

My man is hungry!

We're catching a flight to DC, is there any chance we could ..."

"Take cuts! No, I'm sorry, we don't do that here in Wyoming honey!" The girl said with a stare of disdain, recognizing Trinity's Boston accent.

"It will be about a 30-minute wait," she informed.

Tom's stomach groaned in protest, as Trinity marched into the seating area, dragging Tom behind her. "Hey! What are you doing, we're not catching a flight to DC!" Tom protested still blushing.

Trinity ignored him and stopped in front of an occupied booth by the window and smiled. She looked at the young couple who had just been seated and asked; "Hi, I'm Trinity and this is Tom, and we're running late for a flight to DC, could we share your table.please? There's a 30 minute wait, we'd be happy to buy your lunch!"

Tom silently cussed as the strangers scooted toward the window and Tom found himself sitting next to a young man wearing a Detroit Red Wings hat! Tom despised the Wings, and stared at Trinity in disbelief.

***

Hank closed the gate to his main pasture and walked toward the barn. He swore a repertoire of curse words, one of his watering tanks had sprung a leak.

Hank rifled through the workbench, and several old cabinets looking for his repair kit. But he stopped and stared at his tool pegboard. His hammer, several screwdrivers, and some wrenches were gone. People borrowing his tools and never returning them perturbed Hank. Out of habit, he hollered out Connie's name, she usually came running and asked what the problem was. Connie knew just how to calm Hank down.

But not today, Hank remembered she no longer lived here. He had a lingering headache, his back hurt, and some of his scabs from the fire, itched and bothered him. He also had no wife..and that fact hurt him deeply. He had provided for Connie since before they wed.

Moving her out, and away from her abusive and drunk as a skunk father. Hank moved Connie into one of the spare basement bedrooms, of his parents homestead. He was a gentleman until marriage made them one.

Hank swore and knocked a box of screws to the floor. He had the grumpies and mumbled Trinity's name under his breath. That girl had her fingers in everything and even reorganized the medicine cabinet in his bathroom.

All from looking for a band-aide. Who comes as a guest and reorganizes medicine cabinets? He walked out of the barn and jumped into his pick-up truck. Maybe a burger in town would lift his spirits, and he'd buy a new repair kit at the Hardware.

***

"Hi, I'm Jason and this is Jessica, it's nice to meet you two! You're so young and look really in love! So where are you flying to?" Trinity and Tom held hands across the table and stared into each other's eyes for a moment.

Finally, Tom blurted out. "We're going to Tucson for a few days and attend a sheep herding convention! We're looking to buy a sheepdog."

Trinity about choked on her Diet Coke and corrected Tom; "Honey, don't you remember our chat late last night? We've changed our plans. We're snorkeling in Hawaii and then learning how to grow banana trees hyponically! Men can't remember anything!" Trinity snorted to Jessica.

Trinity dragged out a coy smile and said to Jessica; "your dress is beautiful! Was it sourced locally?" "Actually it's from Southern Nevada.

A lady who lives near Area 51, created this fabric by fusing molecules of lambswool with seat fabric from a flying saucer. It has to be washed in a bucket and dried in a microwave, and its molecules realigned with a lava lamp. It's so comfortable! Here do you want to feel it?"

Tom turned red and quickly pulled Trinity's hand away from Jessica. He changed the subject and asked;

"So what are you all up to today?"

"Looking for a storage locker actually, we need something with a place to wash cars too. You know like a garden hose and buckets, next to the storage locker. But we've been to 4 storage places and they're so weird about letting us use their hose!" Jason replied.

"That is strange!" Tom moaned.

Trinity smiled and said, "Well what about a barn?

We have a huge barn I'm sure you could store stuff in one area and there's like 3 water faucets inside. I'm sure we could find a hose someplace!" "Seriously, that sounds awesome! Is it in Hope Valley?" Jessica asked.

"Just 10 minutes out of town!" Replied Trinity.

"When could we see it? When are you back from Hawaii?" Jason asked excitedly. "Well, what about right after lunch?" Trinity replied.

"But I thought you were catching a flight?" Jason interjected with a confused gaze.

Trinity looked at her cell and replied;

"Oh look! I just got a text from Delta, our flights have been canceled! Airlines are so irresponsible these days!"

Their food arrived and Tom wanted to crawl under the table.

But he whispered to Trinity, "you're taking that Lava Lamp back today! I'm allergic to aliens!" Trinity laughed so hard she almost choked on her veggie burger.

***

"Grandpa?" Tom hollered out the back door. "I'm over here Tom." Hank called out from the chicken coop.

Let's Get Married

In a second Hank handed him a basket of eggs. "Can you take these in the house, Tom?"

"Sure, but I need to talk to you, Grandpa. Trin and I had lunch today at Edith's Diner and we met a young couple, Jason and Jessica. They're engaged to be married."

'Marriage should be illegal. It's bad for your health." Hank interjected.

"Well, anyways Jason is a survivalist and he's looking for a couple of acres to park his camper and grow crops. He believes in living off the land and being prepared to survive a nuclear war. He wants to construct a root cellar to store canned goods, escape the summer's heat, and be his bomb shelter.

Jessica collects vintage cars and is decoding messages from space aliens." "They sound like pretty whacked nut cases.

You should be careful who you talk to Tom.

The world is full of lazy people who have no idea how to keep a real job, and make money. And they take advantage of others! They're probably from Boulder. That town is full of fruitcakes!"

Hank replied with a roll of his eyes.

"See, that's just it Grandpa, they have money, they seem intelligent and Jason needs to lease a couple acres and Jessica is looking for a storage locker. We need the money, I mean your sheep farm needs an influx of money to keep running.

So I agreed to let them lease 4 acres and use some space inside the barn. They'll pay us $950.00 a month cash, for a one-year lease. I told you I want to help you run your farm and be a partner. I found a leasing document online, they signed it, and here."

Tom handed Hank an envelope.

"What's this?" Hank asked without looking inside.

"Grandpa, it's $950.00 cash for the first month's lease, which starts tomorrow. But I wrote in a clause on the lease, that it's pending your approval. I want to be your partner Grandpa, I want to help you run this place and maybe take over once you're old."

Hank stood his broom against the wall and stared at his grandson in amazement. "You're only 17 years old and you came up with this all on your own?"

"Well Trinity helped a lot, I mean she did like 90% of this Grandpa! She's more than a pretty girl." "That girl is sharper than a pencil and damn she can cook; when are you going to marry Trinity?" "I thought you didn't believe in marriage anymore?" Tom asked.

Hank grinned and opened the coop door.

"Let's go get a beer, I need to talk to you about women, they're quintessentially paradoxical!" Tom laughed.

***

Trinity sat at her table in the barn loft, filling out online forms, while BTS blared through her headphones. She had sold 1 dozen roses in 24 hours. She opened her flower fridge and stepped back from the intense bloom fragrance. She called them her children and stared at the huge inventory. She had spent over $150.00 for online flower ads and hadn't received any inquiries or orders.

She sighed and decided to stay positive.

A text came in, she stared at her mother's name, then hit delete without even reading it.

Memories floated through Trinity's young mind of laughter on their last family vacation, 3 years ago. Spending 2 weeks in the Greek Isles was fabulous and constant fun. She lost count of all the young, bare chested men checking her out in her white bikini.

Trinity kissed 3 boys on that vacation, but what she really yearned for was a hug from her mother.

Her emotions rose like a tidal wave, filling her eyes with tears. "Tom." She whispered as she ran down the stairs, 2 at a time. In moments she dashed into the side door of the house and saw him standing in the family room.

Tom turned and whispered, "Trin." Just as she flew into his arms.

Her tears fell onto Tom's shirt as Hank suddenly excused himself. But she had heard Hank's last comment.

"Thomas, you're a man now, you love Trinity, you need to buy her some earrings. A woman needs to know you love her."

***

The next morning, Hank stepped outside at 5:00 am, Tom was right behind, his eyes barely open.

"Thomas, you need to start getting out of bed at 4:00 am. None of this sleeping till noon anymore, if you're going to be a farmer." "There's frost on the grass Grandpa, the moon is still up, and everyone is still in bed, except me."

"That's not all that's on the grass, look way out there!"

Hank pointed way to the back of the farm, past the old mill. "You see it?" "See what Grandpa, I don't see anything."

"It's a motor home, Winnebago, a new model, your new $950.00 friends wasted no time setting up camp, on my property. They better not be dumping their holding tanks here!"

Tom groaned slightly as he pulled the big barn door open. Hank stepped in and stared straight ahead, "when did they park all these old cars in here?" Tom gasped, half the barn was filled with old junker cars.

Suddenly he jumped, as two arms slid around his stomach. He felt Trinity's soft kiss on his neck. "I love you!" She whispered. "You going to kiss me or what?" She slid her soft hand up his t-shirt, and felt for his heartbeat.

Tom spun around and sighed as his lips met hers. They kissed for a long half minute.

She was soft and warm and Tom so wanted to crawl into her lap and sleep 2 more hours. But, he was a farmer now! He had to wake up! "Good morning Grandpa!" Trinity said to Hank.

"Hi Sweetie, did you sleep ok?"

"Yeah, not too bad, but I was cold all night, I could have used this big strapping young man to keep me warm!" "Well, on my farm a young couple needs to be married to share a bed. No exceptions!"

Hank ordered, then looked up at his tool board, with half the tools missing.

"Trinity, I don't mind you borrowing my tools but could you put them back at the end of the day?" "Oh, I'm sorry, I'll try and be better with that.

They're all upstairs, come on Tom, you can help me." "Hey, when did they park all these cars in here?" Hank asked Trinity.

"Um, about 2 am, Jessica likes to be outside between 2 and 5 am cause that's when the flying saucers are out."

"Ya know, I've lived here my whole life, and I never saw no flying saucer. She's got to be a real wack job, this Jessica!" Hank groaned. Trinity grinned and grabbed Tom's hand and ran to the loft stairway.

They raced up the 3 flights of stairs, giggling and laughing. At the top Trinity pushed Tom against the wall and kissed him passionately. In 5 seconds, she stared longingly into his eyes and whispered.

"We should get married!"

***

"Married! Trinity..we're way too young to get married! I'm not even 18! I'm in high school!"

"But, if we love each other....that's all that matters."Trinity replied, and un phased by Tom's hesitation. "You're serious?"Tom asked straightaway.

"Of course, I'm serious!

We're in love, marriage comes next, then children." "Trin, I'm only 17, and you're 18.

We're not ready for marriage or kids!"

"So, why does age matter, I love you, isn't that enough for vows!" She asked.

"I don't have a job, I have no way to support you, I don't have a college education yet." Tom replied with a look of shock.

"I thought you decided not to go to college Tom."

"I never said that. If I marry a girl, I want a college degree to get a good-paying job."Tom replied.

"I've got a good-paying job, Tom! 3 jobs actually! Teaching Yoga, my flower business, and teaching martial arts." "What if you get pregnant?" Tom asked in an alarm-filled voice.

"One issue at a time Sweetie, and I promise we'll be careful!! It's ok Tom! Love is all that matters. Will you think about it please? We could live in the guest house! You could keep me warm at night.

Let's Get Married

Besides, your grandfather said we should get married!" Trinity exclaimed. "He did not say that Trinity!"

"Yes he did Tom!"

"No……he did not! There's nothing to think about Trinity! Maybe someday, but not now!" Tom fired back.

"Tom, could we talk about this again when you turn 18? Please!" Trinity pleaded.

Tom stared at Trinity in disbelief, then shook his head yes, and couldn't help thinking, this was some half-baked idea to boost her flower sales. Tom manned up, smiled and whispered, "I love you Trin." But it was the first time he felt uncomfortable dating Trinity Smithe.

***

Eric awoke every day at 4:43 am, every minute of his day ran like a bus schedule. Except when he worked as a pharmacist at his dad's pharmacy. Customers have a way of demanding time, asking questions, and getting a guy off schedule.

At 4:49 am, Eric began a 58-minute regimen in the small gym he'd built in the basement. A little yoga, a few stretches, and a lot of weights.

At 20 years old, Eric had never actually asked a girl out on a date. He graduated from High School at the age of 14 and obtained his State of Wyoming Pharmacist's license at 18.

Graduating from the University of Wyoming and getting his driver's license the same year, put Eric on a different path than most guys his age. Eric was 6'3", weighed a lean 180 pounds and his eyes had been on Tori Anderson for years.

Tori was gorgeous, and no matter how busy her day was, she always gave Eric a pretty smile. Tori worked next door at the doctor's office.

She was blond, petite, 18 years old, and wore a smile that stopped Eric's heart. They had chatted out front the last few months and even had lunch together every Friday at 1:04 pm in the Pharmacy break room. Eric ate the same thing every day for lunch, but Tori insisted he share her randomly chosen fresh vegetables, and the various small dessert items from her lunch. She often reminded Eric of the benefits a varied diet can bring.

All his Co-workers promised Eric, that Tori liked him, and he should ask her out.

But for an insular young man, with Asperger's Syndrome, looking a girl in the eye and laying his heart out there, was a formidable obstacle to cross.

His grandfather convinced Eric that girls like soft-spoken, physically strong men, with a high IQ, and well-manicured hands. He should hold her hand gently, but firmly, in case she trips on a sidewalk bump.

His mother had insisted kindness be first in his mind, every day of the year. Eric's Aunt Molly had convinced him of the benefits of opening a door for a girl and treating her like a princess.

Let's Get Married

Tell her she's beautiful and most importantly be a good listener.

Eric was terribly handsome, auspicious, and had memorized all of his family's admonishments. At 7:07 am, he started his new red

Toyota Forerunner, looking like the kind of man, all the girls would notice.

***

"Hey! That's Bob the land developer guy, get down out of sight!

I don't want him to see us!" Sherry exclaimed to Trinity in a whisper. They sat in a booth in Edith's diner. Bob slowly walked past and accidentally spotted them. "Sherry! Omg, it's sooo good to see you again!

I've been thinking of you and Hank for days.

The school district is looking for a new location for its high school. I met with their planning board and mentioned your place. They love the location, and want to see it like yesterday!

I'll tell you, these are the sales I love you know!

Helping you sell, and your farm going to the betterment of society, omg, it's awesome sauce! Awesome chili too! Have you tried the homemade chili here? It's sure to curl your toes it is! Well sugar! It's terribly good to see you, beautiful Sherry!

Mike Hurley

Say, how's Tom? He's a lovely young man and I swear he's going to have girls chasing him down I-25! He is so handsome!

Say, what about your sheep? Should I be looking for a buyer, I don't know anything about sheep. But you know I had a pair of sheep's wool slippers for years! They were soooo warm and cuddly, and then our dog Sadie had pups.

You met Sadie I think! Anyway, her pups devoured my slippers. I was soooo upset!

Say, is the sausage good here? I usually get the bacon. But 2 weeks ago, no let me think. Yes, that's right. It was 3 days after my mother-in-law's colon surgery, I read an article. Oh my, all science-based data on how bacon can get stuck in your appendix!

Say, who is this pretty young lady, sitting here all quiet and lovely like a flower on a Wyoming noonday!

You're sure a pretty thing, blonde hair and blue eyes! Oh my! God know a thing or two about creating beauty! Yes he does! You should be on a magazine cover! Yes indeed you should!

My oh my, have you ever thought of being a model!! I know a guy in Cheyenne, I'll get you his number! Say! What's your name honey?"

"Her name is Trinity, and if you'd be so kind, we need to look at our menus.......Bob! Good day." Sherry replied like she was ripping up a defendant in court.

Trinity looked out the window.

It was obvious every guy in the world, had the same thing on his mind. And this guy creeped her out. Yet another reason to marry Tom and wear his wedding ring! Trinity told herself.

Just then, Bob's cell rang. He answered it and waved good-by to Sherry and Trinity, as he trotted off and found a booth a ways down. Sherry laid her head on the table and moaned.

"That guy is a human creeping tornado!" Sherry moaned.

"Yes, a creep extraordinaire, I thought about standing up and using my high heels to turn him into a girl!" Trinity added with a grin. They both burst out laughing!

***

The next morning, Trinity taught her first

'Brazilian Jiu-Jitsu' class, while Tom walked through the flock of sheep in the main pasture. Ewes ran up to him and seemed happy he was out visiting. A few licked his hands and followed him.

The 2 sheep dogs wagged their tails and kept an eye out for predators. Grandpa Hank had taught Tom how to listen and watch to ascertain the flocks' overall health and happiness.

Tom looked up just as a red

Toyota Forerunner entered the back driveway. It slowly drove up and stopped close to Tom. A tall and good looking young man stepped out and waved, yet never made eye contact.

Tom waved back and walked over to the stranger who stepped over the short fence, with ease. Tom noticed straightaway the young man was built like a running back, and handsome enough, that the Statue of Liberty would turn her head.

"Good morning! I'm Eric, from the Pharmacy.

I thought I'd pay a visit and check on Willow, your horse."

Tom grinned and shook Eric's hand, the young Pharmacist had a firm handshake and easy smile. "Hi, I'm Tom, Hank's grandson. He told me about you coming over and helping with Willow.

You're sort of a hero around these parts.

Thank you for what you did with Willow, she's feeling much better. Do you have time to see her?" "Yeah, I'd like that. Willow is a sweet horse."

Eric replied as he stepped into a fast pace, walking beside Tom up to a pasture by the barn. "So how is it a pharmacist is also a veterinarian?" Tom asked.

"I've taken a few veterinary classes, and humans and horses have anatomical similarities. And a few common medicines too. Not as many as we share say with dogs, but horses are beautiful and kind creatures. Both dogs and horses have been our friends for thousands of years.

So are you from around here Tom?"

Let's Get Married

"No, back east, and I've been in boarding school in Boston and recently decided to move in with my Grandpa and help with the farm. I'm a senior at Hope Valley High. I brought my girlfriend with me, she wanted to see Wyoming and try life on a farm. She's a city girl."

"What's her name?" Eric asked politely.

"Trinity, Trinity Smithe. Her dad's sort of a well-known owner of hundreds of hotel and restaurant franchises from coast to coast. Headquartered in Boston."
"Trinity is a pretty name. You must be a lucky guy for a girl of her standing to up and move to Wyoming with you." Eric said.

The two young men climbed over a couple of fences and kept talking.

"Yeah, she's really pretty too, I have no idea what she sees in me." Tom replied with a grin.

"Well, your grandfather Hank is very respected in town. He's always been kind to me and when I was younger and ran the register at the pharmacy he always asked how I was and took a minute to be friendly. I can tell you're his grandson."

Eric replied, complimenting Tom.

Tom smiled a little but didn't reply, he instantly liked Eric, a lot. Tom was looking for a few guy friends to hang out with and wondered if Eric might be one of them. "So do you have a girlfriend Eric?" Tom asked.

"No not really, but I talk to this girl named Tori a lot. She works next door at the medical clinic. We have lunch once a week and I'm dying to ask her out, but I don't know. I'm not sure she'd want to go out with me."

"Why wouldn't she want to go out with you!

You're smart and easy to talk to. Girls like tall handsome guys. You drive a cool truck. What do you have in common with her."

Tom asked.

Eric stopped and forced himself to look Tom in the eyes and excitedly replied.

"We both love to skateboard, she talks about skateboarding non-stop." Eric looked away and added.

"I like being with Tori, she makes me feel good about who I am, you know. A few girls have the ability to lift people up and cheer them on. Tori's like that with everyone, I might even love her."

"Well ask her out, what's the worst that can happen?" Tom replied with a grin.

Tom watched Eric clench his fists, and stare at the ground, then he nervously replied.

"I have Aspergers Syndrome and it's hard for me to look people in the eyes, and how would I ever hold her hand! And then you're supposed to kiss a girl after the first date! I scared to death to kiss her. I mean it sucks to have Asperger's."

"Yeah, I suppose it does, but you're tall and handsome. And I'm short, and it sucks being short, but I asked Trinity out over a year ago, and she said yes. Man, everyone's got something that pulls us down. Buy your girl lifts people up. You should just be brave and ask her out Eric!"

Eric stopped and stared at the mountains.

Asking Tori out was as foreboding as climbing the Rocky Mountains in winter, blindfolded. But Tom decided he wanted Eric as a friend.

The two young men clicked and felt relaxed around each other. So Tom kept encouraging Erik.

"You're a pharmacist! You have a doctorate degree hanging on the wall. There's no way I could ever get a doctorate degree. But you did! And you know, if this girl likes you, she'll be understanding and kind! If she's not, I wouldn't want a girlfriend like that. But my guess is Tori would enjoy going skateboarding with you.

And holding hands with a girl is no big deal.

Girls' hands are soft and they feel good in a guy's hand. And kissing a girl isn't scary, it's really nice actually. Just ask her out! Just do it man! You want me to ask her for you?"

Erik looked Tom in the eyes and said, "ok, I'll ask her tomorrow at lunch!" Making friends was usually difficult for Eric. But today was different.

He got a new friend without even trying.

He really liked Tom, he was kind, encouraging, and fun. The type of friend Eric needed. Just then Willow approached Eric, and nuzzled him fondly.

***

Tom watched Eric drive off, then felt doggie paws on his legs. Scratching furiously for attention and to give kisses. He bent down and whispered 'Hope! How are you girl?"

The wild and crazy puppy licked Tom's face and made him laugh!

He looked up and watched Trinity open the farmhouse door and carry groceries in. She was gorgeous and she was Tom's girl!

He had no idea why she agreed to go on a first date with him.

Tom grinned and loved how spontaneous Trin was. She often embarrassed him, but he was crazy about her! Tom hoped she'd forget about getting married, for at least 10 years.

"Come on girl!" Tom said as he and Hope ran to the farmhouse.

Chapter 11

MY CHERIE AMOUR

There was a sharp rap on Sherry's door.

"Who is it?" she asked, sitting up in bed with a yawn. She looked over at the time. 7:30 am. She got into her bathrobe and went to open the door. Who knocked at 7:30 am?

It was Roland the caretaker.

"Roland, do you have any idea what time it is?" Sherry asked in an irritated tone. "Well, there's a young man here to see you," Roland replied.

Tom had come to see her at 7:30 a.m. He liked to sleep in even more than she did. Was everything okay at the farm? "Where?" she asked, putting on her slippers hurriedly.

"In the front lobby," Roland explained. There had to be something really wrong for Tom to come out here that early. Did something happen to Hank? She rushed down the stairs.

A young man was standing in the front lobby that she knew well, but it wasn't Tom. It was Cooper.

Cooper looked so out of place in his white cotton Vans and jegging-style Guess pants that Sherry would have laughed if she hadn't been so surprised. Cooper was the last person she had expected to see in Hope Valley. He thought traveling to the Bronx was going 'to the country.'

"Oh my God, Cooper, what are you doing here?" Sherry cried.

"Sherry babe," Cooper replied, smiling widely. "I thought I'd surprise you."

"Well you certainly did that," she said putting up a hand self-consciously to her hair which was all mussed up from bed. "You should have told me you were coming." "But that would ruin the surprise Sherry babe," Cooper said. He tried to take a step towards her to hug her, but Roland stepped in between.

"Roland, this is my boyfriend, Cooper," Sherry explained. "Boyfriend?" Roland repeated his eyes bugging out. "That's right," Sherry replied.

Roland looked Cooper up and down. Finally, he replied, "Well you got the boy part right." Sherry glared at Roland as she nudged Cooper up the stairs to her room.

"We'll be down for the complimentary breakfast soon," Sherry said. "Oh, you missed that," Roland called after them.

"What?" Sherry said, "It's 7:30 a.m."

My Cherie Amour

"That's right," Roland said. "It ends at 7:00 a.m., but you can still get breakfast." "Oh good," Sherry said.

"At the diner," Roland continued.

Sherry looked at Cooper and shook her head. "Just come on." She led Cooper up the stairs to her room.

"I still can't believe you are here," Sherry said.

"Believe it or not, old man Jenks gave me some time off so I thought I'd surprise you. Which I obviously did, mission accomplished!" He turned and surveyed her wreck of a room. "So is this how people live out in the country?" he asked.

"No, don't be silly," Sherry replied, grabbing the last few things from the nightstand. "The motel is being taken over by some rodeo club coming through, can you believe it? I thought I'd be back in Manhattan by now, but my father is being a bit more obstinate than I thought so I can't leave yet. I'm moving to a bed and breakfast," she explained.

"What's that?" Cooper asked.

You don't know what a bed and breakfast is? Sherry replied. Cooper shrugged.

" a b and b?"

Cooper looked like a light went off in his head. "Oh a b and b," Cooper replied, "why didn't you just say so?"

Sherry sighed. Cooper was cute, but sometimes a bit daft, she tried to chalk it up to his young age. She gave him a quick hug. She could smell his sharp-smelling cologne, a welcome and comforting smell after all the sweat and animal manure odors that most locals carried around.

"I'm so glad you're here," Sherry announced. "You are?"

"Does this make you feel welcome"?? She said and kissed him.

Sherry remembered she was supposed to meet her mother for lunch at noon.....and be out of her motel room by 11:30.

"I wish we could hang out here, but we can't," Sherry explained as she slipped out of his tight embrace. "I'm supposed to meet my mother at noon, it's going to be so much better with you with me.

Sherry quickly dressed in front of him and threw clothes into her suitcase. Cooper splayed himself on her bed and used his phone. Sherry was soon ready and had her suitcase packed.

Can you help carry my suitcase to the car?" she asked. "I would babe but I can't," Cooper replied.

Why not?

"Well, I'm not dressed to work out babe. Why don't you just get the busboy to do it?"

She was going to say there were no busboys in motels and that carrying her suitcases to her car wasn't really working out but she didn't want to get into it. Sherry knew Cooper could be a bit of a diva, he was from the city after all.

And perhaps he was tired after the long flight. Besides, he made the effort to come all the way out to Wyoming to surprise her. Sherry chuckled slightly as she carried her suitcases to her SUV.

For a motel that was supposedly going to be full that night, it was certainly devoid of many customers just then. The only movement in the parking lot was the dust wheels blowing across it. She saw Roland watching her from the motel office.

She knew Hope Valley enough to know the whole town was going to know Cooper was there in a matter of a few minutes.

When she went back into the room to get more of her stuff, instead of lying down Cooper was taking selfies of himself next to one of the many pictures of cows that dotted the walls of the motel room.

I thought you were resting. she said to Cooper as she picked up her purse and toiletry bag. I am resting, you know they say taking selfies has been found to be very relaxing."

They do, do they? Sherry said, who says that?

"Oh I don't know," Cooper replied between snapping pictures, "Google I guess." he made various faces at the phone, ranging from fierce to cute to sad to outraged. Sherry rolled her eyes and picked up her purse and the room key from the desk near the door.

"Well come on, I've got to drop off this key to Mr. Branson, you can meet your first cowboy. "Oh wow," Cooper said, "so kitsch!"

He followed her out to the car where she loaded the rest of her stuff and then to the office. Here's my key Roland

Roland nodded at her and she could have sworn she heard him say 'they're just leaving," as she exited the office.

They drove the 2 miles on Route 10 into Hope Valley talking about New York and the firm. As they drove through town Sherry asked, "So what do you think of the town?" She was curious as to what a total city boy like Cooper would think of a town like Hope Valley that had all of one stop sign.

Cooper looked around confused. "Wait, This is it? Cooper asked. "I thought we were at a rest stop?"

Sherry chuckled. "Nope, this is the town I grew up in. Now you know why I left." She parked in front of Forest Glen.

Cooper got out of the car and looked around. "You've got to be kidding Sherry, this is Hope Valley? But there's no one around.."

"Oh they're around, the kids are in school, and most of the other people are in the diner. See there are people right over there." She pointed towards the Earlee Mug where people stared at them through the window.

"Is there a reason why they're all staring at us?"

My Cherie Amour

"Because you're a stranger," Sherry replied. "C'mon," she gestured for him to follow her. "Aren't you going to lock the car?" Cooper asked.

This is where my mom is staying. Sherry said. "No one locks their doors here Cooper, so there's no reason to worry about the car," Sherry told him.

I'll take you over to meet my dad at the farm later, and I can't wait for you to meet Tom." Oh yeah has he convinced your dad to move yet?

No, but he's so smart Cooper, if he could just get his act together, he always did so well in school. He was always top of his class at Midtown Elementary."

He got that smart gene from you Sherry "He's adopted," Sherry replied.

They reached her mom's apartment. She was glad to see her mom had planted a few azaleas in a little area outside her apartment. It would be a nice place for her father to garden once he moved in with her.

Before she knocked on the door she said now remember Cooper nothing about the plan you know with Tom, no one knows about that but me and you and Tom and-"

Just then the door swung open and Connie stood there. "Sherry you said you would be here at ten, it's almost twelve,

Sorry, Mom, I lost track of time and I didn't know Cooper was coming. Mom this is Cooper, I think I mentioned him to you before. Oh yes, your boyfriend," Connie said.

Sherry cringed.

I'm surprised you didn't know we were coming. I did know

How was that? Cooper asked.

"Roland from the motel just called," Connie said like it was the most natural thing in the world. I told you everyone around here knows everyone else.

He also told me some disturbing news Sherry, that you are moving into Edith's place. Sherry sighed. What's disturbing about that?

Why would you have anything to do with that woman? She obviously is trying to interfere with your father's and my relationship. Well, I don't know anything about that, and there's nowhere else to stay, Sherry explained.

Hey, why don't you stay with your mom? Cooper interjected.

No, Sherry practically shouted, giving Cooper a warning look. "Oh, look at the time, I think we ought to be going c'mon Cooper." You know, I think Cooper is on to something here. There is an opening in a condo a little ways down, her mother said.

No, this place is for old people, I'm not living here, Sherry blurted out before she realized how it sounded.

Well, I'll have you know we do quite a bit here Sherry, we're not all one foot in the grave you know. Besides, you're no spring chicken anymore yourself.'

My Cherie Amour

I wasn't trying to insult you Mother, I'm just not interested in you know canasta clubs and stuff. Besides, I already told Edith I would stay at her bed and breakfast. What? You're staying at Edith's?

It's not like I wanted to, it's just that besides the motel, she's the only other place open. Trinity's in the guest house.

So you're going to stay with that..witch after the way she's treated me? But you know what could I really expect, I mean it's not like you understand decorum. I mean you're letting that, that girl live with Tom."

She's not living with him, she's living in the guest house.

But Connie dismissed this piece of information and instead said lowering her voice, and this Cooper, I mean how old is he anyways? Maybe that's the way you do things in NY Sherry it's not how we do things here!

Now Sherry was really angry. How dare her mother lecture her when her own behavior was so ridiculous. Oh, and this is how you do things here? You move out of the home you've lived in for like forever??

I guess this means we're not drinking the tea? Cooper said reappearing at the door with a tray with little tea cups on it.

It was nice of him to make them tea but there was no way in hell Sherry was spending even a minute more with her mother. Of all the nerve. She grabbed her coat off the couch and left. She got in her car and sat there seething.

A minute later, Cooper joined her.

"Sorry about that," she said. I just needed to get out of there.

No need to apologize, Cooper said. But that tea I made was really good. You could have waited to have that argument after we drank the tea.

I'm sorry, you're right. But she makes me so furious! The nerve of her saying I shouldn't let Tom have his girlfriend staying with him, but then it's okay for her to move out on my dad after being married for fifty years." She was so busy talking and looking for her keys she didn't notice someone was walking right towards her and she bumped into them.

"Sorry," she mumbled. Years of living in New York had made her adept at not making eye contact with random strangers she bumped into on the street so she hadn't even noticed the person she bumped into was no stranger at all, it was Arlo.

"If it isn't my old sweetheart Sherrie Traylor," Arlo crooned. "And no need to apologize, I think the last time we bumped into each other was in tenth grade and we ended up going out for 2 years."

"Arlo, is there some reason every time we see each other you bring up ancient history?" she asked him, and who can remember all that, and by the way, it wasn't two years, it was more like two months."

My Cherie Amour

Arlo gave her a wry look. "I guess you remember," he remarked. Then he added, "You must be Conner, Sherry's boy..friend?" Sherry gritted her teeth. "It's Cooper."

"Cooper? Oh even better," Arlo chuckled. Sherry didn't even bother asking Arlo how he knew about Cooper, it was obvious to her that the Hope Valley gossip train was the one thing in town that moved at lightning speed.

"So I'm surprised to see you out here," Arlo said.

"Well, I wanted to see what life was like you know, on the range," Cooper replied. His meager attempt at 'rural humor' made Sherry cringe. "Well, we'd love to stay and talk more, Sherry said in a heavily sarcastic tone, "but we're on our way up to Windy Hill to see my dad and Tom." "Oh, meeting the family huh," Arlo said looking at Cooper, "it must be getting pretty serious then?"

Sherry replied, "You know Arlo, as usual, it's been just great seeing you, but we'll just be on our way." She got in the car and slammed the car door just a little harder than she normally would and motioned Cooper to do the same.

But she should have known Arlo wasn't going to let them get away that easily. He rapped on the window. Sherry sighed and rolled the window down.

"What now Arlo? You know, don't you have work to do Arlo? You know like solving crimes, a fire, maybe finding a real suspect and not arresting little old ladies?" "I'm working on it," Arlo replied. "I just thought you could relay something to your dad for me, save me some time so I can work on all that crime-fighting you just mentioned."

"What now?"

"Let him know that Jason Jorjani and his girlfriend Jessica Copton check out, no criminal records or anything."

Sherry blinked at Arlo, She had no idea what he was talking about. "Who are Jason Jorjani and Jessica Copton? And of what are you speaking?"

"Oh, you don't know?" Arlo said leaning heavily on the car. "Hank is looking to rent out part of his land to them. They're some new age types looking to live off the land, you know how young people are these days Sherry, going back to nature and crap. You into nature Cooper?"

"Oh God no," Cooper replied.

"He's renting out part of his land?" Sherry said aloud.

"Yeah, so it doesn't seem like he's looking to sell anytime soon would you say?" Arlo remarked.

What in the world was her father up to now? Sherry wondered. Renting out part of his land to survivalists? "Goodbye Arlo," Sherry said and put the car in reverse.

"Well he was nice," Cooper said as they drove off.

"Not really." Sherry said shortly adding, "I know you want me to go back to New York with you but I think I'm going to have to stay here a bit longer, especially now that my dad has this new crazy idea of renting land out to some random people.

"What? No Sherry, you have to come back. Besides, you heard what the Sheriff said, your dad is renting out part of his land to these people, sounds like the farm is doing fine."

"That's not fine, Cooper, my plan is to have him sell the farm and move in with my mom, not start new businesses at the farm!" Whatever…..I mean you have to come back. What about buying the highrise?

Sherry sighed. She had been so busy thinking about Windy Hill she had forgotten all about the fact that she had promised Cooper they could buy the highrise in New York.

Is that why you came out here? To get me to come back to New York with you?? Yeah, I miss you, I mean who do I have to go to Shilo's with?

Sherry thought about it as she took the turn off Route 10 and onto rural Highway 141 which led to the turn-off for Grove Creek.

I don't know actually, I guess I was hoping that I could be here for Tom. He's been having a tough time with.. pretty much everything.

But I thought he had his girlfriend here with him right? He's 18 babe, time to let him live his own life, and you should have your own life too. I mean I might be a lowly paralegal but if I was an attorney like you up to be partner I wouldn't be wasting my time out here in Nowheresville. I mean if you become a partner you'd have enough money to buy that highrise on Lipton Street we wanted right? Or are you planning on using the proceeds from the sale of the farm?

Sherry bit her lip. She had forgotten that she had told Cooper that when she sold the farm she could use part of the proceeds to buy the spacious highrise they had looked at back in New York.

I told Tom that the proceeds from the farm would go to him. We don't need it, I'm going to make partner soon so- Not if you stay out here you won't Cooper said.

What? What is that supposed to mean? Did you hear something, is that idiot Blackburn going behind my back while-"

"Watch out!" Cooper said and Sherry saw a stray sheep cross the road. She swerved sharply to the side to avoid it. This usually would have been fine except the road was dirt and the back wheels spun wildly causing the front of the car to pitch sending them headlong into a ditch. The last thing Sherry saw was a fence post crashing through the windshield before everything went black.

***

Hank walked slowly up to the farmhouse. It had been a long day. From administering meds to the sheep, changing the oil and coolant in the tractor, a trip into town for a new truck battery, and replacing a track on a barn door. Hank groaned as he climbed the side door steps.

He was hungry, really needed a cold beer, then washing up in the laundry tub, and hoping someone planned on making dinner tonight.

He opened the door and smelled chicken fried chicken. He heard it sizzling in the seemingly 200-year-old electric skillet that had been his mother's. "Hi!" Trinity said, as she turned from the sink and smiled at him. "Are you hungry?"

"I'm starving! Who taught you to cook?" Hank asked as the delightful smells of frying onion, breading, and chicken wafted up his nose.

"My grandma Lilly." Trinity replied and added, "she was my dad's mom and grew up on a farm in Kentucky. She decided I needed to know all her secret family recipes before she passed on.

This is her chicken fried chicken, and the secret ingredient is cold beer poured into the batter, just before coating the chicken. She said the beer married all the herbs, divorced the breading, and infuriated the eggs. She was a delightful crusty old woman who was an Army Mash nurse in WW2. But that woman could cook, and she thought I could do no wrong!"

"Well, it smells delicious Trinity! Where's Hope?" Hank inquired.

"She's downstairs asleep on Tom's bed.

I took her jogging today and wore her out." Trinity replied.

"Hope sits on my lap at 5:30 and we watch the Cheyenne evening news together." Hank said.

"Well, just holler down the stairs and she'll come up. I'm frying you boys up some chicken livers too. We'll be ready to eat in half an hour. I found this old electric skillet in the basement, I hope it's ok I'm cooking in it tonight?" Trinity asked.

"It was my mother's, and she'd be delighted you were using it. Thank you for cooking dinner, Trinity. I always told Thomas to find a woman who was beautiful and could cook. He obviously took my advice."

Trinity blushed and loved the many compliments this family gave her every day. She lowered the temp on the potatoes boiling on the stove. Mashed potatoes and gravy, fresh green beans, and a tossed salad completed the evening's menu.

In 30 seconds Trinity's legs were each licked by a puppy, Hope ran out of the kitchen and into Hank's lap in the family room.

Trinity wiped her hands on her apron and peeked into the family room. "Grandpa, could you let her outside, she just woke from a nap."

"Sure!" Hank replied and opened the front door and took Hope outside. He wondered if Tom and Trinity might marry in a few years and live in the farmhouse with him.

Trinity drove him nuts most days, but she made Tom happy and was as good a cook as Hank's mother had been. Trinity kept the kitchen and refrigerator spotless. More qualities she shared with Hank's mom.

Hope did her business and sniffed some squirrel and cat tracks.

Hank whistled and she came running. Hope and Hank had become best friends. "Come on Hope! Let's go watch the evening news." Hank said.

***

It was late, as Rory sat at the kitchen table doing homework. Jerry went to bed 2 hours ago. She looked out the window and watched the backyard oak tree, gently swaying in a windstorm; its branches conducting an enormous orchestra of trees.

Lighting flashed nearby, and soon escorted a heavy downpour of rain across the valley. Rory closed her eyes and listened; the dancing raindrops became a symphony of harmony.

Rory was in Mrs. Sampson's 3rd year French class and was writing an essay on European music history, in French. She was exploring the 6 eras of classical music, from the 6th to 21st centuries.

Rory loved the brilliant compositions of Hayden, Mozart, and Beethoven.

The symmetry of these 3 composer's arrangements resonated with Rory. Music helped her maintain a balanced equilibrium in every aspect of life. Rory loved music, French, and creative writing. She was passionate about combining the 3 in many aspects of her life.

Last year Rory translated her European essays into French. This year she began writing them in French. She carried a 4.3 GPA and dreamed of playing a harp in the famed 'Philharmonie de Paris'.

Rory was fluent in French, the piano, harp, and her pursuit of Thomas Whitmore.

Hands down, Rory's favorite contemporary musician was Stevland Morris, also known as Stevie Wonder. She adored the sophistication and creativity Morris weaved into his simple songs. Rory's musical repertoire spanned the traditions of rock, rhythm and blues, hip-hop, pop, rap, and others.

But she usually worked on her homework with the music of Stevie Wonder flowing from her headset. And her all-time favorite song of Stevie's was: 'My Cherie Amour'.

Rory could listen to that love ballad all day long.

Its words reflected the emotions of her heart, whenever she was near Tom.

Suddenly lighting struck one of Hank's lightning arrestors atop his barn. Rory jumped as the ensuing thunderclap rattled the windows.

Seconds later, Jerry climbed into her lap, terrified and couldn't sleep. Rory moved to the sofa and let Jerry snuggle against her and fall back asleep. She covered him with their grandmother's pretty afghan.

Jerry abhorred storms and wished he could fit an entire flock of sheep into his bedroom. Sheep calmed Jerry and surrounded him with peaceful thoughts.

'My Cherie Amour' surrounded Rory, as she closed her eyes and imagined dancing with Tom, in the middle of a dark Paris street, under a single dim streetlight, in the pouring rain.

Chapter 12

MAMA MOOSE

Rory stood on a stool and brushed Whisper. His eyes were half closed, the horse loved being brushed. Millions of dust particles danced on silent beams of light, as Rory hummed quietly. They enjoyed each other's company, Whisper and Rory.

"Hey Rory!" Tom called out.

Tom and Jerry walked into the barn, Snowball crawled out of Jerry's sweatshirt pocket, and dashed up his arm, and leapt up to his head. Snowball stared at Whisper, and his whiskers, vibrated as he tried to sense more about the huge creature.

"Jerry, keep that dumb rat away from Whisper! Horses freak out with rats running up and down their backs!" Rory ordered condescendingly. Jerry had been having a good morning until now, girls had a way of ruining all his fun.

Tom grabbed a brush and stood next to Rory, he was in a chatty mood.

"I met Eric yesterday, he's the pharmacist guy / virtual veterinarian who helped Whisper, you know." "I know." Rory replied while concentrating on a nasty-looking lump on Whisper's rump.

"Look at this horse fly bite, it swelled up bad." She said to Tom with alarm in her voice. "We need to remember horse spray at turn out." Retorted Tom.

"Doesn't Eric seem kind of weird?" Rory asked matter of factly.

"No, I thought he was pretty cool, exceptionally smart, and calm under pressure. He'd be a great submarine captain." Tom replied.

"Seriously! Like he'd give an order!

'Load some torpedoes to fire', and no one would know who he's talking to, cause he won't look you in the eye!" Rory said as she stared at Tom, and added, "See I'm looking you in the eye, this is how it's done!"

"He's on the spectrum Rory." Tom exclaimed and grew frustrated with her. "What's a spectrum, a new kind of drug?" Rory asked

"He's got Asperger's, and has issues interacting socially with people, like looking someone in the eye." Tom replied softly. "He's nice, but he's weird, Tom!" "You're sure in a mood today Rory." Tom shot back.

"I miss my mom, and I'm tired of being a babysitter. Jerry's room is a mess, he doesn't do his chores, and his stupid rat sleeps on top the toaster." "You're cute when you're grumpy." Tom said with a grin.

Rory punched him and moved closer. "Oh, and so you like Eric," she asked.

"Yeah, I do, and if I ever had to go to war, I'd want Eric there with me. He's a good problem solver." "Are you joining the Army?" Rory asked with an edge in her voice.

"No, I'm not joining the Army, geeez, it's just an expression!" Tom retorted. "People from back East are weird." Rory said casually.

"Who's weird?" Trinity asked as she stepped off the main stairway.

"Des filles de Boston!" Rory whispered to Tom in French, as she dropped her brush, rolled her eyes, and stormed out of the barn for some air.

Rory's mood went south whenever Trinity was around, and she had no clue why Tom

even liked Trinity. Rory stopped and turned to face Tom, then said, "you know yesterday I told Justin what happened to Whisper, and the guy suddenly weirded out, you know, like all nervous. Then he walked off without saying anything. Don't you think that was weird?? I mean it made me wonder if Justin knew something!" "Yeah, and you know what else is weird?"

Tom asked as he proceeded to tell Rory about the black sedan he and Edith saw the other night. "What were the people wearing?" Rory asked perceptibly.

"Black suit jackets and white shirts. You know sort of like FBI agents or Ghostbuster." Trinity stepped next to Tom and kissed his cheek, several times, while staring at Rory.

Rory rolled her eyes again and wanted to hurl, Trinity drove her nuts. Rory turned and resumed her storming out of the barn while mumbling in French... "Chicks from Boston are bitches."

"What's up with her?" Trinity asked Tom. "She's a teenage girl, they're all flakes." Tom replied loud enough for Rory to hear. "Is that right!" Trinity retorted, then added,

"Well, technically I'm a teenage girl, so do you consider me a flake too?" "You know what I mean."

"No Tom, I don't know what you mean, furthermore the next time you want to make out in the guest house. I'm going to need clarification on what a flake is.

But you're a guy, and most guys, are far, far away in another galaxy when it comes to understanding their own feelings. Much less those of a girl, or a girl who's a flake!"

Trinity replied while glaring at him. "Trin, I don't want to have a fight!" Tom pleaded.

"Well then you'd better go and apologize to your little friend. Cause she's a girl, and I'm a girl, and I can guarantee you hurt her feelings….because you're a guy." Trinity replied.

Tom turned and rolled his eyes as he walked outside to find Rory. He saw her sitting on a tree stump overlooking the pasture. "Hey, I'm sorry I called you a flake, I didn't mean it, and actually I think you're pretty cool."

Tom said sincerely.

"For a girl." Rory added sarcastically.

"Why don't you dump Trinity, she gets on my nerves. She thinks she knows everything about everything. And you're all uptight and nervous whenever she's around!"

"Around who?" Tom asked nervously.

"Trinity, you dork!! I heard she spent $500.00 on a boatload of flowers and hasn't sold a one.

Why do you even like her? Why don't you get a real girlfriend, a girl who loves and appreciates you."

Tom stared at Rory in disbelief and walked back into the barn. He had no idea how to reply to Rory without looking like a puppy dog.

Yes, Trinity got on his nerves too, but he loved her. She gave him the strength to walk away from boarding school. What did a young girl like Rory know about being a guy, and loving a woman?

Tom picked up Rory's brush and set it into the tack box. "What did she say?" Trinity asked as she sprayed Whisper down with fly spray. "I don't know, I apologized and I think she's still mad or still a girl. I need to get out of here!

I was having a nice day and then bamn!!

I got two women mad at me in under 2 minutes!" Tom complained. "Maybe you need to man up?"

Trinity set the spray down and wrapped her arms around Tom's neck, then kissed him deeply. "What's that for? I thought you were mad,

at me?" Tom inquired.

"Since you're a clueless man, I'll explain it to you." Trinity replied and added…

"You know, my dad never apologizes for anything. He thinks it's a sign of weakness. I'm proud of you Tom, only a strong man would apologize to Rory.

And so, I love you, Mr. Whitmore; I love how gentle you are with me." Tom kissed Trinity and pulled her close.

Rory walked back into the barn, now worried she'd upset Tom. She stopped in her tracks at the sight of Tom and Trinity kissing and ran for home; her heart a storm of emotion.

Rory couldn't see well as tears flooded her eyes.

She ran faster than a honeybee flys and tripped on a broken fence post, and fell hard into a patch of river rock. Intense pain shot through her knee. She rolled over and pulled her left leg up. Her jeans had a big rip, and blood oozed out of 8 jagged tears in her skin.

She lay there for a long minute, staring up at sleeping clouds floating by, and wondering why being a teenager was so hard. Suddenly she giggled as Hope arrived and began licking her knee. The puppy then jumped onto Rory's chest and licked her face.

Rory laughed and hugged Hope, and wished she was a cloud, carefree with no worries like when her mom was coming home next, and no stupid little brother to contend with. And most importantly, no handsome young man named Tom, who didn't even notice she wore a little makeup and mascara today. And a new larger size bra.

Life sucked, and Rory was in the front seat.

She stood and noticed her pretty red hair was full of dirt and leaves and weeds.

Rory limped home, Hope by her side, and wishing one of Jessica's flying saucers would beam Trinity up.

In a moment she opened the back door of her house, walked into the bathroom, and patched herself up as Hope lay in front of the toilet admiring Rory like she was the coolest girl on earth.

Rory hugged Hope and sent Tom a text.

'In case you're wondering, I went home.

I can only take so much of Trinity.

You need to find a girl who loves you before anyone else. A girl who devotes herself to you. BTW, Hope followed me home, I'll bring her back later. And I'm sorry I was grumpy.'

Rory hit send and sat on the sofa with Hope. They both fell sound asleep.

Meanwhile, Tom stared at Rory's text and decided he needed an app to decipher teenage girls emotions.

***

Tom and Trinity cleaned Whisper's hooves and fed him a few carrots, then returned him to his run.

"Do you feel like going into town and trying to sell your flowers on the street corners, then lunch at the burger barn, and later a movie?" Tom asked. "Are you asking me out on a date,

Mr. Whitmore?" Trinity asked with a smile as she stepped outside.

The noonday sun lit her pretty blue eyes, and her long blonde hair sparkled. Tom stopped and stared at her, she was gorgeous.

"What's wrong, do I have dirt on my face?"

Trinity asked as she brushed barn dust off her clothes. "No! But you're beautiful!"

Tom replied with a hypnotic gaze guys get when looking at a pretty girl.

"You're just now figuring that out!" Trinity laughed and ran off to the main pasture.

Her long legs jumped the fence easily and she ran towards the sheep. Tom stopped at the fence and watched as the sheep scattered, revealing Jerry and Snowball sitting on the ground, in the middle.

He'd been reading them a Walt Whitman poem and yelled at Trinity for disturbing the sheep. Jerry loved poetry and memorized lots of it.

Tom's eyes returned to Trinity and her pretty young figure. He adored Trinity and her perky spunk-filled spirit. She reminded him of a golden eagle gliding through the Grand Canyon, on silky currents of warm air. She was carefree and loved life.

Tom's warm thoughts were suddenly interrupted; his phone rang. It was Trinity's mom. He lowered his voice, hoping to sound manly and in control...."Hello?"

"Hello Tom, this is Carol, how are you?"

"I'm good Mrs. Smithe, how are you and your family?" Tom replied. "Tom, is this an ok time to call?"

Trinity's mom asked.

Tom turned and looked at Trinity, she held out her hand and Snowball jumped and ran up to her shoulder. Trinity screamed in delight and dashed around the herd of sheep giggling and laughing.

She was beginning to like Snowball.

"I'm not sure ma'am." Tom replied stoically.

"Tom, I miss my daughter, will I ever see her again?"

"I hope so ma'am, all I can tell you is your daughter is safe and seems happy." "Does she ever mention me?" Carol asked as tears fell down her cheeks.

Tom grimaced, then replied, "I'll tell her you called ma'am."

"Thank you, Tom, and I deposited $5000.00 in her debit card. If she ever needs anything, anything at all, will you call me?" "Yes Mrs. Smithe I will, I promise. And ma'am, I love your daughter very much."

"I know you do Tom, and I think highly of you."

"Thank you." Tom replied as the line went dead. He wished it had been his dad calling. Tom groaned in an overload of emotions just as Trinity slipped her soft arms around his waist.

"Who was it, what's wrong?" She asked.

"No one really, just someone I used to know."

Trinity knew him well, and she heard the emotion in his voice, the way a man sounds when he's upset. Tom missed his father terribly, even though he couldn't remember him. And he had no idea why Trinity couldn't just call her mom or send a simple text, letting her mother know she was ok.

"Why can't you tell me who called, was it your dad?" Trinity asked as she touched Tom's eyes and hidden tears poured out onto her fingertips.

For Tom, it was so absurd Trinity refused to call her mom; while Tom desperately wished he could talk to his father. His emotions rattled Tom, he needed Trinity to comfort him; but she was in her own little reality most of the time. And not truly understanding his male emotions.

Tom pulled Trinity tightly to his chest and kissed her; the warmth of her soft lips and body calmed him. But Trinity had no time to be comforting a man……

"I can't go into town, I forgot to tell you, but Bruce called an hour ago and is picking me up. We're driving into Cheyenne so I can test out and get my black belt. Will you come with me?" Trinity asked.

"Trin, you know I have a bunch of stuff to do today." Tom replied, still not looking at her. "Please," she whispered, while turning his face to look at her.

"Please come with me, you're my family and I need you there."

"Will you do something for me, if I come along?" Tom asked. "Sure, what is it?" Trinity replied sharply. Trinity heard Tom take a deep breath, then look into her eyes, and ask,

"Call your mom, and tell her you're ok, like a 20-second phone call." "She just called you, didn't she.

I want nothing to do with her, she's not my mother. She has no idea how to love her children! She's selfish and full of herself! If I ever have kids, they will know every minute, of every day that I love them!

If they call me and say they're sick, I'll go home and take care of them. Tom, your family is always telling me how pretty I am, and what a good cook I am. Your mother is more of a mom to me than mine ever was.

Why should I call her Tom, I moved here with you to get away from her! Don't you understand? Are you that dense Tom?" "Trinity, she's worried about you! She's called me several times now. Every time she cries and says she misses you!

I mean I wish my dad would call and check on me, like your mom cares about you."

Trinity exploded at Tom….. "She doesn't care about me Tom, she's trying to manipulate me into feeling sorry for her! You really don't know a thing about me and my feelings Tom! You're a typical clueless man!"

Trinity turned and ran to the guest house, with clenched fists and tears. At the same time, a kaleidoscope of butterflies flew into Tom's stomach.

***

Tom gave Trinity 10 minutes, then sprinted to the farmhouse for a peppermint tea bag. Trinity loved peppermint ever since she was a little girl.

He walked into the guest house, and saw her curled up on the sofa, Trinity's long blonde hair covered her face. But he heard her softly crying and quickly heated water in the microwave, dropped in the tea bag and stared out the window. It began raining, and his stomach burned with anxiety.

Tom hated seeing Trinity cry, somehow her sadness seemed his fault. Suddenly a knock, as the door opened and his grandfather stepped in. He stood on the little green doormat with its cheery yellow sunflowers, his old gray hair was dripping wet from the rain.

But right away he could hear Trinity crying and looked at Tom, and the hot cup of tea in his hands. "Is she ok?" Hank whispered and watched Tom's shoulders shrug in reply.

"You know, women are a pain on a sunny day." Hank announced in a loud whisper.

"Grandpa, not now." Tom sternly ordered as Hank took his hat off and replied softly, "If I can get Trinity anything will you let me know? I'm glad you brought her here Tom, she brightens the place up. And her blueberry muffins, oh my God they're delicious!

Everything Trinity cooks is amazing!

If you must marry a woman, make sure she can cook, those were my father's words." Tom smiled in reply and motioned he had to take Trin the tea.

"Have you seen Orly? I can't find him." Hank said with a worried look in his eyes.

"No Grandpa, I haven't. We're going to Cheyenne in a few minutes, I'll help you look when I get home, ok?"

"Trinity has become like a daughter to me Tom; is it warm enough in here, maybe she's cold. Women cry and are cold when they're pregnant, maybe she's pregnant. I could turn the furnace on for her." Hank muttered, now feeling sour about his comment about women.

"It's ok Grandpa, but thank you. Trinity likes hot peppermint tea; and she's not pregnant." "You and Trinity know about using protection right?" Hank whispered.

"Yes Grandpa, we're being safe".

Hank nodded his head and stepped back out into the pouring rain.

Tom smiled at his grandfather, behind all the gruff, stood a powerfully kind man.

"Thank you!" Trinity said with a forced and tear-drenched smile as she took a sip of the tea. Tom sat next to her and began rubbing her feet.

"Why do you fuss over me?" Trinity asked. "Cause I love you, and I like seeing you happy."

"My mom never fussed over us ever, she was like a 12-year-old, and had no capacity to be a mom. All she did was attend board meetings of all her charities and causes. If I texted her and said my stomach was upset, you know, hoping she'd come pick me up at school and take me home.

All I got was a short text telling me to call a taxi, and telling me there were cans of chicken noodle soup in the pantry." Trinity took a sip of tea and stared into Tom's eyes.

"You know, you'd be a better mom than she ever was!"

"I'm a guy, in case you hadn't noticed." Tom said with a grin.

"But you'd come pick me up at school and fuss over me. You'd heat up canned soup and read me a story or tuck me in for a nap. That's who you are Tom. Your family, friends, and complete strangers come first in your life."

Trinity sipped more tea and filled her eyes with Tom's strong shoulders. He was a good-looking young man, with the chiseled body of a wrestler.

"Tom, you know how to love people, encourage them, and fuss over them, with their favorite flavor of tea." Trinity added, then sighed and laid her head on Tom's shoulder.

"If you were at my house and my dad started yelling at me and telling me I was stupid. What would you say to him?" Trinity asked. "I'd ask him to stop, and if he didn't, I would get you out of there." Tom replied.

"You wouldn't be afraid of him?" Trinity asked.

"No." Tom replied while looking into her eyes. Trinity slid closer to Tom and kissed him.

Tom wrapped his arms around Trinity, held her, and said, "your mom put $5000.00 on your debit card and said if you need anything to let her know. She asked if you were happy."

"And you told her I was?"

"Yeah, I told her you were happy." Trinity gently kissed his ear.

"$5000.00! So now she's trying to buy my love." Trinity murmured aloud.

"I wonder if they divorced. I'm almost broke how did she know I needed money?" Trinity moaned. 'Mom's know a lot of things." Tom softly replied.

Trinity wiped more tears, then turned and kissed him again. Tom tasted her salty tears, and his butterflies instantly flew away. He loved holding Trinity.

"What did your grandpa want?" Trinity asked as she traced his eyebrows with her finger. "Orly's missing, he wanted to know if I'd seen him."

"He said something about women too." Trinity said with a grin.

"He said a man can't be happy without a woman!"

Trinity laughed and tickled Tom until he begged for mercy.

"You have 24 hours to tell me what he said! Knowing your grandfather, he probably insisted women are a pain in the ass!" "Grandpa likes you Trin, you're polite and you can cook and bake, and he said you've become like a daughter to him." "Oh wow!! I'll be a real catch for some young man!" Trinity laughed.

"You ready to go, babe." Tom asked.

"With you!" Trinity replied as she stepped into the bedroom, changed clothes and grabbed her bag. The rain had stopped.

They walked out to the street just as Officer Bruce arrived, looking hot enough to melt every woman's heart from here to Hudson, Alberta.

***

3 hours later Trinity wore her Black Belt and posed for photos. She was happy.

Her favorite photo was of her and Tom, standing behind a basket of flowers. Her hand was in his, she wore a big smile.

On the way home, Trinity sat in the back seat of Bruce's big SUV and typed up a group text, with her favorite photos from the award ceremony. She addressed the text with 24 names of new friends here in Wyoming, and old friends, back in Boston.

Trinity almost pressed the send button, but paused, and looked out the windshield at a huge mother moose ahead, escorting her two little ones, across the State Highway. "Watch that moose!" Tom helpfully warned.

Bruce hit the brakes and let the 3 moose cross the road. The mother constantly looked for bears, while her two daughters walked close behind her.

"This is a good mama moose, she's got her young trained to stay right next to her when crossing a road. And she's young, these two are probably her first offspring. Not all female moose make good mothers. Most do, but a few don't have good motherly instincts.

Every year I'm dispatched on at least one moose and car collision. It's usually at night, and they're always a mess." Bruce said soberly.

"I've never seen a moose!" Trinity said, as she carefully watched in awe.

In a moment Bruce hit the gas, and Trinity turned to look out the back window.

"That mama's beautiful, and she's doing the best she can, for being a new mom." Trinity observed, then added, "my mom was 18 when she had me. She was still a teenager, and didn't have good motherly instincts."

Trinity sat quietly, and looked out the window for a few miles. She looked down at her text again and stared at all the names. In a moment, she added one more......
…'mom'.

Chapter 13

YOU'VE BEEN SERVED

"Oh my God, Are you alright?" Sherry cried. No reply. She wasn't even sure what had happened. One minute she hwas driving up the dirt road towards Windy Hill, the next she had seen something in the road and hit a sturdy sapling. She turned her neck gingerly. It hurt a bit but she didn't feel like she was bleeding anywhere so that was good. But what about Cooper? He still hasn't made a sound. She could see his still body slumped against the front dashboard of the car. She froze. Could he be…dead?

"Cooper?" she said. Still no sound of movement, other than the bleating of a sheep. She was sure that was the something she had seen in the road and what had caused her to swerve at the last moment. Looking out the cracked windshield she could even see a sheep, gray speckled staring back at her, bleating away loudly. These godforsaken sheep. She was sure the sheep were the reason her father wouldn't move off the farm, and now one of them had caused her to crash her car. She felt around for her purse. The sensible thing to do would be to call

Arlo and have him check out the accident scene but she bucked at the thought of calling him with every bone in her body. Still, if Cooper was hurt or worse, she had to do it.

Just then Cooper groaned and tried to sit upright.

"Oh my God Cooper, I'm so glad you're alright!" Sherry cried. "What happened?" he asked, sitting back against the car seat.

"We got into an accident on the way to Windy Hill," Sherry explained quickly adding, "Don't try to move too quickly." "An accident? What is that godforsaken noise?" Cooper asked.

"It's one of my father's sheep, Orly I think," she said. "Wait, let me just see if I can get us out of here." She pushed and pushed on the car door, but it wouldn't budge. "Can you get out of your side?" she asked Cooper.

Cooper seemed to think about it for a moment and then said, "well no," as he dusted off his jacket. "Oh no!" he yelled startling Sherry. "What?" Sherry replied worried he had a broken bone or something terrible like that.

"My watch broke," he said.

"Oh God, you scared me," Sherry said, relieved as she was finally able to push her car door open. "I thought something serious happened." "This is serious, it's a Gimalt," he replied.

Sherry stepped out of the car and surveyed the accident scene. The car wasn't as badly damaged as she had first thought. In fact, it looked like it could be almost drivable, just some front bumper damage and a few scratches. The tree she had hit looked like it hadn't been hit at all, and just had the barest of knicks in it. She felt a nudge at her back. She turned to see Orly staring at her.

"Stupid sheep," she said, "do you have any idea how much trouble you've caused?" Orly just stared at her with his rectangle eyes. She tried to shoo him away but he just stood there. "Where's the rest of you?" She knew enough about sheep to know it was extremely rare for a sheep to go off on its own. But Hank had said that Orly was different from most sheep.

She went over to Cooper's side of the car and opened his door. There was no damage to that side of the car so the door swung open easily. "Good news," she said to Cooper, "The car isn't badly damaged. Do you want to come out and take a look?"

"No, I better not," Cooper replied.

"Why not?" Sherry asked, "I thought you said you weren't hurt."

"Sherry, we've just been in a car accident, I could have internal injuries. We should call someone, you must at least have 911 out here, right? And can you get that thing to stop?" Cooper said glaring at Orly who had followed Sherry to Cooper's side of the car and was bleating like there was no tomorrow.

"Quiet! Quiet, you mangy mutt!" Cooper waved his hands. Orly kept alternately munching on grass and bleating.

Sherry fished around in her pocket for her phone and sighed. Cooper was probably right. They should just call for help, though Cooper looked fine to her, the car was a rental and she was supposed to report any accident with it. She dialed 911 though she had no idea if it would work or not out there.

Orly, shush she said as she waited for someone to pick up. Orly looked at her but kept eating grass and bleating. Sheriff Arlo speaking! She heard instead of the 911 emergency what's your emergency like she expected.

Sherry said, "I was calling 911."

"Okay well you got it. Wait a minute...Sherry is that you?

Sherry bit her tongue. She had recognized his voice so why was it any surprise he had recognized hers?

"Yes," she squeaked out adding in a more steady voice, "So I called because-" But before she could explain to Arlo about the accident he cut her off saying, "Sherry, of course I knew it was you. I mean I'd know your voice anywhere, after all, we dated for three years remember?

"Yes I remember, and it was three months, not three years and how can I forget when you remind me every time we talk?" Sherry cried.

"Well I'm sorry Sherr, but it's something I think about a lot. Best time of my life. So did you call me to ask me to the Harvest festival? Remember when we went back in high school Sher, and you wore that purple-

"Arlo!" Sherry screamed. Cooper looked at her in surprise. Orly looked at her too and even stopped his constant bleating, she had screamed so loud. Arlo, can you for once in your life just listen for a minute?" She walked a little aways from the car and spoke in a more measured voice, "we've been in an accident." she explained. "An accident," Arlo said, sounding much more official. "Well, why didn't you just say so? Are you okay?"

"Yes, we're okay," she said.

"Who's we? Arlo asked. "you and Tom? Or Hank?"

"No, not Tom or Hank, I mean we, Cooper, my, uh, boyfriend and I, we're out on Route 147 going up towards the farm. You know near mile marker 48. Orly, I mean one of my dad's sheep just came out of nowhere, and I lost control I guess. Anyways, we're fine but you know I thought it was best to call."

"Sure thing Sherr. Okay, I've already texted Vince about the volunteer ambulance and we'll be up there in a few minutes. Sit tight and don't worry about anything." Now Sherry felt bad for yelling at Arlo a few minutes earlier. Sometimes when he wasn't constantly joking and harassing her she guessed he could be halfway decent. "Thanks Arlo," she said and hung up. She turned to Cooper, "okay, the ambulance is on its way."

"Oh good, because I think I might have whiplash."

"Whiplash?" Sherry responded in concern, "Why? Does your neck hurt?" "No," Cooper replied. "I just think I might have it."

Sherry knitted her brows. She didn't bother trying to explain to Cooper that if he had whiplash he would know it. Was it her? Did she just find crazy men to date? Just then she saw her dad's red pickup truck winding its way down the road.

As they got closer Sherry could see that Tom was in the truck too and he was wearing one of her dad's old cowboy hats and an old red checkered plaid shirt of his too. Tom was turning into a local, she realized. She needed to get him out of Hope Valley fast. They pulled up near her car. Tom jumped out of the passenger side of the pickup and raced over to her.

"Mom, what happened?" Tom said.

"It's okay Tom, I'm fine, we're fine," she gestured to Cooper who waved at Tom from the car. "I just got into a little accident. I was avoiding Orly here and ended up in the ditch."

"Car doesn't look too bad," Tom said, walking around it. "Is it not drivable?"

"No it probably is, I haven't checked, it's just Cooper wants to get checked out, you know by emergency response."

"Hi," Cooper waved at Tom from where he sat in the car. "Sherry, is there some reason I can only get two bars out here?" he waved his phone around. "You're actually lucky it works at all," Tom responded, "we rarely have any service up at the farm."

"My God," Cooper said, his mouth open in astonishment, "what kind of a place is this?" he said to Sherry. "Sherry are you alright?" Hank said as he walked up from the truck to the accident scene.

"I'm fine dad, it was just a little fender bender," she explained.

"Well that's good," Hank said then he spied Orly, "Orly, there you are!" Hank said patting the gray sheep on the head. "We'd wonder where you'd got to," he pulled rope out of his jacket pocket and tied it around one of Orly's shoulders.

"He's the one who caused the accident," Sherry said.

Hank walked around Sherry's rental. "Well it doesn't look like it was too bad, just a little knick here in the front. Why don't you guys come up to the house now?" "Cooper wants to get checked out first," Sherry explained.

"Checked out?"

"Yeah, but emergency services, see if he needs to go to the hospital."

"Why?" Hank looked confused, he turned to Cooper and said, "you look like a healthy young man, are any of your bones broken?" "Not that I know of," Cooper answered."But I'm not a professional."

"I'm not sure why you would need a professional to tell you that all your arms and legs are working."

"Dad," Sherry interjected, "if he wants to get checked out, it's fine. I already called for an ambulance anyways." "You want me to call Eric?"

"Is he a doctor?" Cooper asked Sherry.

"Pharmacist," Sherry replied. Then she saw a police car and an ambulance making their way up the road. "He fixed Whisper up really good though," Hank said.

"Who's Whisper?" Cooper asked.

"He's a horse that someone is boarding up at Windy Hill," Sherry explained. "A horse?" Cooper echoed.

Arlo and 2 paramedic types snaked their way through the grass over to them. "Everyone okay here?" Arlo asked nodding at Hank and Tom.

"Yes, we're fine," Sherry said.

"I'm not!" Cooper protested raising his hand. The paramedics kneeled beside him. "What seems to be the problem sir?"

"Okay, we can take you. Just wait here we'll get the stretcher." "The problem is I want to get checked out by a doctor, not a pharmacist or a vet."

Cooper nodded at them. "Wait!" Both paramedics looked back in alarm at this sudden cry. But then he said, "do either of you have a decent hot spot I can use?" The paramedics gave each other a look and Hank whispered under his breath, "typical city slicker."

Sherry gave Hank a dirty look. "Dad give him a break, he was just in an accident"

"If he reacts that way from something like this I'd hate to see how he'd be when he had a real problem."

Sherry didn't reply, Sure Cooper was a bit silly, something that she hadn't noticed as much when they had been in New York considering there they just spent all their time either working or dining at posh Manhattan eateries.

"Sherry!" Cooper called as the paramedics carried the stretcher back to the ambulance. "What honey? Cooper looked like he was going to say something serious. "remember...remember to refrigerate my night time face lotions."

Tom and Hank could hardly contain their laughter as they got back into Hank's pickup and she had just about had it with them. "You want to ride with us up to the farm Mom?" Tom asked her.

"No, I better deal with the car. I'll be up in a bit."

"Don't worry about her," Arlo said, putting one arm on Sherry's shoulder which she immediately shrugged off. "Do you want me to have your car towed into town by Greg Watson?" Arlo asked.

"No, I better let the car rental place deal with it. I'll get a ride up to the farm with Tom and my dad. And call the rental place from there." "Why don't you ride with me?" Arlo offered, "I was heading up there anyway.."

Sherry hesitated for a moment, she was not really in the mood to deal with Arlo's jokes and quips, but riding squished between her dad, Tom, and Orly the sheep wasn't going to be a dream either, especially with how they were acting about Cooper.

"Okay fine," she said. She slammed the police car door shut a little more forcefully than she usually would. "Whoa, I know you're upset but Copper is going to be fine."

"It's Cooper," Sherry explained. Then she sighed. "You know what I'm sorry it's not the accident. It's just now I'm going to miss my flight and I don't know why my dad and Tom were acting like such jerks about Cooper."

"He did seem a bit, uh, pampered."

"See this is exactly what I mean, everyone is hung up on his age.

"I didn't say that, I said pampered. Though now that you mention it, I did hear from Edith that he was a young whippersnapper."

"Look Arlo, he's not that much younger than me, and besides, I don't really think you're one to talk about relationships. I mean how many girlfriends have you had? And I'm not even counting the ones that you had while we were dating!"

Arlo chuckled as he pulled into a parking spot in front of the sheep barn. "Hey, I can't help it if I'm popular." He put the car into park and turned towards her, his expression got serious. "But about us, back in high school, I know I probably should have said this a long time ago, but all joking aside, I just want you to know that I regret how I acted back then."

Looking straight at her, even with his laugh lines on his face now and his hair in a short buzz cut which was so different from his curly shag he had back in high school, Sherry could glimpse the boy he had once dated and for a moment she felt disarmed, but she snapped out of it quickly.

"It doesn't matter," Sherry replied, though she was secretly appreciative of the fact that he had finally apologized, "it's ancient history."

"So have you been able to find out any more about how the fire started?" She asked Arlo, more to change the subject than anything else. The atmosphere in the squad car had become too intimate for her liking.

Arlo nodded. "I was actually going to talk to you about that. I have a hunch it was Bob. it just all fits together. He has motive, opportunity."

Sherry groaned inwardly. She knew it wasn't Bob but she couldn't say anything about that to Arlo. Arlo had no idea that she and Bob already had an understanding that she would sell the farm to him, so there would be absolutely no need for Bob to burn down any of the property.

"It's not Bob," she said to Arlo.

Arlo replied, "I really think it is Sherry. Just listen to this. He had a motive right? He wants the farm, Hank won't sell, so he sets the fire to scare him off the property. Then he or some lackey he hired whacked Hank on the head so he can't identify them."

Sherry could see how the theory would make sense to Arlo, even though she knew he was probably on the wrong track. "So that's it? That's your theory that it's Bob? No one else? What about what my dad was saying about the kids throwing field parties down there? Couldn't they have set a fire and then it got out of control? Arlo scratched his head. "Yeah, of course, that's possible. But it can't be Brady Johnson and his crew."

"Why not?"

"Because Bruce swears he was with Brady the night of the fire down at his house watching a game, so Brady has an airtight alibi." "Okay so what about Mr. Genshin, the guy my mom said owns another carding mill in Pine River?

"His motive isn't very strong, I mean, everyone knows carding mills have been on the down and out for a while now. New machines can do the same work in half the time…and his operation is twice as big as your parents. Sorry to say this but they couldn't really compete with him, not the other way around. So there goes his motive."

"So that's why you arrested my mom then? Do you still think my parents had something to do with it?" Sherry asked. She could see Rory leading Whisper and Tigger down to the front field. Whisper seemed to be a lot better than the last time she'd seen him.

"No, and I'm sorry we even brought your mom down to the station. Especially with all the issues they are having now. How's that going anyways? Any chance of them getting back together?"

Sherry shrugged but she wasn't about to let Arlo change the topic of conversation. "So what's your plan? Arrest Bob Hoffman?"

"No, I can't do that without any evidence. And though he has a motive, I haven't found a shred of evidence tying him to the crime scene." Well thanks for the ride Arlo

She expected Arlo to pull back out of the driveway but instead he turned the squad car off and got out. She hoped he didn't expect her to entertain him now, fix him a lunch of something like one of his little girlfriends. She might not have been hurt in the accident, but all the excitement had made her quite tired.

I wanted to check in on Rory, and see how she's making out with the horses, Arlo said.

Okay, I'm going to go call the rental car company, let them know what happened, and if I need to bring the car back and get a different car or just keep driving it as is," Sherry said.

Arlo looked surprised. "Oh so you're sticking around then, Arlo said.

Well I have to now, with Cooper in the hospital and all, Sherry replied. But once he's better.

You're out of here? Arlo finished her sentence. It's the longest you've been here so I guess we should appreciate it huh?

Rory came walking by pulling the leads of 2 of the horses behind her. One of them Sherry recognized as the horse that had been sick before. "He looks all better," Sherry said.

"Yeah, he's been fine ever since Thursday, the fluids Eric gave him seemed to do the trick," Rory said. Hey boy, Arlo said, patting Whisper on the trunk. Rory have you seen Justin around?

Not much, and truthfully I'm glad. Ever since what happened with Whisper he seems so angry. He just comes by and goes into the office, checks on the horses really quick, sometimes grabs some hay, and then leaves."

"Well that's strange, Sherry said, you'd think if your horse was sick you'd come around more, not less. "Yeah, you'd think," Arlo said and Sherry felt like he was trying to say something about her.

I'm starting to think there's something a bit fishy about our neighborhood friendly veteran here. "Like what?" Sherry said.

"He has priors," Arlo replied. "For what?" Sherry asked.

But Arlo didn't reply. Instead he was looking at Tom as he walked over to them, with Gruff trailing behind him. "Where are you off to Tom?" he asked. I'm off to get the sheep from the backfield Tom said, pulling on yellow work gloves.

Look at you Sherry said, it's like you've always lived on a farm, you have time for all these chores with your school work? Yeah, school in Hope Valley is super easy.

Well that's not a good thing Tom, thats not preparing you for the Ivy leagues. Ivy leagues huh? Arlo asked. You looking to follow in your mom's footsteps?

Actually I've been thinking about criminal justice

"What? You mean become a cop?" Arlo said, "that would be great." "I don't think so," Sherry snorted.

"What were you saying about Justin? I heard you tell my mom he has a criminal record?" "Back child support," Arlo said.

"That doesn't prove anything," Sherry replied.

"It proves he's not as squeaky clean as he pretends to be," Arlo said.

Just then there was a shriek from the chicken coop, and before any of them could even react Trinity came barreling out of the chicken coop, arms flailing, scaring all the chickens in the run, making them squawk and run in every direction.

Arlo, Sherry and Tom ran over to investigate.

"What is it? Is there a fox in there or something?" Sherry cried.

"There's something in there, something really big!" Trinity shrieked. Arlo and Sherry looked at each other. Could there be a coyote or a fox in there? Once when Sherry was young she remembered a raccoon had gotten into the coop and made a huge mess, besides the fact that Sherry had been the one who had happened upon the ringed-tail raccoon having its egg dinner and it had scared her half to death so she knew how Trinity felt.

"I'll check," Arlo said, putting his hand on the holster of his police revolved as he walked over and peeked inside the coop. Sherry put her hand on the quivering trinity's shoulder and held her breath while Arlo was inside half expecting to hear a gunshot or something scary come running out of the coop. But there wasn't a sound and after a minute Arlo emerged looking like he was hiding a smile.

"Well, no fox or snake, but something a lot more scary..he stepped back and Jerry emerged from the coop with a cracked egg dripping from his head. "What the heck?" Trinity cried, suddenly going from sounding frightened out of her wits to indignant, "what were you doing in there?"

"Sleeping," Jerry replied as he picked pieces of eggshell out of his hair.

"Why were you sleeping in the chicken coop? Shouldn't you be at school? Trinity continued. "No," Jerry replied.

"Why not?"

"Because it's Saturday," he said matter of factly.

"Ugh! Trinity said, "and look what you did, egg doesn't come out of suede you know!" She pointed at her boots. "Ready to go back to Boston?" Arlo asked Trinity in a wry tone.

Tom and Arlo laughed. Trinity gave them both a withering look and said to Tom, "we need to talk," before storming off towards the guesthouse. "What did I do?" Tom called after his retreating girlfriend, but Trinity just kept walking.

"You're in trouble, boy," Arlo said but Tom shrugged and said, she'll be fine. Hey, I've been meaning to mention to you about something weird that happened last Friday night."

"What's that?" Sherry said, "what happened?" "It's about Justin."

"What about him?" Arlo asked. "I was saying bye to Edith-"

Wait, Edith was here?" Arlo asked.

Yeah, she came to bring over a uh, pie for us, and stayed for dinner. Tom said. And we noticed a car parked down there, he pointed towards the bottom of the hill "Who was it?"

"That's just it, I don't know."

Arlo nodded, "Seems suspicious!! What business would anybody have to be parked down in the front field at night?" "That's what Edith and I thought too, so we drove down to investigate-", Tom said.

"What?" Sherry interrupted. "Why would you do that Tom? Investigate? That's dangerous. And despite what ridiculous ideas Arlo here has put into your head, you should not be galavanting around like that!" What was going on with Tom anyways? Not only was he talking about not going to college now he was putting himself in precarious situations. She had taken him out of Boston to get him away from these types of situations. But all coming to Hope Valley had done was make everything worse.

"Wait a minute, I never told him to do anything of the sort-" Arlo began. "Well, he must have got that idea from somewhere!" Sherry snapped.

Arlo put his hands up in frustration. "Okay, if I say guilty as charged can we just let poor Tom here finish his story?" Sherry nodded.

"There were two people in the car dressed in black sitting in the car and they had computers on their laps. They showed Edith and I a picture of Justin and asked us if we'd seen him before. After I said yeah that's Justin they said to each other that's him and just drove off."

"That's him?" Sherry echoed. Tom nodded.

"I knew it, Arlo said I just knew it! "Knew what?" Sherry asked.

"They sound like feds, that's what. But what I want to know is what has that guy been up to have feds tracking him?"

"Maybe it's just the child support thing, his ex is trying to track him down," Sherry said. "Nothing earth-shattering. But you," she turned to Tom, "you shouldn't be getting involved in this type of thing. Regardless of who they were, what were you thinking Tom? Your job is to concentrate on school, not getting involved in all this garbage. I'm starting to think this was all a mistake. Maybe we should just pack up and head back to New York."

"Yeah because New York is way safer than it is here in Hope Valley," Arlo retorted chuckling. His walkie went off crackling. "Excuse me," he said walking off from them with the walkie in his hand.

"You know what Mom, I used to think you were this big attorney, this bigger-than-life figure that knew more than everyone, but now, I'm not sure if you know anything. You certainly don't seem to know me, like at all," he said, his dark eyes flashing.

Sherry was taken aback by Tom's words. "What is that supposed to mean?"

"It means exactly what I said. If you'd been paying any attention to what's going on here you would realize I don't want to go back to New York," Tom said, "that I actually like it here. That this is Hank's home, and that trying to make him get rid of his animals, get rid of this farm to suit you and your ideas of what people should do and shouldn't do is just wrong. So why don't you just go back if you want…I mean I'm sure that's why you had Cooper out here right? So you had an excuse to go back?

Sherry replied, "No, I didn't even ask him to come. But yeah of course I'm thinking of going back. I'm up for partner Tom, what do you think is going to happen if I don't go back? That's always been my dream, being a partner at the firm, it's what people work so hard for."

You don't think I already know that, Mom??

Well I wouldn't want to stop you from pursuing your dream. Not like you would ever let anything stand in your way. You know what Mom, just go," Tom turned and started walking back to the house.

Sherry stood in stunned silence watching Tom's retreating back walk up to the house. What had that been all about? She had always thought she and Tom had such a great relationship, that he enjoyed his independence and freedom. And it was like he wasn't grateful at all. The time she had spent working, the money she had spent on him. If she could just make him understand, "Tom wait!" she called after him but Tom just kept walking and walked into the house slamming the door behind him. Sherry started walking up to the house too.

As she climbed the steps up the house she noticed Hank was sitting in his rocking chair on the front porch hidden by the evening shadows. "I guess you heard all that?" Sherry asked him.

"Hard not to," he replied, rocking a bit.

"Well can you believe that? Tom about being an ungrateful spoiled teenager. After all I've ever done for him? I'm the one who should be mad. "Can't say I'm surprised," Hank replied.

"Yeah exactly, I mean I can't believe he's acting like this!"

Hank shook his head, "No, I mean I'm surprised you even stayed a few days. I mean the last time you came home was over five years ago Sherry and you stayed for a total of one and a half days."

"I had to work, Dad. I can't believe you are trying to make me feel guilty. Besides that has nothing to do with the way Tom is acting."

"It has everything to do with it, Sherry," Hank retorted. "Sherry, did you even want a kid or did you think it was like having a cool decoration." "What is that supposed to mean?" Sherry demanded to know.

Sherry was getting really angry. Did her father have any idea how much trouble it had been for her to adopt a baby from Korea, and the cost? How dare he ask her a question like that.

"Well you dump him at that fancy private school you were sending him to in Boston, and now you dump him here," Hank cried, "that wasn't the way you were raised, why did you think that would work for Tom? Your mom and I did everything with you, and for you. We didn't send you to some boarding school in Montana. You're our daughter we raised you up right here where we live.!"

Sherry couldn't believe that Hank was trying to guilt trip her and say he was the better parent. He had no idea what he was talking about. His world was just this small little place in Wyoming. Sherry said, "I've given Tom opportunities, opportunities he never could have gotten here in Hope Valley. And besides, you say you and Mom do so much for me, what do you call all this? All you are doing now is causing me tons of trouble," she added angrily.

Hank's face became hard. "Sherry, I've lived on this farm for 55 years. I'm not about to leave it now."

Suddenly Sherry thought of something. "What if I told you leaving the farm would be the best thing for me, and the best thing for Tom?" "How?"

With the money we get from selling the farm it would easily pay for the finest ivy league education for Tom, and I could finally buy that apartment in Manhattan I've been wanting for Cooper."

Hank looked at her for a moment without answering and then said, "So that's what this has been all about? Money?"

"No, Dad, that's not what I meant. Let's just talk about this and then you can see this is the best solution. I've thought about this a lot."

"I can see that," He got up slowly and Sherry never thought she'd ever seen her dad look so old. "I think I'm through with talking." he walked past her and into the house.

Sherry sat down heavily on the porch steps. Now not only was Tom angry at her, so was Hank. But she was glad she had said what she did. Maybe he would come to his senses and realize her plan was the best solution for all of them. She wondered how Cooper was doing. She was surprised he hadn't called her by now to pick her up from the hospital. At least Cooper wasn't mad at her. At least Cooper understood her and what her needs were, like getting back to New York and getting that high-rise apartment together. They were sort of a power couple in a way she thought to herself.

A black Lincoln town car came guzzling up the driveway and Sherry wondered who it could be. When a man wearing a dark suit jacket stepped out of the car. He looked very out of place and awkward walking up the old dirt driveway. Could he be one of the mysterious people Tom had mentioned he saw that night at the farm looking for Justin?

The man walked up to Sherry in silence. She stood up and said, "If you're looking for Justin he's not here." "I'm not looking for a Justin. I'm actually looking for Sheryl Whitmore, Sheryl Ann Whitmore."

Sherry was surprised. What could this man want with her? "I'm Sherry, um, Sheryl. What's this all about?"

The man in black handed her a yellow envelope he had been carrying under his right arm and said, "Sheryl Ann Whitmore, you've been served."

Chapter 14

DAVID AND GOLIATH

Rory finished her quiz in French class quickly. She drew a picture in an app on her phone.

Shania leaned over and stared at the drawing and whispered, "Let me guess, that's you and Tom dancing in the street in front of the Eiffel Tower, at midnight. The music is Stevie Wonder's My Cherie Amour."

Rory smiled and replied, "Wow, you're good." Then, Shania laughed and said,

"Non, je vous connais trop bien!"

***

Tom's mind flew among the clouds like an angry RAF Spitfire. He didn't like being grumpy, it went against his happy-go-lucky personality.

And usually, being angry wastes time. But his 3rd-hour teacher, Mr Johnson was 23 minutes into a god-awful boring dissertation on economics. Tom's mind had lifted off the runway 19 minutes ago. He sat by the windows, in classroom 214, his hands on the throttle of a massive 12-cylinder Rolls Royce engine, in a famed WW2 fighter plane.

He flew the warbird among the lazy clouds floating high above Hope Valley. The British-made Spitfire handled like a dream, sleek and powerful! As the Spitfire roared, Tom wondered how real moms operate, you know, moms who are home when their children walk in the door from school. Or the moms who text their kids from work.

Moms who ask how your day was, offer real solutions to tummy aches or give answers to children not understanding what caused the 1929 Great Depression. Even moms who travel for work, have viable and loving solutions for a kid feeling sick at school.

But Tom realized he would never know, the loving touch of a real mom. His mother delegated everything. Like sending her kid off to boarding school. Where a school resource person would hand him a business card of a tutor, who specialized in economics.

The school nurse passed out gallons of

Pepto Bismal for tummy aches and had no real concern that Tom's indigestion was caused by a pretty girl.

But if a guy lacked the self-confidence to ask a beautiful young girl to the school dance. What school nurse had a pill for that?

Tom thought about Trinity and her ever-increasing bossiness. Until a month ago she'd never actually seen a real sheep, but now she was a sheep expert and had a list of barn chores to pass out daily to Rory.

Tom wondered if he really loved Trinity, or was he simply hypnotized by her stunning beauty.

In all reality, the little neighbor girl Rory had bloomed into a woman overnight and seemed more interested in Tom's opinion than Trinity ever would be.

But not soon enough the bell rang and everyone stood and filed out the door. Economics class was over, and even though no clouds had been injured in the making of Tom's daydream.

He still felt sick to his stomach from Trinity refusing to kiss him good night, 14 hours ago. Tom was just beginning to learn about the power, a woman held over a man's heart.

"Hi Tom!" A beautiful young girl softly said as he passed her in the hall. Her smile stopped his heart, as his eyes stared at her young figure. It was not the first time, Allison Haggar dive-bombed his heart.

Tom turned the corner for a quick locker stop and saw a huge derogatory 4 letter word written in pink lipstick, on his locker door. Brady and his minions stood next to Tom's locker and sneered at him like a heckling herd of hyenas.

They blocked Tom's way.

"Get out of my face", Tom scowled with agitation in his voice. Brady laughed and snatched Tom's pen from his shirt pocket.

"You think you're pretty tough, don't you Whitmore! But your little girlfriend is not here to protect you! So what are you going to do, huh? Fight us all? Call 9-11 and have the police come save you!

'Save me, Save me, oh Mr. Policeman sir'." Brady mocked in the pitch of a female voice.

"You're such a freak Whitmore! We don't like your kind here. So pack your crap and move back to SissyLand!" Tom glanced behind him and saw about a dozen students gathering. They smelled a fight brewing.

"Brady, I'm going to count to 3. If you and your girlfriends, don't move out of my way. I'm going to break your left leg, right under your knee, and then smash your face in." Tom said as he stood tall and stared up at the linebacker-sized Brady.

Brady's demeanor shifted immediately as he knew Tom was the Wrestling Teams captain, and unbeaten boxer. Brady remembered the rumor about Tom breaking a 2x4 in half in the men's locker room last week, with his teeth. "You remember what I said Punk!

And don't show up at the Harvest Festival Dance! We don't let your kind date our women!" Brady snarled as he dropped Tom's pen on the floor. The bully stomped on it and ink bled out onto the floor tile.

"You better clean that up, son!" Brady sneered.

In a second he and his minions were gone, laughing like a horde of hormonal crows.

David and Goliath

Tom opened his locker and stared at a selfie photo of him and Trinity on their first date. He hated having Trinity mad at him. And her accusations of Tom liking Rory were ridiculous. He thought again of Trinity refusing to kiss him good night, at the guest house door. And his mom was all upset about Tom's plans for his future. Tom turned and walked fast for the west exit, and headed to Edith's diner. Milkshakes always calmed his nerves and Edith's shakes were out of this world! It was almost lunchtime and Tom was hungry.

He hoped Rory was there, she was a good listener. Cute too, for a 15-year-old.

It seemed like yesterday she was only 12, and a fullblown Tom Boy. Climbing trees and building go-carts with her friends. She excelled at softball and being a brat. But now, Rory was 15, beautiful, and a young woman.

Her emotions were that of a typical teenage girl. But Tom saw a softness in her pretty eyes.

She'd ask pertinent questions and never interrupt. Somehow Tom saw a gentle sophistication in Rory. Yes, she was funny and giggled a bit much sometimes. But Rory seemed to understand Tom's almost 18-year-old male emotions. He was excited, hoping he and Rory could now become good friends.

If he was a year younger, he'd ask her out and infuriate Brady!

Tom could smell the diner's burgers and onion rings cooking. He walked faster and in 5 minutes stepped into the diner and spotted Rory. She smiled at him. She was so pretty.

***

3 hours earlier....

Trinity carried a raspberry popsicle as she walked slowly through a sea of sheep.

Every few seconds she carefully plunged her left hand deep into white wool. So deep her hand disappeared. The sheep didn't seem to care. Trinity heard 3 sounds, the wind as it danced across the meadow, an occasional 'baaaah', and Jerry's sing-songy boyish voice reading his sheep friends yet another story. Jerry loved reading stories of sailboats, pirates, and warships, to the sheep.

The sheep listened intently, mesmerized as Redbeard the pirate evaded the American warship: USS United States in 1799.

The 'United States' massive guns could easily blow holes in the pirate ship's hull.

After sinking his ship, survivors would be hauled aboard and tried in an American court of law. Redbeard had no intention of rotting in some damp New York prison.

"Raise the Jib and flying jib! We need more speed!" Redbeard ordered in a rattled voice. "Jerry!" Trinity called out from 20 feet away.

"I'm sorry to disturb story hour, but I have a favor to ask of Captain Redbeard, and I brought him a raspberry

Popsicle. She slid off the wrapper and held out the ice cold treat.

"Captain Redbeard loves popsicles!" Jerry exclaimed with a grin as he reached out for the wooden stick and immediately bit off a chunk. "What's your favor," Jerry asked as raspberry juice dripped down his chin.

Trinity sighed and explained;

"Well, I assume you know I'm in the flower business, and this town is far from sophisticated. Farmers, ranchers, and hicks, evidently have no use for flowers. So I'd like to pull out the remaining good flowers and you and I go downtown in an hour and try to sell them. My plan requires you to wear a disguise.

I'll pay you $10.00 and buy you lunch at the diner when we're done." Jerry closed his book and asked:

"A disguise you say, can I dress up as a pirate?" Trinity gently replied "No."

"Will Tom be having lunch with us?" Jerry asked hopefully.

"No, he will not be joining us, we had a fight last night and he's busy with school and the farm. Are you ready to go? Do you need to use the bathroom before we drive downtown?"

"I'm 10! You don't ask a 10-year-old guy about using the bathroom! Duh! I'm not a little kid you know." Jerry replied with a roll of his eyes.

Snowball stuck his head out of Jerry's pocket and glared at Trinity. Anyone who upset Jerry automatically upset Snowball. They were best friends. Hope came bounding across the field and circled Trinity and Jerry. She loved them both.

"Hope sit!" Trinity ordered with a closed-fisted hand signal. Hope obediently sat and looked up at Trinity. "Good girl!" Trinity praised the dog and fed her a treat.

"Does she know any new tricks?" Jerry asked as he gulped down the last bite of popsicle. "Tom taught her to roll over, but he uses a special hand signal. Maybe he'll show us later." "Why are you and Tom fighting?" Jerry asked with a dismal sadness in his voice.

"I don't know, we'll figure it out." Trinity replied softly, as the image of Rory standing atop a ladder in the barn, filled her memory.

Rory wore shorts designed to light a man's desire. And her top was tight enough to throw fire on a man's imagination. Trinity's memory played on. She had seen everything, it all happened so fast.......

She stood watching as Rory felt unsteady on the stepladder. She reached way high to change a light bulb and screamed, as she fell off the ladder and into Tom's waiting arms. He was just feet away, and heard her scream and ran like a cheetah to save her.

She lay safe in Tom's strong arms. Their lips were just an inch apart. They stared into each other eyes. It was like a scene in a romantic movie.

Rory smiled at Tom, he was hallucinated with her beauty, the softness of her body, and the loveliness of her voice. He didn't set her down, or ask if she was ok. Tom just stood there in a trance, holding Rory in his arms, and staring into her eyes. Trinity remembered running to her guest house and sobbing into her pillow. Oh of course Tom said all the right things and desperately tried to console the broken-hearted Trinity. She knew it was just a moment of weakness in a man's armor.

He said the whole thing scared him. Rory fell off the very top step of a 12-foot ladder and Tom was stunned he actually caught her. And Trinity's memory played on……

Rory was just a little thing, all petite and beautiful. But it was the way she and Tom looked into each other's eyes that shocked Trinity. They had a chemistry she had never seen before.

"My mom and stepdad used to fight and my stepdad up and left one day and like never came back." Jerry said sadly. "I'm sorry!" Trinity said as she held Jerry's hand.

"When did he leave?" She asked.

"Like 7 years ago, I was 3 and don't remember him. Rory does and says he used to play with us a lot. He was nice." Jerry replied.

They walked out of the field, Hope ran on ahead, chasing anything that moved. Jerry talked about pirates, Snowball fell asleep, and Trinity wondered if Officer Bruce was a good lover.

That thought was the crux of Trinity's conundrum, and she knew it. She was attracted to Bruce like a moth to a flame. Their practice sessions alone in the martial arts studio were way more than the young Trinity could resist.

Bruce was gorgeous and handsome rolled into one. He picked Trinity up, like she was stardust. His eyes saw clear into Trinity's heart, melting all resistance she had. She tasted his lips, just as Bruce's radio crackled with an emergency out on the State Hwy. He was off duty but needed to direct traffic around a horrific semi- truck and school bus crash. He set Trinity down, grabbed his revolver, holster, and jacket with his silver star of a Wyoming police officer, and ran out the back door. Trinity stood and watched as hidden police flashers on his SUV lit up the entire street. Traffic stopped and yielded to his authority. He roared off to save the world. Trinity was burning with desire for this powerful superhero of a man.

She helped Jerry into her BMW and knew her love for Tom was eternal. But the memory of being in Bruce's arms, and kissing him, refused to leave her heart.

***

Tom crossed Main Street and could see the diner. With all the road noise he didn't hear a text from Trinity come in……. "Hey, I'm hungry and it's after 11:00. Can you meet me at Edith's Diner in a few minutes for lunch?" Jerry is with me. But, we to need to talk Tom…… about us.

I love you!"

***

Rory and Shania were deciding what to order for lunch when Rory looked at the front door of the diner. "Do I look pretty? Is my hair a mess? Can I borrow your lipstick?" Rory asked as she quickly adjusted her bra, for a man's eyes.

"He's headed right towards us Rory, you have no time for lipstick, and your heart is racing. Rory O'Connor, can you explain why your heart is racing?" Shania asked with a giggle.

"Shut up!" Rory commanded, with a grin.

Her pretty blue eyes were glued onto Tom and his lean muscular body. "God! He's an Adonis!" Rory whispered to herself.

"Hey, Tom come sit with us, are you hungry?" Rory asked in a pretty and feminine voice. I'm starving!" Tom complained as he slid into the booth, and sat next to Rory.

"Hey!" He said to her with a grin.

Rory punched him in the arm and replied,

"Hey to you too!" Tom instantly relaxed. Sitting next to Rory calmed him.

Rory passed Tom her menu and his fingers briefly touched hers. She wanted to kiss him, but had no idea how a girl kissed a guy. Instead, Rory asked Tom….

"So are you going to college?"

"Yeah, but I'm not sure for what though.

My mom wants me to be a doctor or attorney.

I really like farming though, it's a blend of science and art. Don't you think it's amazing how a farmer helps feed the world?

I mean he inherits some land, marries his girl, they have babies, and he buys a John Deere! Then they grow enough crops to fill 12 grocery stores." Tom said as he looked at the menu.

Shania kicked Rory under the table. Seconds later, Rory said: "You know, Trinity is a real peach of a girl, but I just can't see her wanting babies. I can't imagine Trinity being a mom, can you Tom?"

"What?" Tom replied as he looked into Rory's eyes. "Trinity? I guess I've never imagined Trinity being a mom. But, someday I want a family, maybe 4 kids, a dog, and two cats. And I'll kiss my girl 24x7!

A summer vacation every year, and I'd be a hands-on dad. I believe in a man and a woman being partners in everything. I'd be changing just as many diapers as she does. You know, helping with homework and teaching them to drive. There'd be no boarding schools. But you're right Rory, finding the right girl to share a dream with is critical. Finding the right girl is key to any man's equation."

"Well, I wouldn't sweat it Tom, there are lots of girls right here in Hope Valley who'd want to share your dream of being a farmer. It would be a lot of work, but very rewarding." Rory softly said.

"You really think so?" Tom asked.

"Yeah, I do. But you need a girl who adores you!" Rory said with a big smile. "Did you know almost half of American farmers have college degrees?

They have degrees in agriculture, animal, and soil sciences, just to name a few." "Really!!" Tom replied.

"Yeah and Colorado State University is the highest-rated agricultural school in North America, and it's in Fort Collins, that's like 3 hours from here!" Rory explained. "Really!" Tom replied with a grin.

"Yeah, you should go there and get a degree. If you decide to drive down to Ft Collins and check out CSU, I'd go with you." Rory offered.

"Really!" Tom replied, now trying not to laugh. Rory smacked him over the head with her menu.

"Is that all you can say is 'really? You're such a boy!" Rory gave Tom a shove, and was in heaven, sitting next to him.

Tom tickled her ribs and Rory screamed and jumped up and tickled him back. She crawled into his lap, and he grabbed her hands and they wrestled in the booth for a few moments.

Tom could easily overpower Rory, but he didn't. They were both laughing and becoming real friends.

Rory laid her head on Tom's shoulder, still laughing, and wishing this moment would never end. Whatever love looked like for a girl almost 16 years old, Rory wanted so badly to experience it with Tom.

"You're a trouble maker Tom Whitmore!"

Rory giggled. She leaned close and looked at Tom's menu, their faces almost touching, and asked, "What looks good?"

Tom sighed and felt the stress flow out of his mind. He looked at Rory, she was gorgeous with long red hair hanging over her shoulders, and pretty blue eyes. He could see the curves of her young female softness protruding from her sweater. But most of all Tom loved how fun it was to be with Rory. She was a beautiful girl in every way, funny, intelligent, kind, and thoughtful.

Tom wondered what it would be like to hold Rory and kiss her. He let his face wander closer, and their cheeks touched. Rory felt his sand papery facial skin, on her soft cheeks and purred. She slid her hand under his, and Tom closed his fingers around hers. For 10 minutes, love awoke and their heats danced together in Paris, under the Arc de Triomphe. An attraction exploded between them. They both felt it and knew it was real.

But Tom took a deep breath and moved a few inches away from Rory. He knew Rory was attracted to him. And for the first time, Tom realized he had feelings for her too.

Real feelings, not just the ones guys get around pretty girls. But Tom had a girlfriend, and he would never cheat on Trinity. They were a couple, and in love. Tom's mind wandered, he thought of the intense attraction he and Claire shared back in Boston. And now, his urge to kiss Rory. He had no idea what his heart was telling him. But he fought his feelings for Rory, and let go of her hand. She looked up at him, not understanding the cues he was giving her.

Rory fought back tears. She had wanted this so badly, and she was careful not to flirt with Tom or manipulate his emotions. Rory was being herself and had shared a real moment with Tom.

An honest moment. But now it vanished, like the dew at sunrise. Shania looked at Rory and saw invisible tears forming in her best friend's eyes. She reached across the table and took Rory's hand just for a moment. Their eyes met and Rory knew Shania was telling her to be patient.

The best things in life, are often the most elusive, and require the most patience.

Rory composed herself and looked at Tom and said…
.."thank you for catching me when I fell off the ladder."
"It was nothing, and you're welcome."

Their eyes lingered together for more than several seconds then returned to the menu. Tom had also seen the hidden tears in Rory's eyes and wanted to kiss her, and take away any pain in her heart.

***

I think I'll get a burger, fries and a soda.

Tom announced. But suddenly he watched Rory's demeanor change from relaxed to tense. She grabbed Tom's muscular bicep and clung to him. Her gaze was focused on the front door. Tom looked up and saw Brady walking in with 2 of his minions.

"Maybe we should go!" Rory said with alarm in her voice. "He's always hitting on me, he's a creep!" She gathered her cell phone, and wallet to leave. "Has he ever hurt you?" Tom asked quietly.

"He's tried to kiss me too many times, but I've always gotten away." Rory answered, then added, "I want to leave. Shania let's go out the back door."

Rory was scared, and gave Tom an angry shove to let her out of the booth. "Would you move!" She barked at him. Tom saw the same fear in Rory's eyes he had seen in Claire's.

Rory stepped into the aisle and made eye contact with Brady.

The two girls stood and Tom grabbed Rory's hand and said, "No one's going anywhere, Shania sit down please." Tom ordered.

Rory was scared and Tom slipped his arm around her. He pulled her close and felt her trembling. He gently guided her back to her seat. Tom saw tears in Rory's eyes. She wasn't cold, yet Tom set his light jacket over her shoulders. She clung to it with all her might.

Their few fleeting romantic moments had slipped away. But Rory could feel Tom protecting her. No man had ever protected her before. Her young emotions were now a wreck, and tears ran down her cheeks.

Rory knew Trinity was in Tom's heart, that's why he pulled away. But right now, she cherished Tom's overwhelming need to keep her safe. Rory told herself love had taken root in both their hearts, she calmed her emotions and focused on being a warrior. Rory knew how to fight and stick up for herself and Jerry.

Brady was headed right towards them. "He's such a creep." Shania murmured.

Brady walked up to their booth like an angry dinosaur and grabbed Tom's menu and began reading, then said, "OMG, look at this! Right here on the menu. No Asian boys allowed!

And Gee Whitmore!! You're an Asian boy!"

He stared at Tom and saw his arm around Rory.

"Go bug someone else, Brady, you're as obnoxious as a horse fly!" Tom said.

"You better clear out right now Whitmore, and what did I tell you about dating our women?" I'm dating Rory....get your hands off her Tom!" Brady said in a booming and angry voice. "I'm not dating you! You creep!"

Rory shouted back as she clung tightly to Tom's arm, and Shania crawled under the table and sat on the other side of Rory. Tom was in the aisle seat. Shania looked up at Brady and calmly said,

"I'm calling the Sheriff's office!"

Brady became more agitated at that remark and replied, "You call the Sheriff and I'll be sure your mom's tires are all flat in the morning! You stupid chic! You're as dumb as a rock Shania!"

"Get out Brady!!" Rory ordered, and pointed her finger towards the door.

"You going to make me leave Rory? Or maybe Tom the sissy wants to try?" Brady sneered and smacked Tom in the face with the menu. Rory unknowingly pulled herself closer to Tom and in a quiet voice whispered to him,

"I'm scared Tom!"

Brady grabbed a glass of water and tried to throw it in Tom's face. But Tom stood, and twisted Brady's wrist and the water glass fell to the floor and shattered. Brady grabbed Tom by the shirt, but Tom shoved the bully hard, and said,

"I've had all I'm going to take from you Brady! You and your pals clear out of here!" "No! You clear out Whitmore!" Brady shouted in reply.

Edith saw the commotion and called Arlo's cell.

Arlo answered and said he had just arrived at the diner for lunch. He'd be right in. Tom stood close to the tall and chunky Brady.

But Brady reached for Rory's hand, Tom threw a punch at Brady's face and knocked him onto the next table. One of Brady's friends swung at Tom. But Tom ducked and came up with an undercut punch to the kid's chin and decked him so hard, he crashed to the floor, unconscious.

Brady stood and reached for Tom, but Tom jumped out of the way, then flipped Brady onto the floor and twisted his arm behind his back so hard, tears came. Tom knelt on Brady's back and kept him immobilized.

Tom motioned for the 2nd kid to come closer, but the now terrified teen helped his friend up and they dashed out the door and right into Sheriff Arlo. Tom was calmly furious and said to Brady,

"I'm going to let you up punk, and you will walk out the front door. If you don't, I'm going to mess you up so bad, they'll need to call an ambulance! You ever upset Rory again, and I'll ruin your life!"

Brady gathered his strength and tried to force Tom off of him. But Tom put all his weight on Brady's back and twisted his arm more. "What's it going to be Brady? You want to fight me, let's go. Right now, out back in the alley. Just you and me!"

"What's going on here!" Arlo barked in a commanding tone and set his hand on his police revolver for extra drama. Arlo was a big and powerful man, and many fools had made the mistake of making him mad.

Rory knelt and wrapped her arms around Tom's chest and pulled him off of Brady. "Tom! The Sheriff's here!" She whispered in his ear.

In seconds Arlo walked up and helped Brady up from the floor. Then asked in a loud voice, "Who started this?" Brady groaned in pain and pointed to Tom.

"He started it and I think he broke my ribs"

Rory pushed Tom down into his seat and whispered to him in a frantic voice, "You need to calm down, your face is beet red!"

She held Tom's hand as more tears filled her eyes.

Rory didn't like fights and her entire body trembled in fear. Tom stood and told Rory and Shania to stand behind him, in the aisle. Rory held Tom's hand tightly and wrapped her other arm around his waist. She hid behind him, hoping Brady would go away.

Just then Tom looked at the front door and stared into Trinity's glaring eyes. Jerry stood next to her, still dressed up as a blind homeless kid trying to sell flowers on street corners. They stepped into the diner slowly and walked closer, as Trinity saw Rory holding Tom's hand and clinging to him.

Trinity shook her head in disbelief. "Get your paws off my boyfriend, you little wretch!" Trinity shouted out in an angry Boston accent.

"I'm going to break your face Rory!" Trinity warned.

Arlo turned to face Trinity and Jerry, and ordered them to sit and shut up! Not a peep out of either one of them. Trinity reached for her cell and typed off an angry text to Rory, and hit send.

She sent one to Tom too, "Boys start fights, but I thought you were a man. I hope the sheriff arrests you. We're done!" Trinity hit send as her emotions wanted to explode.

Arlo was not happy his early lunch had been interrupted.

He glared at Tom, "Is Brady right Tom, did you start this fight?" "Yes, sir, I did!" Tom replied.

"Oh God!" Rory moaned and whispered to Tom, "I love you." But he didn't hear her. Arlo turned to Brady and said, "Did you say something to Tom that pushed his buttons? Did you initiate any harassment or bullying?"

"No sir!" Brady replied. Rory peeked out from behind Tom and shot lightning bolts at Brady. He squirmed as Rory's angry demeanor scared him.

Finally, Rory calmly said, "Brady, if you don't tell the Sheriff what you said to Tom, I will. And I will quote you! And don't forget how you tried to throw ice water in our faces. You're a coward and a bully!"

Arlo stepped forward and saw the water, and shattered glass on the floor.

Brady suddenly looked sick, like he was about to vomit. He was secretly in love with Rory and was devastated by her hostility towards him.

He had dreamed all year of asking Rory out on a date. Maybe a movie and ice cream. He knew her favorite was Chocolate Rocky Road in a cone. And she adored cotton candy.

Brady was smitten with Rory, but now he was certain this idiot Tom was ruining everything. Arlo interrupted his thoughts, "Brady, who is going to tell me what you said to Tom?

You or Rory, and you're interrupting my lunch so hurry it up."

Brady looked at the floor, as he said, "I think I did make a negative comment about Tom being Asian and other stuff. But I didn't think he'd take it so personally, I was just joking around. Tom and I are friends, we tease each other."

Arlo turned to Tom and asked, "Are you friends with Brady?"

"Yes, sir, I am. We hang out at school too. We were just having fun and things got out of hand. The broken glass was an accident. I'm sorry, I'll pay Edith for the glass, sir."

Tom held his hand out and Brady shook it. Their eyes met and negotiated a truce.

Arlo had the stamina of a buffalo, and stood tall like a Texas Ranger and softly said, "This friend's stuff is the biggest crock of BS I've heard in months, and I'm not buying it.

But gentlemen, you two had better think hard and fast about becoming real friends. If I ever catch the two of you fighting again in my town, I'll toss you both out of WyomingDo not test my resolve gentlemen.

"Yes sir!" Brady replied. "Yes Sheriff." Tom echoed.

David and Goliath

10 minutes later, Tom and Brady sat in Arlo's patrol car, in handcuffs.

***

Trinity took Jerry across the street to the pizza joint and Shania tried to help Rory stop her tears. She admitted to being in love with Tom, and wanted to kiss him so badly, it hurt.

"Honey, from what I've seen, loving a man is full of emotions. But if you find a good man, every tear is a drop of gold. My Grandma told me that last year." Shania said.

Rory had a toughness in her, and she pulled herself up out of her tears, and said,

"I watched Brady try and throw a glass of ice water at us and Tom rose up and stopped him. Brady is huge, and Tom is small.

Yet, David had Goliath pinned to the floor in under a second. For years, my mom has spent most of her life in Casper. I've been the mother and father at our house. I protect Jerry, I pay the bills, get groceries, cook, and clean. I mow the grass and watch YouTube videos on how to replace a garbage disposal. Shania, taking care of Jerry is a full-time job. Jerry tells people he's 10 when he's only 9. And he acts like he's 5. He's a boy, and boys have the focusing ability of a lizard. When Jerry gets in trouble at school, they call me to come get him. Not my mom…..me!

I'm just a girl Shania! And for the very first time, a man named Tom Whitmore told me to sit down and relax. He stood and protected me Shania. No one has ever protected me before.

I love him Shania and I can't live without him. And did you hear what I told him?" Rory asked. "No," Shania softly replied.

Now Tom thinks I'm a stalker. What am I going to do Shania?" "I told Tom I loved him! I'm such an idiot!

"Rory…..Tom has feelings for you. He likes you a lot. I think he even loves you Rory. Just bide your time, and when his

Boston-bitch-girlfriend dumps him, you pick up the pieces of his heart, and you be his girl. I'm shy and I don't say much, Rory. But I watch and listen and Tom Whitmore is dying to kiss you!"

'Shut up!" Rory replied with a grin. She stared out the front window and had no idea what she would say to Tom, the next time they met. "Tom has no idea how I feel about him, I'm just the stupid little neighbor girl who used to climb trees and sold Kool-Aide up at the corner.

I'm wearing a bigger bra now, but he can't see that I've become a woman."

"Rory, this is just my opinion, but I think you're wrong. 1 second after you told Tom you were scared, he stood up and confronted Brady. To me, that seems like a man protecting his woman. And I've seen Tom looking at you, you know how guys look at a girl they want.

He's a man, and I'd bet 50 dollars he's noticed you're wearing a bigger bra now. Guys notice those things." Rory smiled and blushed,

She hugged Shania and said,

"Let's get out of here, I don't feel like a burger anymore! And what was Trinity doing with Jerry? I want her to stay away from my little brother. Do you feel like pizza?" Shania shook her head yes.

"I love you, Shania! You're my very best friend, and you look extra pretty today!" Shania grinned and followed Rory down the Diner's main aisle.

They headed across Main St. to the pizza shop, where a new storm awaited them inside.

Chapter 15

SHERIFF ARLO WOLFF

Rory and Shania walked across the street to the Pizza Shop as Rory read aloud her text from Trinity.

"Rory, it's been brought to my attention that you have been remiss in keeping your end of the 'Windy Hill Horse boarding/leasing Contract' you signed a year ago. As partial compensation for boarding/leasing fees, you agreed to sweep the main barn aisleway and empty the trash daily.

Plus clean the bathroom twice a week, and dust and vacuum the office. Obviously, you have no idea how to use a broom, toilet bowl brush, or vacuum. Effective immediately, you're fired.

And you had better keep your paws off my boyfriend! If you want a man, find your own." Sincerely,

Trinity P Smithe. Manager."

Rory went off on a fulminate.

"Trinity thinks she's the mayor of Hope Valley, and God rolled into one! And who died and made her barn manager? She's afraid of horses!

It makes me sick thinking about Tom kissing her! That chic is such a witch; she can't fire me, I work for Hank! You think Tom is ok?" Rory asked Shania. "I'd wait an hour and call him." Shania replied.

"Call him! No one calls anyone, why can't I text him?" Rory asked, still agitated from Trinity's note.

"Tom kept you safe, and then he got arrested. He's probably shaken up and nervous, and maybe scared if he's in jail. Hearing your voice would probably help his emotions, and show you care about him." Shania replied.

"How'd you get so smart about relationship?" Rory asked.

Shania grinned and replied, "I've seen Amy and Ty make lots of mistakes with their relationship on Heartland. But it's the little things that make love strong."

***

Arlo walked past a decrepit old mailbox on a leaning post, the name said, Primo. He stepped up onto the rotting front porch and gingerly approached the front door.

19 large and disorderly spider webs loomed over his head. 11 Wolf spiders stared at Arlo and creeped him out. One growled and another was chomping on a pretty monarch butterfly. Arlo had shot a few spiders since becoming a lawman. He saw the broken front window with glass shards by his boots.

Frosty the Snowman stood half dead in the corner, a glass shard shoved into his right eye. A foul smell crept from the house. Arlo felt nauseous and thought about leaving.

He looked behind and saw Tom and Brady talking in the back seat of his patrol car. Brady never carried a conversation with anyone. He took after his mother Delores, constantly spewing insults.

Delores Primo, coincidently, was a classmate of Arlo's from 1st grade to 12th. She married Nathaniel Primo, the class troublemaker right out of high school, who has been in a Wyoming State Prison, for the last 9 years for murder. Arlo would rather be stuck in an elevator with Nathanial, than Delores.

City gossip claimed Delores drove Nathaniel to drink, anger, and murder.

But the real interesting twist here is Arlo and Delores dated in high school, sophomore year. They were inseparable and planned to marry after graduation.

Arlo raised his hand and knocked on the screen door, it promptly groaned and fell off its hinges and hit Arlo in the head. He was way past hungry by now and grabbed the screen door and angrily threw it off the porch into a sea of man-eating 8-foot high thistle weeds. "Delores!!" He yelled. "It's Arlo, I need to talk to you! Now!!"

"Go away, Arlo, I don't need no promise-breaking man in my life.

The man I married knocked me up and murdered the Williwsby sisters. So get off my property, I'm not kissing you today." Arlo swore and hit talk on his radio.

2 seconds later, Casper Police Department Dispatch answered. "Good morning Sheriff," a female voice said.

"Hey Tina, I'm at 229 Plum Street and I need backup. I've got 2 juveniles in my patrol car and I need to enter a house for a safety check. Over", Arlo said. "10-4 Sheriff, car 17, Mary Turner is en route to you. She's in downtown Casper, eta 23 minutes. She's new here, 9 years with Detroit PD. Over."

"10-4 Tina. Much appreciated, how's your newborn?" Arlo asked. "She's a crier Arlo, she rules the house at night! Over."

"Try playing classical music, I've heard it puts babies right to sleep. Over." "Thanks, Arlo, please stay safe. I mean it, Arlo! No heroics today! Out." Arlo's stomach grumbled as he stepped back a few feet, and boomed out;

"Delores if you don't come down here right now and talk to me, I'm coming in!" "On whose authority are you entering my home?" Delores yelled back in anger. "On the authority of the

People of the State of Wyoming, and the badge on my chest.

You have 1 minute Delores!" Arlo boomed.

"You need a warrant Sheriff!" "Delores, you have 30 seconds! Don't trifle with me!"

Delores used to be a beautiful young woman who caught the eye of every young man in Hope Valley.

But now she was late 30's, with a body rotting like the front porch floor boards. She pickled her mind with alcohol and cigarettes. She lived on public assistance, and never cleaned house.

Her freezer was packed full of high-carb TV dinners, pizzas, and waffles.

She swore constantly and watched TV in bed 12 hours a day. She was also Brady's mother.

***

Trinity and Jerry sat at a booth in the pizza shop. Their lunch order had been taken and the waiter brought Trinity a soda, and Jerry a milkshake.

Trinity decided she was done with her flower business, but with Jerry's help this morning, she made over $200.00 selling flowers to motorists. She handed Jerry a 20-dollar bill and thanked him. She liked Jerry a lot, he was quickly becoming a little brother to her.

"Hey! You doubled my pay!" Jerry said with a big smile!

"You're a hard worker Jerry, and a great salesman! Plus your costume was very effective!" Trinity replied. Trinity heard the front door open and groaned at the sight of Rory and Shania walking in for lunch.

Rory immediately spotted them, dashed over to Trinity's table, and grabbed Jerry by the arm. She pulled her little brother out of the booth and glared at him. "Jerry, I don't want to see you with her ever again! Do you hear me! Come sit with me and Shania, I'm buying your lunch."

Rory glared at Trinity with laser eyes.

Jerry fought to get away from Rory just as Snowball jumped out of his pocket, leaped up to Rory's shoulder, and bit her right ear lobe. Trinity screamed at the sight of a rat and stood on the table.

"Get your rat out of here Rory...now!" Trinity ordered.

Rory grabbed Snowball and shoved him back into Jerry's pocket as several drops of blood dripped from her ear. She yelled at Snowball, with a slew of French swear words.

She turned and faced Trinity and went off like a canon!

"I want you to stay 10 feet away from my brother at all times. You are not to look or smile or say a word to him. Jerry is my family! You lay one paw on him and I'll dump 100 rats into your stupid guest house at 2:00 a.m.

And your rude text about my supposed lack of cleaning skills......I signed that contract with Mr. Hank! Not you! And who do you think you are Trinity!

Ever since you flew your broom into this town, you act like you own it. Take your obnoxious Boston accent and get the heck out of Wyoming! You don't know the first thing about farm life, or flowers! And you're terrified of horses! I'm warning you chic! 100 rats at 2:00 am!!

Oh, and Tom is my friend, and don't be telling me who I can hang out with! You're lucky I didn't kiss him! And maybe I will kiss him tonight!"

"Tom is almost 18 and you're a mere child!" Trinity replied with a nasty smirk.

"100 rats!" Rory said loudly, as she stomped back to her table and dragged Jerry with her.

Trinity sat back down and stared into her mind, at 100 rats running through her bedroom. Each rat wore a 5-foot-long tail. In a second, 17 rats jumped onto her head! Trinity stood and screamed, then ran out the Pizza Shop's front door. Her imagination had seized her mind!

Rory burst out laughing and gave Shania a high five!

Jerry was convinced girls were the weirdest creatures in the entire universe. And Snowball quietly laughed and nibbled on a cracker, deep and safe in Jerry's pocket.

It was just another afternoon in Hope Valley!

***

The front door swung open at 90 mph and Delores stood staring at Arlo. She wore an ancient blue dirty nightgown, held a can of Coors beer in her left hand, and her brunette hair was full of houseflies.

"What do you want Arlo? Can't you see I'm busy!" "When was the last time you had a shower?"

Arlo asked.

Delores pulled a pocket-sized copy of the

US Constitution from her nightgown, and threw it at Arlo. She put her hands on her hips and snarled at the lawman, "there's nothing in the constitution giving you authority over when people shower. I'm in no mood for one of your lectures Arlo, and you'll need a warrant to inspect the cleanliness of my home, so get your sorry butt off my property!"

She looked past Arlo to his patrol car and saw her son Brady in the back seat looking at her. Delores pointed her finger at Arlo and said,

"And don't be dropping Brady off here and telling me what a lousy mother I am. He doesn't live here anymore. I threw him out a week ago after he sassed off to me!"

"Delores, the boy is 17, you can't throw him out of your house. You're his parent. Until he turns 18, he's your responsibility!" Arlo replied forcibly.

"You think you're all high and mighty don't you Arlo? Slap that Sheriff's badge on, and you turn into Mussolini! Well let me tell you something Mr Lawman! My life sucks, and you know why?

I'll tell you why! You couldn't keep your hands off me in high school. You gave me a promise ring and talked about marriage and getting a big house and buying me a brand-new Ford Thunderbird. You wanted kids someday and we were going to move to

Madison, Wisconsin, and live the good life!

But then one day Sherry Whitmore wore a cute little outfit that grabbed your eyeballs. And you dropped me like a rock and kissed her non-stop 24x7. You made me promises Arlo, I loved you!

But no, your promises were Grade-A garbage.

You ruined my life, Mr. Lawman! Are you happy now?" Delores stared at Arlo with a menacing hate. "And I've had enough of your honor and integrity lectures!" And last I heard, Sherry dropped you, good for her! You freaking loser!

I heard you got that stupid sheriff's badge in a Cracker Jack box!

Now take your stupid Sheriff's badge and get off my property. I'm not taking orders from you or any other man!"

Arlo was in shock and frozen still, but jumped when the door slammed and he heard Delores sobbing. He picked his heart up off the rotted floorboards and stumbled back to his patrol car.

Delores was his kryptonite.

***

Dear Diary,

I witnessed something today I've never seen before. Tom and Brady got into a big fight at the Diner. Brady started it and should have been thrown in jail, he's such an ass. But Tom took the blame for the fight and told the Sheriff he and Brady were friends and things just got out of hand. Why would Tom do that? Why would he be kind to Brady? It makes no sense to me. But somehow, in a way, I don't understand.

I'm proud of Tom. I think it took a real man to do what he did. And Tom kept Shania and me safe. I told him I loved him. And I do, very, very much.

***

Arlo steadied himself against the driver's door and stared up at the Rocky Mountains.

He remembered noticing Sherry Whitmore's pretty figure back in high school. He stood behind her at the drinking fountain. She took a long drink, stood too quickly and became lightheaded. She fell against Arlo, and he held her for a long moment. Sherry was drop-dead gorgeous, he asked her out, and she accepted. He dropped Delores like a rock and never looked back.

No explanation, no telling her he was breaking up.

But what do teenage boys know about love, and the rules of dating?

But, right now, Delores had just punched him in the gut; her cancerous insults left Arlo feeling sick. He took a deep breath and remembered the oath he took to protect and serve the people of Wyoming....all the people, not just the kind and nice ones.

His jurisdiction was the entire state, but he was permanently assigned to Hope Valley. He opened the back door, stared at Brady, and said,

"You never told me your mom kicked you out."

"You never asked." Brady replied with a deadpan expression.

Brady was a product of his mother, and now she was slipping deeper and deeper into a depression.

Somewhere deep in Arlo's heart, he thought fondly of Delores. He once loved her. And in due time the US Navy had chiseled honor and integrity into his heart. Arlo always regretted how he treated Delores back then. He did apologize once years ago.

But now he had a job to do and looked at Brady and said,

"She's refusing to let you live here, but if you want I can get State Social Services involved and they can apply some legal pressure and maybe your mom will change her mind. But look, Brady, I need you involved in this decision, do you want to move back in with your mom?"

"I can't live here, she makes my life a living hell. But she's my mom and I love her, ya know?"

"Yeah, I know Brady, we all have moms, and we all make mistakes. And I'm still paying for one I made when I was your age." Arlo softly replied.

"Can you get her some help?" Brady asked. "I'll try my hardest, you have my word.

Where have you been living?"

"In an abandoned house up on Hwy 227. I sleep there." Brady answered. "OK, I need to find a place for you to stay until we can figure all this out. Tom, I'll drop you off at the police station,

I'll call your mom and she can pick you up.

I'm letting both of you go, with a warning that there had better not be any more fighting in my town! Now, are you two going to try and be peaceable with each other?" Arlo asked while looking at Brady. Both Brady and Tom said yes.

"Ok let's go to the station and drop you off, Tom. Brady, I've got a small apartment above my garage you can stay for a while under one condition. I want you to find a job."

"Arlo, I've tried, and no one will hire me because of what my dad did. Everyone knows I'm his son!" Brady complained. "OK, then I'll find you a job. That won't be a problem." Arlo replied.

"How are you going to find me a job, Arlo?

My dad murdered 2 women, or did you forget about that?" Brady asked. "Let me worry about that." Arlo replied, as a

Casper police cruiser came roaring up the dirt road at 82 mph in a 45 mph zone. Its flashers were all lit up. Its 6-liter turbo-charged engine was napping at 82 mph.

"I'll be right back." Arlo said to the boys. He went and talked to the new Casper officer, then in 10 minutes was headed east to the police station, and chatting with Sherry on the phone.

Meanwhile, in the backseat, Brady turned and looked at Tom. "What!" Tom asked him.

"I want to know why you covered for me at the diner and told Arlo you broke the glass and we were just having fun and it all got out of hand?" "Brady, just because you're a jerk to me, doesn't mean I have to be a jerk to you.

And I don't throw people under the bus, not even you!"

***

30 minutes earlier.........

It was 1:00 pm in Hope Valley and Sherry had overslept when there was a knock at the door.

Sherry opened her eyes and sighed. Why was it that everywhere she stayed in Hope Valley people were constantly knocking at her door? Had they ever heard of a little thing called privacy here? No, of course not. Who was she kidding? This was Hope Valley, the fishbowl of fish bowls, where your neighbor practically knew what you were doing before you even did it.

There was another knock, a little louder this time.

She sighed again and sat up in bed. She looked over at her alarm clock and was a bit shocked to see the time was 1:01 p.m.

She had known she was sleeping in but she hadn't realized she had almost missed lunchtime. She supposed that it wasn't that strange for someone to be knocking then since it was past 1:00 in the afternoon and she hadn't left her bedroom. Still, she barely had the will to get up after the dreadful day she had had the day before. The day had started off good enough with Cooper surprising her with a visit but then quickly became horrible as they had gotten into a car accident caused by that stupid sheep Orly, but worst of all was when Cooper had sent a processor over to the farmhouse serving her with papers for nonexistent injuries from the accident. She remembered everything that had happened as if it had been yesterday, which of course it had been: A man with a short crew cut and a pronounced chin had handed her an envelope and informed her that she had been served. Stunned, she had looked at the envelope to see the return address stating it was from a law firm in New York, actually a rival law firm to Sherry's that she knew quite well. Togart and Mead. Why would she be getting sued by Togart and Mead? The last time she had had any dealings with them had been that big tort claim she had made against a solar electric company they had been the defendants for. She had won the case and their client, Moon Solar, had been forced to pay out hundreds of thousands of dollars in damages to irate damaged roof owners, but that would not be grounds for them to sue Sherry for anything personally. She ripped open the envelope and read through the complaint form on the top quickly. The name Cooper Thompson caught her eye. She read quickly through the complaint again. Cooper was suing her for injuries sustained in an automobile accident in Hope Valley Wyoming and alleging negligence on the part of the complainant which was her Sherry.

Negligence Sherry thought indignantly. He had been the one talking a mile a minute while she had been trying to drive. And what injuries did he have? The paramedics had said it looked like he hadn't broken anything, just a sprain. But Cooper was very sly in the complaint. It didn't say anything about broken bones, instead, it said whiplash. Whiplash? So that's why he had kept complaining about his neck, saying he couldn't move. That crooked little weasel! The complaint also alleged Loss of Consortium. Loss of Consortium? Being a lawyer Sherry knew this meant he was suing for his inability to be in a relationship with someone while he was injured. But the person he was in a relationship with was her! Or it had been. Not anymore, that was for sure.

But worse than that was that she and Tom had had a terrible fight in which Tom had accused her of not caring about him or her dad. Worst of all was the look she had seen on her dad's face when he found out she had sent Tom to live with him to convince him to sell the farm. She had never seen him more devastated. She groaned and lay back down again, burrowing her face into her pillow a bit more. Maybe she would just stay in bed all day.

"Sherry, are you in there?" Edith called out.

Not wanting Edith to walk in, Sherry called out, "I'm here." She wanted to add 'go away' but not only would that be extremely impolite, but she knew it wouldn't work anyway.

"It's almost 1 o'clock dear," Edith said.

"I know, I'm just uh, busy," Sherry replied. "Everything's okay." She was going to add thanks for your concern but was afraid the words would come out too sarcastic. "Okay then, I'm off to the diner dear," Edith said and Sherry breathed a sigh of relief to hear Edith's steps walking away from the door. She wasn't surprised Edith was off to the diner. Off to tell everyone there how Sherry was still in bed at 1 p.m. It didn't matter, Sherry had to get up anyway and make some decisions on what to do. This whole time she had been in Hope Valley and even when she had been in New York, she had been so sure that her parents moving off the farm was the best thing for them to do, but now, she wasn't so sure. Tom's words kept going through her mind over and over again. "Taking Hank away from everything he loves is not the best thing for him," he had said. Was that how Tom had felt when Sherry had put him into MPI when he was in seventh grade? She had only done it for his own good, but now she wasn't so sure if she knew what that was. She got up and reached over to the bedside table for her cell and punched in Bob Hoffman's number. He answered quicker than she expected. "Sherry, I've been expecting you to call," he said. "we need to talk."

"I know, I know," she replied quickly, "and I'm sorry I got all your texts and calls wanting to know what's been going on with the property but I've been a bit, uh, busy. Do you have time to meet for lunch?"

"Sure," Bob said. "I was about to go down to the diner so I can be there in like ten minutes?"

"Okay," Sherry replied, knowing there was no way she could be ready that fast but wanting to be accommodating, knowing Bob was going to be quite miffed with her when she told him she no longer was interested in convincing her dad to sell Windy Hill. She was surprised that Bob had sounded as cheerful as he did, she was sure he would be miffed at how long it had already taken.

She hurriedly got dressed but took time to throw on some makeup and pearl earrings so she would at least look semi-professional and put together. When she stepped outside she was surprised at how nice a day it was. Since the diner was only a five-minute walk from the bed and breakfast, Sherry decided to walk. She had almost reached the diner when her phone rang.

She recognized the number as Arlo's and considered not picking it up as she was already running late to meet Bob and had been mentally psyching herself up to give Bob the bad news that the farm was not going to be sold after all, but decided to take Arlo's call, on the off chance that he had finally found a non-ridiculous lead on the fire or something else sensible.

"Arlo?" she said into the phone.

"The one and only," Arlo answered with a chuckle.

She could see Bob was already sitting at one of the tables near the front of the diner. He had his back to her so he didn't see her. Still, she didn't want to keep him waiting, adding insult to injury with the bad news she had for him.

"Arlo, this better be good, I'm busy," Sherry said.

"Hot date?" he asked her, "with uh what's his name, uh Copper or something like that?" "It's Cooper," she replied, adding, "No, that's over.."

"Oh really?" Arlo said, sounding more interested. "What happened?"

"It's hard to explain," she answered. She didn't want to get into the real reason with Arlo right then. Maybe never. "Arlo, seriously, I don't have time for this. It's 1:08 pm and I'm late for an appointment.

Hey, what's that siren I hear blaring at your end of the call?? I'm on my way to a domestic disturbance report.

Is there something important you need to tell me, because if this is a social call we'll need to continue this at another time." "Unfortunately Sher, this isn't a social call. I've got Tom down at the station."

Sherry was shocked. "What? What happened? Is he okay?"

"It's nothing to get all frantic about. He's fine. He just got into it with a boy from his school, Brady." Arlo answered. "Brady? The one Tom thinks might have set the fire?"

"Yeah, well they were down at the diner and I guess they had some words. Words that Tom didn't like so he decked the guy. Brady can be a punk so I can't say I blame Tom and I'm not going to arrest him or anything Sher.

Look, I just wanted to get Tom the heck out of there. So he's down at the station now. Can you pick him up there?? I've got a lot going on right now, but I diffused the fight. I've got some stuff with Brady I'm dealing with too. His family is a bunch of losers.

"Okay, thank you, Arlo!! I'll be right down to get him. But hey, did you tell Tom there's zero tolerance for fighting in school? Oh yeah, I shook 'em both up pretty well!!

Sherry put her phone in her purse. She had to get down to the station to see Tom and figure out where his head was, but first, she had to let Bob know what was going on as he was staring right at her from inside the diner. She wasn't sure if he had been there when the supposed altercation between Tom and Brady had happened.

But as soon as she was about to walk into the diner Rory came running over to her from the pizza shop across the street with a girl Sherry didn't recognize. "Mrs. Whitmore, is Tom alright?" Rory cried. I, we were there, when he had that big fight with Brady. It was pretty crazy."

"I don't know. I'm going down to the police station now," Sherry replied.

"Brady and his goons were the ones who started the whole thing," the girl with Rory said.

Rory realized Sherry didn't know who Shania was, and introduced them. "Nice to meet you, Shania," Sherry said, "I'm sure everything is fine girls. I'm going down to the police station now to get Tom."

Just then a loud horn blared in the street and a big black pickup truck with deer headlights on the top pulled up next to Sherry and the girls.

"Just the girl I was looking for," someone barked from inside the truck cab. Sherry was surprised to see that the someone was Hank's boarder, Justin. "We need to talk," he was looking at Rory.

Rory looked confused. "Uh, is something wrong with one of the horses?"

"Now that's exactly what I wanted to talk to you about. Nothing is wrong with those horses. But strangely I was just up at the farm and I heard from Hank you had some kid up there nosing around the barn. I told you before that I don't want anyone else in there besides you. So why'd you have some stranger in there poking around? A pharmacist or something?"

"You mean Eric? Rory replied. "Yeah, he's a pharmacist but he's also really good with animals. Everyone around here calls him when they have an animal that's sick or hurt."

Well, whatever, I don't want him or anyone else around my horses. You have a problem with one of them, you call me, you got that?"

Sherry could no longer keep quiet while Justin yelled at Rory. Who did this guy think he was? Sherry was sympathetic to the fact that he was a veteran and maybe used to being a bit rough around the edges but there was no need for him to act like this.

She stepped forward, "Justin, is it? I don't know if we've met before, I'm Sherry Whitmore, Hank's daughter." She held her hand out for Justin to take but he didn't take it, instead, he just gave her a quick nod.

"I know who you are," he said shortly.

"Okay then well I understand you're a bit upset here but I can assure you Rory is taking very good care of your horses and I was there, she did try to call you but you weren't around."

Justin didn't reply for a moment and when he did he addressed Rory only, "Just see you don't let strangers around my horses again," he grumbled and with a roar of his truck he drove away leaving them standing in his exhaust fumes.

"Jerk," Sherry said as she watched his truck peeling away.

"I can't believe my father lets that guy board his horses at the farm," Sherry said. "I guess they are his horses," Rory replied meekly,

"Sure, but that doesn't give him the right to act that way, how rude," Sherry said.

"Speaking of rude are you planning to ever join me for lunch?" Sherry turned around to see Bob standing at the diner door.

"Bob I am so sorry but I need to go do something really quick," she said not wanting to disclose she was on the way to the police station to pick up her son though she was sure since the incident had happened in the diner and half if not the whole town already knew what had happened.

She added, "I understand if you want to reschedule."

Bob looked at his phone. "When do you think you'll be back?

Sherry estimated the time to drive Tom back up to Windy Hill Farm and get back to the diner, "Thirty minutes or so?"

Oh, that's it? He said taking his eyes off his phone, "Take your time, luckily for you, a client of mine pushed their appointment back to the late afternoon. Another piece of pie Edith!"

As soon as Bob went back into the diner Sherry turned towards the girls. "Do you guys need a ride or anything?" "No thanks, Shania lives right here in town and we can walk right over to her house."

Sherry said her goodbyes to the girls and quickly made her way back to the bed and breakfast for her rental car and then drove to the police station. When she got there she was surprised to see Tom waiting outside, alone. He looked none too happy to see her.

"Arlo called me," Sherry said as she pulled away from the station. They drove out of the town and onto Route 63 in silence. Sherry was hoping that Tom would volunteer what had happened but he just sat there saying nothing. Finally, she burst out, "So now you're getting into fights? Threatening people?"

Tom sighed. "Look, Mom, you don't know Brady but that guy is a class-A jerk. I can tolerate it when he calls me a Korean cowboy but just wouldn't stop with the insults."

"So this is why you decided to say you were going to kill him? Your temper is getting out of control "I know I know Arlo already gave me the third degree."

Well, you're lucky Arlo didn't decide to throw you in jail for assault and then how would you get into the Ivy's?" Here we go again, Tom said, scrunching down in his seat.

"Tom, I just want what's best for you!" Are you sure about that?

"Of course I'm sure. She turned up onto the narrow road up the farm passing the tree she had hit the day before. And this is exactly why I didn't want you to stay in this podunk town.

I know how narrow-minded people are in holes in the walls like this. Tom, you don't think they said stuff like that to me back in New York?

That was something that had never crossed Sherry's mind. New York was so diverse, she figured kids would be nicer to someone different from them. Seems she was wrong. "But you never said anything," she said to Tom.

It's not something you go around talking about, Tom replied, slouching even farther down in his seat, "besides you never asked."

Sherry felt terrible. Tom was right. She had been so wrapped up in her climb of the corporate ladder she had never asked Tom more than a cursory how are your classes going?

A few times a week when she remembered to call him on the phone. She wondered if that was why he had gotten into so much trouble at school. Then she remembered Hank's words. Sometimes to go forward, you have to go back. Maybe Tom talking to her about what had happened back at

Massachusetts Prep Institute, was helping them to heal their relationship and go forward.

She could see Hank was out in one of the lower pastures with his flock. She parked the car near the house and turned to Tom who was already getting out of the car. "Tom, wait. I know you are mad at me and I just want to say, I'm sorry. I never realized I was hurting you. I thought I was making you into this strong independent boy by putting you into private school you know. Her eyes filled with tears, as Sherry continued: but I can see now that I've just made a mess of everything. You hate me, Hank hates me, even Cooper."

"Cooper? What do you mean?"

"He's suing me," Sherry blurted out, as she parked the car in front of the farmhouse and continued, "he's suing me for his imaginary injuries in the accident. "Are you serious?" Tom asked, looking incredulous.

"Sadly, yes. Anyway, I really don't want to talk about that right now. I have something way more important to talk to you about. I made a decision. You'll be happy to know I'm going to stop trying to convince my Dad to sell the property."

"Well that's great," Tom replied, they both stood by the car, staring out at the fields, quiet for a moment, and then Tom spoke. "But you're wrong about one thing mom, I don't hate you, it's the opposite of hate. I just realized from being out here and hanging out with Grandpa what I'd been missing with you and Dad too. Oh, shoot! I told Bob I'd be back in thirty minutes. But I'll see you at the festival tomorrow, she said as she backed up.

She sped back down to Hope Valley and parked with a jolt at the diner. There was a Closed sign on the front of the diner as it was past 2 but when she tried the door it was still open. Bob was sitting at the counter now on one of the bar stools with Edith nearby cleaning the bar with a dishtowel.

"Oh thank goodness you're back Sherry, my waistline thanks you," Bob said brushing pie crumbs off his suit.

Sherry smiled and sat down next to him. So thank you for waiting and I'm so glad we were finally able to connect because we really need to talk. Yeah, we do, Bob said.

And I'm sorry that you know I've been taking so long on the property but the thing is, we've decided not to sell. What? Bob said almost choking on his pie.

"Yeah, I'm sorry Bob."

Oh, you don't know. I'm the one who should be sorry, I thought you invited me here to talk about the details Details for what?

Details of the property transition. I thought it was strange too. Your father just showed up out of the blue and said he wanted to sell lock stock and barrel. So we sat down and signed everything. It's all a done deal. As of last night at 4:55 pm I'm the proud new owner of Windy Hill Farm soon to be known as Windy Hill Development Corp."

re was a Closed sign on the front of the diner as it was past 2 but when she tried the door it was still open. Bob was sitting at the counter now on one of the bar stools with Edith nearby cleaning the bar with a dishtowel.

"Oh thank goodness you're back Sherry, my waistline thanks you," Bob said brushing pie crumbs off his suit.

Sherry smiled and sat down next to him. So thank you for waiting and I'm so glad we were finally able to connect because we really need to talk. Yeah, we do, Bob said.

And I'm sorry that you know I've been taking so long on the property but the thing is, we've decided not to sell. What? Bob said almost choking on his pie.

"Yeah, I'm sorry Bob."

Oh, you don't know. I'm the one who should be sorry, I thought you invited me here to talk about the details Details for what?

Details of the property transition. I thought it was strange too. Your father just showed up out of the blue and said he wanted to sell lock stock and barrel. So we sat down and signed everything. It's all a done deal. As of last night at 4:55 pm I'm the proud new owner of Windy Hill Farm soon to be known as Windy Hill Development Corp."

Chapter 16

10,000 MILES TO BOSTON

Tom opened his eyes and yawned. He rolled over and glanced at the clock, 5:17 a.m. He hated mornings.

He looked out his bedroom window just as Rory walked by leading Whiusper. He wondered where they had been so early. His eyes followed Rory.

The early morning sun lit her face and beautiful long red hair, which she had put into a ponytail. He stared at the front of her t-shirt and saw her pretty curves. He suddenly realized Rory was a woman and no longer a girl.

Tom sat up and pulled his clothes on, he had never really noticed Rory before, until this week.

His entire life, she had been Rory who lived up the road. Card-carrying tomboy who had climbed over 100 trees and beat up 3 boys. He looked out the window again, his eyes glued to Rory, as she stopped under the old oak tree and began brushing Whisper. Tom was surprised at how pretty she had become. He figured any day now a trove of boys would be lined up to ask her out. He was entranced with her confident and calm mannerisms with Whisper.

His mind kept returning to the 10 minutes they shared at the diner. He remembered her arms around his chest, pulling him off of Brady and telling him to calm down. That's the kind of girl Tom had always dreamed about, a girl who cared deeply for him, no matter where they were.

Tom reminded himself Rory was just a young girl, yet his thoughts returned to her pretty figure. But she probably still had a room full of dolls and stuffed animals. He stood and walked to his bedroom door and stopped and listened. His mom and grandfather were in the living room upstairs watching the morning news.

He could hear their voices perfectly, through the furnace vents.

It soon became apparent his grandfather had sold the farm. The sheep and, everything. For a moment Tom wanted to punch a tree.

He had begun to love this place. It had come to feel like home. His many summers spent here as a boy were treasured memories. Now he belonged here, but suddenly it was all ending.

Tom quietly left his bedroom and ran up the basement stairs, out the side door, and then to the old oak tree just as Jerry walked up. Hey Rory. Morning Jerry. Tom said in a sullen and agitated voice.

Rory stopped and looked at Tom. "What's eating you," She inquired, and added, "you look pretty upset." "Nothing's wrong." He replied in a huff, and curious how Rory the little neighbor girl suddenly became an expert on his emotions.

Rory turned and locked her eyes on Tom like lasers. "No, something's upsetting you, it's all over your face Tom." She said emphatically. "What's wrong?" She asked in a concerned and poignant voice, as she set her hand on his chest. Like a girlfriend would do.

Tom had no idea how Rory suddenly could decipher his emotions. Yes, they shared a 10-minute romance at the Diner a few days ago, but what can a girl learn about a guy in 10 minutes?

He examined a horsefly bite on Whisper and ignored Rory. He wasn't in the mood for an interrogation. "Tu es un gars typique, tu le sais!"

Rory said to him.

"Can you stop with the French crap!"

Tom snapped and added, "This is Wyoming, can you speak English." Rory, now agitated, rolled her eyes and replied to him.

"What I said in French was,

'you're a typical guy, you know that'. Seven words." "What are you, Dr Phil now?.

Rory ignored him and looked hurt. He had protected her at the diner, Rory had hoped he had feelings for her. Like she did for him. "I don't understand how I just said good morning and you're like Mr. Spock and mind melding into my emotions." Tom moaned. "Who poured lime juice in your coffee,

Mr Grumpy Bear!" Rory replied.

"You girls thrive on figuring out men." Tom shot back.

"Look, we all know women are the superior sex, and part of that is knowing everything about a guy." Rory said with a wink of her eye. She tried to lighten the mood with some humor. But it wasn't working.

"I just thought we were friends Tom, and friends know you better than ordinary people." Rory replied. Tom saw the hurt in Rory's eyes and wondered what he said to upset her. He paced around the tree a bit, hungry for breakfast, missing Trinity, and confused with his ridiculous attraction to Rory. Trinity insisted Rory was a mere child. His mind began to swirl and further agitate him. He stopped and stood a few feet from Rory and watched how gentle she was with Whisper. Tom was an emotional mess as Rory was cleaning out Whisper's frogs and humming to her. Like everything was fine in the world.

Tom looked at Rory and went off in a huff.

"Ok, you want to know why I'm upset, I'll tell you why, Mr Spock! I just overheard my grandpa say he sold the farm!" Tom stood still and stared at Rory. Her phone call had calmed Tom when he was at the sheriff's office waiting for his mom.

Rory had a way with Tom's heart, and he knew it. "This farm?" Jerry asked.

Snowball stopped cleaning his paws and stared at Tom too, with a shocked expression. "Why would he do that?" Rory asked in a worried voice.

"Cause he's a typical guy." Tom replied and stormed off to the barn. "Wait, Tom!" Rory called out as she ran after him.

She stood close and spoke softly to his rattled emotions. "Have you had breakfast?" She asked.

"No, not yet."

"Well, you'll feel better if you get some food in your tummy. And you should ask your grandpa for details and ask why. Jerry and I will both be devastated if your family sells this farm. But I can't imagine how sad it will be for you. But my mom always says when one door closes, another one opens in our lives. I could scramble you some eggs." Rory offered.

"No, I'll get something in a minute, but thank you." Tom replied, and added, "I'm sorry, I'm a grump."

"It's okay, but will you let me know what Hank says?" Rory asked as she gave Tom a deep and sincere hug. Tom felt the softness of her young bosom on his chest. Now he was further confused and rattled as he realized Trinity's assertion that Rory was a 'mere child' made no sense. A mere child does not have a bosom and Rory was of generous size. So logic stipulates Rory is not a mere child, she's a woman. And Tom's attraction to Rory was a real and natural thing.

"You look deep in thought about something Tom." Rory observed. Tom looked at her and without thinking, said, "You're very pretty Rory, I just think you should know that."

Rory froze and looked at him, she blushed and smiled and touched his hand.

She was esoteric to realize Tom had finally noticed……

"Thank you!" She blurted out, with joy bursting from her heart. "Your shoe is untied!" Rory said with a fiery tease.

"Are you my mom now?" Tom retorted with a grin as he leaned over to tie it.

Rory ran back to Whisper and Tom's eyes automatically followed her pretty curves. Rory stopped brushing and stared at Tom.

He returned her gaze and knew she was up to something. Girls always are.

Rory gazed at his well-defined physique and wondered how much he could bench press, he was a wrestler and boxer. She was beginning to understand his emotions.

During their brief time together at the Diner, and the ensuing fight with Brady, Rory learned a lot about Tom.

The more she got to know Tom, the more she wanted to be his girl.

He was frazzled and upset as he ran up the barn loft steps two at a time.

"About time you get up! You know you sleep a lot, and we're not going to be billionaires with you dreaming of Rory all night long." Trinity said to him as she entered numbers into her calculator. He tried to kiss her, but she turned her face.

"You think you know everything Trinity, but you don't." She ignored him.

"What are you doing?" Tom asked softly, as he massaged Trinity's back, and desperately sought a kiss from her. She tossed him the calculator.

"Ok, so what's $37.39 supposed to mean?" Trinity rolled her eyes and replied:

"It's what I lost on my first batch of flowers. I spent $500.00 and only took in $462.61.

I lost money, Tom! If you had taken some initiative and helped sell, I could have at least broken even! But no, instead of helping me you're sharing a milkshake with Rory at the diner!

Why was she holding your hand? Her arm was around you…..why? Did she kiss you?"

"What is that supposed to mean?" Tom replied in a huff. They stared at each other with laser eyes. "It means she likes you and wants you to kiss her, duh!" Trinity shot back.

"You're crazy Trinity! Rory is just a friend.

And you're starting to piss me off with your talk of me kissing her!" Tom shot back. "Tom, if you stopped obsessing about Rory maybe you could sell more flowers."
"And I'm not interested in being a billionaire Trinity!" Tom replied.

"Newsflash......Rory doesn't look like a kid to me Tom, she could easily appear on the cover of Cosmo!! Long chestnut hair, blue eyes, and a pretty petite figure. She's a young woman, and I've seen your eyes glued to her! And she's got a crush on you as big as the Grand Canyon!"

"I have no interest in Rory." Tom replied in a loud voice. "Besides, she's only 15!"

"Why are you so agitated this morning, Tom do you have PMS?" Trinity jabbed at him. She could see the anger rising in his eyes and she enjoyed making him mad. "I'm not agitated, Trinity! You are! You threw that calculator at me and suddenly it's my fault your flower business is a failure.

You never bothered to go out and sell flowers till yesterday and you made Jerry do all the work. Did you pay him anything?" Tom demanded.

"Of course, I paid him, $20.00 and I bought him lunch. But your little girlfriend ruined lunch by coming into Pizza Palace and threatening me like I was a terrorist! She's a nasty girl Tom!

Full of herself and she thinks she's hot with the guys. You need to stay away from her! I'm warning you!" Trinity replied with hostility in her voice.

"Don't order me around Trinity!

Rory and I are just friends!" Tom shouted back.

"Oh like, Bruce and I are just friends, and for your information, Bruce is a man, while you're still a boy!" Trinity replied with yet another jab to his heart. "That hurts Trinity, and I've been really supportive of you, ever since we met!

Are you kissing Bruce after you teach class?" She ignored his comment and shot back…. "Why are you starting a fight, Tom?"

"I didn't start it, you did! And you know if you were more focused on your business, a woman with your superior intelligence would have figured out my grandfather has plans to sell this farm!"

Trinity turned her back to Tom and began cleaning her office table. "When do we need to be out?" She asked in a matter-of-fact tone.

"I don't know," Tom replied as he started pacing back and forth. "Aren't you upset we're losing a place to live?" He asked her. "I want us to move back home." Trinity replied.

"Move home! Why? You hate it there!" Tom replied.

"I hate it here too. There are all these stupid rules about everything. Rory comes in here and makes a mess in the barn aisle. She leaves tack scattered all over and Grandpa Hank accuses me of doing it! Rory cleans the barn bathroom and the mirror is streaked and she doesn't disinfect the toilet bowl." Trinity complained. "You know Trinity, all you seem to care about is how incompetent everyone is."

"Is that right, well at least I can clean a toilet."

"Trinity, no one even uses the barn bathroom, yet you torment Rory about keeping it immaculate. No wonder she doesn't like you!" "I want to leave Sunday, we can drive straight thru." Trinity announced.

"Where will we live?" Tom asked.

"At my mom's house, she likes you. And we won't have Rory to deal with." Trinity replied. "You called your mom?" Tom asked.

"Yeah, this morning. She divorced my dad and she said she loved me. She apologized for being a lousy mom and she wants me to come home. She was crying. She put money into my debit card." Trinity answered.

"I already told you that Trin." Tom replied.

"Can you change the oil in my car and wash it?" "Why?" Tom demanded. "OMG Tom! You're a guy and you don't know a thing about mechanical things!

You have to do maintenance on a car, just like a girlfriend. But you have no clue with either.

Tom replied, as his anger rose. It's due for an oil change and driving home to Boston will put like, 10,000 miles on it! Are you that stupid Tom?" "It's not 10,000 miles to Boston."

"Can you be ready to leave Sunday at 6:00 am?" She asked. "Are we breaking up Trinity?" Tom asked.

"I don't know, are we?" She replied flippantly. "Are you coming with me to Boston, Tom?"

"No, I'm not going, Hope Valley is my home now." Tom announced with a stare.

"Suit yourself, and get your crap out of my BMW," Trinity said in an arrogant voice as she kicked her computer table over and stormed down the stairs.

Tom stared at her 1-year-old, $5000.00 ultra fancy laptop, now smashed on the floor. He almost yelled out; your laptop needs maintenance! But instead, Tom knew he needed to calm down, he forced his mind to focus on Rory.....

Tom thought of how pretty Rory was, he wanted to kiss her to calm his rattled nerves.

Tom suddenly realized his conundrum, Rory calmed him while Trinity rattled him. They were two different women, with completely different outlooks on life and him. Tom was 10 shades of angry, he swore and walked down the stairs, wishing he had never met Trinity. Yet Tom knew……he still loved her, very much. He couldn't imagine living without her.

Tears ran down his face as he imagined Trinity driving off and leaving him in Wyoming. Several days ago, Trinity wanted to get married. But today, she suddenly ripped Tom's heart out and thrust a spear into it.

***

Tom walked outside looking for Trinity, but her BMW was gone and Hope sat at his feet, looking upset and despondent. Tom immediately looked for Rory, he needed her desperately.

She could calm his nerves, and knew exactly what to say to him. Rory was only 15, but she had a maturity that far outpaced Trinity. He saw her out in the pasture. Rory and Jerry were standing in the middle of a flock of sheep, they both looked upset.

Tom ran to them, sensing a problem.

"What's going on?" He asked, just as he saw blood all over Rory and Jerry's hands. "Jerry tripped on this rock and cut his hand."

Rory replied matter of factly, trying to keep Jerry from crying, as she held a tissue to his wound. "Let's go to the house for peroxide and a

Band-Aid." Tom suggested.

The 3 walked off towards the farmhouse and Rory jumped into one of her chatterbox moods. "Why are you so sullen all of a sudden?

You seem more upset now than you were 30 minutes ago." Rory observed. "I don't know. I have PMS I guess."

Tom replied flippantly.

"That's not funny Tom, PMS is tough, and don't appreciate you making jokes about it." "I'm sorry Rory." Tom quipped.

"I think Trinity made you mad!

You know, yesterday Trinity took Jerry downtown to stand in traffic and sell her stupid flowers. Later I found them in Pizza Palace and I politely asked her to check with me before she takes Jerry off to do whatever. And she went off at me like a bomb, ranting and yelling like she's the mayor, and makes all the rules!

Then, this morning I heard Trinity yelling at you upstairs in the barn, Tom, you need to dump her and find a girl who cares about you!" "Yeah, I guess." Tom replied.

"She wants us to move back to Boston." Tom mumbled. Rory stopped dead in her tracks and stared at him. "Well, you're not moving right! I mean

Hope Valley is your home now. Maybe Mr. Hank will stop the sale if you tell him. You like it here. You have friends here now, who care about you. I'm just so tired of Trinity!"

Rory softly said.

Tom heard tears in Rory's voice, and said; "You're crying!"

"I'm not crying! I'm allergic to those stupid weeds over there, and your grandpa depends on you for help with the farm. He's old you know, and you're a deterrent to Brady.

He hasn't pestered me since you beat him up at the diner." "I didn't beat anyone up."

Jerry ran off ahead chasing an imaginary pirate.

"Call it what you want, but you were impressive how you nailed him to the floor at light speed!

I've heard about 3 girls wanting to ask you out. And Jerry would be broken-hearted if you moved away. You can't move Tom! You just can't!" Tom watched tears pour out of Rory's eyes.

He pulled her close, and held her, Rory laid her face on his chest and closed her eyes. Tom awkwardly tried to hold Rory, and neither knew what to say. They stood in the pasture, holding each other, both scared and uncertain about their future. Tom knew he was holding a girl with more maturity than Trinity would ever have.

He heard music from

Rory's headphones and asked. "What are you listening to?" "Stevie Wonder." She replied.

"Cool, and you're fluent in French like you can speak the language, and read and write in it too." Tom said, hoping to dispel her sadness.

"Oui monsieur."

Rory replied with a tear-drenched smile, as she pulled away from Tom and looked up into his eyes.

"Maybe we can catch a Stevie Wonder concert in Denver someday, just you and me." Tom suggested. Her smile beamed brighter than a sunflower.

Tom was mesmerized by the beauty of her tear-drenched blue eyes. They sparkled at him. Rory played with the zipper on the old vest he wore, and said; "You don't understand my feelings for you Tom."

"What do you mean?" Tom replied as he struggled to understand his own emotions. But Rory's eyes told Tom what he suspected, they were becoming more than just friends.

Just then a big Sheriff's patrol car pulled into the driveway.

"Rory can you take Jerry inside, the bandages and stuff are under the bathroom sink. I'm going to see what Arlo wants." Their eyes met for a fleeting forever and Rory very softly said, "Je vous aime."

Tom had no idea what 'Je vous aime' meant as he looked into her eyes for a clue to her heart.

Tom's eyes were glued to Rory as she turned and ran to catch up with Jerry. He saw the curves of Rory's young figure and knew he loved her.

She was strong and fearless, and her emotions were honest. Rory cared about people and not becoming a billionaire. She drove a 21-speed Trek bicycle, instead of a BMW. She solved problems at home by herself. Problems that a parent would usually tackle, like changing out a garbage disposal or replacing a light fixture. Rory had no concierge service to call. Her bedroom was small, she shared a bathroom with Jerry.

No one held Rory at night when she was scared or cold. Tom was in awe of her. Rory's resiliency reminded Tom of his father. Men who wear a Navy Cross do not have a concierge service to call. They face the enemy in hand-to-hand combat. They fight impossible odds to save their fellow soldiers. Courage flows through their veins.

***

Rory held the side door for Jerry and turned to look back at Tom. He was still standing there staring at her. Their eyes met again, they both sensed the chemistry between them.

"Tom!" Arlo called out. Tom snapped out of his trance and ran to Arlo's car.

Rory walked through the kitchen and followed Jerry into the bathroom. Blood dripped onto the floor. "Look at all this blood, am I going to die?" Jerry asked in a frantic voice.

Rory smiled and softly whispered, "No, a captain of an American warship is fearless, and he gets his hands cut up some days. It's a tough job fighting pirates!" Rory was just 15, but she knew exactly how to stop the bleeding in Jerry's hand, and in Tom's heart. She lifted Jerry's little chin up and softly said, "Je vous aime." "I love you too!" Jerry replied as he hugged her.

Chapter 17

SKIPPING STONES

"Good morning Sheriff Arlo."

"Morning Tom. Is your Mom or Hank around?" The lawman asked. "No, they're off running errands, can I help you with something sir?"

"Well, you can give them a message. I had a very interesting call with a Denver FBI agent this morning. Seems they've arrested your renter, Justin, at the airport. He had a one-way ticket to Mexico and they're interrogating him now on drug dealing charges, and a host of other crimes."

"What's going to happen to Tigger and Whisper?" Tom asked.

"Can they stay here, with you for the time being? The county will reimburse you for all expenses." Arlo asked politely. "Absolutely." Tom replied with a cheerful grin.

"Good! So how's it going with you and Trinity? Deputy Bruce can't take his eyes off her."

"I don't know, girls are hard to figure out. Just when you're happy and getting along, they get mad about something. It's like a weekly occurrence." Tom sighed as he stared at the Rocky Mountains, and thought of Claire.

"Tom, relationships with women are like a chess game. You need to think 6 moves ahead, but the real conundrum is, women write the rules, and change them." Arlo grinned, stepped into his car, and asked Tom;

"So are you going to make Hope Valley your home?"

"Yeah, I think I am sir, a friend told me when doors close, new ones open in our lives. But how do you know when a girl really loves you?" Tom asked.

"She does little things for you, like making you a sandwich before you said you're hungry."

Arlo smiled, then responded to a call on his police radio. He turned his roof flashers on and roared down the road. In a moment, Tom stepped into the house.

"Hey Tom, check out my cool Band-Aid!

See it's the Flintstones!" Jerry said excitedly. Tom looked at Rory and asked,

"Did you wash it well with soap and water, and a splash of peroxide, before the bandage?" "Yes, Doctor!" Rory replied with a cute grin, and salute.

"Do you guys feel like some lemonade?" Tom asked. "Yeah, that sounds good, but I'm not a guy."

Rory replied with a tiny giggle as she pulled 3 glasses out of the cupboard. She felt Tom's eyes on her young figure. He noticed again how pretty Rory looked today. She even wore tiny earrings.

"Hey Tom!" You want to play tic-tac-toe?" Jerry asked hopefully. "Paper and pencils are in the desk drawer."

Tom replied, as they sat at the kitchen table.

In a moment Tom and Jerry banged out game after game of tic-tac-toe. Rory found a pan, broke and whipped 3 eggs, and set them on the stove. She put 2 pieces of bread in the toaster and chopped ham into the egg. In a minute, she set a plate in front of Tom, with strawberry jam.

He took her hand and said; "thank you!"

Rory smiled as their eyes met, and sat at the table with the boys.

She silently watched and marveled at how patient Tom was with her little brother. She quickly deciphered Tom's strategy. Every other game, he let Jerry win.

Rory loved his kindness to a 9-year-old boy. She loved how upset he got about things that mattered. The two boys laughed and told jokes while Rory pulled her phone out and began texting Shania.

She also built a new photos folder and labeled it:

'Tom Whitmore'. She snapped a photo of him. Rory wanted a selfie with Tom, so she slid close and tickled him. He made a face at her, she stuck her tongue out at him, and snapped the photo.

Rory wondered again if it was hard to learn how to kiss a man.

A 17-year-old man who had boarded her heart and taken it hostage.

Rory snapped out of her daydream and sent the photo to Shania. She got a heart emotive in reply. "I need to check on Trinity," Tom announced after their 17th game.

"Why, she's just somewhere being obnoxious.

You should just chill and tell us about your first boxing match."

Replied Rory, as she took a photo of Tom and Jerry.

Jerry pulled another piece of paper off the notebook, as Tom watched Rory typing quickly into her phone. "Who are you texting?" He asked.

"No one!" She quipped at him curtly. Rory raised her eyes and met Tom's.

Not a word was said, but they burst out laughing.

He blushed a little and didn't understand why, but his heart understood everything. Tom stole a lingering glance at Rory's bosom, she had pretty curves and was bigger than he remembered. Obviously, she was a woman now. Rory looked up and saw what he was looking at. Tom blushed and quickly looked away.

"I'll be 16 in a few days, and I'm no longer 12 in case you haven't noticed." "I noticed!" Tom quipped with a grin, as Rory rolled her eyes at him.

Skipping Stones

"Will you have a party?" Tom inquired as he let Jerry win another tic-tac-toe game.

"I don't know, maybe. I'm not sure who would come, I don't have a ton of friends." Rory replied. "If you have chocolate cake, I'll come."

Tom said.

"What if I don't like chocolate cake?"

Rory teased. She quickly wrote her initials on his arm. "What'd you do that for?" Tom asked in a surprised voice.

"To piss off your girlfriend." Rory replied with no emotion. "Gee, thanks!" Tom quipped.

"Anytime!" Rory replied with a smile. "Your earrings are pretty!"

Tom softly said. Their eyes met and danced together for a mere moment. "Thank you!" Rory replied as she took Jerry's pencil out of his hand.

"Hey, give me my pencil back, you're such a girl!" Jerry shouted as Rory evaded his hands. "Jerry sit down, I'm going to play the

Tic tac toe master one game then we better head home."

Jerry moaned and watched as Tom and his sister took turns filling the page with

X's and O's. In a quick few seconds, Rory won and punched Tom in the shoulder and said, "See, I told you women are smarter than men!" Tom growled and jumped up from the table.

Rory screamed and dashed out the side door. Tom stood on the porch laughing and watched Rory run across the driveway. Her pretty figure held his eyes hostage. She was beautiful and looked like a Wyoming girl standing on a rainbow.

Rory turned and waved, she was incredibly happy. "You like her, don't you?" Jerry asked politely. "Like who?" Tom replied.

"My sister……she likes you, ya know." "How do you know that?"

"I heard her talking to Shania, but girls are a pain ya know.

They always have to win at every game and Rory is always telling me what to do. So I'd steer clear if I were you! Just get a rat, Snowball never tells me what to do." "Duly noted!" Tom replied with a grin.

"See ya, Tom!" Jerry gave Tom a high-5, then jumped off the porch like Superman, and ran to catch up with Rory. Snowball hung on tight in Jerry's pocket. Tom tried calling Trinity but just got voice mail.

Next, he texted his mom.

'Mom, I want to talk to my dad, I need his phone number.' 'What do you need to talk to him about?'

Sherry texted back. 'Girls.' Tom typed.

'Don't bother, your father is clueless. And I'm not giving you his phone number. I'm tired of you asking for his number Tom!'

Just then Hank stepped in the side door. "What's Trinity cooking for dinner tonight?" He asked.

"I have no idea Grandpa, she's in a mood. Do you know my dad." Tom asked.

"I know him well, he was here with his 2 girls last month." Hank replied. "He comes here to visit?"

"Yes, he owns a bunch of car repair shops in Cheyenne and Denver so he stops here often to see us." Hank explained. "You mean he has daughters?"

"Yes, he re-married. He and his wife Melanie have 2 daughters, Katie and Kathy. They're 10 and 12 years old. They're into horses and fishing right now."

Hank opened his wallet and pulled out a photo.

"So, they'd be my sisters, sort of." Tom asked as he stared at the little photo. "Yup, half-sisters." Hank replied.

"But I'm adopted." Tom stated.

"So what does that matter, Matt is yours and the girl's legal father." Hank explained. "My mom never told me I had sisters; what's my dad like Grandpa?"

"I've never met a finer man, than your father.

He has a firm handshake, he's a kind man and a good listener. He walks with a cane, but God help anyone who messes with his family." Hank replied. Tom smiled and asked.

"So you like my dad?"

"I've always liked your father, he went through some tough stuff when you were little and your mother divorced him and played hardball. She took him to court and got custody of you. She nailed him to the wall."

"Is it true he has a Purple Heart and a Navy Cross?" Tom asked.

"Yes, I've seen them both, when he wears a suit or sports jacket he sometimes pins them inside his jacket, they help him manage his PTSD." Hank explained. "So he still has PTSD?"

Tom asked. "Yes, but he knows how to manage it now. The VA helped him and Tom….."

"Yes, Grandpa?" "All the men he saved in that battle are still alive. I've met each of them. Your father and his men are close. They're all like brothers. Your mom never understood any of that, she was too busy suing people."

"What do his medals look like?" Tom inquired.

"They look like medals that heroes wear." Hank replied, and added, "Arlo and your father are good friends. Arlo was a Navy man, your father a Marine. You should ask Arlo about your father."

"If he's a hero, then why won't my mom let me call him, or write him a letter, or anything? I don't even have a picture." Tom complained.

"Your mother is stubborn Tom." Hank replied. "Do you have his number, Grandpa?"

"Yeah, but your mother would flip out if I gave it to you."

"I'm old enough to call and talk to him and make my own assessment. Maybe I'd like him." Tom insisted. "I know you'd like him! And every time I talk to your father he always asks about you, he misses you as much as you miss him." "Really?" Tom asked.

"Your father loves you very much!" Hank replied as he turned on the television, and sat in his chair. Tom walked into the kitchen; tears fell from his eyes.

Hank sent Matt Whitmore a text......'your son is asking about you, maybe it's time you battle my daughter. He wants to meet you, Matt. Tom is turning into a fine young man. He reminds me a lot of you.'

***

Late that afternoon, Tom and Jerry walked up to the guesthouse door. Tom knocked, but no one answered, so he pushed the door open.

"Trin?? Trinity," He called out. Tom's heart sank.... Hope's water bowl was gone, the small frig was empty and everything was cleaned immaculately. There was not a speck of dust anywhere in the entire house.

Tom's eyes teared up as he softly called for her; "Trinity? Anyone here?" Their fight had been rough but he never expected this.

Her bed was made with clean sheets, and the closet was empty. Tom wanted to vomit, it was as if Trinity moved out of his heart. "She probably went to the grocery store for peanut butter," Jerry whispered, trying to console Tom.

"No, I think she's driving home to Boston." Tom replied.

***

Rory had been searching for her friend Tom for 35 minutes. Jerry told her about Trinity moving out and Tom crying. It was getting late and her Mom was coming home tonight for 2 whole days.

Rory decided to look one last place, but she had to hurry.

McIntosh Lake was a 15-minute walk up the same dirt road, Rory and Windy Hill Farm were located. It was a beautiful secluded lake, with calm waters perfect for skipping stones.

Rory walked quickly up the road, a little nervous being by herself in such a remote location. Her mom had warned her for years never to visit the lake, or be on the road alone.

She had tried calling and texting Tom, but she guessed his heart wanted to be alone.

Two giant chestnut trees cast long eerie shadows across her path. Rory shivered, zipped up her sweater, looked behind her, felt for her cell phone, and began jogging.

Rory knew if Tom wasn't at the lake, she'd be walking home, alone in the dark.

Fall had crept into Hope Valley unannounced.

A few crickets tuned their fiddles and further creeped Rory out.

In 15 minutes, she walked through the entrance to McIntosh Park. Empty picnic tables and swing sets seemed to be asleep.

Rory continued on a piece and reached the crest of the hill and saw the lake below. She smiled as a west wind blew her long red hair, and she spotted Tom sitting by himself at the end of the dock.

The last rays of sunshine danced with tree shadows on the water. The oscillating wind sounded like waves on the ocean. In a minute Tom heard footsteps and looked behind to see who it was.

He smiled and stood, like a gentleman stands when a lady enters a room.

He reached for her hand and helped Rory take a seat on the wooden dock. He sat next to her and sighed, several pounds of sadness suddenly evaporated from his heart. Rory dipped her feet into the cold water next to Tom's and giggled. Their toes touched, and hers were pretty and painted a light red to match her hair.

They were quiet and simply enjoyed being together. Rory could see his eyes were wet from rancorous tears. Trinity had broken his heart. Rory disliked Trinity for all kinds of reasons, but she hated Trinity for breaking Tom's heart.

"Your earrings are pretty!"

Rory grinned and replied, "you already told me that." "Well, I'm telling you again," Tom said as he gave her a shove. Rory giggled, and then her eyes became serious as she said, "I'm sorry Tom."

"Jerry told me Trinity is gone, probably on her way back to Boston."

"Yeah, I was supposed to wash her car and check the fluids, but I guess she left early and was anxious to get home." Tom replied "Did she take Hope with her?" Rory asked.

"Seems like." Tom answered sadly.

"I loved Hope, she always licked my nose and made me laugh. I'll miss that dog." Rory said, then asked, "Is Trinity a good driver?"

"She's a bat out of hell, kind of driver. She does 55 in school zones." Tom answered with a forced grin. "Sounds like Trinity." Rory laughed, then added.

"Trinity drove me nuts, but I worry about her being safe on such a long drive."

Tom rolled his eyes and said, "Trinity makes a plan and jumps in without thinking it through. Then everyone cleans up her mess." "You sound angry and hurt."

"Wouldn't you be?" Tom replied, then added, "I wish I could talk to my dad."

"I've never heard you mention your dad before Tom. Your parents are divorced, right?" Rory asked.

"Open your hand." Tom said to her. Rory held her left hand open and Tom dropped 5 stones into her palm. "Whats this?" She asked.

"Skipping stones, you know, you skip stones on the lake. My highest score here was 2 summers ago. I got 8 skips with a flat-bottomed black round stone. It was sweet! My dad taught me when I was a little boy. It's about all I remember of him. He had PTSD after several tours in the Middle East with the Marines.

"My mom was fed up and divorced him.

And in her typical Manhattan attorney mindset, she threw him under the bus and left him for dead. I was 5. But see, for my mom, winning a case meant a pound of flesh." Tom observed.

"Shakespeare's Merchant of Venice." Rory replied.

Tom nodded and continued, "she ruins everyone she opposes in court. So she got custody of me and bolted the door on my ever seeing my father again. My mom believed my father was making up his PTSD. Even though the Marines had test results that proved he suffered from acute post-battlefield emotional stress.

My mom won, and me and my dad lost." "I'm sorry Tom." Rory softly said.

"My Grandpa called my father the finest man he's ever met. So I'm out here throwing rocks, and sad about

Trinity breaking up with me and I can't even call my dad for advice on women."

Rory hid a laugh and replied, "we're a handful, that's for sure!" "Can you teach me how to skip a stone?"

She asked suddenly.

"You've never skipped stones?"

Tom asked, with bewilderment on his face. "What did Arlo want earlier?" Rory asked.

"Um, he got a call from the Denver FBI, they arrested Justin at the airport with a one-way ticket to Mexico. He's been smuggling drugs and other crazy stuff." Tom replied.

"Wow! He always seemed weird to me, and what about Whisper and Tigger?"

Rory asked. "Well, I told Arlo you'd cry and blow a gasket if the Feds confiscated them. So they decided we could keep the horses for a while. They'll pay for feed and expenses."

Rory glared at Tom and said, "I could easily push you into the lake, Mr Thomas Whitmore, and I might even blow a gasket doing it!"

"You don't scare me!" Tom shot back while Rory reached over and tickled him ferociously. She pulled his shirt up and tickled his tummy. Tom begged for mercy and the two friends laughed and sat close watching the sun fall asleep. Tom loved being with Rory.

"Are your parents divorced?" Tom asked.

"My mom doesn't know who my dad was. She had like 4 boyfriends in the month I was conceived and by the time she realized she was pregnant, they were all gone. She didn't want a permanent man in her life so she raised me on her own.

Jerry has a similar story. So, I never had a father to teach me how to skip a stone.

Your grandfather and my Uncle Ernie are the closest things Jerry and I have to fathers." Rory said matter of factly.

Tom stared at Rory in complete shock.

"Seriously, your mom doesn't know who your dad was?" "Nope." Rory replied.

"Come here." Tom said as he took Rory's hand and they stood together. In bare feet, they walked along the sandy shoreline to Tom's favorite spot.

For the next 15 minutes, he taught her the intricacies of stone skipping. They laughed and cheered each other on, but they were just good friends. Yet they each felt gentle waves of love wash across their hearts.

Rory soon shivered and Tom held her in the grass as darkness crept across the lake. "Why did you come here looking for me?"

Tom inquired.

"Do you really need to ask that? Haven't you figured out my feelings for you Tom?" Rory gently asked him.

Tom looked into her eyes and rubbed her cold feet, as Rory shivered in his arms. In a minute moonlight guided Tom as he ran to the dock for their socks and shoes.

He set his jacket on Rory's shoulders and whispered, "you're beautiful you know, inside and out." Rory smiled and Tom observed a simple elegance in Rory as they walked home in silence. He held her hand the entire way, keeping her safe.

Somehow Rory reminded him of Claire, they both wore an aire of elegance, and grace. Tom saw Rory to her front porch.

She turned to him and asked, "are you and Trinity officially broken up?" Tom shook his head yes, and then said,

"Tomorrow is the Fall Festival. I'm going to call Trinity and say goodbye. What hurts the most is how she just walked away. I don't deserve that! We need to each go our own way, but as friends, with a proper goodbye. Trinity owes me that, I've been good to her."

"Tom, you remind me of a knight in shining armor. Always doing the right thing. Always polite and protecting others.

I'm proud of you Tom, in your standing up to Trinity, but I know you'll be gentle with her. She did love you."

Tom and Rory were good friends, who cared for each other, and nothing more. But sometimes love falls quietly on two people like dew on a spring morning. Tom forced a smile and said,

"Thanks for finding me tonight Rory, you're the best friend I've ever had."

She watched him disappear into the darkness as he walked up the dirt road to home.

Rory sat alone on the front porch glider. Tom's jacket kept her warm, she forgot to give it back to him. Rory cried a little, tears of joy for her budding friendship with Tom, and tears of sadness that Trinity broke his heart. Rory knew he was devastated. She wondered what his father was like. Rory had heard Mr Whitmore was a war hero, his son was her hero. She needed more from Tom, but Rory was wise enough to give him space. She hoped someday soon he would kiss her, and they would be a couple.

Friends and family would call them, Tom and Rory.

She put her hand in Tom's jacket pocket and pulled out a perfectly sized skipping stone. She felt its smooth edges and flat bottom; somehow it reminded her of Tom.

Rory walked into the house, and checked on Jerry. He was in bed asleep. She kissed his forehead and whispered "good night." She took a photo of the little stone and sent it to Tom in a text. "Can I keep this?" She asked. He replied with a smile emoji.

Rory set the little stone into her jewelry box, and kept it in her heart forever.

Chapter 18

FALL FESTIVAL

Matt Whitmore was sound asleep in his bedroom in NYC. But he was in a dream wrestling an enemy combatant in the dirt thousands of miles away. He had his pillow in a choke hold, as he fought to rescue his team. His daughters Katie and Kathy stood outside their parent's door scared and unsure what to do. Their father had not dealt with a PTSD episode in years.

"Matt!! Honey!! You're having a dream!

Wake up Matt! You're here with us, your family. Matt! Wake up." Melanie Whitmore held her husband and patiently reached in and pulled him out of his nightmare. "Oh! It seemed so real! He had a knife to my throat Mel, but I….."

"Matt, let it go. You've been having your dreams again. The last 3 nights you woke me up wrestling someone. Tonight you woke the girls. What's changed Matt? Has work gotten hard? Your PTSD hasn't bothered you much in years."

Matt sat up and threw the covers off, he was sweaty and tense.

"It's Tom, I've been thinking about Tom a lot in the last month. I worry he doesn't remember me Mel!" "Of course Tom remembers you Matt, you're his father.

Maybe you should call your ex and ask to see him?"

"Mel, talking to Sherry is like talking to a brick, there's no way she'll let me see my son. She'll start yelling and cussing, and call me a creep."

"You're a Marine Matt, if you can fight the enemy in your sleep, you can fight for your son. No knives, just face Sherry and be brave. Don't let her intimidate you with all her fancy lawyer jargon. You're Tom's father, you need to act like it.

Mel rubbed his back and kissed him. "Matt I'm sorry, I shouldn't have said that.

I found her office yesterday, maybe I'll go talk to her." Melanie said matter of factly.

Matt turned and looked at his wife, she was calm and composed in any situation. Mel was an ER nurse.

"You're not scared of her are you?" Matt asked.

Melanie pulled her husband close and held him, then replied, "No Matthew I'm not afraid of Sherry. I've never met her, but we're both mothers, so we have something in common. And I want our daughters to know their brother."

Mel could feel the Marine in him, fearless and on a mission.

But Matt's eyes were glued to a family photo on their bedroom dresser. Tom held an apple and looked so happy. It was a beautiful photo with Matt and Melanie, their two young girls, and Tom.

***

Brady hung his mop up, put away the vacuum, and double checked all 3 bathrooms.

He smiled....the mirrors even shined. It was 3:08 am as Brady locked the back door of Edith's Diner, and walked home. 20 minutes later he stepped into Arlo's garage and walked up the stairs to his tiny but cozy apartment.

He stepped into the kitchen, took his shoes off and noticed several large bags on his bed from Hillar's Department Store on Main Street.

He looked inside and found 3 pair of jeans, 5 shirts, a sweatshirt, jackets, winter hats and gloves. A pair of pajamas, comfy slippers, T-shirts and underwear. Plus a gift card for Turner's Shoe Shoppe for a new pair of cowboy boots.

A note from Arlo said to dress nicely for the

Fall Festival tomorrow, and be ready to leave the house @ 7 am.

Brady stepped into the shower and washed away all sorts of emotions. He was overwhelmed with the kindness of Edith who not only gave him 3 meals a day, a job, but hugs and compliments too. He made a note to contact the Vatican in the morning and suggest Arlo for sainthood. But the thing that amazed him the most was Mr Grumpy Bear, Felix the night shift cook stayed late and helped him with his homework. He has no idea a mere cook could be an expert on trigonometry.

***

As Sherry walked down the stairs of BeeSweet B&B she wondered if she had worn the wrong shoes. But there were no options, the nearest shoe store which sold anything beyond cowboy boots, was an hour away in Cheyenne.

Her 2 day trip with light packing, had evolved into 2 weeks, with multiple trips to the laundromat. Sherry stopped and glanced at her shoes.

She had chosen silver sparkly heels to match her silvery lavender dress which was strapless, skimmed her waist and flared to her knees. She knew her outfit would likely make her the most overdressed person at the annual Harvest Festival, to which she was headed.

Sherry swore at the last step......the shoes pinched her toes something awful!! But one thing was for sure, every citizen of Hope Valley would remember the year Sherry attended the

Fall Harvest Festival and stopped the sheriff's heart cold. She giggled.

***

Trinity walked along a new trail she found, Hope ran ahead of her, sniffing profusely. The young dog loved her walks with Trinity, especially their early morning runs. Plus consistent exercise kept men's eyes on her. In particular, a handsome young police officer named Bruce, who she discovered recently was quite the intense kisser. He was also her boss at the martial arts studio.

***

Thinking she was alone, Sherry was startled to hear an: "Oh my goodness dear!" as Edith came sashaying in from her living quarters behind the dining room. She looked Sherry up and down. "What a beautiful dress, dear!" She added.

Edith wore a dress too, but it was more the style one would expect to see at a country town dance than Sherry's. Edith's dress was made of a gingham cotton material and had a pattern of little flowers and a lapel of white lace. "Thank you," Sherry replied, "you look nice as well."

"Wait, isn't that the same color dress you wore to your cotillion back in high school?" Edith asked. Did Edith have to mention high school every time she talked to Sherry?

Sherry sighed, that was something she would not miss about Hope Valley. "I don't think so, that was a purple dress." Sherry replied as she wondered how anyone could remember such detail……

But then again Sherry surmised that years of being the town gossip had helped Edith hone her keen memo-

Fall Festival

ry of extraneous detail. "Well I'm off to the dance, Edith announced, seeming to ignore Sherry's remark, and then adding………"I'm going alone thanks to you." "I wanted to talk to you about that, you going alone to the dance and all, Sherry said.

"I can't believe I'm saying this, but I'm sorry for the way things turned out between you and my dad. You two got along better than my parents ever did." "Well, all's well that ends well I suppose. Hank's a special man. I'm glad your mother appreciates that now," Edith replied with a mysterious smile.

Sherry picked a piece of lint off her dress and said, Well I don't know about that. I mean who knows what will happen when they move in together in that small place?"

I worry about them you know. They had a huge farm to get away from each other for hours. Now all that's going to change.

"Well, your mother was always a firecracker even back in school. I always felt I was more mature than she was even though she's quite a bit older than me." Edith replied.

"Aren't you guys only six months apart?" Sherry asked.

Edith rolled her eyes. "Well regardless, she better treat Hank right, because next time I won't back off so easily!" Edith stated and looked out the door. "Well, I'm going to be off to the festival dear with my pot of world famous chili here. My friend MaryLynn is catering the evening meal this year, but 52 ladies volunteered to bring potluck food to help. Should be interesting!!

Don't be too late, dear."

"I won't, Sherry said, "I'm just waiting for Tom to pick me up."

Shame about that Trinity huh? Edith said as she picked up her chili pot with both hands.

I guess, but she was sort of flaky and not the best influence on Tom so I have to say I'm not completely upset she went back to Boston. Back to Boston?" Edith said putting her chili pot down and giving Sherry a confused look.

"Oh you don't know, do you!! "Know what?" Sherry replied.

"Well, you know how I've been looking to sell off one of my businesses?

Trinity bought my Highridge Apartment Complex as well as a few office buildings downtown." She paid me just over $12 million dollars.

And she pulled out her checkbook and wrote me a check for the 12 million. I mean seriously!

Who goes around writing checks for 12 million dollars! And she's only 18! What's the world coming to dear!" "What?" Sherry replied, stunned.

Trinity was selling flowers this week! Like a homeless person.

"Well, she's a talented girl and evidently loaded with cash. Edith replied.

And you know how much of a money-maker those apartments are. So I guess Trinity finally has a successful business." She laughed and peered out the window. "Oh, it looks like your very handsome chaperone to the dance is here," Edith said with a smile as Tom opened the door for her. "Thank you, Tom, see you both at the dance!"

Tom stepped inside after Edith left. He was wearing a plaid shirt, a bolero tie, and a cowboy hat. Sherry couldn't help but stifle a laugh.

"What?" Tom said, looking down at his outfit with a sheepish look. "Nothing it's just you look very Hope Valley'ish"!

Sherry kissed Tom's cheek and made him blush a little.

"I just wanted to look appropriate for a country dance. This is all Grandpa's stuff."

"I know," Sherry said, "I remember him wearing that shirt,… like thirty years ago?"

"Very funny," Tom replied.

"I'm just joking Tom you look very nice."

Tom grinned. "Yeah right. Anyway, I have all my luggage in the back of Grandpa's new truck. He dropped me off, and went back to get Grandma." "That's fine, we can just put your suitcases in my car, right before we need to leave for the airport, you know, when we say our goodbyes." Sherry couldn't help but notice, that Tom looked sad at her words.

"Are you sure you don't mind leaving Tom?"

Tom sighed then nodded. "Yes I'm sure, what am I going to do here now anyways? My mission is over. The farm is sold and Grandpa is going to be moving out soon so I'll have no place to stay.

"Okay," Sherry said and grabbed her purse off the table, then added "I forgot to tell you. Edith told me Trinity stayed in town." She looked at Tom with concern, not sure how he was going to react to the news. "What do you mean she stayed in town?"

Tom replied with emotion in his eyes.

"Edith said Trinity wrote her a $12 million dollar check and bought her HighRidge Apartment Complex and some commercial buildings downtown. Trinity didn't tell you?"

"No, she didn't tell me!! She moved out of the guest house unannounced and isn't returning my calls or texts. I just assumed she drove home to Boston, with Hope. That was her plan."

Tom answered.

"But she was such a nice girl Tom, a little immature in ways, but she's young, you know." Sherry replied softly and touched Tom's arm.

"Well, Rory's younger than Trinity and she doesn't act like that. She wouldn't just up and leave and not say

Fall Festival

goodbye. Rory doesn't kick computer tables over or yell at me, or treat me like her servant."

"But what does Rory have to do with Trinity?" Sherry asked.

"Nothing I guess but they drove each other nuts."

"Does Rory like you Tom? She's a very pretty and impressive girl." Sherry asked. "How should I know, she's just a neighbor girl, Mom. Geez!"

"Well, girls grow up overnight, and become young women, and they notice young men like you.

You're smart, kind, and very handsome. You have a promising future too. I think highly of Rory, maybe you should get to know her better. Maybe invite her to New York for a visit once you get settled."

Sherry said with a subtle smile.

"If you have to know every minutia of my life, we've actually become good friends just this summer. But that's it, we're just friends." Tom replied.

"I hear Rory loves to dance and she adores classical music. Maybe you'll ask her to dance tonight." Sherry exclaimed. "Mom! I'm not into dancing anymore."

"But you loved dancing Thomas, it gave you a huge edge in boxing and martial arts." "Mom, would you stop trying to run my life!

Can we just go to the festival, I don't feel like discussing women with you." Tom replied. "What about you and Trinity? Is there a chance you can patch it up with her?" Sherry asked.

"Let me sum it up Mom, our family welcomed her in. She had free room and board, she didn't have much money and now she does, and all of a sudden, I'm a loser in her eyes. Young women confuse me and I have no father to call for advice." Tom moaned. "Well you can ask your grandfather about women." Sherry cheerfully suggested. Mom, most days your elevator doesn't reach the top floor. Grandpa thinks women are only good for like 3 things."

"Tom, don't talk to me like that, I'm your mother!

Look, somehow the girl got money, and money can change a person." Sherry said. "Grandpa always told me, our integrity is all we own in this world.

I mean what good is a Monopoly Board full of expensive properties when a person can't even say goodbye." Tom moaned. Sherry watched her young son, now almost a man, fighting back tears. She didn't know what to say to him.

"Well, if I see Trinity today, I'm going to rip her up over what she did to me. And I wish I could talk to Dad." "Tom, I don't want to hear another word about your father. He's a loser and don't waste time thinking about him. And don't be ripping people up Thomas,

It's not good manners!" Sherry scolded.

"You ripped Dad up really bad Mom, and you destroyed my relationship with him!" Sherry had enough and took Tom's hand and opened the door.

"Come on, let's go to the Fall Festival, you've always loved this event. You'll see some friends and have fun. Tom, build good memories of your last day here, ok?

Grandma and Grandpa are spending the day at the festival, spend some good time with them. They seem happy again."

***

"Rory! Let's go! Why are you putting on makeup? We're going to be outside having fun all day! Hello! It's a festival! Oh wait, maybe Tom will be there!

Are you going to kiss him?" Jerry taunted with a laugh.

"Would you shut up!" Rory complained. "Ok let's go, where's Mom?" She added. "How should I know?" Jerry whined.

"Hey, you're a little boy, maybe you should use the bathroom before we go!" Rory teased. "You're such a goof Rory!" Jerry replied with a smirk.

"Hey!" Jerry said to Rory.

"Hey what!" She replied staring at him, and anxious to get going.

"You look extra pretty today! Are you getting married? Then you'll have a baby." Jerry asked and stuck his tongue out at Rory.

Rory grinned and pulled her little brother's ear extra hard! "You're a baby Jerry, why do we need another one?" Rory snapped back. "Haha, you're so funny Rory!"

"You kids ready to go?"

"Yes Mom! We're ready, I set a dress, and matching shoes in the car for the dance tonight." Rory said. "Is there a young man in particular you're going to dance with?" "I don't know."

Rory answered coyly. "That sweater is lovely, is it new?" "Yeah, Uncle Ernie sent it for my birthday." "Well it looks beautiful on you Rory."

Mom, I need you to sign a paper for me to take drivers training at school. I want to get my license." "When do you turn 16 Rory?"

"Mom, today's my birthday!" You don't even know when my birthday is, and you were there when I was born!" Rory moaned in a perturbed voice.

"Honey I've just got tons of work on top of me, and I'm a bit stressed." "Yeah, and that's not all you've got on top of you!"

Rory mumbled to herself and wondered how many men her mom was dating.

"Honey, just sign my name on the forms, there's money in the checking account for any fees, and do what you need to do. I trust you to take care of things around here while I'm gone.

Fall Festival

And once you've got your license, go and buy yourself a nice used car so you can get around easier.

I'll drop $40K on your debit card. Sign my name on the sales agreement. Oh and get a 4-wheel drive, they handle good in the snow. Rory, you're a responsible young lady and we'll celebrate your birthday once my work slows down, ok? Just remind me, ok?"

Jerry, honey, remind me when your birthday is."

Rory was sad and stared out the car window and wished she had a real mom who knew today was her birthday. And March 17th was Jerry's. She didn't want a $40K used car, Rory wanted a mom who loved her children before anything else. Rory glanced into the back seat and saw crocodile tears in Jerry's eyes.

Rory reached for his hand.

"I'll make you a birthday cake," Jerry whispered. "I love you!" Rory whispered back.

Snowball threw Rory a kiss, and wondered when his birthday was.

***

Sherry and Tom arrived at the Fall Festival, walked up to the athletic field, and parted ways. "Call me when you want to meet up for a carnival ride, or a meal, ok?" Sherry said to Tom.

"Hey Tom!" Rory yelled as she jumped out of her Mom's car and ran to him. You just getting here too?" She asked. "Yeah, my mom took off somewhere!" Tom laughed. "You feel like some cotton candy?" Rory asked excitedly.

"Um, actually I found out Trinity didn't leave town. She's staying in Hope Valley and I sort of want to call her before I explode with anger." Rory softly said, "it's ok, you find Trinity and I'll find Shania and maybe we can hang out later and catch some rides and stuff."

"I'd like that a lot, Rory!" Tom said with a smile.

He reached for her hand and held it for a long moment. Their fingers intertwined. She smiled at Tom and kissed his cheek. Tom grinned and said, "What's the kiss for?" "It's to remind you to call me so we can hang out together. I thought maybe we could start with the roller coaster."

"Awesome plan!" Tom said. They had a hard time parting ways and stood by each other and chatted. Rory knew he was dreading calling Trinity, so she asked, "do you want me to be with you when you call Trin?"

"Thank you but I need to do that on my own! I'll text you soon."

They finally separated and walked off in different directions. Rory caught up with Shania and hugged her.

"What's that for?" Shania asked with a grin. "It's for being my bestie!" Rory replied,

"So hey, what's the chance of Tom kissing you today?" Shania asked.

Fall Festival

"Zero to none. I saw him just now. He looks pretty devastated about his breakup with Trinity. He needs time, you know." Rory replied.

Shania laughed and said, "Tom's a guy!

He won't remember Trinity when you smile at him! And once you take your sweater off, your yellow halter top is going to launch his spaceship!" "Shut up!" Rory replied with a big grin.

***

Connie and Hank spotted their daughter, "Sherry, what's wrong? You're crying and your mascara is running!" Connie called out and let go of Hank's hand. "It's nothing, Mom, my boy is becoming a man, and I'm all emotional because of it!

I need to stop crying like a girl!" Sherry laughed as she dabbed her eyes with a tissue.

"Come walk with us, we're headed over to the petting zoo to check on the 5 sheep we brought."

Sherry watched how her parents had found a brand new affection for each other and began crying all over again.

***

Rory, Shania, and two other girlfriends headed for the carnival. They rode the 'Zippy Squirrel' roller coaster, and a scary ride named the

'Tippy Tornado" twice. An hour later they took two benches on the enormous Ferris Wheel. Shania and

Rory shared a bench and chatted about the usual topics that fill teenage girls minds.

"Did you get a new ring?" Shania asked. "Yeah, at Wardens Drug Store, it's no big deal" Rory replied in a melancholy tone.

"Well it's really pretty, I love gold and it goes with your red hair." Rory shrugged her shoulders and stared off at the crowd below.

"Rory, you need to face facts, you don't have a chance with Trinity hanging all over Tom. She's a woman….. you're a girl." Shania said. "They broke up," Rory replied.

"Who broke up?"

"Jerry told me Tom had tears in his eyes when they walked into that little guest house you know where Trinity was living. It was empty, all cleaned and vacuumed, Trinity is such a germ freak, she wanted the barn bathroom cleaned like every day. Half the time no one even used it.

She just moved out and moved on and didn't say a word to Tom! Not even goodbye." "No way! Trinity is so weird." Exclaimed Shania.

"Trinity is such a spoiled bitch I'm like glorified she's gone," Rory mumbled. "Well, now you can make a move on Tom!"

"Yeah right, I have no idea how to kiss a guy but I'm going to ask Tom out!" Rory replied and rolled her eyes. "He needs to know you care, Rory!" Shania softly said.

"You know there's this scene on Heartland where somebody steals Amy's horse......Spartan.

And Ty is like obsessed with trying to find Spartan for Amy, but he can't. So Ty buys Amy a horse at the auction house named Harley. And Jack the grandfather guy finds out and tells Ty, 'if someone's dog dies, you don't just go buy them a new one'.

That's sort of how I feel about Tom, he's hurting and I need to just be his friend, and he needs time to get over Trinity." Rory explained. "Yeah, I see your point, Rory.

So where did Trinity go?" Shania asked.

"Rumor has it she bought Edith's apartment complex and is living in one of the vacant apartments. And my cousin Trisha said she saw Trinity kissing Officer Bruce last night on a bench by the Dairy Queen." Rory replied.

"Officer Bruce is the guy who runs the new martial arts place?" Shania asked. "Yup and he's screeching hot, and Trinity Smithe works for him."

"OMG! But where did Trinity get enough money to buy an apartment complex? Isn't she just 18?" Shania asked.

"Her father is a billionaire back in Boston, her parents divorced and her mom got half of everything. She put like 50 million dollars in Trinity's piggy bank to buy a new life!"

Rory exclaimed.

"What a bitch! I'd be happy with a $1000.00 and she has $50 million. Chicks like her make me sick!" Shania replied. Rory stared out across Hope Valley and said,

"The more I think about Trinity, the less I want Tom facing off with her, alone. He's going to call her soon and I have a hunch they're going to meet face to face. I need to be there for Tom, I won't say a word, but I'll be by his side. And if she starts yelling at Tom, I'm taking her out!"

Shania, will you help me find him?" Rory asked. "Absolutely! Chic's to the rescue!"

Shania shouted as they stepped off the Ferris wheel. Rory grinned and hugged her best friend.

"Which way?" Shania asked.

Rory had no idea, but she pointed east, and they took off running.

***

Tom stood by the athletic field concession hut. He made a mental list of all the attributes of Rory and Trinity. But his heart already had chosen. Rory was right, he needed a girl who really cared for him.

There was no getting around this, Tom needed to call Trinity and end their relationship respectfully. He swiped through photos of her, she was breathtakingly beautiful.

Prettier than any model on a grocery store magazine cover.

Tom had no idea why Trinity fell in love with him. But in reality, Trinity was attracted to Tom's calm protective stance with her. He would even stand up to her father to save Trinity from tears.

She loved Tom's calm and confident demeanor.

Tom stared at her cell number in his phone and pressed send. He stood tall and solid like a fireman, he was ready for anything she'd throw at him. "Hello." He heard a familiar female voice, with a Boston accent.

"Where are you?" He demanded. "I'm at the Fall Festival, why?"

"You said.....". I know what I said, but I'm staying here now. I'm not moving home. What do you want Tom?" Trinity inquired.

"We need to talk Trinity." "About what?" She demanded.

"You know what Trinity. You've never played games with me before. Why are you starting now." Tom replied forcefully. "What do you mean Tom?"

"Seriously Trinity, we had a fight, and the next thing I know, you moved out of the guest house and disappeared. My grandfather is all upset and is worried about you. He drove around

Hope Valley 3 hours last night looking for you. He opened his home to you. And you just up and left without an explanation. Not even a note, or even thanking him. Homeless people have better manners than you! I think you broke up with me Trin., but you can't face me, and tell me, why."

"Do you even care Tom?" Trinity asked flippantly.

Tom felt his blood begin to boil but forced his feelings to calm. Wrestling had taught him control over his emotions. "Of course I care Trinity. I love you, but my best guess is I did something to hurt you or

I don't know. Maybe I'm no longer good enough for you. Why all the drama? You couldn't say goodbye or go to hell or whatever?" Tom replied.

"Tom, don't be such a drama queen! My parents divorced. My mother got over $2 Billion dollars in the settlement. She deposited a chunk of money in my account and said she loved me. We're launching a real estate business together, Tom, you should be happy for me. My mom really loves me Tom, and she actually said the words, I love you to me."

"I am happy for you Trin, and I like your mom, but have you forgotten that I love you too? And how exactly does $2 Billion dollars involve me, Trinity? Am I just a low-class disposable boyfriend with sheep manure on my shoes?" Tom mused.

"Tom, money changes things, it's nothing personal," Trinity said with emotion in her voice.

"Is that right, so thoughtless behavior, is just business? You're the one who walked out on me. But a few days ago you wanted to get married. What the hell Trinity, you've turned into your father. His relationships are all built on money; that's what you told me on the flight out here."
"Don't you ever compare me to my father again!" Trinity snapped, then added, "Look I've been busy, I just didn't

have time to say goodbye." They were both silent for over a minute.

Then Tom spoke from his heart.

"I'm leaving tomorrow, and I want to see you. I need a proper goodbye. I need us to close this chapter of our lives together. Maybe you don't care about us, but I still do. I still love you, Trinity, and I always will.

I'm sorry if you can't understand how I feel."

Tom said as his emotions began to overwhelm him. "What do you want from me, Tom?"

Trinity coldly replied.

"I just asked to see you, Trinity, can't you understand English?" Tom slammed his fist into a young oak tree.

Tears fell from Tom's eyes. He had lost all control over his young emotions. He lost his father, and now Trinity was walking away from him. Tom had a sadness in his heart the size of The Milky Way.

Trinity was his first serious girlfriend, and this hurt like hell. "Are you at the Festival?." She asked abruptly.

"Yes, and I'm headed to the petting zoo, by the sheep. My Grandfather's sheep. I want 10 minutes from you Trinity. Are you going to bill me for that?"

Tom watched drops of blood drip from

his knuckles onto the grass below. The little oak tree was already solid as concrete. It was a surreal moment in his life.

"Are you crying?" Trinity asked. "What do you care Trinity?" Tom snapped at her, then added. "You don't have time to care Trin, you're busy, so I guess this is it… good bye Trin."

Tears welled up in Trinity's eyes; "wait Tom! We'll be at the petting zoo in 20 minutes." "Who is 'we' Trin?" Tom asked.

He heard the line go dead.

Tom had no idea what to say to Trinity, in 20 minutes.

He called his mom, as he walked toward the sheep exhibit.

"Hi honey, are you having a fun day?" Sherry asked with a smile. "Mom, I want Dad's phone number. And I want it now!"

"Tom, what is this all about honey?" "I want to talk to my father."

"Tom I don't want you talking to him, you know that! It's not negotiable. You're not allowed to see him or talk to him. I have legal papers that spell all that out. We've been through this before Tom! No! Your father doesn't love you, Tom. I'm sorry but that's reality."

"Mom, I'm going to say this one more time.

And I'm not in the mood for your attorney style of motherhood. I don't care about your legal papers and all that crap!

I want my father's phone number. I need to talk to him. My father's name is Matthew Whitmore, in case you forgot." Tom announced loudly. "Don't smart off to me Thomas, I'm your mother, in case you forgot."

"Don't treat me like a child Mom!" "You sound upset Tom."

"I am upset Mom! I'm mad as hell that I can't remember what my father looks like!

He was a Marine……he must be a powerful man. And I'm not flying out with you tonight. I'm tired of being told my father doesn't remember me. I'm tired of you telling me where I'm going to live and go to school.

I'm tired of you and your lies Mom.

And I want nothing to do with you until I talk to Dad!

If you don't want to give me his phone number, then fine! Have him call me!

And why didn't you extend a little grace to Dad at my custody hearing years ago? Grandpa said my dad is a good man, and you treated him like crap! I miss my dad mom!" Tom softly said as tears now poured out of his eyes.

"Honey, what's wrong……just tell me, Tom! What's gotten into you? Let's talk this out!" Sherry pleaded.

"I told you what's wrong mom; talking to you is like talking to a tree! And I have 2 sisters! Their names are Katie and Kathy; why did you never tell me?" Tom swore and hit end. He hung up on his own mother.

***

Sherry was so scared her hands trembled.

"Tom hung up on me," Sherry mumbled to herself in complete shock. "What if I never see my son again!" She moaned.

Tears fell from Sherry's eyes as she scrolled through her cell phones contact list.

She remembered her father's words from years ago, at the custody hearing. "Sherry, your meanness to Matt will come back and bite you someday!"

Chapter 19

U-TURN

Matt Whitmore stared at his phone.

The call from his ex was so bizarre, she begged for his help.

He had pulled into a grocery store parking lot to take her call. She was crying, and so upset.

He opened his car door and walked a ways, he stopped and looked around for a US flag. Matt spotted one flying high a top a flag pole, and stared at it, his racing heart instantly slowed.

Matt opened his text and found Sherry's message, she sent him Tom's phone number.

He returned to his car, opened his glove box, and pulled out two small US military medals. Matt's fingers picked up his Navy Cross and felt the sailing ship atop a gold cross. He looked at the Purple Heart, and stared at the image of George Washington, who centuries ago faced insurmountable odds, yet gave the order to get into the boats. He looked at the phone number again and said a quick prayer.

Matt tapped on the phone number and waited for the ringing to begin. He was a retired US Marine. But most people do not understand that Marine's never really retire.

He was ready for anything.

Matt heard ringing as memories flew through his mind at light speed…..

He was on the side of a mountain in the Middle East. He found the last two and circled up from behind. They were shooting at a group of his men. They were using a pick up truck mounted machine gun and had his men pinned down. Matt's team had no way to retreat and were low on ammo.

Matt grabbed the first guy out of the passenger seat and silently slit his throat. The other he wrestled in hand to hand combat for over 5 minutes. They were all over each other, he got the man's neck between his knees and began to suffocate him.

But suddenly Matt felt a knife slicing into his boot over and over and over.

Finally Matt broke free and spun up and drove his knife deep into the guys chest.

Matt Whitmore called for an extraction and limped to a clearing and waved an Australian Royal Marine Apache helicopter down. It swooped in, 50 yards ahead and retrieved his men. The chopper began to lift off, but threw a rope out for Matt.

He grabbed the rope as the chopper flew 20 feet above, and shouted to the pilot to go! The chopper climbed fast, and soon

Matt dangled 3000 feet in the air, then climbed the rope up into the chopper. An Aussie Medic pulled Matt's boot off and blood poured out everywhere. His foot was nearly cut in half. A tourniquet and bandages were applied and his men gathered around, as Matt sat up to count each of them, and made sure everyone was on board. He gave a thumbs up, then passed out as the Medic ripped his shirt open and injected adrenaline into his heart.....

***

Tom was halfway to the petting zoo, and he felt like a caged animal. His mother wanted to control his life and emotions. How could his father not love him?? And Trinity had stomped on his heart.

Suddenly Tom's phone rang, it was an unknown New York number, but he knew who it was. 5 kaleidoscopes of butterflies flew into his stomach. He took a deep breath and said:

"Hello."

"Tom, this is your father, Matt Whitmore, and I've been waiting for this day for 12 years. How are you son?" "Are you ok Tom?" Matt Whitmore asked with concern in his voice.

"I'm ok Dad," Tom replied, as his heart was racing. He stopped and sat on a park bench, and knew this had to be a dream. Tom quickly took a selfie, to always remember this moment, a treasure in time he would forever cherish.

"Your mother called just now in tears and said something is wrong? Where are you, Tom?"

"I stood up to her dad, I told her I never wanted to see her again, unless she let me talk to you." "Sherry said you hung up on her Tom, that really upset her. She's your mother."

"I'm sorry Dad, I'll apologize to Mom for that. I had no right to hang up on her. I'm staying with Grandma and Grandpa in Hope Valley," Tom replied. "Everything's going to be ok Tom! Whatever it is, we'll handle it together, ok! I'm going to come tonight to be with you. I just made a U-Turn, I'm headed to the airport. Is it ok if I fly out to see you?"

Tom was speechless. His emotions just ran off the tracks, but he gathered everything he had and said,

"I can't wait to see you, Dad. I've thought about you every day for as long as I can remember. Year after year I asked mom for your phone number. She said you were a homeless person who forgot about me."

Matt Whitmore laid his head on the steering wheel and closed his eyes. A Marine never cries, but huge tears ran down his face. All his Special Forces training, and years as a businessman, never prepared him for a moment like this.

"Dad, is this phone call real, or are we having a dream?" Matt sat up and smiled, "it's very real Tom. You had real courage in confronting your mom, I'm proud of you!"

"Dad, I just needed to hear your voice, do you remember me?" Tom asked. Tom was speechless as he heard emotion enter his father's voice.

"Tom, I have your photo in every room of my house, in my garage, my bedroom, the basement, on the fridge, my office, in my briefcase, my wallet, the living room, our den, my car, and one on my keychain. My daughters, Katie and Kathy who have never met you, have the same photo in their bedrooms.

Your Grandmother sent the photo to me two years ago. You were up in an apple tree picking fruit. My wife Melanie took that photo to a professional studio in Manhattan, and had you photo-shopped into our last family vacation photo. "You're a part of our family," Matt said.

"Oh my God!" Tom whispered to himself, he now understood exactly how much his father loved him.

"You had a very cool smile in that photo Tom, and you were wearing a New York Yankees hat, they're my favorite team. I took Katy and Kathy to a game last week."

"They're your daughter's dad?" "Yeah, and you're their big brother." "I never knew I had sisters,

Grandpa mentioned them recently and showed me a photo.

I remember that apple tree Dad, it was a McIntosh tree and I threw an apple to Grandpa in the next tree. He caught it and threw it back. He spoke very highly of you Dad, and he said you're friends with Sheriff Arlo."

Matt smiled and replied, "Arlo is like a brother to me, he was a Navy man. I was a Marine. And I love your grandfather, he still introduces me to people in town as his son. Years back when I wasn't doing so well, Hank flew out twice to get me help at the VA. He loaned me money to open my first auto repair shop. He's an incredible man." Matt replied.

"How did you meet Melanie?" Tom asked.

"Ski trip in Winter Park. Mel was a new skier and she made a wrong turn and couldn't stop. She sort of ran into me on an intermediate run; we both wiped out bad. She was with a bunch of her friends that day and went off by herself for a few minutes. I um, helped her down to the chairlift, then rode with her to the lodge. She broke two fingers so I got her to the resorts clinic. Afterwards she offered to buy me lunch. And I said yes.

Melanie is from Farmington, New Mexico. After we married she moved to New York and we bought a house, we had 2 kids, and we have a dog named Molly." "What kind of dog is she dad?" Tom asked excitedly.

"Molly is a poodle, a miniature poodle, and her IQ is higher than mine." Tom grinned, he loved talking to his dad!

Silence entered the phone call as both men were in shock to be talking to each other. Tom's emotions were overloaded.

Trinity dumped him, and now his father was lifting him up. It was too much for a young man to process. "Tom, are you there?" Matt asked.

"Yeah, I'm at the Fall Festival and my girlfriend broke up with me, I'm angry Dad, and it hurts something awful. I feel like I just want to die. I never imagined she'd do this. She didn't even say goodbye."

"You loved her?" Matt asked softly.

"Yeah, I did, I really loved her," Tom replied.

"I'm sorry Tom, sometimes love bucks us off like a horse who is spooked. It makes no sense, but just remember, your mother and I both love you. No matter what happens, you're our son, and we're very proud of you Tom."

"Dad, do you hate Mom!" "No, Tom, I don't hate your mother. She did what she thought was best for you, and she could never cope with my PTSD." "But how can you not hate her dad, after what she did to you…..and us? I don't remember what you look like, how can that be good for me?"

"Tom I don't hate anybody. Hate destroys everyone it touches."

"So if I don't hate Trinity, does that mean my pain will be less." Tom asked.

"No, not necessarily, but not hating someone is a choice, Tom. Part of being a man is being strong enough to get up, face the day, and move on. Someday you might have fond memories of Trinity. Maybe you'll remain friends, and someday, you'll find another girl to love.

It's not easy being a man, but trying to be a better man, day by day builds integrity and strength in us. Those are traits others will see in you. And someday another girl will notice how you live your life to a higher standard, and she'll want to get to know you better. ….I'm sorry, I'm sort of rambling on here Tom, I don't mean to give you a lecture."

"No it's okay, what you said makes sense to me. Is it true you have a Purple Heart and Navy Cross?" "Yeah, I got them for courage in battle.

But they really belong to the men and women who fought over there and never made it home.

They're the real heroes. This is hard to explain Tom, but I see those men and women when I look at a US flag, and they help me battle my PTSD. They help me every day and I owe them my life."

"Dad, I need your advice, I have feelings for another girl. But I'm not sure how to proceed with that relationship."

"What's her name, Tom?"

"Rory,…but she's only 15. Actually, she's 16 today." "What do you like about her?" Matt inquired.

"She cares about me, Dad. I told her about you and my custody hearing, years ago when I was 5. Rory said Mom should have shown you some grace and kindness.

Rory listens to me Dad, she asks questions, she tries to help, she makes me laugh and feel good about myself. She kind of fusses over me, and she's beautiful inside and out, and she's got a calm strength about her, that I like. She focuses on me Dad, and not on herself. I'm falling in love with her dad. But she's 16 years old. The girl I broke up with is 18.

I mean Rory is still a girl. I know she likes me, but I don't know what to do. I want to kiss her dad, I love being with her. Do you think she's too young for me?" "What does your heart tell you when you're with her?" Matt asked.

"My heart is super happy when I'm with her; when I'm stressed out I find her, and she calms me down."

"There's your answer Tom, I think you love Rory. Son, with teenage girls, their level of maturity is often more important than their age. It sounds like Rory is helping you become a better man.

She sounds quite mature for 16, and she has wisdom far beyond her years. Rory cares about you, and that quality in a girl is priceless." Matt said.

"Today's her birthday, I'm going to buy her a gold necklace, I've already picked it out."

"Nice! I know Rory will love it, Tom. Do you need any money for the necklace? I'll give you my credit card number." Matt offered. Tom's mind was numb, his father just offered to help buy Rory's necklace.

"No I'm good Dad, but thank you.

I taught Rory how to skip stones last night up at the lake. I held her when she was cold. I love being with her."

"If I were you Tom, I wouldn't let her get away, she might be the catch of a lifetime! You better hurry up and get that necklace!" Tom grinned and listened to the fun spontaneity in his Father's voice. He sounded like a big brother, and a dad rolled into one. "Tom, I'll be at JFK in 20 minutes. I'll catch the next flight out to Cheyenne or Denver."

"Dad, I don't remember you, how will I know you when you get here?" Tom asked.

"I'm your father, Tom, you'll recognize me. I'd better hang up now, traffic is heavy, and I'm losing my signal, but I'll see you tonight Tom, I promise!" Tom hung up from his father and walked quickly to meet Trinity. He knew now what he was going to say to her.

***

The call with his father had been a transformative experience for Tom. His father was a retired Marine Corps officer. A natural leader of men. His gentle words and demeanor instilled courage and confidence in his son.

Tom no longer needed his tears and brushed them aside. He no longer hated Trinity. He arrived at the petting zoo and saw her walking quickly to him.

Officer Bruce held her hand. Trinity looked at Tom, and her heart instantly changed. She still cared for Tom, and would never forget him. Tom faced Trinity like a man.

"I'm so sorry Tom!! I was mean and rude, I didn't mean to hurt you. It's just all that's happened, in the last few days has been overwhelming. My mom......we're friends now!

You remember Bruce?"

Tom stepped forward and shook Bruce's hand. "It's good to see you again Tom."

"It's good to see you too Bruce," Tom said sincerely. Trinity stepped closer and asked, "Are you ok Tom? You look different somehow like Moses walking down the mountain." Trinity sensed a new resolve in Tom, she had never seen before.

"Tom, I'd like for us to remain friends. You stood by me when my family was dysfunctional. I want to always be your friend Tom!" Trinity blurted out nervously. "I just got off the phone with my dad. He's on his way here." Tom said as he looked at Trinity with no emotion.

"He's coming here? But why?" Trinity asked. "He's at JFK now, catching a flight."

"That's so great Tom. OMG, that's incredible! You and I have had amazing weeks, right?

Are you nervous? Can I meet him while he's here? We could go to dinner!

Um you know....you and Rory and me and Bruce, and your dad. Could we do that Tom?" "Maybe," Tom replied stone-faced. He saw Bruce's arm around Trinity's small waist and wanted to vomit. Tom's heart was shattered, but he was trying to be kind and graceful with Trinity and move on. Advice he'd recently learned from Rory and his Dad.

***

Rory stopped and climbed up an old red oak tree to about 25 feet. She looked toward the petting zoo and saw them about 100 meters ahead. She gasped and saw Tom facing off with Trinity.

Officer Bruce was there too! Rory scampered down the tree and jumped from a branch 10 feet high, and hugged Shania, then charged off like a mountain lion, all alone.

***

"OMG, your hand is bleeding Tom, you should look after that, I saw a first aid station somewhere.. Well, we'd better run, we're putting on a martial arts demo behind the high school," Trinity said, but she froze and stared as Rory came flying up like an F15 Eagle.

"OMG! Rory's here!" Trinity nervously mumbled to herself. Her memory was suddenly full of 100 rats.

Tom felt a small and soft hand slide into his.

He turned and Rory's smile was waiting for him. Tom instantly calmed. She stood extra close, her long chestnut hair resting on Tom's arm. Rory was panting and out of breath, but she stood by Tom's side, like a best friend. She saw his bloodied knuckles and pulled 2 paper towels from her pocket and wrapped his hand. She fussed over him and applied pressure, but his bleeding soaked the paper towels in seconds.

Next Rory took her new sweater off and used it as a wrap. "Are you ok? Did you punch someone?" Rory whispered. She saw the answer in his stalwart eyes.

"Don't let her push your buttons, she's the one who left…..not you." Rory whispered, and she wanted to say more, a lot more, but she clung to Tom's hand and looked at Trinity and decided to be kind.

"You look extra pretty today Trinity. Will you be going to the dance tonight?" Rory asked.

Trinity stared at Rory's eye catching yellow halter top and became rattled. "Yes, we're planning on dinner and dancing tonight. Maybe we'll see you there." Trinity replied.

"That would be fun." Rory said with a simple yet elegant smile.

Tom looked at Rory and wondered how a 16-year-old girl could have such poise and grace. He remembered his father's words.

Trinity suddenly became timorous and wanted to run. While Rory stood perfectly still and composed with a pleasant and kind demeanor. Not unlike Eleanor Roosevelt at a State Dinner.

Trinity looked at Tom, then found a courage and panache all her own. She set aside the memory of Rory's 100 rats, and with a smile posed a question to Tom's brash young friend.

"Rory, I have a favor to ask of you.

I'm sort of starting a new job with my mom, and I'll be traveling some. I won't have time for a dog.

Would you be interested in taking Hope? She's a good girl and I know she loves you.

I could write you a check for her future food and medical bills."

"Thank you, Trinity!! I'd love to take Hope, but I don't want any money. And I know Hope will miss you terribly." "Are you sure you're ok taking her?" Trinity asked.

"I'm positive, and thank you, Trinity, that's very kind of you." Rory softly said, then added,

"I promise I'll love Hope and Tom and I will give her a good life. And you can come visit her anytime. You know where I live, you have my number, and you're always welcome at my house Trinity."

Trinity smiled and was overwhelmed with Rory's kindness to her.

"Can I pick her up tomorrow? I can't wait to see her!" Rory asked with excitement in her eyes.

"Let's text in the morning Rory and figure it out. Maybe we can take Hope for a walk and grab lunch together. There's a new Chinese place downtown." Rory grinned, and replied,

"I'd like that a lot Trinity, I love Chinese food!"

"Hope chewed up her dog bed last night, so I'll pick up a new one. Thanks again, Rory!" Trinity said with a pretty smile.

"You're very welcome Trinity and good luck with your new job, I'm very excited for you! Maybe I can meet your mom someday." Rory sincerely added.

Trinity was captivated by Rory's sweet kindness. She stepped close and hugged Rory, then kissed Tom on his cheek. She turned to go, but stopped and asked,

"Are you two a couple?"

Tom looked Trinity in the eye and said, "Yes, Rory and I are a couple."

"Well, you're very cute together," Trinity said with a grin. "I want a photo of us!" Trinity said excitedly as she handed her iPhone to Bruce, and stood next to Rory. They all 3 smiled at the camera.

Then Trinity and Officer Bruce disappeared into the crowd. Trinity began to cry, and realized letting Tom go was the worst mistake she'd ever made. Officer Bruce was scared to death of her roller-coaster emotions. A week later he broke up with her.

Tom wrapped his arm around Rory's waist and pulled her close.

He looked into her eyes……and desperately wanted to kiss her. But it was too soon, Trinity had broken his heart.

Rory gazed into Tom's eyes and softly said: "Everything's going to be okay, and I'm sorry Tom, I know you loved her. Trinity is a lovely girl; do you want to talk about anything Tom?"

"Yeah, thank you for coming, I couldn't have faced her without you," Tom replied as he squeezed Rory's hand and they started walking. "I like it here, in Hope Valley." He said.

"I know you do." Replied Rory with a big smile.

"I'm sorry about your sweater; it's beautiful; well it was before I got it all bloodied." "It's no big deal." Rory replied.

"Yeah but it's impossible to get blood out of white clothes." "Not if you know how to do laundry". Rory quipped. Tom grinned and tickled her ribs. "That's a really cute top you have on!"

Tom said as his eyes locked onto her halter top. "I figured you'd like it." Rory said with a subtle laugh. They walked silently for 20 minutes. Rory giving Tom time to sort out his feelings. Soon they approached the Rafferty River and sat on the wooden pedestrian bridge in the sun.

Rory looked into his troubled eyes and said,

"Hey, you!" She kissed his ear and gently rubbed his back, and wondered what thoughts fill a man's mind. But like a tulip pops from the earth, rises quickly, and opens. Both Tom and Rory knew they were falling in love.

They hadn't kissed yet or made an announcement, but they were a couple. And it felt incredible.

Tom was still hurting over Trinity, but being with Rory made it bearable. He felt the softness in Rory's hands. He smiled at her and noticed again her pretty female curves beneath her top. She sat perfectly still next to Tom, not charging off every 30 seconds to do this or that.

Their feet hung over the bridge, and their reflection danced with rays of dappled sunlight, on the fast-moving water. The Rafferty River began high in the Rocky Mountains and brought cold and pure water to Hope Valley. Tom and the way he lived his life brought a breath of fresh air to Rory. She loved the way Tom cared for her and for Jerry. And she loved being with him.

"Something else is bothering you, Tom, can you tell me?" Rory asked as she watched his eyes stare into the past. Tom pulled a skipping stone from his pocket and threw it into the river, and then opened his heart to her.

"I was born in Korea, my mother died just after giving birth to me." Tom opened his wallet and held a tiny faded photo of a Korean girl of about 16 years of age. "My mom" Tom said affectionately.

"Do you know her name?"

"Mi Cha….her name means 'beautiful daughter'."

Rory pressed her soft cheek against his rough face and pulled him close.

She stared at the photo for a long moment and said, "She's beautiful Tom, and you have her smile."

"A month later Matt and Sherry Whitmore adopted me. 5 years later, they divorced, and my mom Sherry got total custody of me and refused any contact between me and my dad. I haven't seen or talked to him since I was 5."

Rory looked into Tom's eyes and listened intently as he continued.

"I blew up at my mom like an hour ago and said I want nothing to do with her unless she lets me talk to my dad. He called me 10 minutes later and was driving to John F. Kennedy Airport for a flight to Cheyenne.

He's coming to see me, Rory....tonight, and I don't remember him.

He's going to have dinner with us, you and me."

Tom turned and stared into Rory's eyes and continued, "my dad said he loves me." Rory stood and jumped up and down on the bridge like an excited little girl.

She yelled "Yes!" and sat back down and hugged Tom excitedly. "Tom this is so exciting!! I'm so happy for you." Rory exclaimed.

"But what if he's not proud of me, you know, of the man I've become? I'm not a US Marine or some tough guy." Tom said in a melancholy tone. "Don't talk like that Tom! He's your father so

of course, he'll be proud of you.

I mean why would he be flying here if he wasn't proud of you? I'm proud of you!

Everyone's proud of you! Even little Hope about licks your nose off! I'm so excited to get Hope tomorrow, I love that dog!" Rory exclaimed. "Wait, you told your dad about me?"

Rory asked in an alarmed voice.

"Yes, he's looking forward to meeting you."

"OMG Tom! My hair is a mess, and I just brought a simple dress for tonight. I need a shower, and some makeup, and my nails need to be painted. I should be wearing high heels. I'm not prepared to meet your dad!"

Tom laughed and took both her hands in his and softly said, "you're one of those girls who's beautiful no matter what you're wearing! And I want you by my side, not some girl in high heels and painted nails. I just want you with me when he comes Rory. I'm nervous and being with you calms me. I don't know what your dinner plans are but would you be with me when he arrives?"

"Are you asking me on a date

Mr Whitmore?" Rory said with a big grin.

"Yes, I guess I am!" Tom replied with a happy look in his eyes. Rory smiled and said: "I accept!

Do you know much about your dad?"

"All I know is he's remarried, and has 2 teenage daughters. He lives in New York. He was a Marine and was awarded the Purple Heart, and Navy Cross." Tom said.

"So that's good right? I've always heard it's tough as hell to become a Marine. So he must be an incredible man, I heard he's a war hero!"

Rory paused and saw the tension in Tom's face. She took his hand and gently said, "maybe we should hit a few rides, you know, to get your mind off tonight, grab some lunch. We can take a little nap together under a tree. With each other."

"Absolutely, but there's something I need to do at the arcade first. Would you come with me?" Tom asked. "Sure!" Rory replied. Tom handed her a stone and she threw it far into the river.

"That's an impressive throw!" Tom exclaimed.

"I used to be a Tomboy!" Rory giggled. "And now it seems I'm Tom's girl!"

They laughed and Joy entered their hearts. Tom took Rory's hand as they ran across the bridge, like 2 cheetahs in love.

Chapter 20

HIGH OCTANE

Sherry stood over a jewelry counter of a vendor from NYC. She smelled cotton candy as two young boys walked by. It was a bright and sunny day at the Fall Festival. Suddenly someone swooped her up in his arms.

She started to scream but recognized the man's strong arms and Police Academy ring on his right hand.

"Put me down Arlo, you ape!" Sherry demanded as she cherished and despised the experience of a man swooping her off her feet like she was 17 again. "That's a lovely dress, Sher!" Arlo complimented sincerely.

He set her carefully down on her high heels, then said. "So that guy you've been hanging with….Cooper. He looks like a drowned tumbleweed someone pulled out of the lake. You ever date any real men Sher? Could I take you to dinner tomorrow night? Just as old friends catching up, and nothing more." He asked.

"I'm flying home tonight Arlo," Sherry said in a flippant and annoyed voice, as she continued gazing at diamond earrings. She put him on ignore.

Arlo was suddenly quiet. Sherry looked up and watched hurt flood into his eyes. He was a powerful man, and Sherry was shocked to see she had hurt his feelings. Arlo stood tall and went off on an unrehearsed rant.

"So, that's how it's always been, Sherry. To you, I'm just an uneducated Barney Fife of a man.

A classless goof who has no hope and no potential to ever be anything in life, and definitely not your friend. In fact you're probably embarrassed to be seen with me right now.

You go to dinner with influential, high-octane men.

While all my friends wear cowboy boots and smell of honesty and hard work. Enjoy your life, Sherry."

He tipped his Wyoming Sheriff's hat to her, then abruptly turned and walked off into the crowd.

Sherry watched as dozens of ordinary people stopped to greet Arlo and shake his hand. He smiled and chatted with them all. His silver Sheriff's badge glistened in the late afternoon sun. Several little boys dressed up like cowboys wanted their picture taken with the Sheriff. He knelt and put his arms around them, and smiled for the camera.

All 3 wore silver stars, the cowboys had toy cap guns in their holsters. Arlo carried a Colt-45 Magnum.

He was a part of Hope Valley, a man born and raised here. A simple man who could be obnoxious and even rude at times. But kindness and integrity flowed through his veins.

He had spent his own money to buy Brady new clothes. That's just who Arlo was. A big man with a big heart, in a small town, a man who everyone loved.

***

"What are we doing here?" Rory asked inquisitively. "I'm buying something for a friend, hurry, there's no line!" They ran towards the timeless 'Turner Big Game Arcade', and stared at the prize wall. "I've never been in one of these places, what do you do?" Rory asked as she looked around.

Tom pointed to a moving conveyor belt with small replicas of old glass bottles on the back wall.

The belt changed speed every 3 seconds randomly from slow to fast. Tom put his hand on Rory's hip and pulled her close. "So, I'm going to use this electronic rifle and try and 'shoot' as many bottles as I can on the moving belt.

I need 10 hits to get what I want. It's all electronic, there's no bullets. They give me 30 seconds and for every hit, I earn 50 points towards a prize.

"So that's 500 points," Rory said as she looked in the prize area and saw only one that cost 500 points. It was a stunningly beautiful gold necklace with a heart- shaped locket, its retail value was $275.00. She watched as Tom handed the cashier 5, ten dollar bills.

He picked up the rifle and sighted at the bottles. Rory stood behind Tom and wrapped her arms around his waist. She laid her head on his back and listened to his calm and steady heartbeat.

"In 10 seconds the bell will ring for you to begin," The cashier said as he pushed the start button.

A crowd had formed. Tom had to hit 10 targets in 30 seconds. He was allowed 30 shots with the electronic rifle.

Rory stood on her tippy toes and peeked above Tom's shoulder and watched the timer count down to zero. She closed her eyes when the bell rang. She felt Tom frantically moving the rifle and shooting at the targets. She wondered if he had ever done this before and who the necklace was for.

To Rory, the 30 seconds seemed like forever.

A buzzer sounded, plus celebratory music, plus the crowd was cheering. Rory opened her eyes and found Tom looking at her with a smile.

"I can't believe you got all 10," She said excitedly, and hugged him.

The cashier handed Tom the necklace and a coupon for Barrett's Photography for a tiny photo to put in the locket.

Tom slipped the necklace into his pocket and they walked hand in hand to the Ferris Wheel and rode up to the top. Tom's arm was around Rory, as if she was his girl. They chatted, and pointed to sights they recognized far below.

"Tom, who is the necklace for?" Rory asked. "Close your eyes,"Tom said as he hung the gold necklace around Rory's neck and said; "Happy Birthday Rory!" She kissed his cheek and whispered;

"Thank-you, it's beautiful?" Rory was not a girl who cried a lot, but her eyes moistened as she opened the locket. "Our picture will go here?" She asked. "Yeah, you and me," Tom whispered.

Rory was hoping for a kiss from Tom, but she knew he was still upset about Trinity. They stared out across Hope Valley and could see the City of Casper, in the distance. Rory's head lay on Tom's shoulder. She had never been so happy.

***

Minutes later they walked to the outdoor food court and chatted.

Rory looked at Tom and asked, "Did I tell you, I found a stash of 25 dead grasshoppers in Jerry's room last week? Who keeps dead grasshoppers in their bedroom? Were you goofy when you were a boy Tom?"

"Yeah I was….and I never outgrew it!

I need to find you a dead grasshopper Rory!

How about grasshopper earrings? Chicks love those you know!"

Tom tickled Rory, and she screamed and laughed, then dug her fingers into Tom's ribs. He laughed and dashed on ahead, evading her capture!

"You're a goof extraordinary!" Rory shouted at him. "That's a pretty big word for a girl!"

Tom replied with a grin.

Rory growled and sprinted after Tom and tackled him right in front of a Hope Valley policeman. "Is everything okay here?" He asked.

Rory grinned and said, "Arrest him for tickling me!" She laid on top of Tom and had him pinned to the ground. Her eyes just inches from his. Tom watched as Rory looked at his lips.

She touched the tip of her nose to his. Rory had never been this close to a man before, and she loved it. Tom stuck his tongue out at her. They burst out laughing.

"You hungry?" Rory asked.

"I'm starving, do you like Mediterranean food?" Tom asked. "With you!" Rory answered.

She pulled out a brush and quickly removed some grass from her hair. "I have a cramp in my calf, I need to stretch it out, it'll just take a minute." "Which leg?" Tom inquired.

Rory pointed to her left, then pulled a clasp out of her pocket and set her hair into a ponytail. Tom carefully pulled Rory's jeans up a few inches above her knee and gently massaged her calf. He felt a knot in her muscle and worked it out.

"Does that hurt," Tom asked, as he dug a little deeper into her calf muscle. "No…that feels good. If I do some yoga stretches every night it doesn't bother me." Rory replied.

"I like yoga too, I do a few poses after wrestling practice," Tom replied. "Which poses help you?" Rory inquired.

"My favorite is the downward-facing grasshopper." Tom replied while trying his best not to laugh.

"Oh is that right, Mr Whitmore!

Maybe you'd like to demonstrate this grasshopper pose, right here, right now!" Rory stood glaring at him and also trying not to laugh.

"No I don't think so, it's hard to do on an empty stomach." Tom complained with a giggle.

"You're such a boy!" She added with a pretty laugh. They met Jerry for lunch, then the 3 of them jumped on some more rides. Rory's plan had worked, Tom relaxed and enjoyed the afternoon.

The day slid by with fun that rivaled the Wyoming State Fair.

Soon folks meandered over to the gymnasium where dinner was being served, followed by dancing. The band 'Wyoming Wind' was slated to begin playing at 7:30.

Tom, Rory, and Jerry walked back to the parking area, where Rory pulled a small bag from her Mom's car. They entered the high school and the boys looked at the trophy cases as Rory slipped into the women's locker room.

In 10 minutes she walked out and stood near Tom. He turned and gasped. She wore a pretty green dress that fell several inches above her knees. Tom was speechless, Rory was resplendent.

Tom saw the lovely shape of her hips. His eyes rose and lingered a quick moment at the curves of her breasts. Tom couldn't take his eyes off her. She took his hand and the 3 walked over to the gym.

"You like my dress, Mr Thomas Whitmore?" Rory asked with a flirty grin.

"You're gorgeous Rory, and green is my favorite color!" She smiled at him. Jerry snapped their photo, then woke Snowball and showed the little rat the picture. Jerry whispered to Snowball,

"They're going to kiss tonight, I just know it.

You know, I warned Tom not to get involved with girls. But my sister and her goofy green dress like put a trance on Tom. He's toast!" Snowball rolled his eyes and agreed.

***

Matt Whitmore looked out the window of a

Boeing 737 at 41,000 feet. He was somewhere over South Dakota, en route to

Cheyenne Regional Airport. He replayed a call in his mind to Melanie, Katy, and Kathy, at JFK airport. They were all so excited. But right now, Matt was preparing for war with Sherry.

There was no flag to stare at inside the jet, but in his mind, Matt saw the face of the Aussie medic who did CPR on him in the helicopter.

He was just a kid from Brisbane, Australia, who had fought death dozens of times. That kid refused to let Matt slip away, and now Matt was refusing to walk away from his son.

***

About an hour later, Tom received a text from his father. His plane had landed in Cheyenne and he was in line to get a rental car. He was going to grab a drive-thru meal in Cheyenne since his plane had been late.

***

Tom, Rory, and Jerry were in line for dinner. Snowball was asleep in Jerry's pocket, his tummy full of yummy hot dogs, popcorn, and pink cotton candy. The family rendezvoused at a table in the front, and close to the band.

Sherry could see Arlo enjoying a slow dance with a blonde girl, and Hank and Connie were dancing too. Connie must have felt Sherry's eyes on her because she broke off from Hank mid-dance, said something in his ear and then walked over to where Sherry stood.

"I'm glad you came dear, I was afraid you might leave without saying goodbye!" "I wouldn't do that," Sherry said. "I'm glad to see you and Dad getting along."

"I'm glad to see he cared enough about me to give up something very important to him. I never thought he would do that. But now that it's all said and done, I wonder if I was too hard about it. I never thought I would say this, but I miss the old farm a little bit."

Sherry was astounded. "What? Are you serious?"

"I mean, maybe I was pushing too hard. You know, we had a lot of good years up at that farm, I wouldn't have minded living back there, having family and friends over, you know how cramped that apartment complex is and did you hear about the new owner?"

"Yes, Trinity!" Her mom laughed. "To think I was excited when I heard Edith had sold it until I found out it was Trinity." "So you have regrets now?"

"Yes," Connie said, then looking to where Sherry was looking at Arlo and his girlfriend dancing she added, "But we all have regrets I think." With that she squeezed Sherry's arm and walked off to where Hank was sitting with Eric's dad Ed.

What had her mom meant by regrets? Sherry wondered.

The only thing Sherry did have regrets about was her scheme to sell the farm. If she hadn't started the whole chain of events her mother probably would have never moved off the farm in the first place, and her dad would have never sold it. Now no one was happy. Not Connie who had regrets about moving. Not Tom who had grown attached to the old place. Not Hank who had just resigned himself to doing what Sherry wanted. Sherry felt she had seriously messed up.

Sherry watched as the song ended and Arlo disentangled himself from his 'friend' and walked past her and up to the podium which was perched on a small platform on one side of the room. What antics was he up to now?

Arlo poked the mic with one hand and it made a loud screeching noise that made everyone cover their ears. "Sorry people, but can I have your attention for just one moment? I need to announce that one of the sponsors, Bob Hoffman will not be here tonight. Just know that he was looking forward to giving y'all a speech here, but he's been uh, otherwise detained. Anyways, thank you all for your time, now go back to your slow dancing, your fry bread, and your huckleberry pies, but for God's sake Rick O'Leary save a piece for me!"

Arlo fake glared at who Sherry could only assume was Rick O'Leary, a youngish-looking man of considerable weight wearing a pair of dirty overalls and hiking boots over what used to be a white t-shirt who had at least three pieces of pie piled high on his plate. Sherry made her way over to Arlo as he walked down from the podium.

"So why isn't Bob going to be here?" Sherry asked. Arlo looked at her in surprise." Oh, you don't know?"
"Know what?"

Arlo scratched his head. "I figured everyone already knew."

Sherry sighed. "I'm sorry that I'm not part of the Hope Valley gossip train. So why isn't he here? Did something happen to him? I just saw him the other day and he seemed fine."

Arlo gave her a wry smile "Seemed might be the operative word there, Sherry," he said adding, "You know what? Let's go outside for a minute for some privacy." "Arlo, I'm leaving to go back to New York tonight, I don't have time for your games. Just tell me what happened." Sherry said irritated. "Besides, what about your girlfriend?"

"What, her?" Arlo replied. "She'll be fine. Just, come on," he said and he held his hand out to Sherry which she quickly squatted away but she was curious enough that she followed him out of the main hall out to the area near the back football fields.

"So why are we out here then?" Sherry said, gesturing all around and inadvertently shivering. The sun had dropped and so had the temperature. She should have known better than not to bring a shawl. October in Wyoming yielded warm days but below-freezing temperatures at night.

Arlo grinned. "It's a beautiful night and I just wanted to be alone with you," Arlo said, patting the bleacher seat next to him. "remember the last time we were out here together?"

Sherry sighed and thought here we go again. Then she said, "Arlo, as much as I'd like to go down memory lane with you, I have a plane to catch so can you focus?" Arlo nodded. "Okay, but can you blame me for trying one last time? I know I made a mess of things."

Sherry snorted at that. "Maybe, but truth be told I've made a mess of things too. And I'm sorry for being rude to you earlier.

If I was staying, yes I'd go to dinner with you Arlo. You drive me nuts, but we are old friends. And without friendship what do we have?

And I need all the friends I can get after I've screwed everything up here.

What you? Arlo was surprised. You are literally the most put together person I've ever known Sherry."

She shook her head, "hardly," Sherry replied, "But it's just too late to do anything about it now. So, can you just tell me what happened with Bob? Well, that story starts with Jake.

Jake? Who is Jake?

Jake is the real name of Justin leClerc. Also known as Jake Clark, aka Jake Stone, aka Jake Rosenfeld Jr."

"Okay, so he had a lot of aliases. We knew he was a small-town hustler, you told me that back when you were looking for him up at the farm. So you found him." She was going to add "Surprising" but she bit her tongue. She knew Arlo enough to know that arguing with him or adding more commentary was just going to make his story that much longer. She shivered again as a strong wind gust blew by.

Noticing her shiver, Arlo started to take off his jacket. "Here," he said, handing it to her. She took it and put it on, a bit disarmed by the gesture. "It looks good on you." He said. "Of course, you would look good even in a potato sack."

"Thanks," Sherry said, smiling despite herself. "So what does Bob have to do with Justin? She asked.

"Our friend Bob, well more like your friend because I never trusted the guy. I guess he was getting tired of waiting for Hank to sell the farm. Turns out he hired Justin to set the fire at Windy Hill."

What? Sherry cried, are you sure? She had always thought of Bob as almost a friend. It was hard to believe that he would do anything like that. "Yes, I'm sure. Remember the glove we found near the mill?"

"The one you thought was my mom's you mean? The one you used to arrest her because it was obvious she had set the fire?" Sherry replied sarcastically.

"Yeah, that glove," Arlo replied like it was nothing, "Turns out it was Bob's. He's a small guy, you can see why we thought it was a woman's glove. Anyways, we found the other one at his house."

"So he was actually there? The night of the fire?"

"Yes ma'am, according to Justin he planned and coordinated the whole thing, the only thing he didn't do was set the fire. Justin admitted to doing that. You know Bob, wouldn't want to get his hands dirty. We also think he was the one who knocked your dad on the head and then threw away the glove, probably thinking it was contaminated because it had touched another person."

"So was it Bob who hit my dad on the head?" "Looks like it."

Sherry was having a hard time believing all of this. Bob Hoffman had set the fire? But he was a reputable businessman. A bit of a creep with the young pretty girls, but honest nonetheless.

"But why would he leave a glove on the ground as evidence?" Sherry questioned Arlo.

Arlo shrugged. " He probably thought it would burn up in the fire, but it didn't. The truth always finds a way, Sherry, like I told you."

Sherry stared at Arlo. like he had told her? She had been the one who had constantly told him he was going in the wrong direction in the investigation. "This is terrible," Sherry said.

I don't get it Sher, everything worked out exactly as you wanted.

That's because I thought this was what I wanted, the farm sold, my parents in a nice little retirement community in town, my son going to school in New York, but now that it's all happening everything about it seems wrong. And my gosh Tom and Trinity broke up!! What's that all about Arlo?

"I don't know Sher but she's dating Bruce now, and he's mesmerized by her stunning beauty. But he says she's a flake and a half and simply uses everyone to get what she wants.

Bruce said Trinity was using Tom."

"Wow!" Sherry exclaimed. "But back to Bob and all that. Is there more to that story Arlo?" "Well, the contract is null and void now Sherry. Hank still owns the farm."

Sherry stared at Arlo. "What do you mean?"

"Bob as much as confessed to having Jake aka Justin set that fire so the contract would be invalid, it would be considered a fraud." Before she knew what she was doing Sherry pulled Arlo close to her and kissed him.

"What was that?" He asked her, amazed.

"I don't know I guess I don't know, excuse me," she said and ran back into the dance hall. What was she doing kissing Arlo? It had been nothing she told herself. He had just told her that he had finally solved the case of the fire and that Hank still owned the farm. It was nothing, just the heat of the moment and her happiness that she hadn't completely messed things up after all.

She found her parents talking to Ed the pharmacist. "Excuse us for a second," she said to Ed and pulled her parents away. Mom, Dad, you are not going to believe this.

"Arlo arrested the person who set the fire. It was Justin and at Bob Hoffman's direction." "What?" Both Hank and Connie were astounded.

Sherry shook her head. "I know. The important thing is you still own the farm. The contract you signed was null."

Connie laughed. "I'm never going to be rid of that place, am I? With all the shenanigans Bob pulled and it's still standing." Hank smiled. "I agree, think it's meant to be around for a long long time."

He gave Connie a squeeze.

The band was playing and dancing had begun.

"And I was thinking Sherry, we could ask Tom to live in the guest house. It's a shame that he can't finish his schooling here in Hope Valley. He seems to be having an interesting time here."

"It's interesting all right," Sherry agreed, grinning. "He and Rory seem a thing now.

I've always wanted Tom to notice Rory. She's a high-quality girl, and she cares about Tom."

She looked around at all the smiling faces of Mom and Dad, Arlo, Tom, and Rory. Of course, not everyone was smiling. Trinity didn't look very happy and neither did many of Tom's classmates who sat at the tables staring. Oh well, you couldn't have everything, but this was mighty close, Sherry thought. She had been so focused on her career, her keeping up with the jet-set lifestyle she had been miserable and lost sight of everything that was important. Looking at her family smiling, she realized she hadn't felt more content in years. Looking out at the brilliant sunflower decorations and the hay bales where Jerry sat with Orly helping him eat his dripping ice cream and all the fat-laden food she wouldn't have touched with a ten-foot pole a month ago, beckoned her now in their Pyrex dishes like a comforting blanket. This was the stuff dreams were made of, the smells of Edith's apple pie, the sound of the fiddle slightly off tune, the sight of her family and friends happy all around her, this was life. This was home.

Chapter 21

JE VOUS AIME

Sherry took a photo of her parents, they sat side by side eating pie, and looking like 2 high schoolers in love again. The band played a slow tune, an old song from their youth.

Hank and Connie walked to the dance floor and were suddenly 60 years younger. They stayed and picked up the speed for an

Elton John's song and Hank very carefully spun his bride around. Connie giggled and remembered why she married this charming man who had farming in his blood. After 2 songs they both had sore knees as they ambled back to their table. But their focus was on each other and finding young love again, which was sweet as old strawberry wine.

Jerry was asleep on the floor of the gymnasium.

He hung out with school friends all day and had a fabulous time. So did Snowball, he was asleep too, snug as a bug in Jerry's pocket. The rat enjoyed seconds of lasagna tonight.

Tom ran out to his Grandfather's truck for a blanket for Jerry. Tom fussed over Jerry, he was like a little brother. It was one of many reasons Rory loved Tom.

Connie, Hank, Sherry, Rory, and Arlo were sitting around a long rectangular table, chatting and enjoying the music. Hank and Rory found a box of crayons and art paper and were collaborating on a drawing of the band on the stage. They laughed a lot and Rory gave the drummer purple hair. Connie shook her head but marveled at how the young girl could get Hank laughing again.

Rory saw him first. He was tall, and well built, with a kind face, but chiseled from hard times. He stood straight as an arrow but held a cane and walked with a slight limp.

He was dressed in pressed jeans, a light blue shirt, a sports jacket, and a baseball hat with the emblem of the United States Marine Corps. His right shoe was two sizes bigger than the left, to accommodate a war injury to his foot.

Inside his jacket and out of sight, two medals hung silently side by side. One bore an image of George Washington. The other a gold cross with a sailing ship overlay.

He stood at the main gymnasium door, looking around the room for his Son. As with all Marines, active and retired, he resonated a quiet confidence, that had been built into him in basic training.

Je vous aime

Somehow Rory knew the man had to be Tom's father. Her young woman's intuition……just knew it was him.

She stood and waved to the man and told Sherry she'd be right back. Rory ran to him, somehow wanting Tom's father to be her father too. We all wish for things in life, that simply won't be, but Rory knew, this man was someone very special.

"Hi, I'm Rory!" Her smile lit his face! "Hi! I'm Matt! It's nice to meet you, Rory. Tom talked about you a lot.

And he's right, you are beautiful."

Matt Whitmore stood with a commanding presence.

Rory smiled and blushed at the same time and watched him step through the open front door and remove his hat. Matt still suffered from remnants of PTSD. After years of help from the VA, he pretty much had his memories under control. Until this very moment, when the horrors of war hit him like a rocket-propelled grenade. All the people, all the noise, the dancing and loud music became his kryptonite.

Plus an approaching storm with Sherry.

Matt had steeled himself, he was not backing down this time. There would be no surrender.

Rory watched his eyes quickly scan the gymnasium. Like he was searching a valley for the enemy. But PTSD was his enemy and knew him well. Rory saw his right hand tightly gripping his wooden cane.

He found the US flag high on the gym wall and stared at it for a long second, then nodded to it. Rory figured out what was going on, as he closed his eyes for a moment and relaxed.

"I'm sorry, my acid reflux doesn't like flying."

Matt said. Trying to camouflage the real battle in his mind. Rory set her small soft hand on his and gently said,

"It's ok, we're glad you're here, Mr Whitmore! Tom is so excited to see you again!" "Please call me Matt," he said to Rory.

Matt smiled and saw the same patience and kindness in Rory that his wife Melanie displayed. In mere moments Matt discovered much about his son, by the soft confident smile on Rory's face.

You can tell a lot about a man by the woman who walks by his side.

The VA had taught Matt several mechanisms to stop his memories from overpowering him. "Tom will be right back, he ran out to the truck for a blanket.... My little brother fell asleep. Have you had dinner?" Rory asked.

"No, I ended up coming straight here and I'm starving," Matt replied.

Rory took Matt's left hand and led him to the dinner line. She sensed the battle in his mind and kept him away from big groups of people. He looked tough enough to fight a rhino, but gentle enough to be kind.

The dinner line was closed, and the kitchen crew was cleaning up, and all the leftover food had been packed up. Rory looked into Matt's eyes and said, "I'll get you a plate."

She grabbed a chair for Matt to sit in. "I'll be right back, I promise!"

Rory's smile calmed him.

"But they're closed." He said.

"Trust me!" Rory replied, as she dashed into the kitchen, and saw an older woman putting foil on large tins of leftovers. Her gray hair was tied in a ponytail.

Her wrinkled hands had traveled many miles in life. "Hi, excuse me, I'm sorry to bother you….I'm Rory.

My friend Matt just got here from the airport, you know how flights run late. He's really hungry. Is there a chance I could make him a plate?" Rory politely asked. "Oh honey, we're all closed up, but there's Edith's Diner 2 blocks down on Main Street. They can fix him up, I'm so sorry honey."

"But my friend is a veteran and has two medals for saving 7 of our men in Afghanistan.

He has a Navy Cross. I promise I won't make a mess. All I need is a paper plate and a serving spoon. I could come to your office Monday and wash windows or vacuum, or something." Rory's eyes pleaded for help.

"He has what kind of medal?" The woman asked.

"A Navy Cross for courage and heroism, it's right below the Medal of Honor. You've heard of that one right?" Rory asked. The lady smiled and began taking foil covers off a dozen serving trays, then helped Rory make a plate.

"What time should I come on Monday?" Rory asked politely.

"Oh, you don't need to come honey."

"But I'd like to repay your kindness." Rory insisted.

"But you're in school Monday, right?" The woman asked. "We get Monday off, it's a State holiday."

Rory replied.

"We do need someone to clean our kitchen from top to bottom every week. Could we hire you to do that? Monday's after 3:00. Should take you 4 hours. Are you afraid of cleaning dear?"

"No Ma'am!" Rory replied with a grin. "Do you need a reference?" Rory asked.

"No honey, your friend's Navy Cross is all I need to know. I'll pay you $100.00, every Monday. Here's my card, our kitchen is 1/2 mile from here, it's easy to find. My name is MaryLynn Johnson. I'm a friend of Edith's.

You know Edith from the diner."

Rory jumped with excitement. She was looking for a job. And a $100.00 every Monday!" "Thank you for the food and the job," Rory said.

Je vous aime

"You're quite welcome Rory, and please thank your friend for his service! My brother has a Navy Cross. His name is Tony Firkins, he lives in South Dakota." Rory hugged MaryLynn and took the heaping plate out to Matt.

They found a small table near the door Tom went out. Rory brought Matt a glass of fruit punch and sat quietly while he ate. "So, how long have you and Tom been dating?" Matt asked.

"Oh, this is our first date, but we've known each other for years. My family lives just down the road from Hank and Connie." Rory answered. Matt smiled, then asked, "What do you like about Tom?"

"Everything!" Rory replied with a grin. "So you haven't seen Tom in 12 years, are you nervous?" Rory asked.

"Very nervous!" Matt replied with a grin.

Rory watched his eyes stare at the flag again, like it was an old friend. She glanced at his cane and one big shoe. It was obvious to Rory, this man walked with courage.

"Here he is!" Rory said as Tom walked in the door. She waved to Tom. He stopped and stared at the big man sitting with Rory. She watched Tom fight back tears. He was brave, just like his father. Rory ran to Tom and slipped her hand inside his. She led him to the table, and then said, "Tom, this is your father." Rory let go of Tom's hand and stood still and silent as she watched the two men. They stood in a gymnasium full of people, loud music, and fun.

But Rory didn't hear any of that. It was so quiet, as she watched in awe. "Dad!" Tom said as he walked closer.

Matt stood and shook Tom's hand. They looked at each other for a long time, both overwhelmed and not sure of what to say. "You're taller than I expected!"

Tom said as he fought back tears with all his strength. He knew Marines never cried. Rory took a photo of Tom and his father, then walked off to leave the 2 men alone. "I'm sorry Tom….that it's taken me all this time to come."

"No Dad……it was Mom who put up walls between us," Tom said. "But I'm your father, I should have found a way!"

"But you're here now Dad!"

"So, your Mom is here?" Matt asked.

"Yeah, over there with Grandma and Grandpa, they're at a table up near the stage."

Matt pulled Tom into a hug and felt his son begin to sob. Tears fell out of Matt's eyes too.

He gently rubbed his son's back, like he used to when Tom was a little boy. Rory sat alone at a table across the room and watched them, and cried. She would never get a hug from her real father. Yet Rory hoped this mountain of a man, who walked with a limp, could be a father to her too.

Suddenly Matt saw her and motioned for Rory to come. Rory ran and soon Matt's arms were around her too. She looked up at Tom and whispered……."Je vous aime"!

***

Sherry had a long and lecturing preamble all prepared to attack Matt with. She planned to humiliate him, then get him on the next flight home. She looked up and saw Matt walking to her table, Sherry could see the warrior in his eyes.

US Marines do not enter battles unprepared. Her stomach suddenly churned, this was not the man she pushed around 12 years ago in court. Something had changed, there was no fear in his eyes. Just an unmovable confidence.

Sherry saw Tom and Rory walking behind Matt. They were holding hands and Tom never looked happier. "Hello, Sherry!" Matt said with a big smile.

Sherry instantly dropped her shields, stood and hugged him. He was still a kind and powerful man. With broad shoulders and a massive chest, she had forgotten how small she was in his arms. Matt was gentle with her. He held no grudges. He asked how she was and listened intently to her reply. He invited her to come to dinner sometime and meet his family.

Tom took a photo of his parents standing side by side like old friends. Tom kissed his mother's cheek. "Thank you!" He whispered to her.

Sherry saw Matt's cane and looked up into his eyes. "Did the VA help you, Matt?" He shook his head yes.

"How are Melanie and your girls….

Katie and Kathy?" Sherry asked in a friendly tone. "They're good, thank you for asking Sherry."

He opened his phone and showed everyone photos of his daughters. Rory wrapped her arms around Tom as he looked at his 2 sisters. "They're pretty girls!" Rory whispered to him.

"Thank you for coming Matt!" Sherry said, then added, "It's so good to see you!" She looked at Tom and could see he had been crying. Sherry knew her decision was the right one……love won.

Sherry hugged Rory and said, "I love your dress dear, it's lovely. Have you rescued any more grandfathers since I last saw you?" Rory laughed and smiled at Tom's mom.

Hank stood and shook Matt's hand. Connie hugged him and said, "you look so handsome tonight Matt. You're still our son, you know!" Matt grinned and was incredibly happy.

"Will you stay with us tonight? Your room is all ready." Connie asked. Matt smiled and said, "Absolutely!"

Arlo walked up and shook Matt's hand and gave him a big hug. The two men had become good friends a few years ago. Arlo motioned for Brady to come meet Matt.

"Matt, this is my young friend Brady.

Brady this is Matt, he was a Captain in Special Forces in Afghanistan. Hope Valley is always safer when Matt is here." "It's nice to meet you, sir." Brady politely said, as he shook Matt's hand, and stood close to Arlo.

Edith was helping MaryLynn carry food trays to a catering van. They stopped and said hello to the man who was awarded the Navy Cross. Matt Whitmore was overwhelmed with emotion. He had arrived ready to battle it out with Sherry.

But there was no battle, just smiles and hugs.

Matt saw Rory, standing off a ways and watching the band play a Stevie Wonder song. He set his cane on a chair and slowly walked over and stood beside her.

"You like Stevie Wonder's music?" He asked.

Rory grinned and replied, "very much, he's an amazing composer and musician. All his music exemplifies happiness."

"Come on!" Matt said as he led Rory out to the dance floor. "You can dance?" She asked excitedly. "No, this is my first time in years. I'm hoping you can keep me from killing myself!"

Rory held his left hand, Matt set his right hand on her shoulder for balance and off they went. Their smiles were huge! Arlo ran over and snapped a photo, and gave Matt a thumbs-up.

They stayed and danced 2 more until Matt's foot began to hurt. Rory helped him back to the table and got him into a chair.

She kissed Matt's cheek and for the very first time, Rory had a father. A kind man who knew lots about music and was fluent in 4 languages, including French. She sat next to him, and they discussed the talents of Hayden, Mozart, and Beethoven in French for over 20 minutes. Rory was blown away that someone shared her same passions for music and language.

The family and their friends sat and listened to music, chatted some, and had a fantastic evening. Rory sat on Tom's lap and whispered, "your father is the most amazing man I've ever met! Do you know he's fluent in 4 languages, and plays the piano and sax? We discussed the 3 most influential classical composers in French.

We talked in French for 20 minutes, can you believe it! How are you?" She asked Tom. He looked into her eyes and said,

'Je vous aime!" "I love you too!" Rory replied as she laid her head on his shoulder, and smiled. Tom was her's now. She snuggled into his chest and curled up into his lap. He massaged her calf, and she fell asleep in his arms.

In a little while, Rory woke, stood, and looked intently at the dance floor. She walked up towards the band. "What's going on?" Tom asked as he slipped his arm around her small waist.

"This is my favorite song!

Stevie Wonder's 'My Cherie Amour'.

It's a classic!" Rory replied with excited eyes.

Je vous aime

Tom watched Rory's feet tapping; he picked her up and carried her to the dance floor. She screamed in excitement. In a moment they were dancing and laughing. Rory was beautiful. She saw Shania and waved.

Just as the song began to end. Tom pulled Rory close…. and kissed her. She kissed him back! Her smile exploded into Tom's heart. For a small and quant, off-the-grid town.

Hope Valley was a pretty cool place after all.

***

"Whoever is happy, will make others happy too." Anne Frank

Mike Hurley is an avid writer of fan fiction stories all about the Canadian television series Heartland. His stories appear in the readers app: WattPad. Mike is also an experienced beekeeper and enjoyed working in his small fruit orchard when he isn't writing.

Made in the USA
Las Vegas, NV
19 January 2024